Rainbow Brite ™

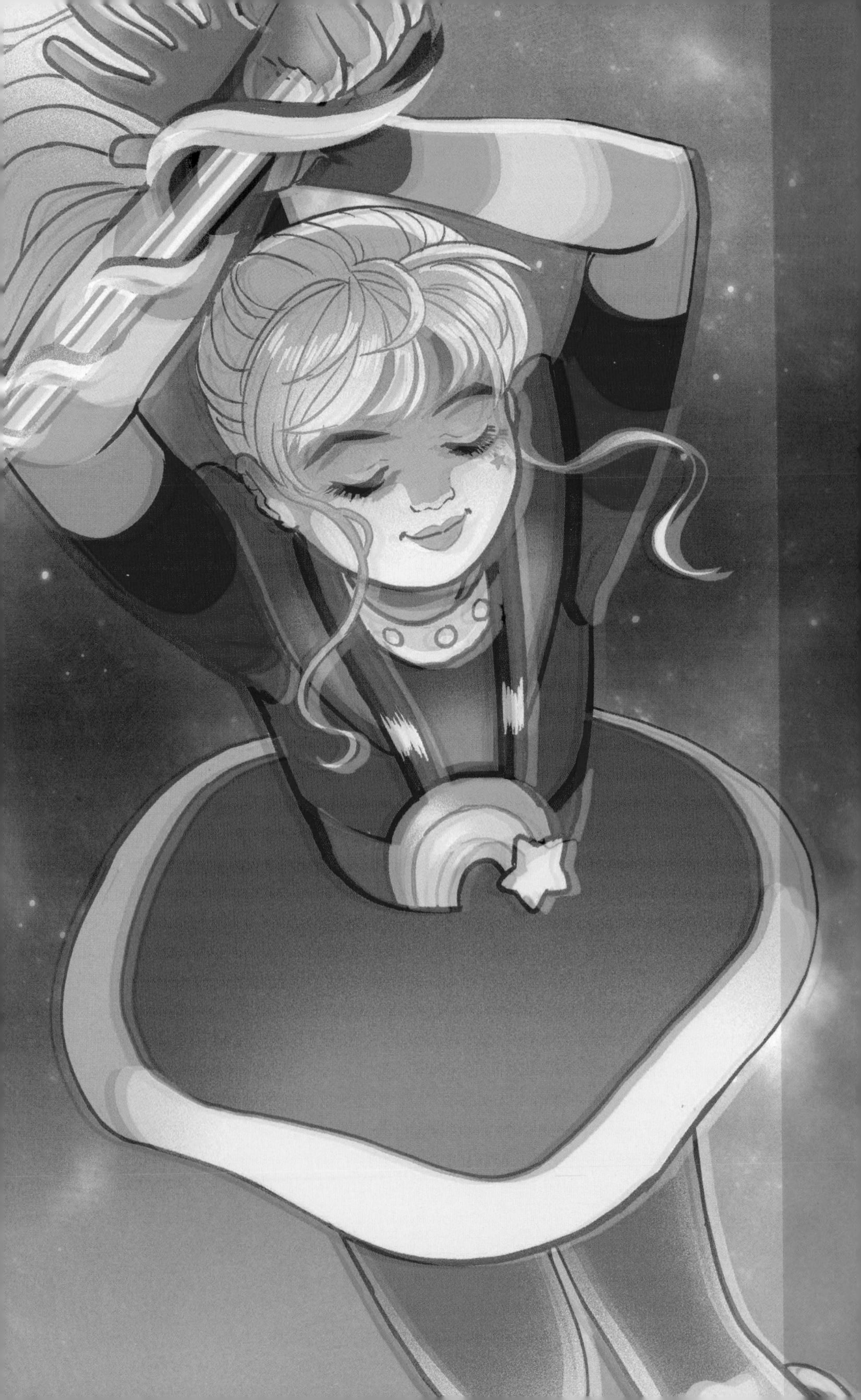

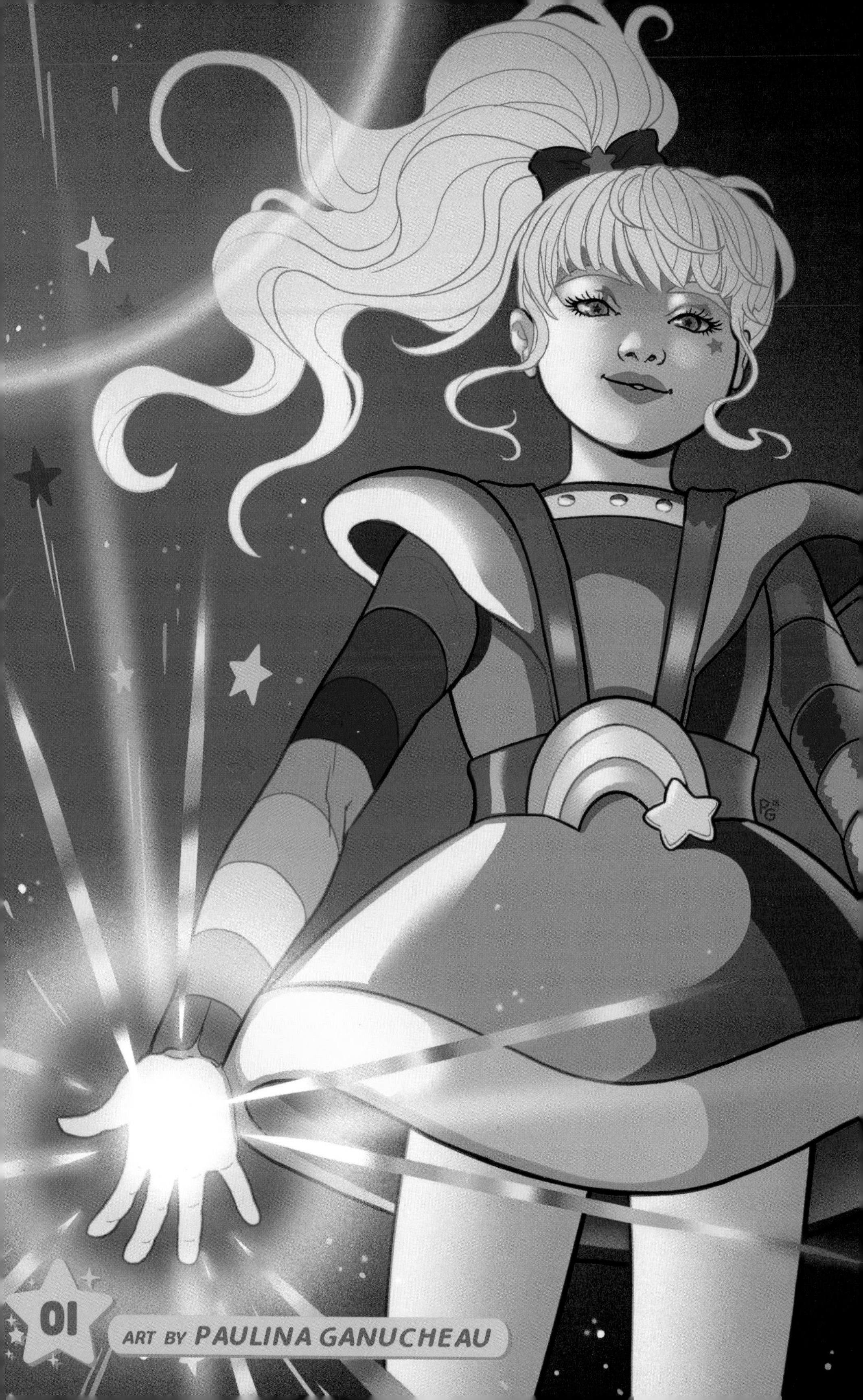
PG 18
01
ART BY PAULINA GANUCHEAU

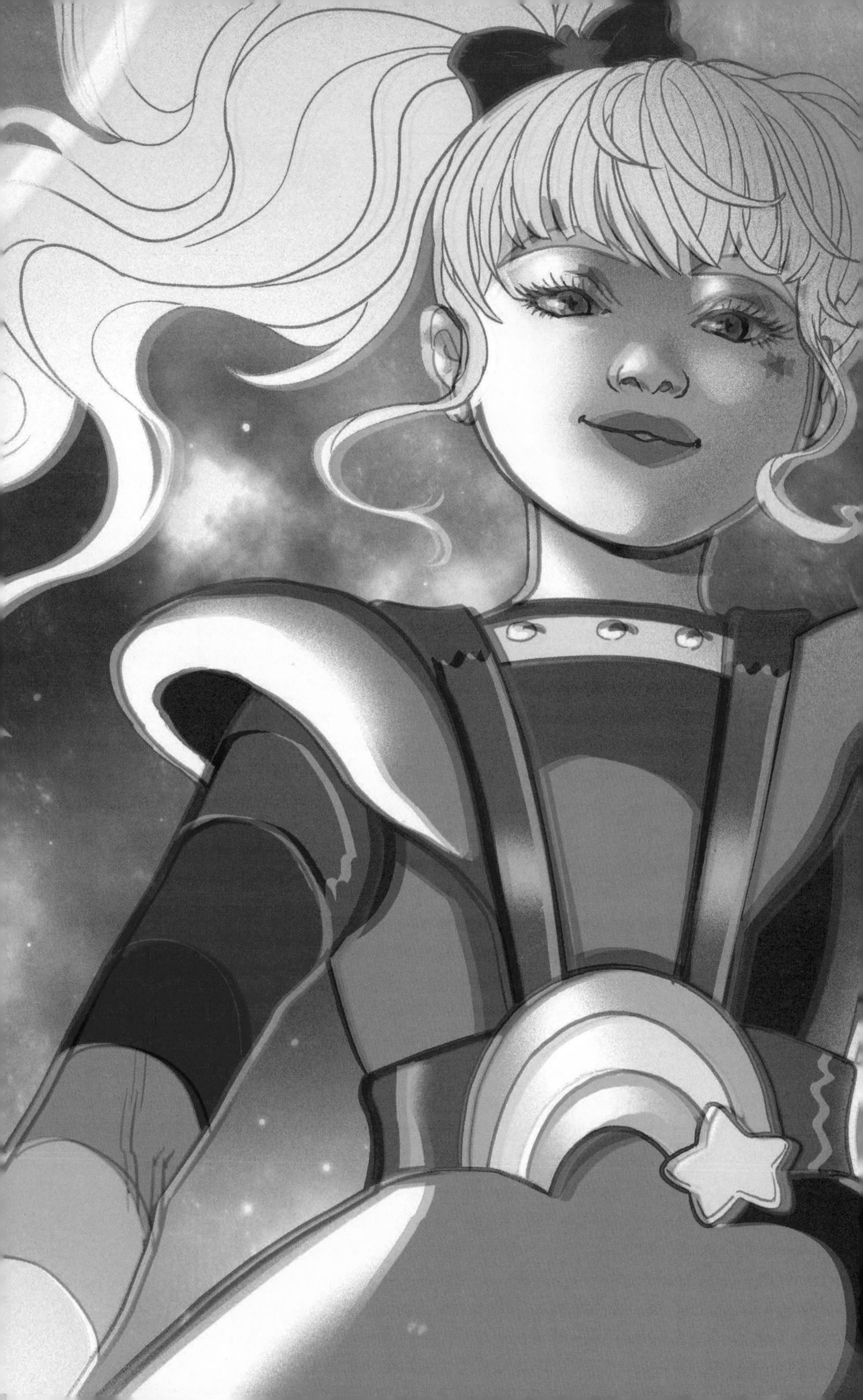

WRITER
JEREMY WHITLEY

ARTIST
BRITTNEY WILLIAMS (01-03)
XENIA PAMFIL (04-05)
CHRISTINE HIPP (05 inks)

COLORIST
VALENTINA PINTO

LETTERER
TAYLOR ESPOSITO

EDITOR
KEVIN KETNER

COLLECTION COVER ARTIST
PAULINA GANUCHEAU

COLLECTION DESIGNER
ALEXIS PERSSON

SPECIAL THANKS TO KATY BRIGGS, HANNAH CAREY,
KEVIN DILMORE, PETER MARTIN, JOHN NENS, ANDY OLSON,
JACK PULLAN AND LENA STONE AT HALLMARK.

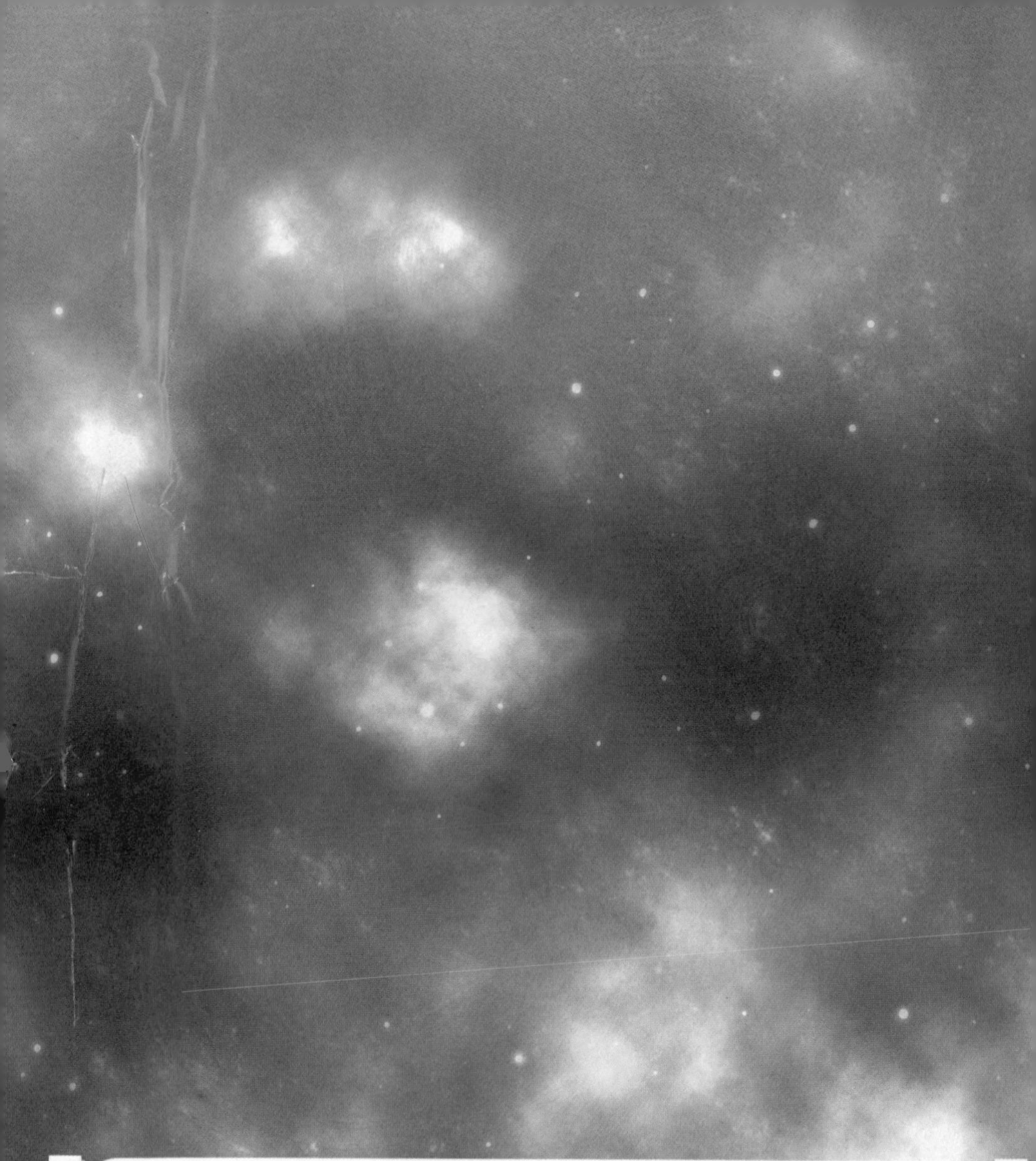

DYNAMITE®

Nick Barrucci, CEO / Publisher
Juan Collado, President / COO
Brandon Dante Primavera, V.P. of IT and Operations

Joe Rybandt, Executive Editor
Matt Idelson, Senior Editor

Cathleen Heard, Art Director
Rachel Kilbury, Digital Multimedia Associate
Alexis Persson, Graphic Designer
Katie Hidalgo, Graphic Designer

Alan Payne, V.P. of Sales and Marketing
Vincent Faust, Marketing Coordinator

Jay Spence, Director of Product Development
Mariano Nicieza, Director of Research & Development

Amy Jackson, Administrative Coordinator

ISBN: 978-15241-1518-0

First Print 1 2 3 4 5 6 7 8 9 10

www.DYNAMITE.com | Facebook **/Dynamitecomics** | Twitter **@dynamitecomics**

RAINBOW BRITE, Volume 1. First printing. Contains material originally published as RAINBOW BRITE issues 1-5. Published by Dynamite Entertainment, 113 Gaither Dr., STE 205, Mt. Laurel, NJ 08054. "RAINBOW BRITE" is © Hallmark Licensing, LLC. "Dynamite" and "Dynamite Entertainment" are ®, and the "DE Logo" is ™ and ©, 2020 Dynamite Entertainment. All Rights Reserved. All names, characters, events, and locales in this publication are entirely fictional. Any resemblance to actual persons (living or dead), events or places, without satiric intent, is coincidental. No portion of this book may be reproduced by any means (digital or print) without the written permission of Dynamite Entertainment except for review purposes. Printed in Korea.
For information regarding press, media rights, foreign rights, licensing, promotions, and advertising e-mail: marketing@dynamite.com

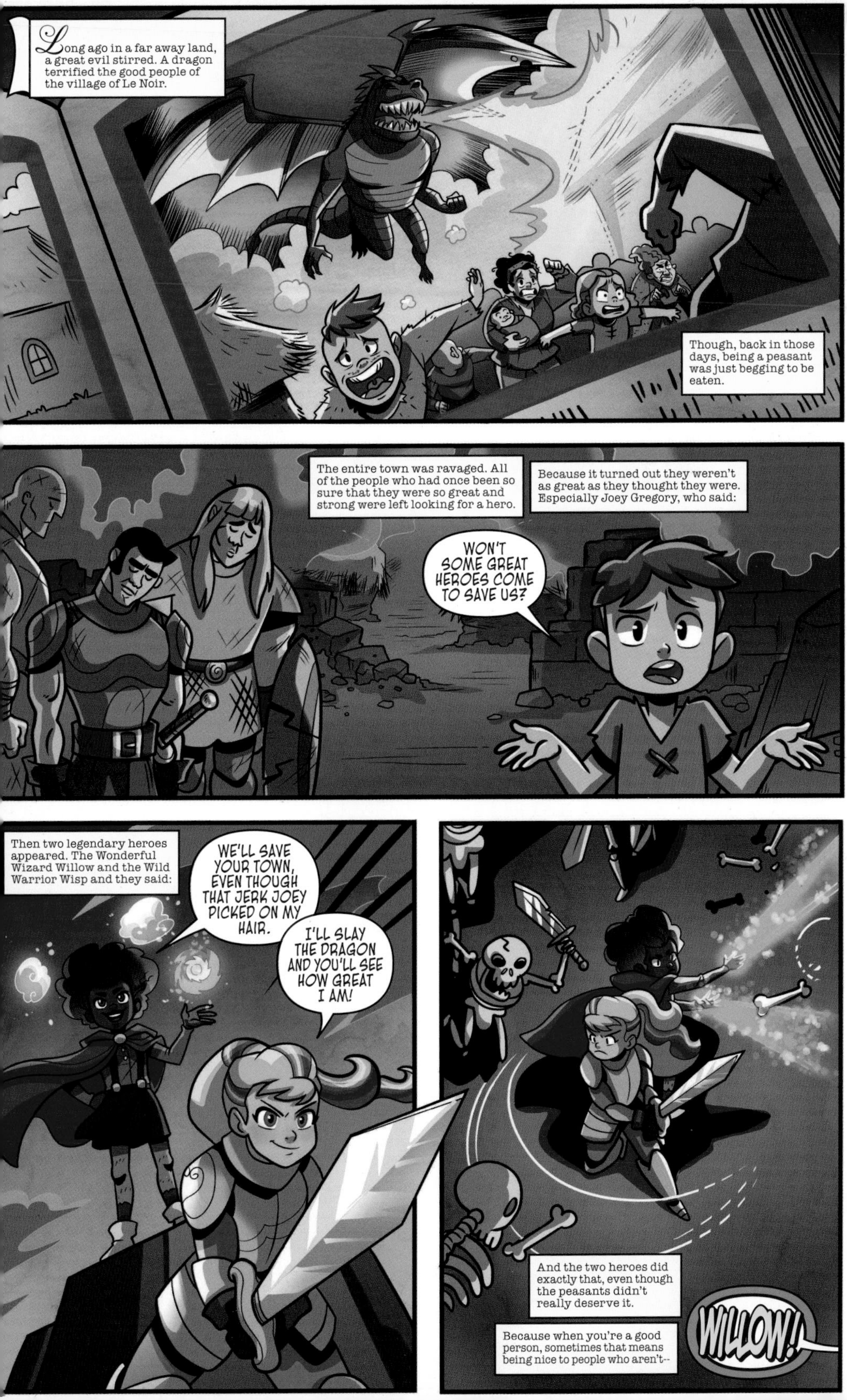
Long ago in a far away land, a great evil stirred. A dragon terrified the good people of the village of Le Noir.
Though, back in those days, being a peasant was just begging to be eaten.
The entire town was ravaged. All of the people who had once been so sure that they were so great and strong were left looking for a hero.
Because it turned out they weren't as great as they thought they were. Especially Joey Gregory, who said:
WON'T SOME GREAT HEROES COME TO SAVE US?
Then two legendary heroes appeared. The Wonderful Wizard Willow and the Wild Warrior Wisp and they said:
WE'LL SAVE YOUR TOWN, EVEN THOUGH THAT JERK JOEY PICKED ON MY HAIR.
I'LL SLAY THE DRAGON AND YOU'LL SEE HOW GREAT I AM!
And the two heroes did exactly that, even though the peasants didn't really deserve it.
Because when you're a good person, sometimes that means being nice to people who aren't--
WILLOW!

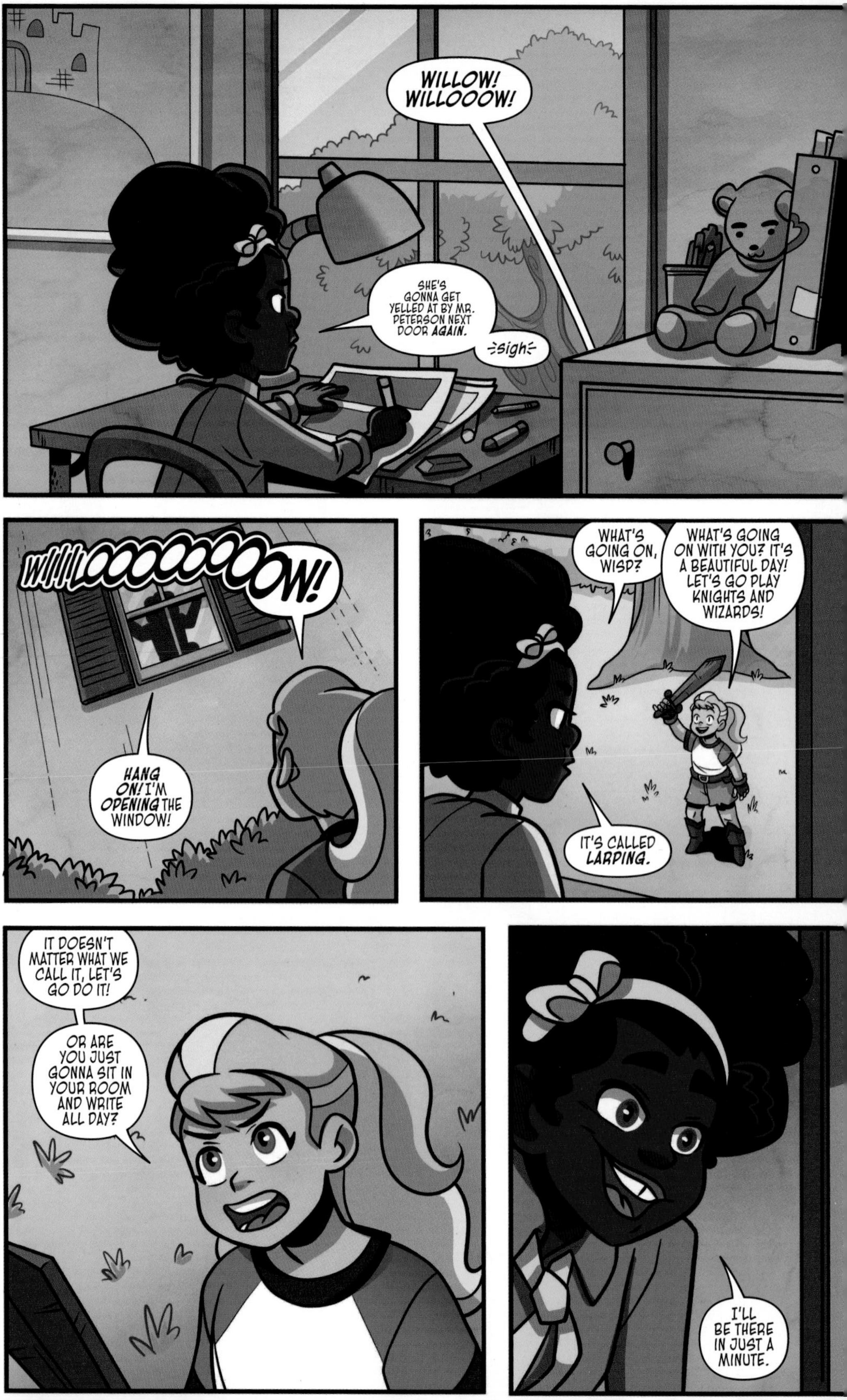
WILLOW! WILLOOOW!
SHE'S GONNA GET YELLED AT BY MR. PETERSON NEXT DOOR AGAIN.
sigh
WIIILOOOOOOOOW!
HANG ON! I'M OPENING THE WINDOW!
WHAT'S GOING ON, WISP?
WHAT'S GOING ON WITH YOU? IT'S A BEAUTIFUL DAY! LET'S GO PLAY KNIGHTS AND WIZARDS!
IT'S CALLED LARPING.
IT DOESN'T MATTER WHAT WE CALL IT, LET'S GO DO IT!
OR ARE YOU JUST GONNA SIT IN YOUR ROOM AND WRITE ALL DAY?
I'LL BE THERE IN JUST A MINUTE.

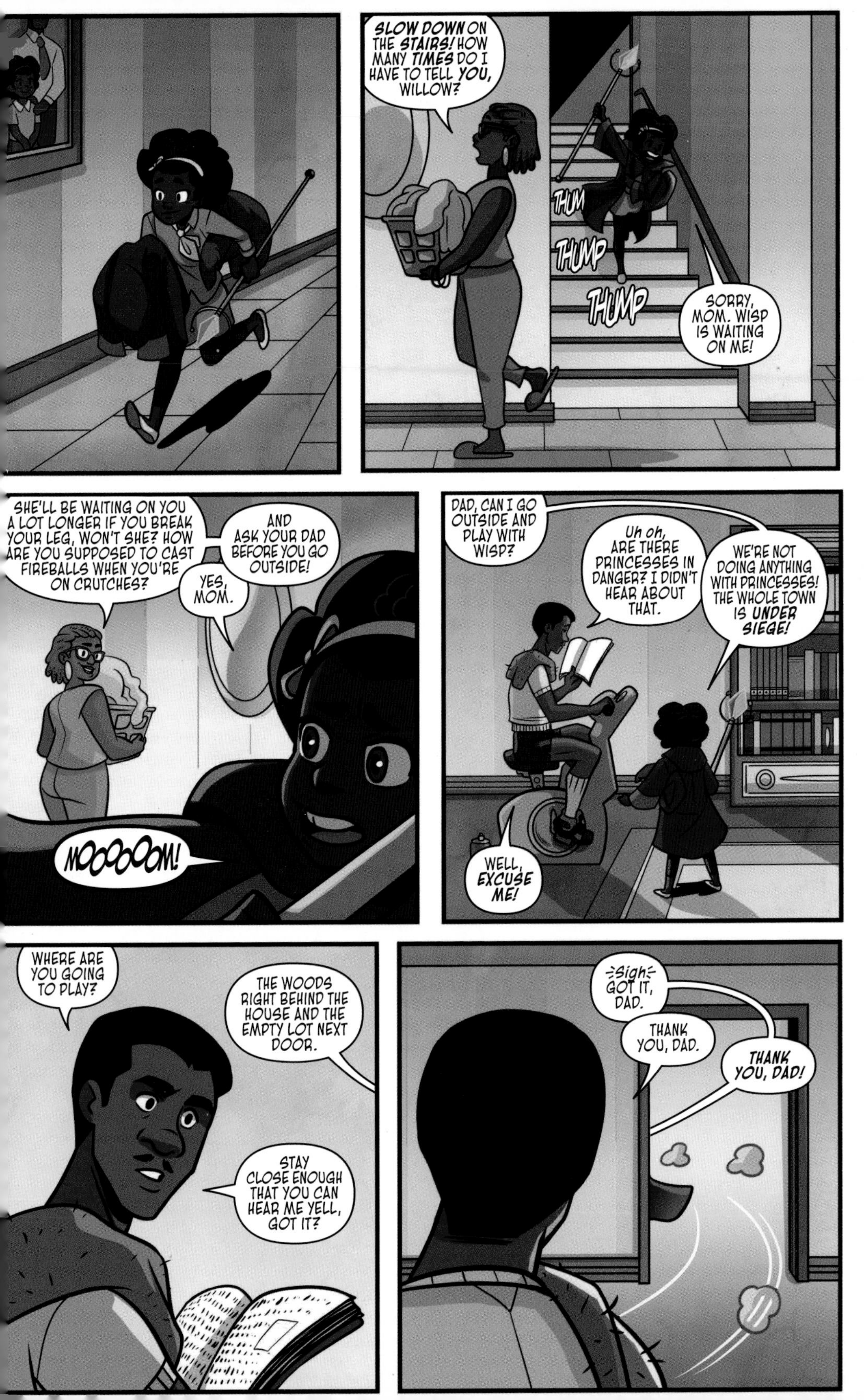
SLOW DOWN ON THE STAIRS! HOW MANY TIMES DO I HAVE TO TELL YOU, WILLOW?
THUMP
THUMP
THUMP
SORRY, MOM. WISP IS WAITING ON ME!
SHE'LL BE WAITING ON YOU A LOT LONGER IF YOU BREAK YOUR LEG, WON'T SHE? HOW ARE YOU SUPPOSED TO CAST FIREBALLS WHEN YOU'RE ON CRUTCHES?
AND ASK YOUR DAD BEFORE YOU GO OUTSIDE!
YES, MOM.
MOOOOOOM!
DAD, CAN I GO OUTSIDE AND PLAY WITH WISP?
Uh oh, ARE THERE PRINCESSES IN DANGER? I DIDN'T HEAR ABOUT THAT.
WE'RE NOT DOING ANYTHING WITH PRINCESSES! THE WHOLE TOWN IS UNDER SIEGE!
WELL, EXCUSE ME!
WHERE ARE YOU GOING TO PLAY?
THE WOODS RIGHT BEHIND THE HOUSE AND THE EMPTY LOT NEXT DOOR.
STAY CLOSE ENOUGH THAT YOU CAN HEAR ME YELL, GOT IT?
Sigh GOT IT, DAD.
THANK YOU, DAD.
THANK YOU, DAD!

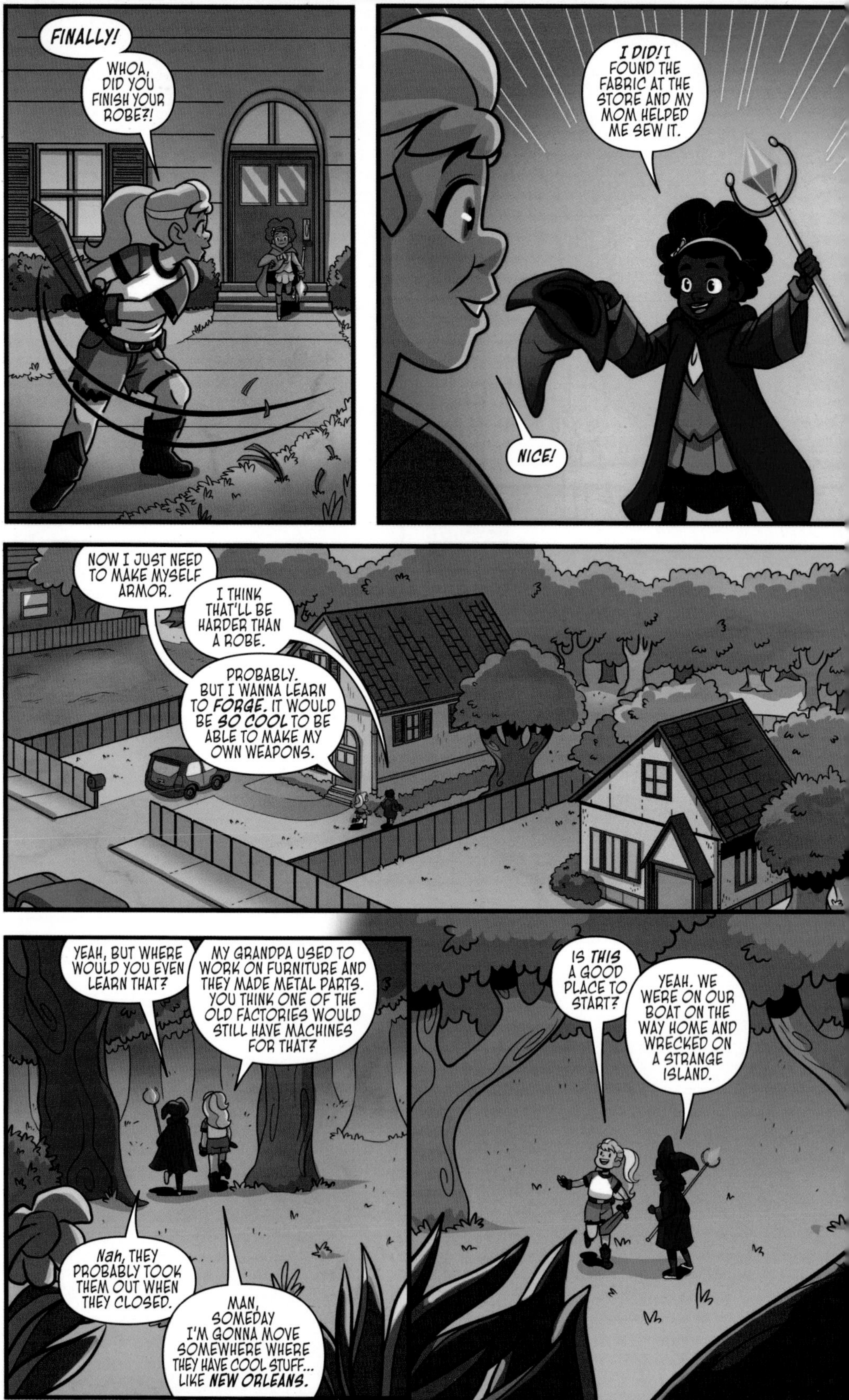
FINALLY!
WHOA, DID YOU FINISH YOUR ROBE?!
I DID! I FOUND THE FABRIC AT THE STORE AND MY MOM HELPED ME SEW IT.
NICE!
NOW I JUST NEED TO MAKE MYSELF ARMOR.
I THINK THAT'LL BE HARDER THAN A ROBE.
PROBABLY. BUT I WANNA LEARN TO FORGE. IT WOULD BE SO COOL TO BE ABLE TO MAKE MY OWN WEAPONS.
YEAH, BUT WHERE WOULD YOU EVEN LEARN THAT?
MY GRANDPA USED TO WORK ON FURNITURE AND THEY MADE METAL PARTS. YOU THINK ONE OF THE OLD FACTORIES WOULD STILL HAVE MACHINES FOR THAT?
Nah, THEY PROBABLY TOOK THEM OUT WHEN THEY CLOSED.
MAN, SOMEDAY I'M GONNA MOVE SOMEWHERE WHERE THEY HAVE COOL STUFF... LIKE NEW ORLEANS.
IS THIS A GOOD PLACE TO START?
YEAH. WE WERE ON OUR BOAT ON THE WAY HOME AND WRECKED ON A STRANGE ISLAND.

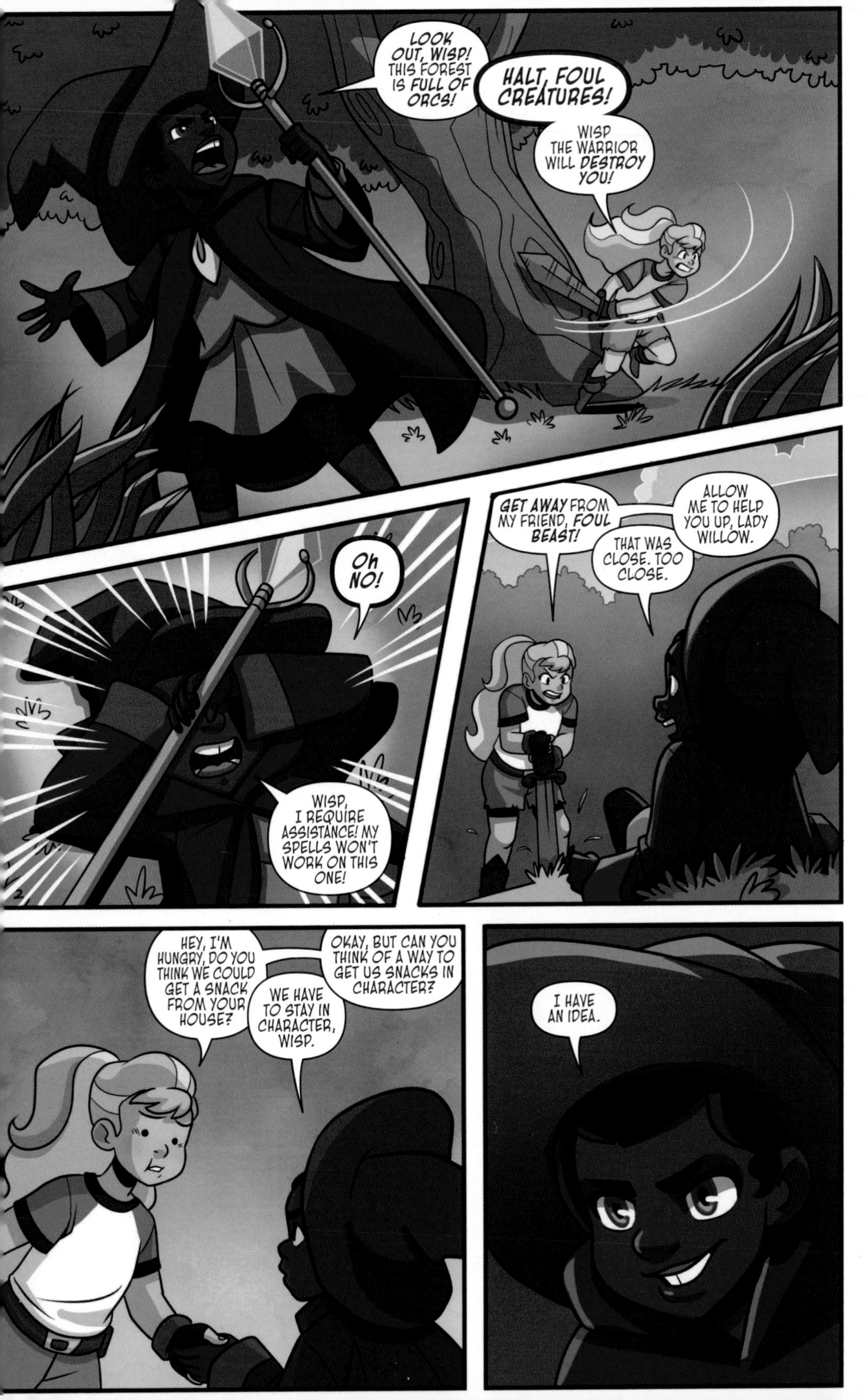
LOOK OUT, WISP! THIS FOREST IS FULL OF ORCS!
HALT, FOUL CREATURES!
WISP THE WARRIOR WILL DESTROY YOU!
Oh NO!
WISP, I REQUIRE ASSISTANCE! MY SPELLS WON'T WORK ON THIS ONE!
GET AWAY FROM MY FRIEND, FOUL BEAST!
THAT WAS CLOSE. TOO CLOSE.
ALLOW ME TO HELP YOU UP, LADY WILLOW.
HEY, I'M HUNGRY, DO YOU THINK WE COULD GET A SNACK FROM YOUR HOUSE?
WE HAVE TO STAY IN CHARACTER, WISP.
OKAY, BUT CAN YOU THINK OF A WAY TO GET US SNACKS IN CHARACTER?
I HAVE AN IDEA.

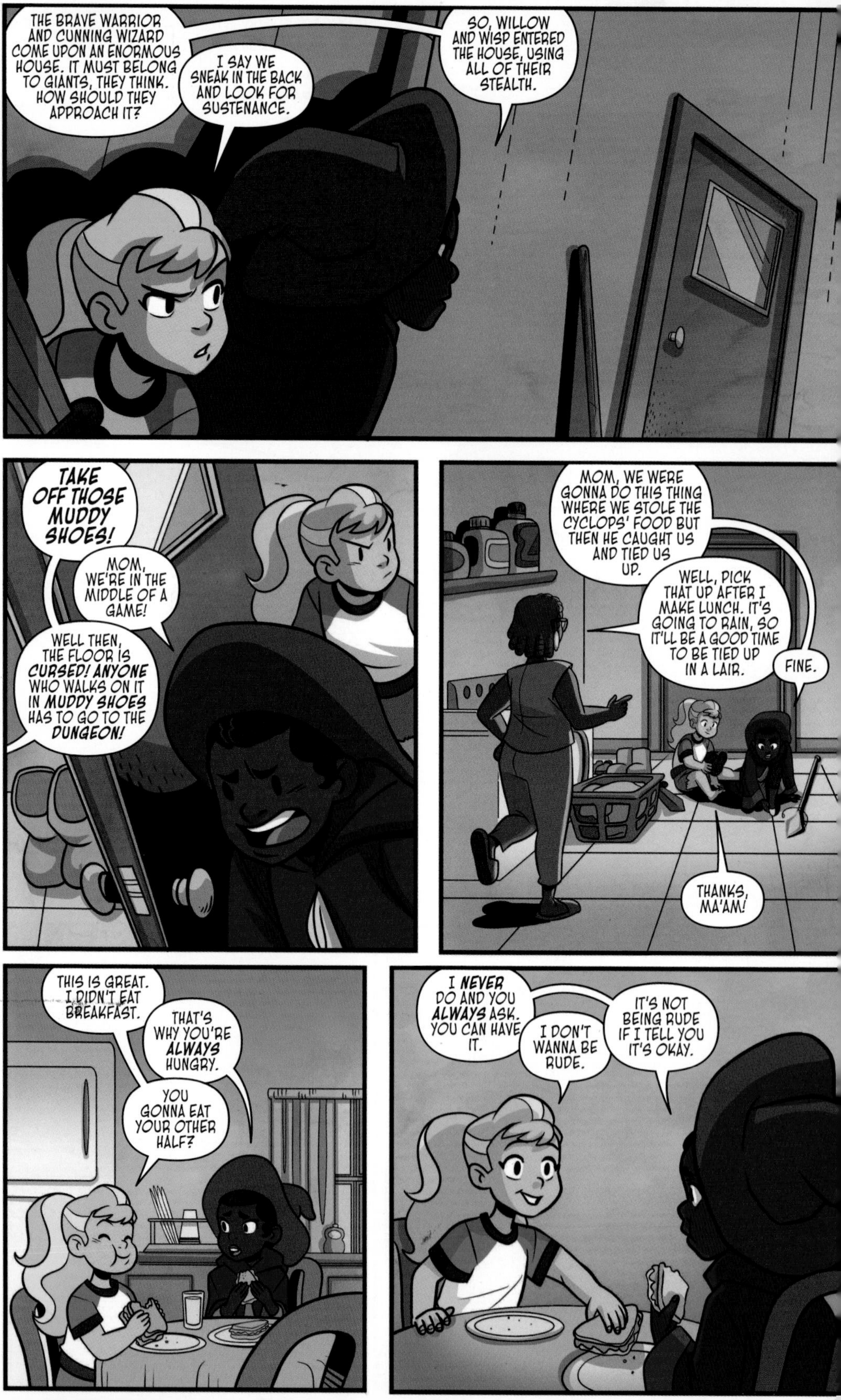
THE BRAVE WARRIOR AND CUNNING WIZARD COME UPON AN ENORMOUS HOUSE. IT MUST BELONG TO GIANTS, THEY THINK. HOW SHOULD THEY APPROACH IT?
I SAY WE SNEAK IN THE BACK AND LOOK FOR SUSTENANCE.
SO, WILLOW AND WISP ENTERED THE HOUSE, USING ALL OF THEIR STEALTH.
TAKE OFF THOSE MUDDY SHOES!
MOM, WE'RE IN THE MIDDLE OF A GAME!
WELL THEN, THE FLOOR IS CURSED! ANYONE WHO WALKS ON IT IN MUDDY SHOES HAS TO GO TO THE DUNGEON!
MOM, WE WERE GONNA DO THIS THING WHERE WE STOLE THE CYCLOPS' FOOD BUT THEN HE CAUGHT US AND TIED US UP.
WELL, PICK THAT UP AFTER I MAKE LUNCH. IT'S GOING TO RAIN, SO IT'LL BE A GOOD TIME TO BE TIED UP IN A LAIR.
FINE.
THANKS, MA'AM!
THIS IS GREAT. I DIDN'T EAT BREAKFAST.
THAT'S WHY YOU'RE ALWAYS HUNGRY.
YOU GONNA EAT YOUR OTHER HALF?
I NEVER DO AND YOU ALWAYS ASK. YOU CAN HAVE IT.
I DON'T WANNA BE RUDE.
IT'S NOT BEING RUDE IF I TELL YOU IT'S OKAY.

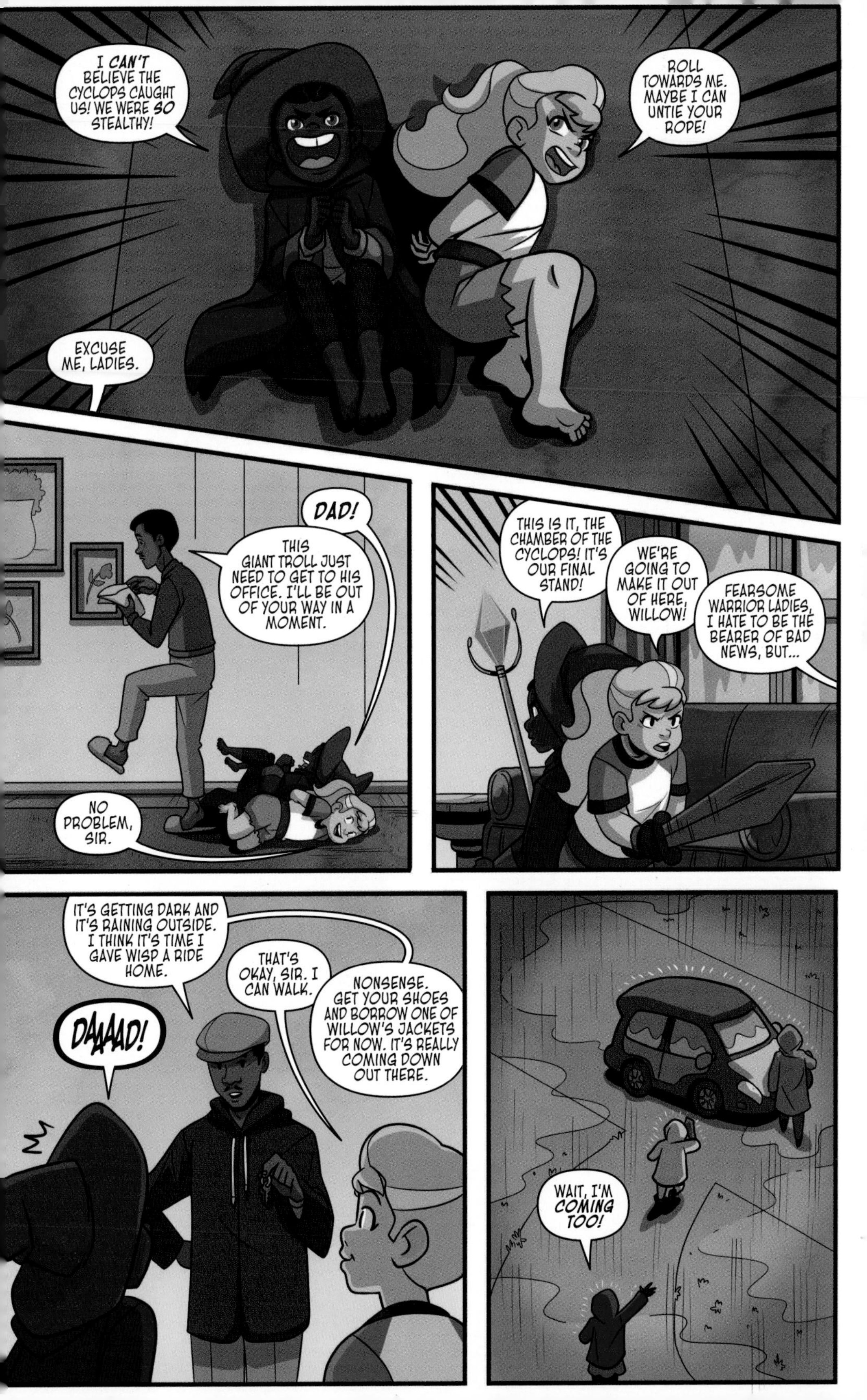
I CAN'T BELIEVE THE CYCLOPS CAUGHT US! WE WERE SO STEALTHY!
ROLL TOWARDS ME. MAYBE I CAN UNTIE YOUR ROPE!
EXCUSE ME, LADIES.
DAD!
THIS GIANT TROLL JUST NEED TO GET TO HIS OFFICE. I'LL BE OUT OF YOUR WAY IN A MOMENT.
NO PROBLEM, SIR.
THIS IS IT, THE CHAMBER OF THE CYCLOPS! IT'S OUR FINAL STAND!
WE'RE GOING TO MAKE IT OUT OF HERE, WILLOW!
FEARSOME WARRIOR LADIES, I HATE TO BE THE BEARER OF BAD NEWS, BUT...
IT'S GETTING DARK AND IT'S RAINING OUTSIDE. I THINK IT'S TIME I GAVE WISP A RIDE HOME.
DAAAAD!
THAT'S OKAY, SIR. I CAN WALK.
NONSENSE. GET YOUR SHOES AND BORROW ONE OF WILLOW'S JACKETS FOR NOW. IT'S REALLY COMING DOWN OUT THERE.
WAIT, I'M COMING TOO!

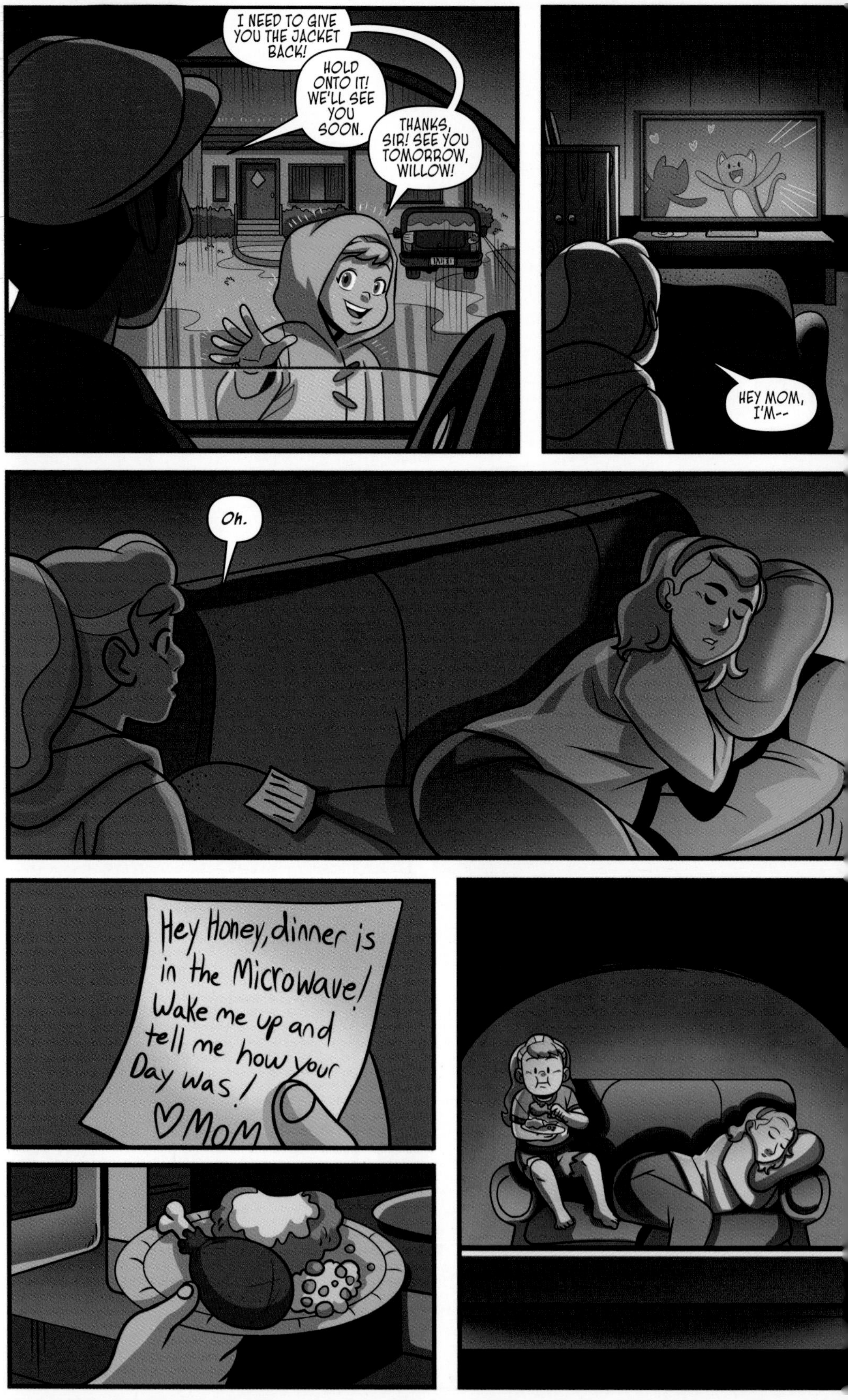

I NEED TO GIVE YOU THE JACKET BACK!
HOLD ONTO IT! WE'LL SEE YOU SOON.
THANKS, SIR! SEE YOU TOMORROW, WILLOW!
HEY MOM, I'M--
Oh.
Hey Honey, dinner is in the Microwave! Wake me up and tell me how your Day was! ♡ MOM

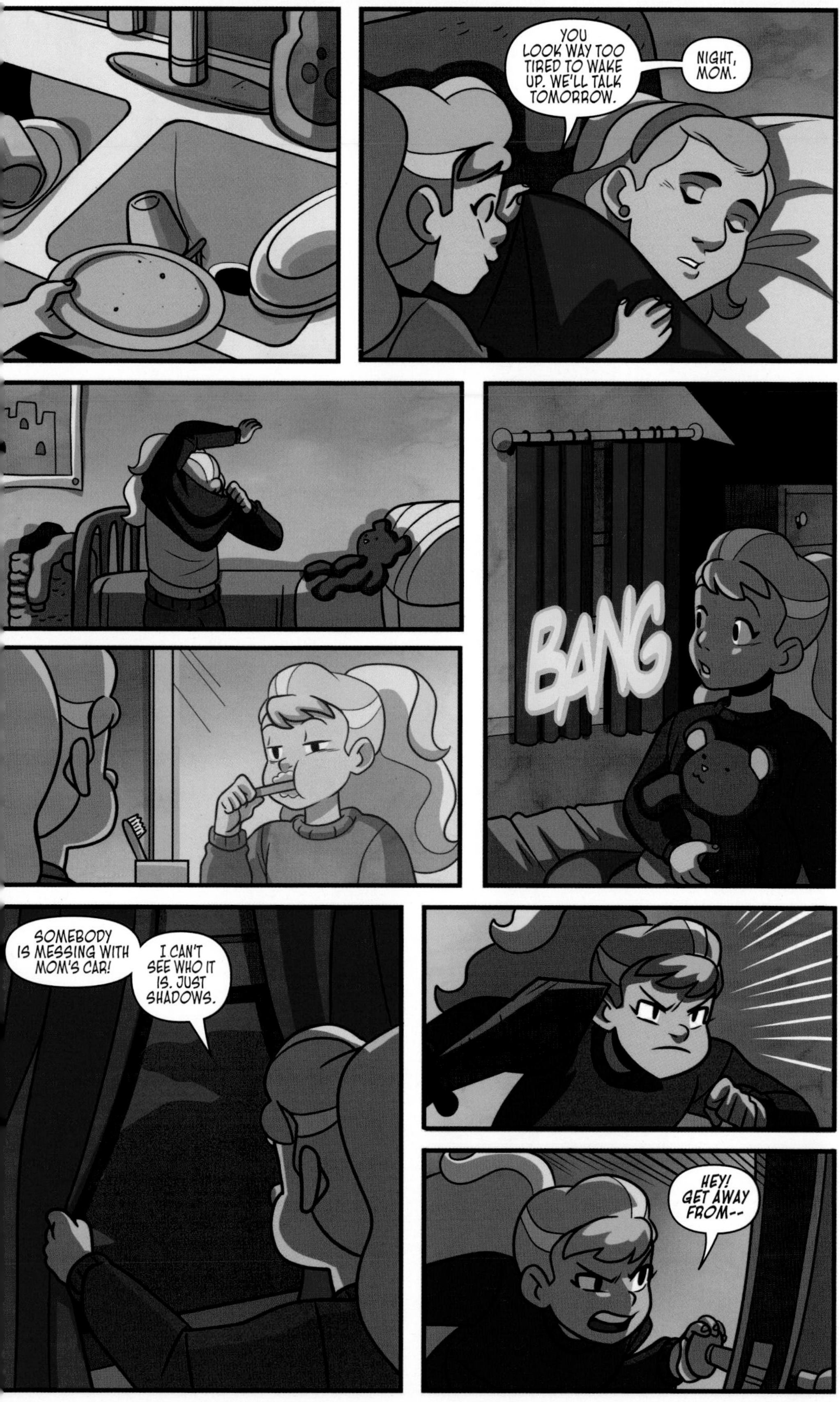
YOU LOOK WAY TOO TIRED TO WAKE UP. WE'LL TALK TOMORROW.
NIGHT, MOM.
BANG
SOMEBODY IS MESSING WITH MOM'S CAR!
I CAN'T SEE WHO IT IS. JUST SHADOWS.
HEY! GET AWAY FROM--

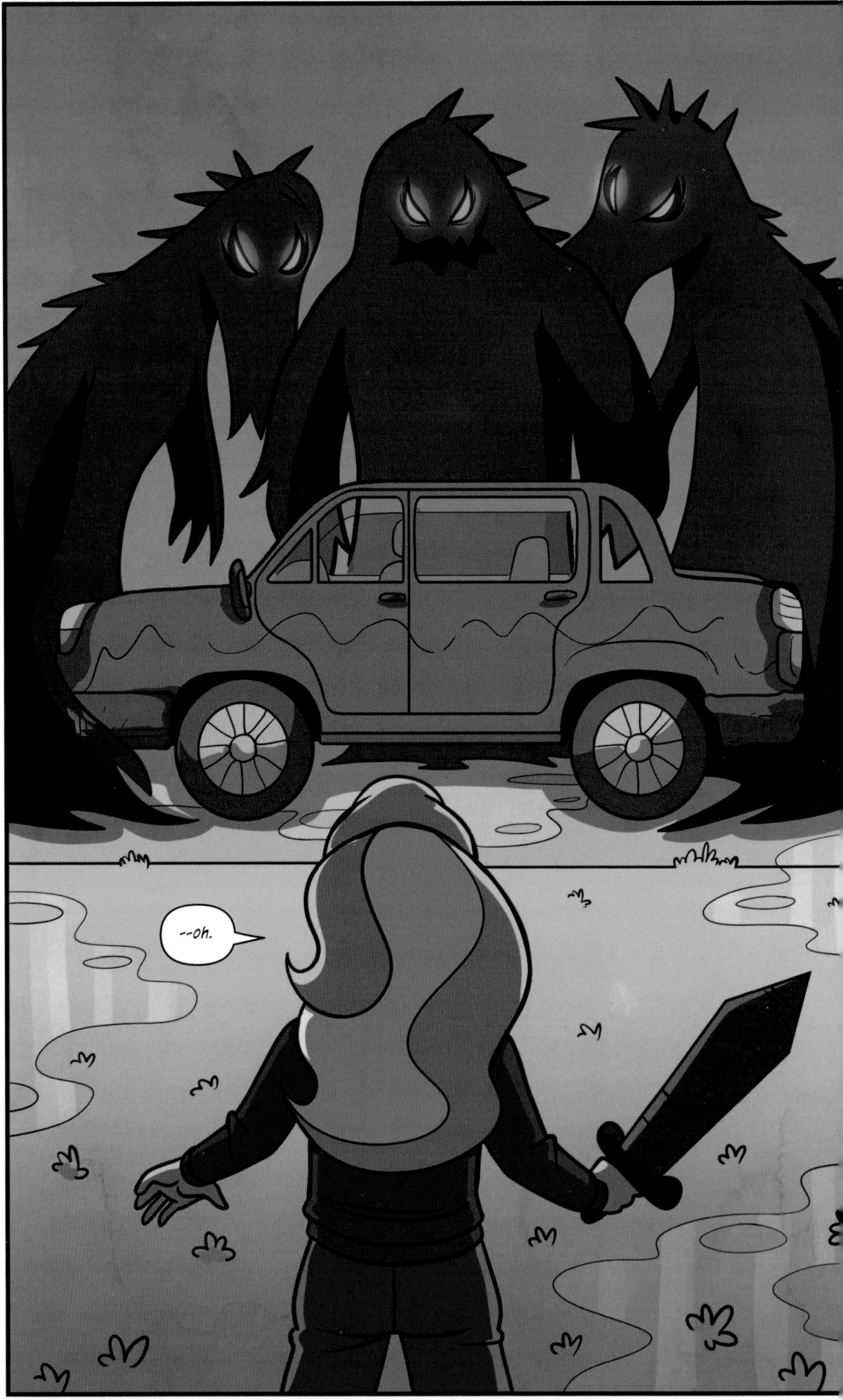
--oh.

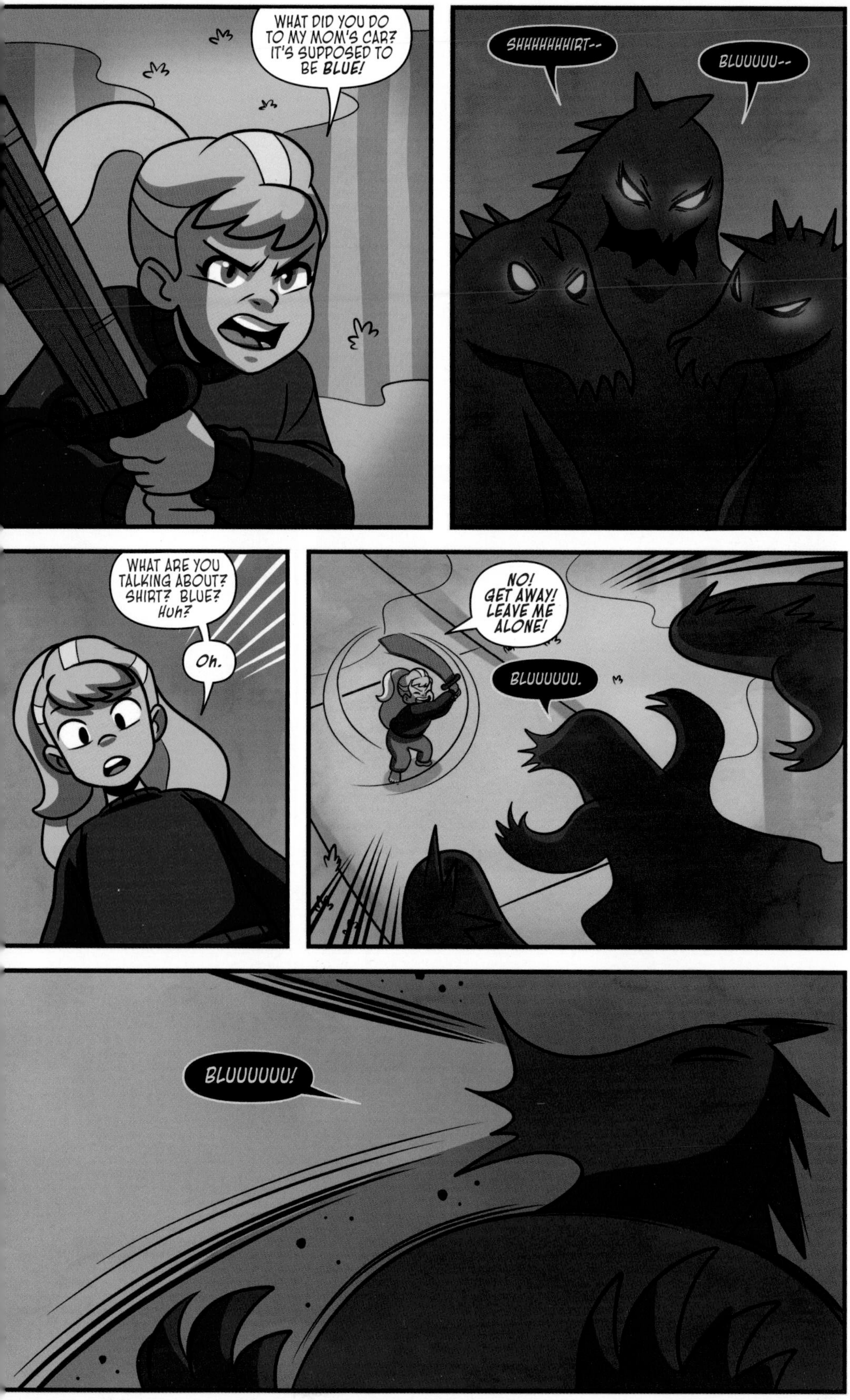
WHAT DID YOU DO TO MY MOM'S CAR? IT'S SUPPOSED TO BE BLUE!
SHHHHHHHIRT--
BLUUUUU--
WHAT ARE YOU TALKING ABOUT? SHIRT? BLUE? Huh?
Oh.
NO! GET AWAY! LEAVE ME ALONE!
BLUUUUUU.
BLUUUUUU!

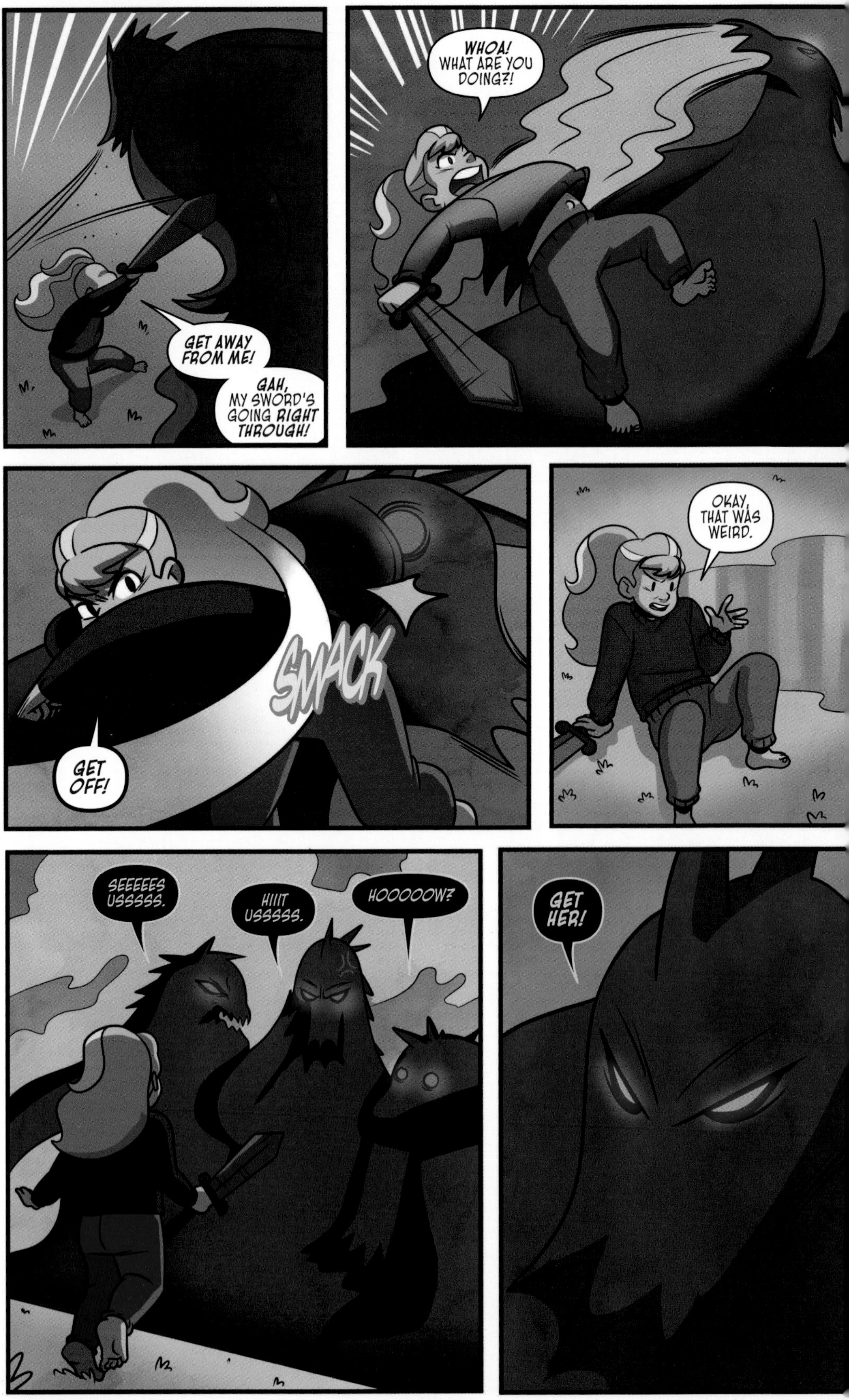
GET AWAY FROM ME!
GAH, MY SWORD'S GOING RIGHT THROUGH!
WHOA! WHAT ARE YOU DOING?!
GET OFF!
SMACK
OKAY, THAT WAS WEIRD.
SEEEEES USSSSS.
HIIIT USSSSS.
HOOOOOW?
GET HER!

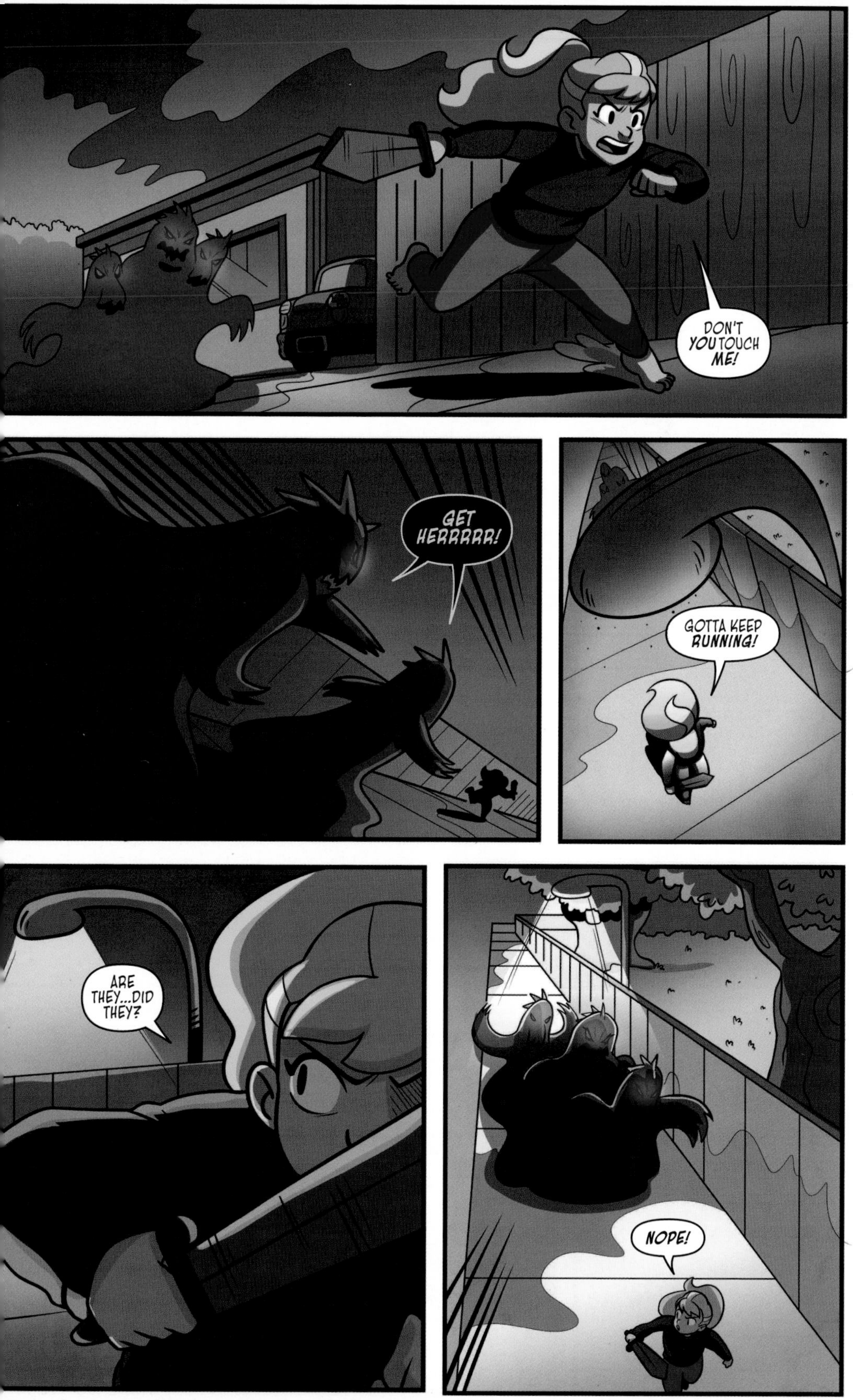
DON'T YOU TOUCH ME!
GET HERRRRR!
GOTTA KEEP RUNNING!
ARE THEY...DID THEY?
NOPE!

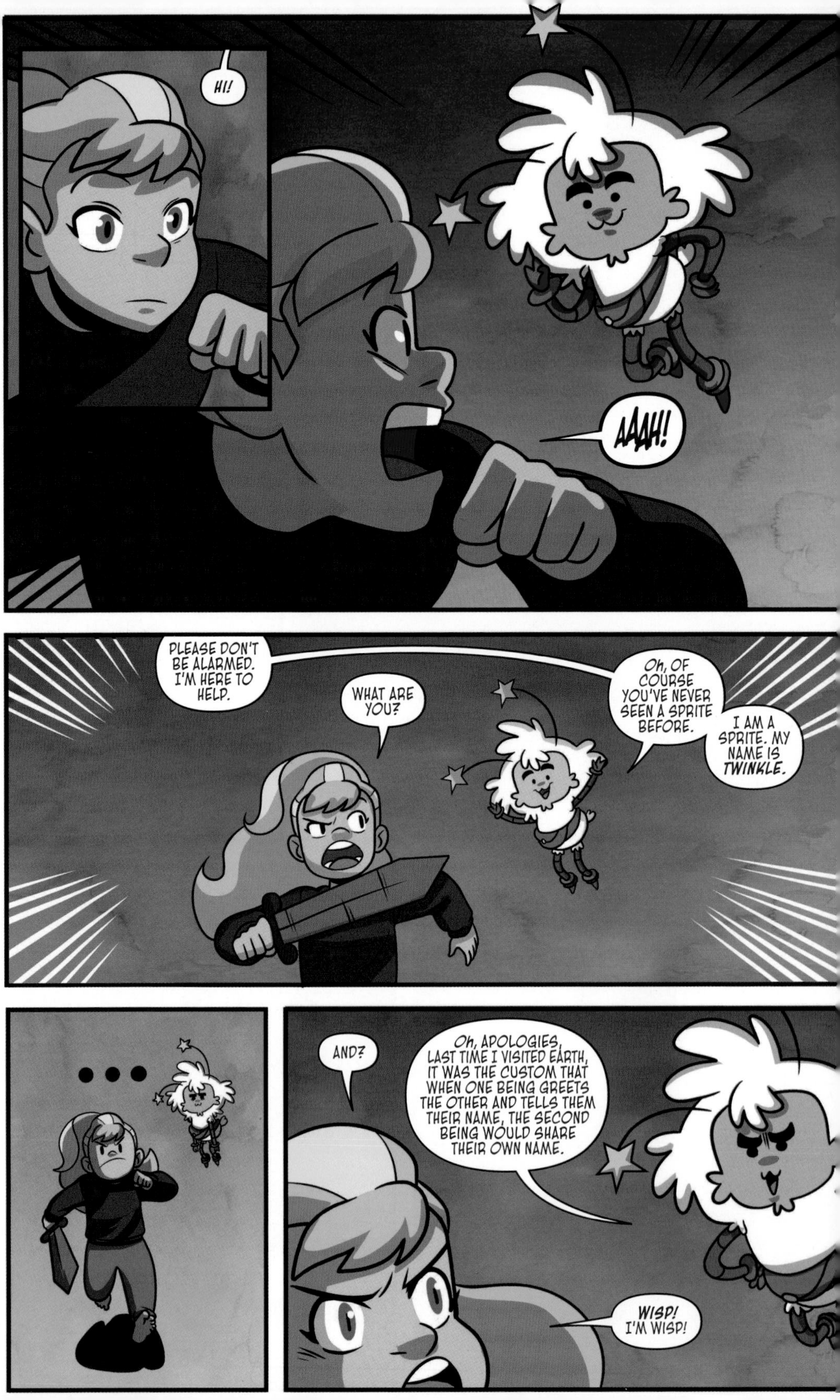
HI!
AAAH!
PLEASE DON'T BE ALARMED. I'M HERE TO HELP.
WHAT ARE YOU?
Oh, OF COURSE YOU'VE NEVER SEEN A SPRITE BEFORE.
I AM A SPRITE. MY NAME IS TWINKLE.
...
AND?
Oh, APOLOGIES, LAST TIME I VISITED EARTH, IT WAS THE CUSTOM THAT WHEN ONE BEING GREETS THE OTHER AND TELLS THEM THEIR NAME, THE SECOND BEING WOULD SHARE THEIR OWN NAME.
WISP! I'M WISP!

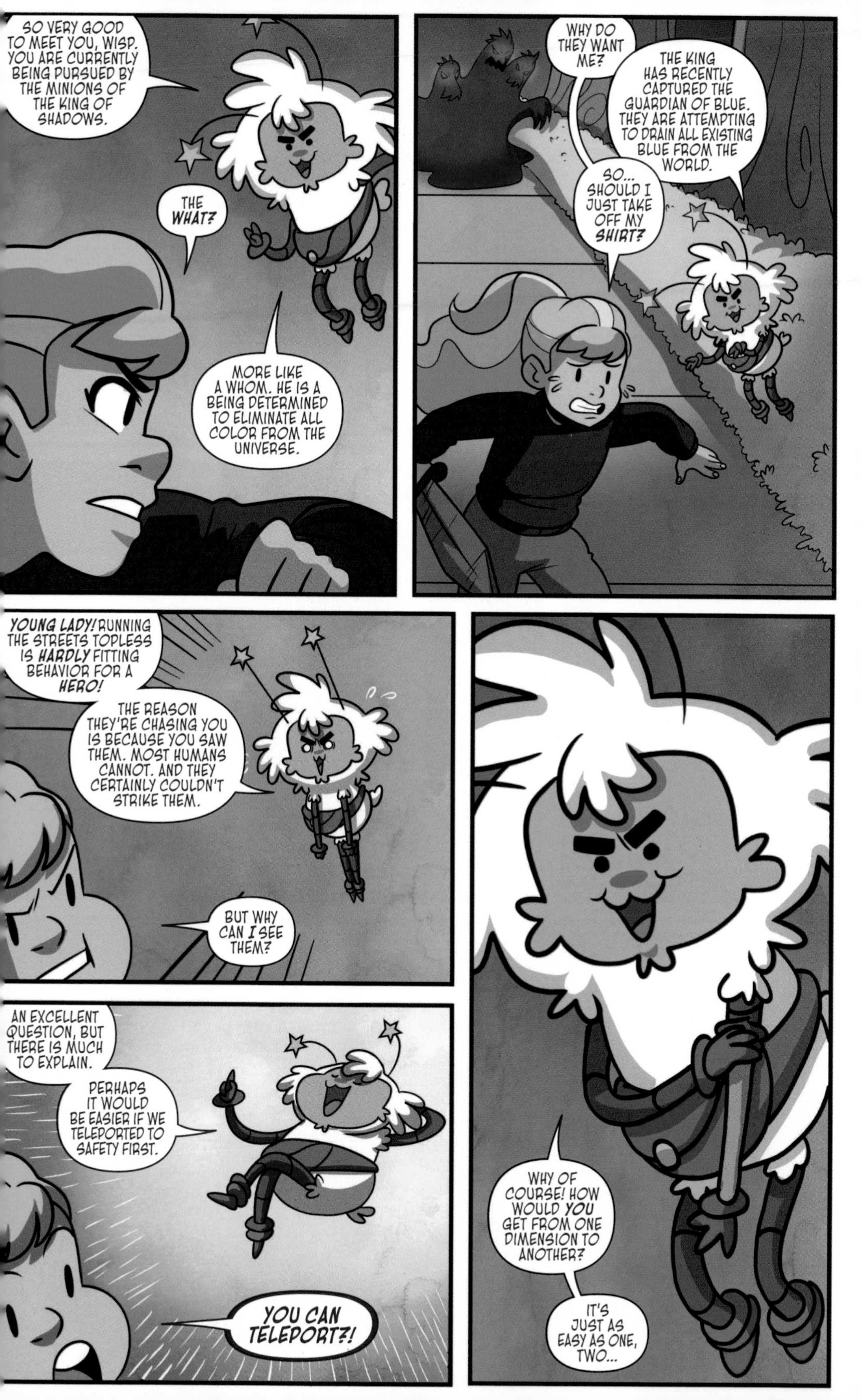
SO VERY GOOD TO MEET YOU, WISP. YOU ARE CURRENTLY BEING PURSUED BY THE MINIONS OF THE KING OF SHADOWS.
THE WHAT?
MORE LIKE A WHOM. HE IS A BEING DETERMINED TO ELIMINATE ALL COLOR FROM THE UNIVERSE.
WHY DO THEY WANT ME?
THE KING HAS RECENTLY CAPTURED THE GUARDIAN OF BLUE. THEY ARE ATTEMPTING TO DRAIN ALL EXISTING BLUE FROM THE WORLD.
SO... SHOULD I JUST TAKE OFF MY SHIRT?
YOUNG LADY! RUNNING THE STREETS TOPLESS IS HARDLY FITTING BEHAVIOR FOR A HERO!
THE REASON THEY'RE CHASING YOU IS BECAUSE YOU SAW THEM. MOST HUMANS CANNOT. AND THEY CERTAINLY COULDN'T STRIKE THEM.
BUT WHY CAN I SEE THEM?
AN EXCELLENT QUESTION, BUT THERE IS MUCH TO EXPLAIN.
PERHAPS IT WOULD BE EASIER IF WE TELEPORTED TO SAFETY FIRST.
YOU CAN TELEPORT?!
WHY OF COURSE! HOW WOULD YOU GET FROM ONE DIMENSION TO ANOTHER?
IT'S JUST AS EASY AS ONE, TWO...

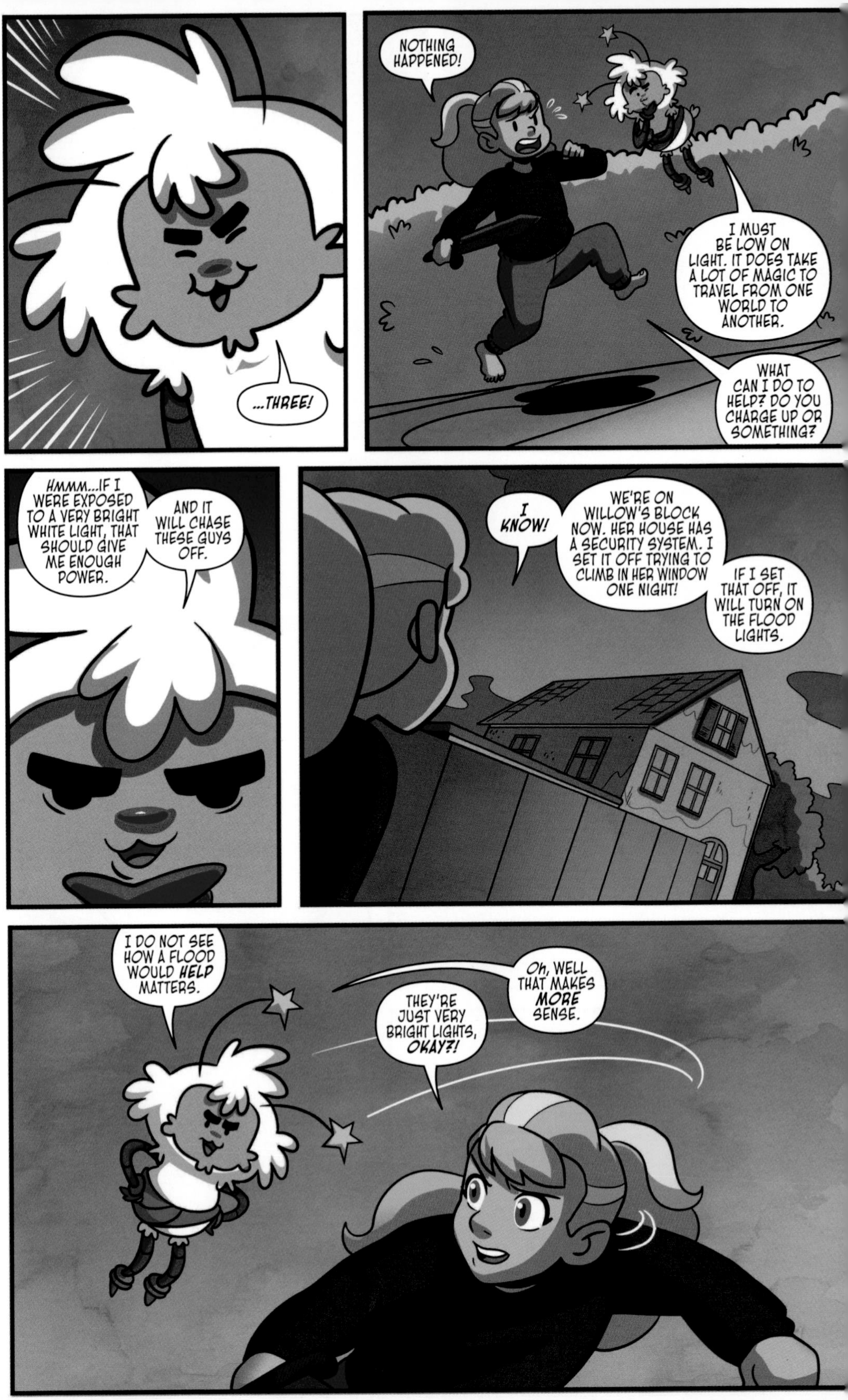
...THREE!
NOTHING HAPPENED!
I MUST BE LOW ON LIGHT. IT DOES TAKE A LOT OF MAGIC TO TRAVEL FROM ONE WORLD TO ANOTHER.
WHAT CAN I DO TO HELP? DO YOU CHARGE UP OR SOMETHING?
HMMM...IF I WERE EXPOSED TO A VERY BRIGHT WHITE LIGHT, THAT SHOULD GIVE ME ENOUGH POWER.
AND IT WILL CHASE THESE GUYS OFF.
I KNOW!
WE'RE ON WILLOW'S BLOCK NOW. HER HOUSE HAS A SECURITY SYSTEM. I SET IT OFF TRYING TO CLIMB IN HER WINDOW ONE NIGHT!
IF I SET THAT OFF, IT WILL TURN ON THE FLOOD LIGHTS.
I DO NOT SEE HOW A FLOOD WOULD HELP MATTERS.
THEY'RE JUST VERY BRIGHT LIGHTS, OKAY?!
Oh, WELL THAT MAKES MORE SENSE.

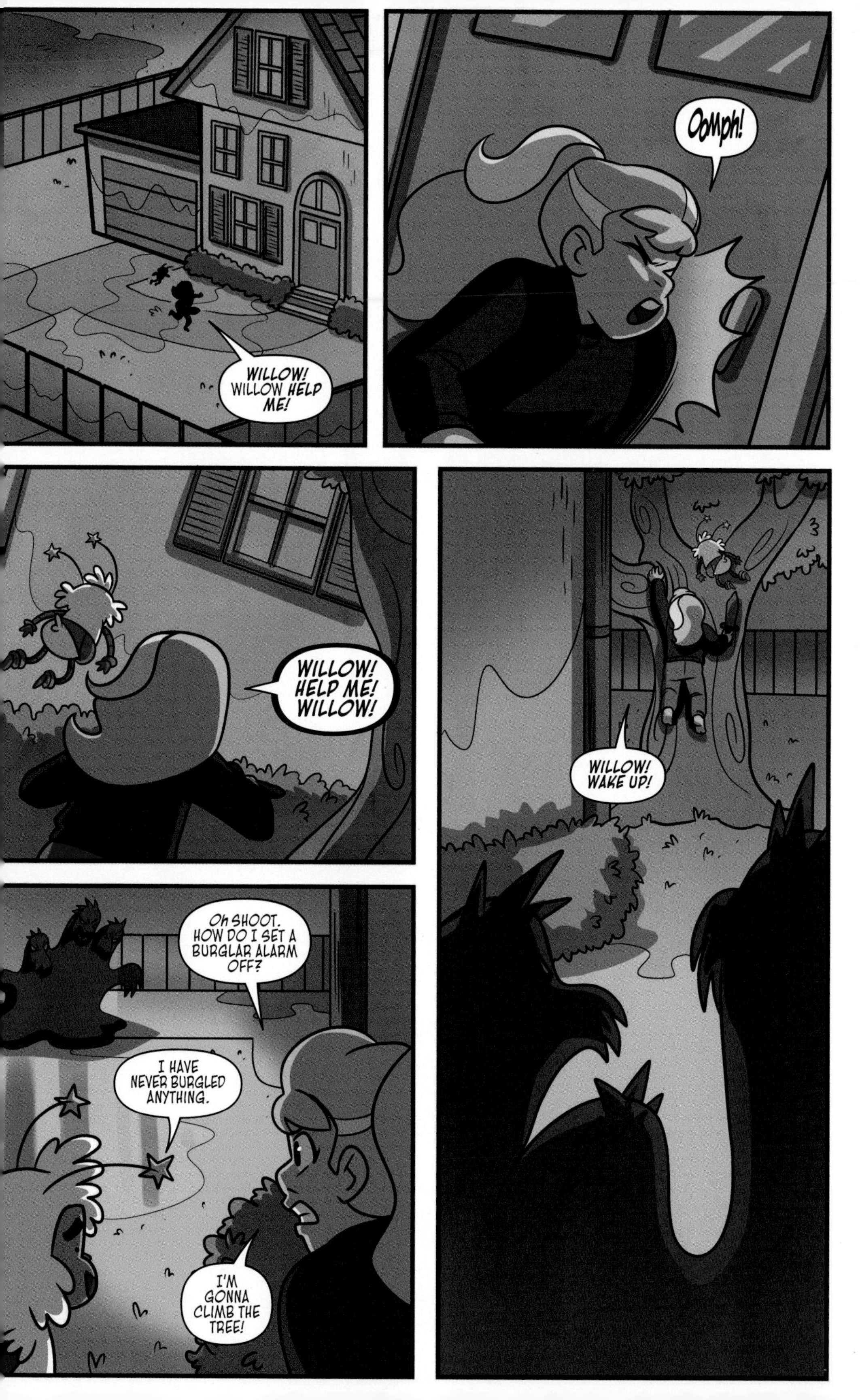
WILLOW! WILLOW HELP ME!
OoMph!
WILLOW! HELP ME! WILLOW!
WILLOW! WAKE UP!
Oh SHOOT. HOW DO I SET A BURGLAR ALARM OFF?
I HAVE NEVER BURGLED ANYTHING.
I'M GONNA CLIMB THE TREE!

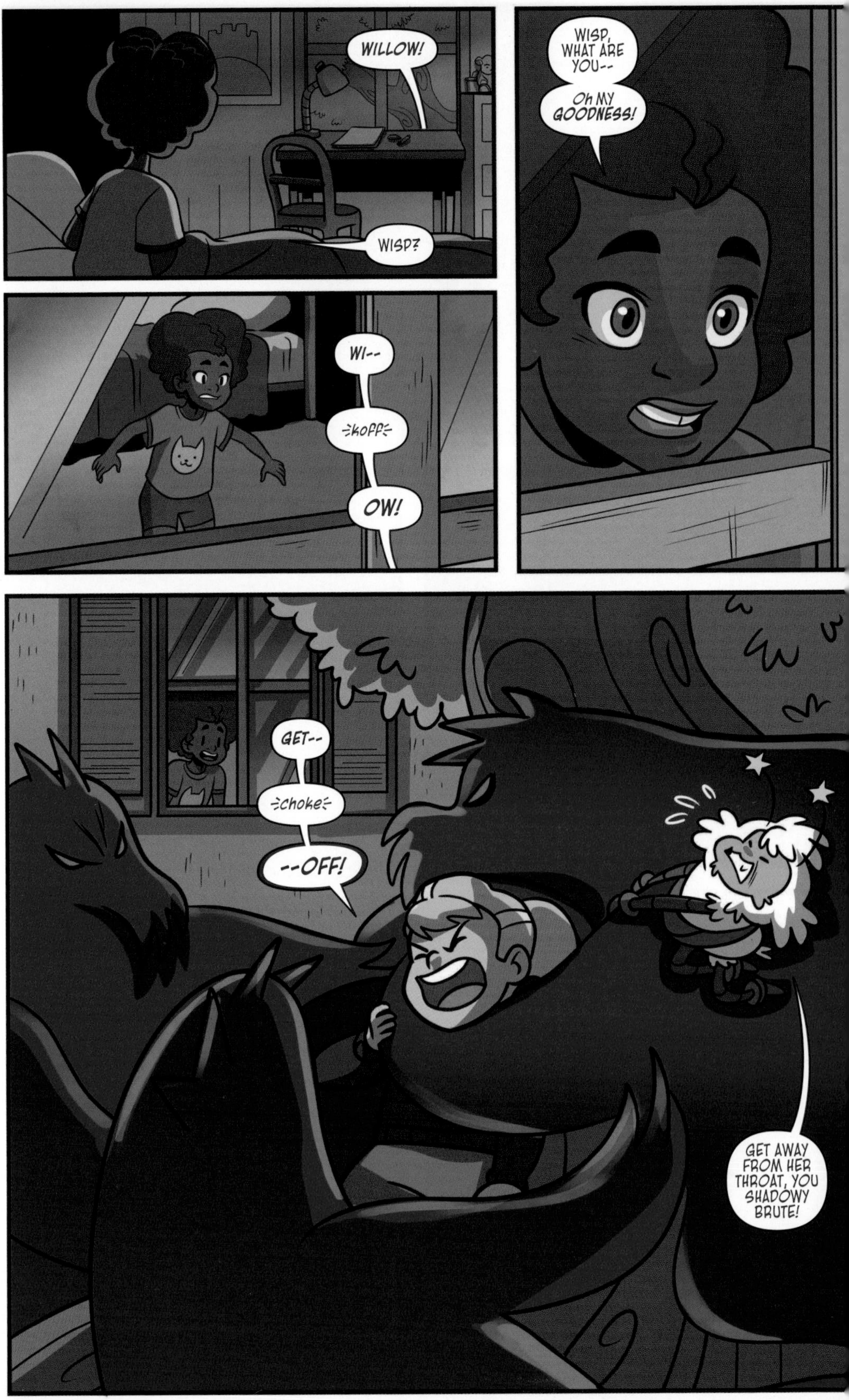
WILLOW!
WISP?
WI--
=koff=
OW!
WISP, WHAT ARE YOU--
Oh MY GOODNESS!
GET--
=choke=
--OFF!
GET AWAY FROM HER THROAT, YOU SHADOWY BRUTE!

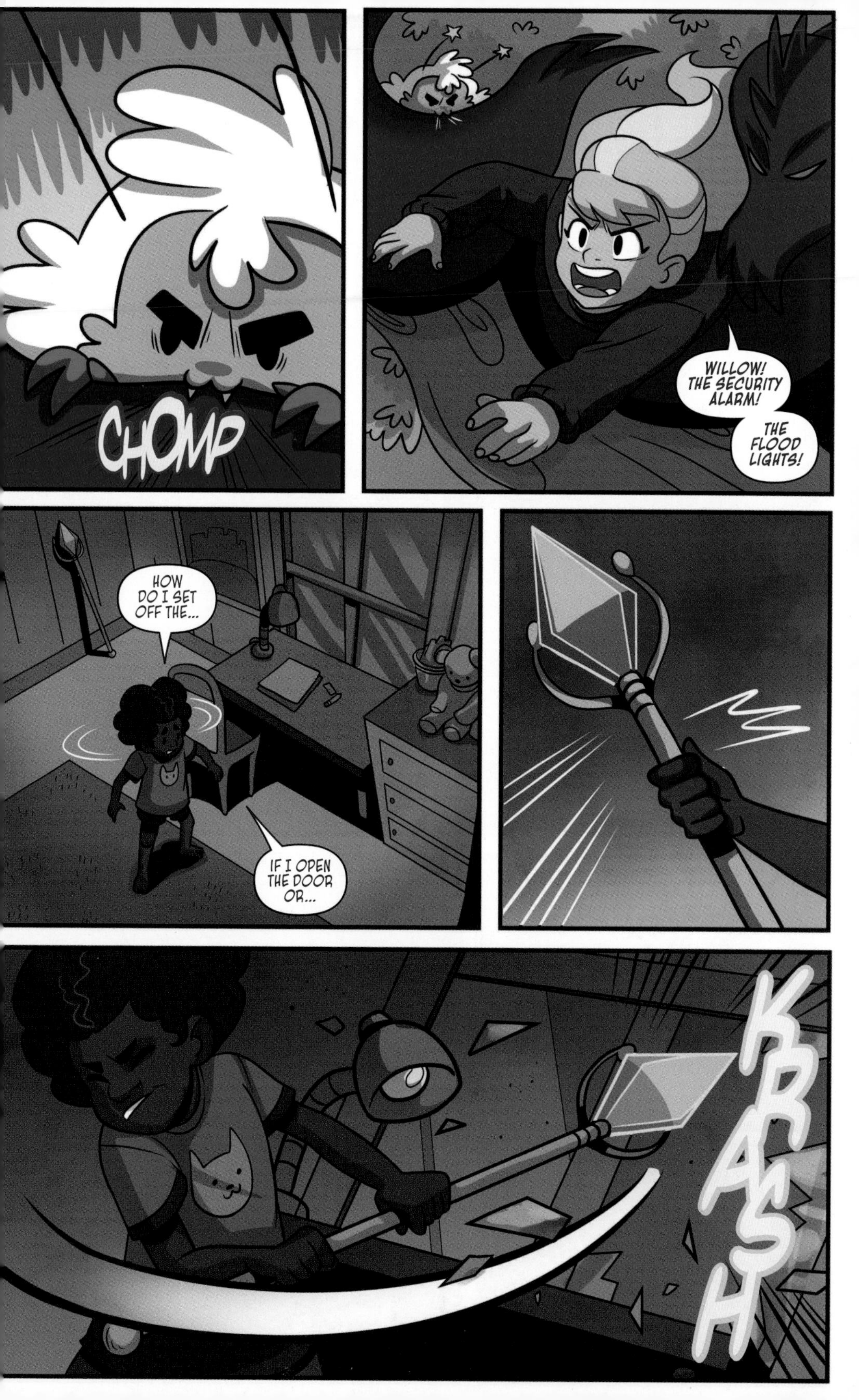
CHOMP
WILLOW! THE SECURITY ALARM!
THE FLOOD LIGHTS!
HOW DO I SET OFF THE...
IF I OPEN THE DOOR OR...
KRASH

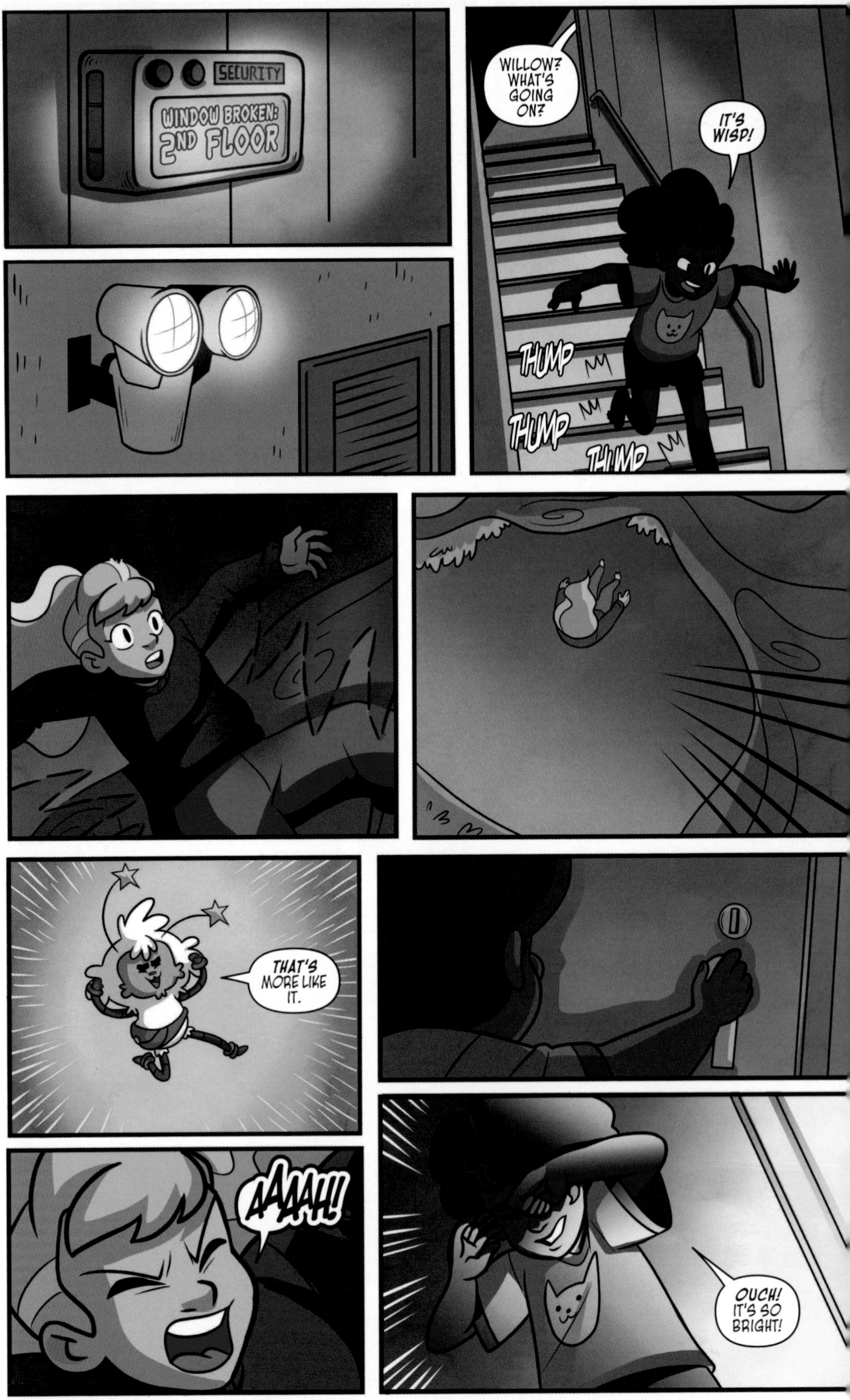
SECURITY
WINDOW BROKEN: 2ND FLOOR
WILLOW? WHAT'S GOING ON?
IT'S WISP!
THUMP
THUMP
THUMP
THAT'S MORE LIKE IT.
AAAAH!!
OUCH! IT'S SO BRIGHT!

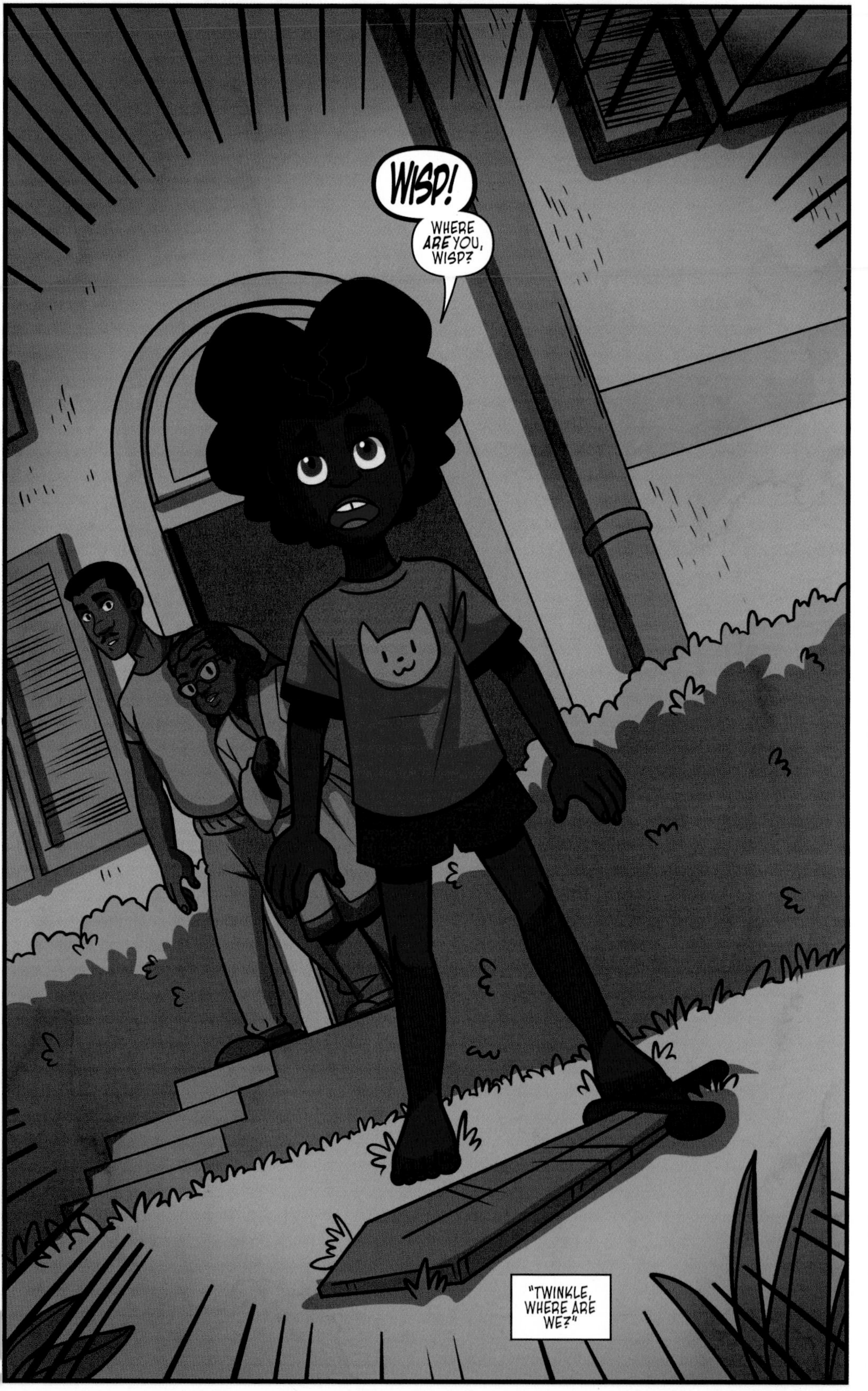
WISP!
WHERE ARE YOU, WISP?
"TWINKLE, WHERE ARE WE?"

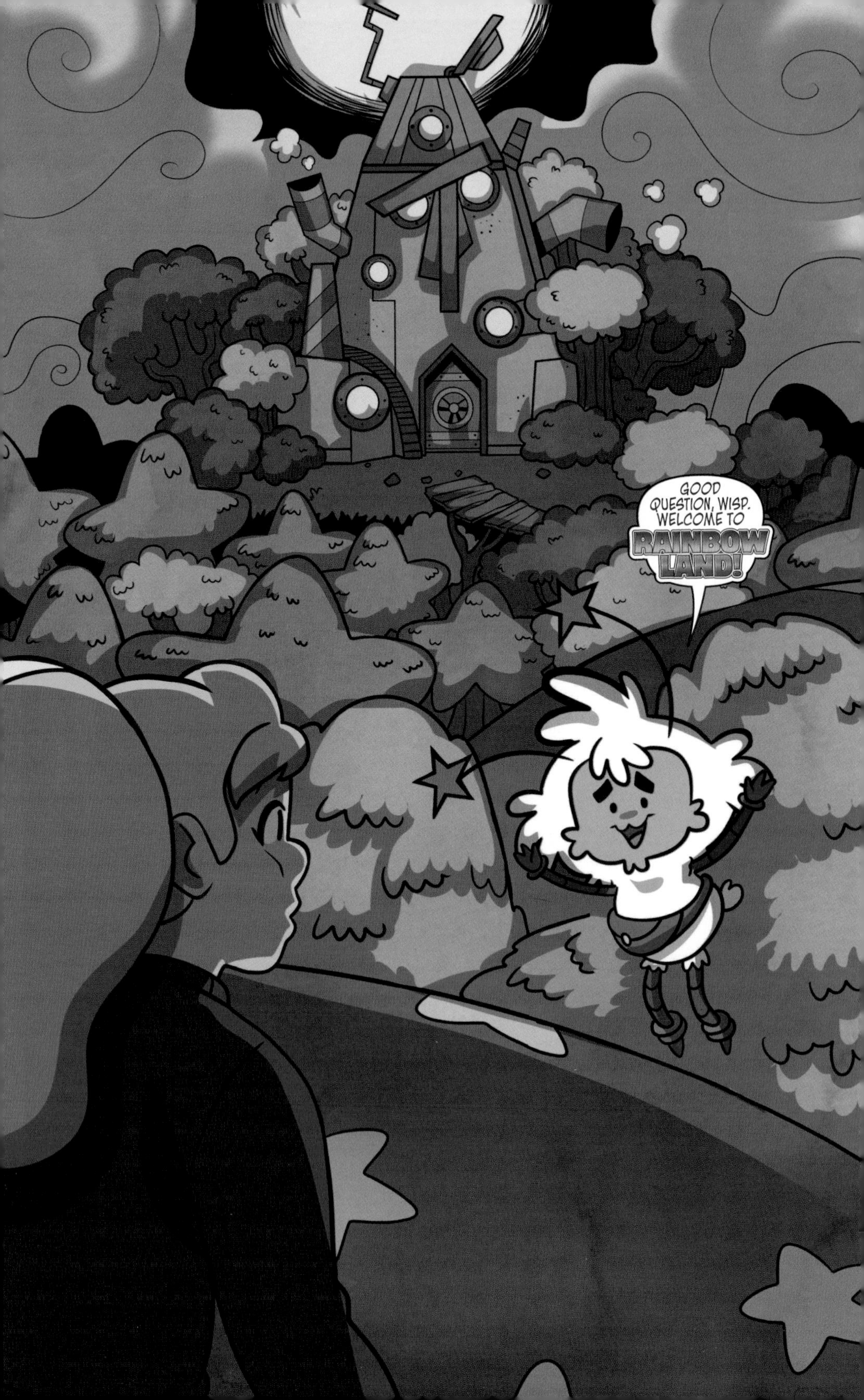
GOOD QUESTION, WISP. WELCOME TO RAINBOW LAND!

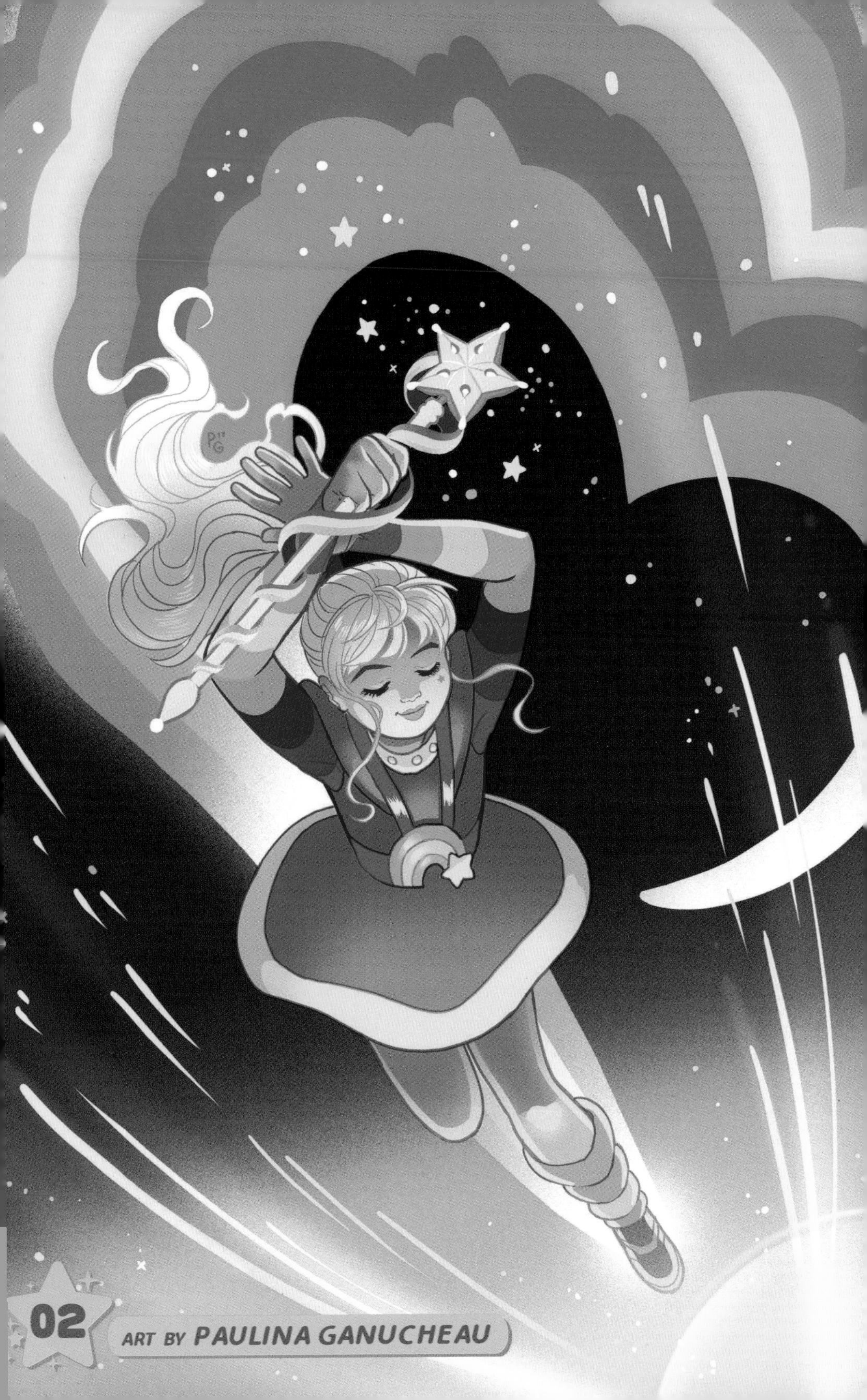

02

ART BY PAULINA GANUCHEAU

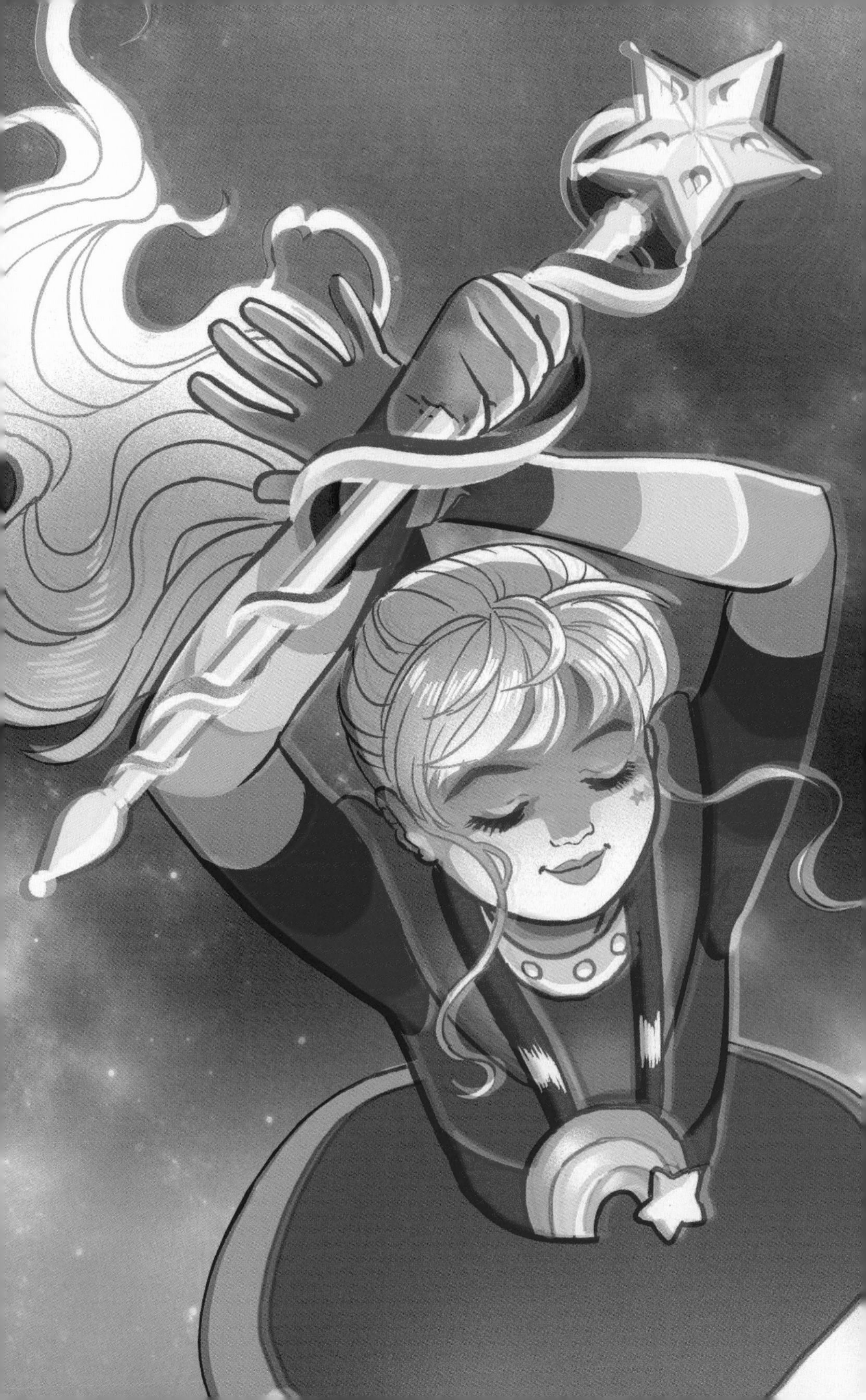

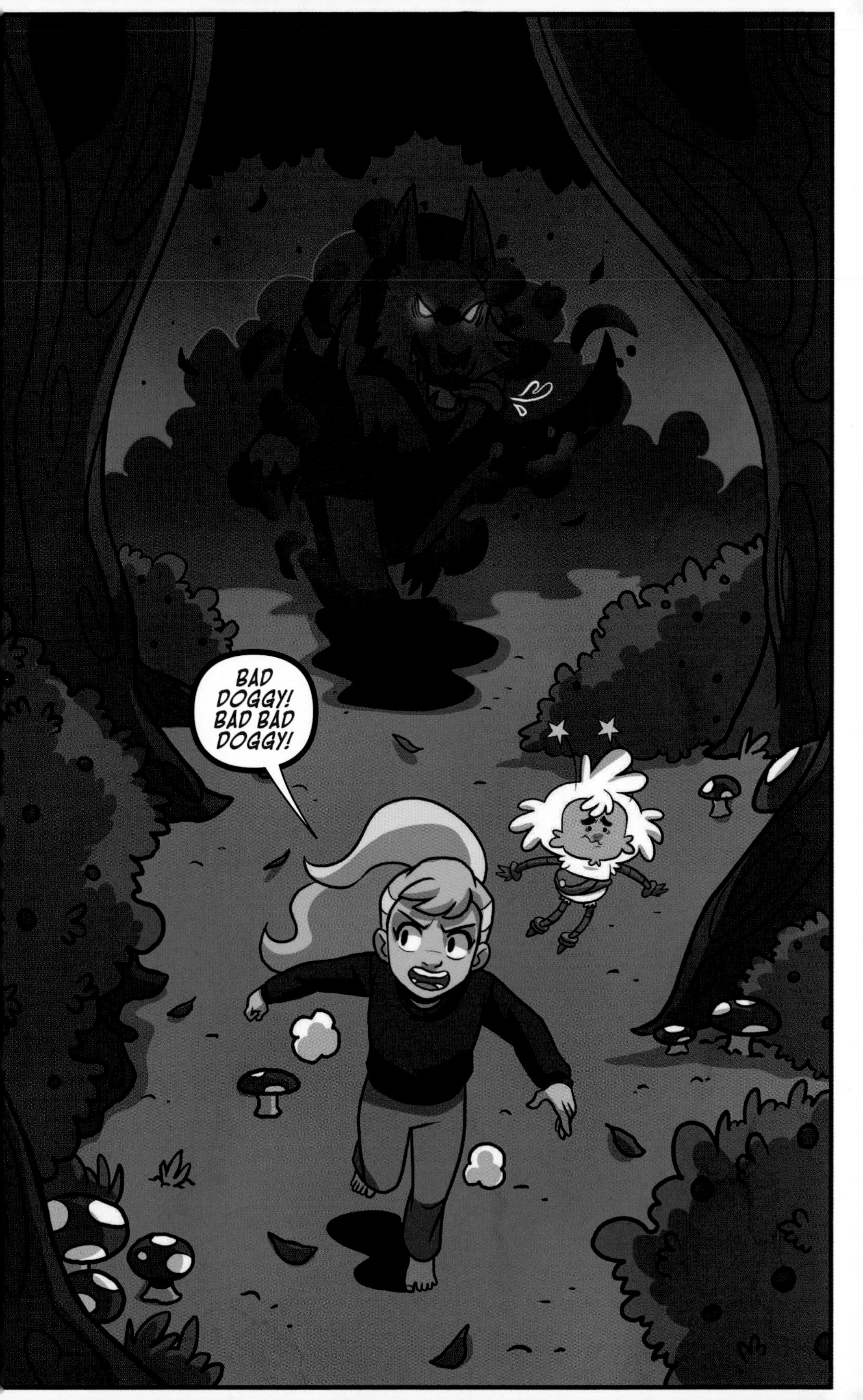
BAD DOGGY! BAD BAD DOGGY!

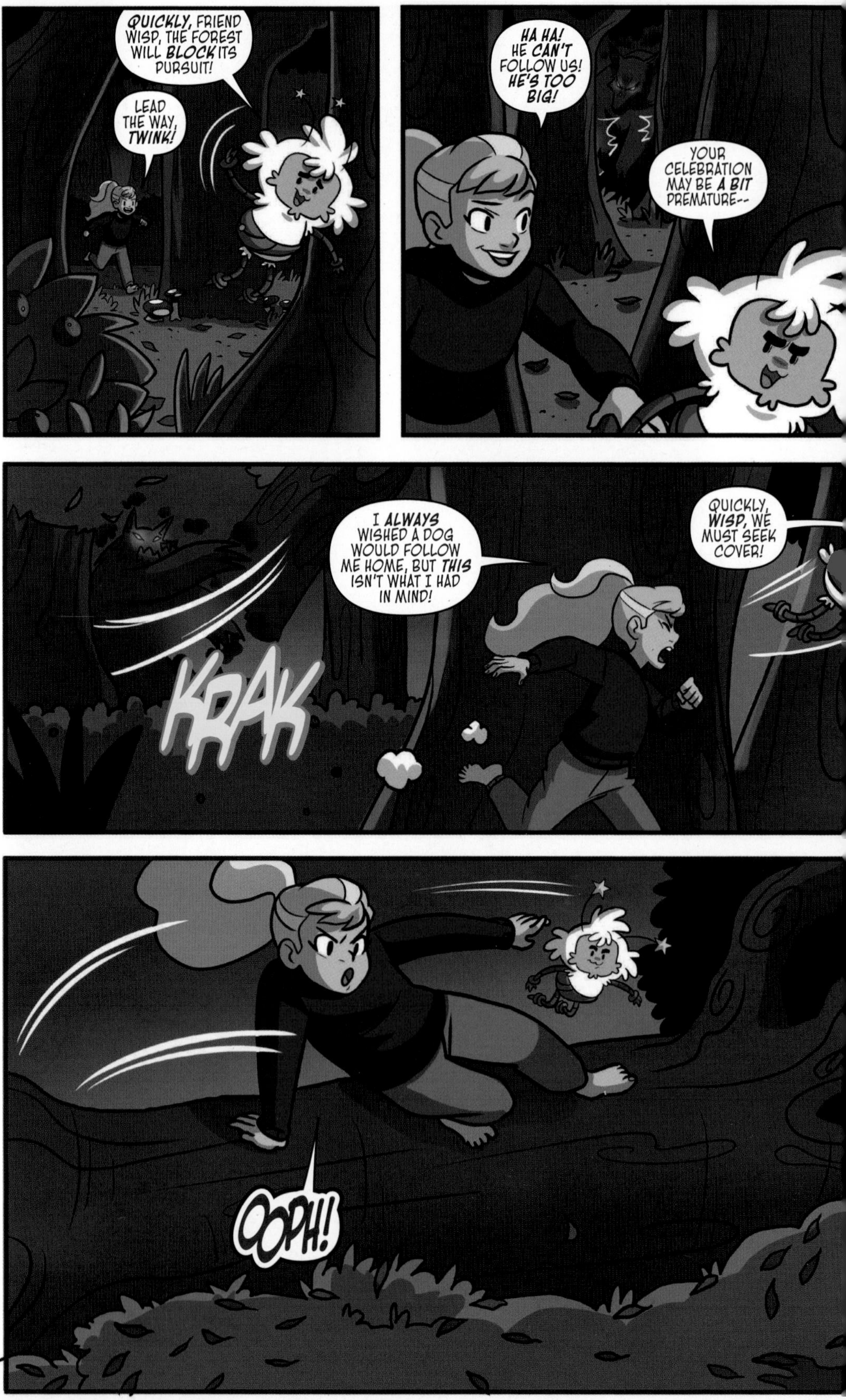
QUICKLY, FRIEND WISP, THE FOREST WILL BLOCK ITS PURSUIT!
LEAD THE WAY, TWINK!
HA HA! HE CAN'T FOLLOW US! HE'S TOO BIG!
YOUR CELEBRATION MAY BE A BIT PREMATURE--
I ALWAYS WISHED A DOG WOULD FOLLOW ME HOME, BUT THIS ISN'T WHAT I HAD IN MIND!
QUICKLY, WISP, WE MUST SEEK COVER!
KRAK
OOPH!

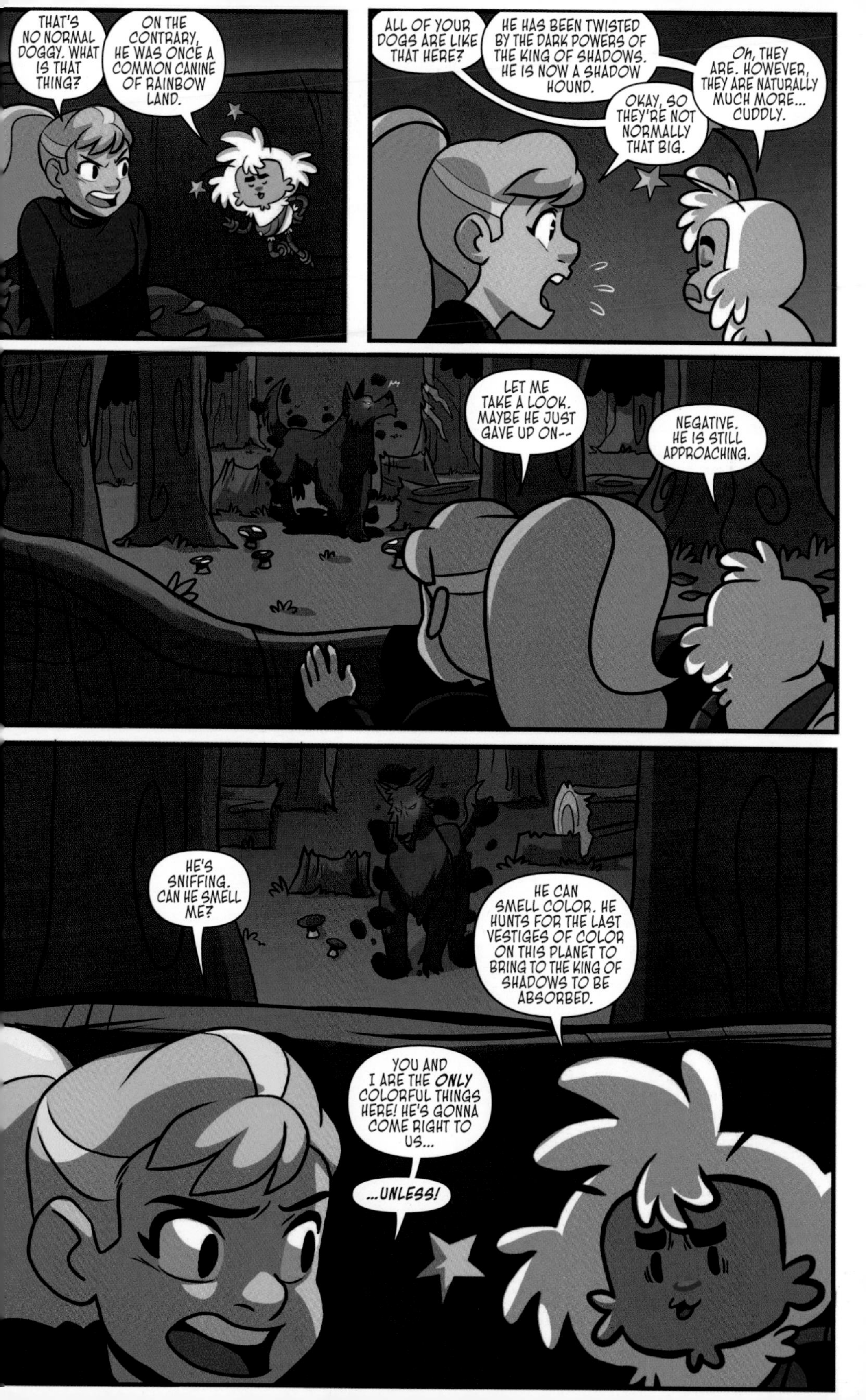

THAT'S NO NORMAL DOGGY. WHAT IS THAT THING?
ON THE CONTRARY, HE WAS ONCE A COMMON CANINE OF RAINBOW LAND.
ALL OF YOUR DOGS ARE LIKE THAT HERE?
HE HAS BEEN TWISTED BY THE DARK POWERS OF THE KING OF SHADOWS. HE IS NOW A SHADOW HOUND.
OKAY, SO THEY'RE NOT NORMALLY THAT BIG.
Oh, THEY ARE. HOWEVER, THEY ARE NATURALLY MUCH MORE... CUDDLY.
LET ME TAKE A LOOK. MAYBE HE JUST GAVE UP ON--
NEGATIVE. HE IS STILL APPROACHING.
HE'S SNIFFING. CAN HE SMELL ME?
HE CAN SMELL COLOR. HE HUNTS FOR THE LAST VESTIGES OF COLOR ON THIS PLANET TO BRING TO THE KING OF SHADOWS TO BE ABSORBED.
YOU AND I ARE THE *ONLY* COLORFUL THINGS HERE! HE'S GONNA COME RIGHT TO US...
...UNLESS!

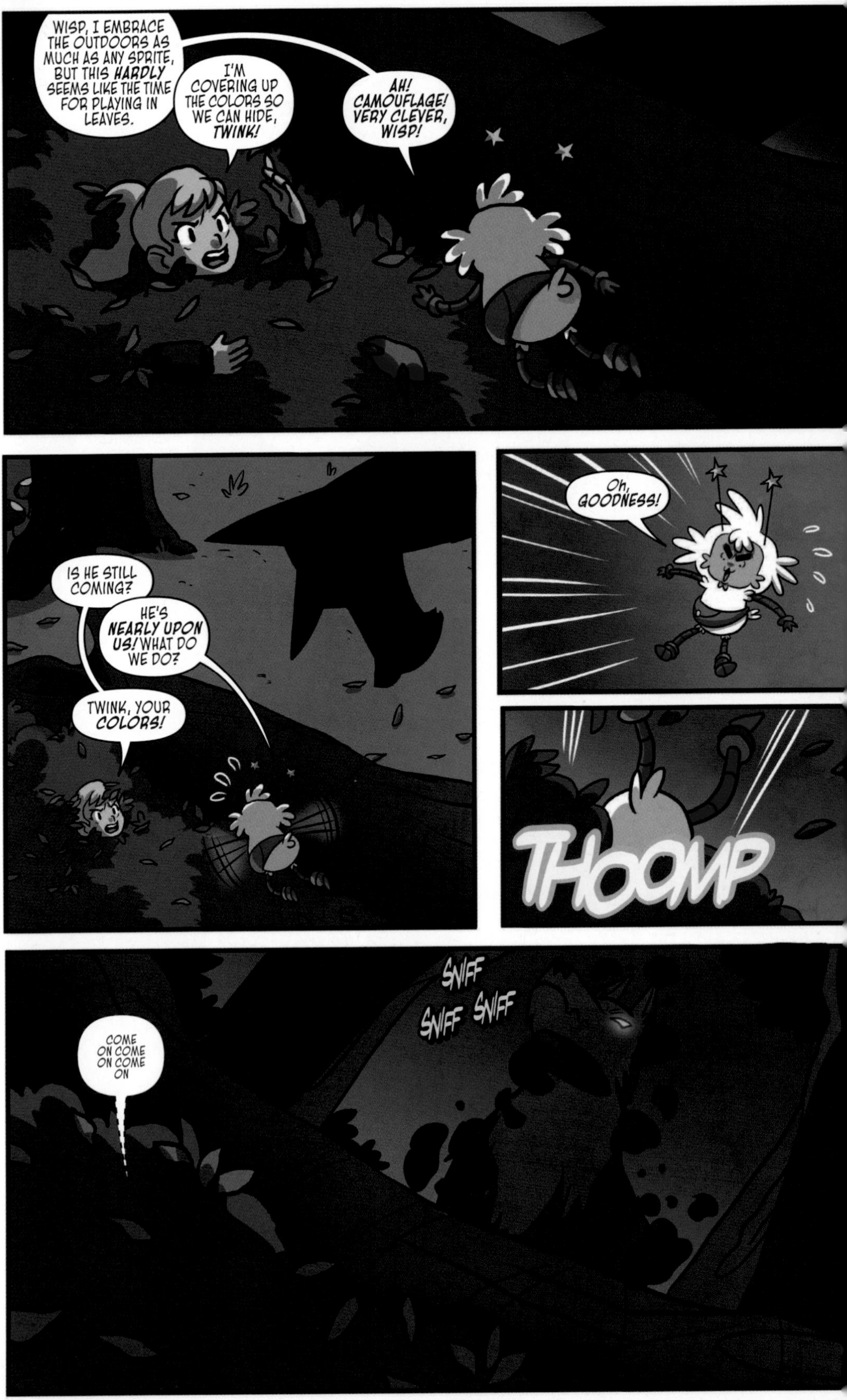
WISP, I EMBRACE THE OUTDOORS AS MUCH AS ANY SPRITE, BUT THIS HARDLY SEEMS LIKE THE TIME FOR PLAYING IN LEAVES.
I'M COVERING UP THE COLORS SO WE CAN HIDE, TWINK!
AH! CAMOUFLAGE! VERY CLEVER, WISP!
IS HE STILL COMING?
HE'S NEARLY UPON US! WHAT DO WE DO?
TWINK, YOUR COLORS!
Oh, GOODNESS!
THOOMP
SNIFF
SNIFF SNIFF
COME ON COME ON COME ON

POP
SHHHH

CURSE YOU,
YOU CONFOUNDED
CONTRAPTION!
CEASE YOUR
SPUTTERING!

KLLINK

WHINE

THAT'S IT!
THIS IS THE **LAST**
TIME I TRUST **LURKY**
WHEN HE TELLS
ME **HE'S FIXED**
ANYTHING!

Huh, HE
IS JUST A
NORMAL
PUPPY.

SQUEE

HOW
DO WE
HELP HIM,
TWINK?

TWINK?

GRIND

BANG

KA-
B
L
A
M
M
O

ARE
WE SAFE
NOW?

I DON'T
KNOW, BUT
THE HOUND
LEFT.

YOU SAID
HE WAS TWISTED
BY THE KING OF
SHADOWS. HOW DO
WE HELP HIM?

THE KING
HAS A STAFF WHICH
DARKENS THE LIGHT
WITHIN A LIVING
CREATURE. THE ONLY
WAY TO REVERSE THE
EFFECT--

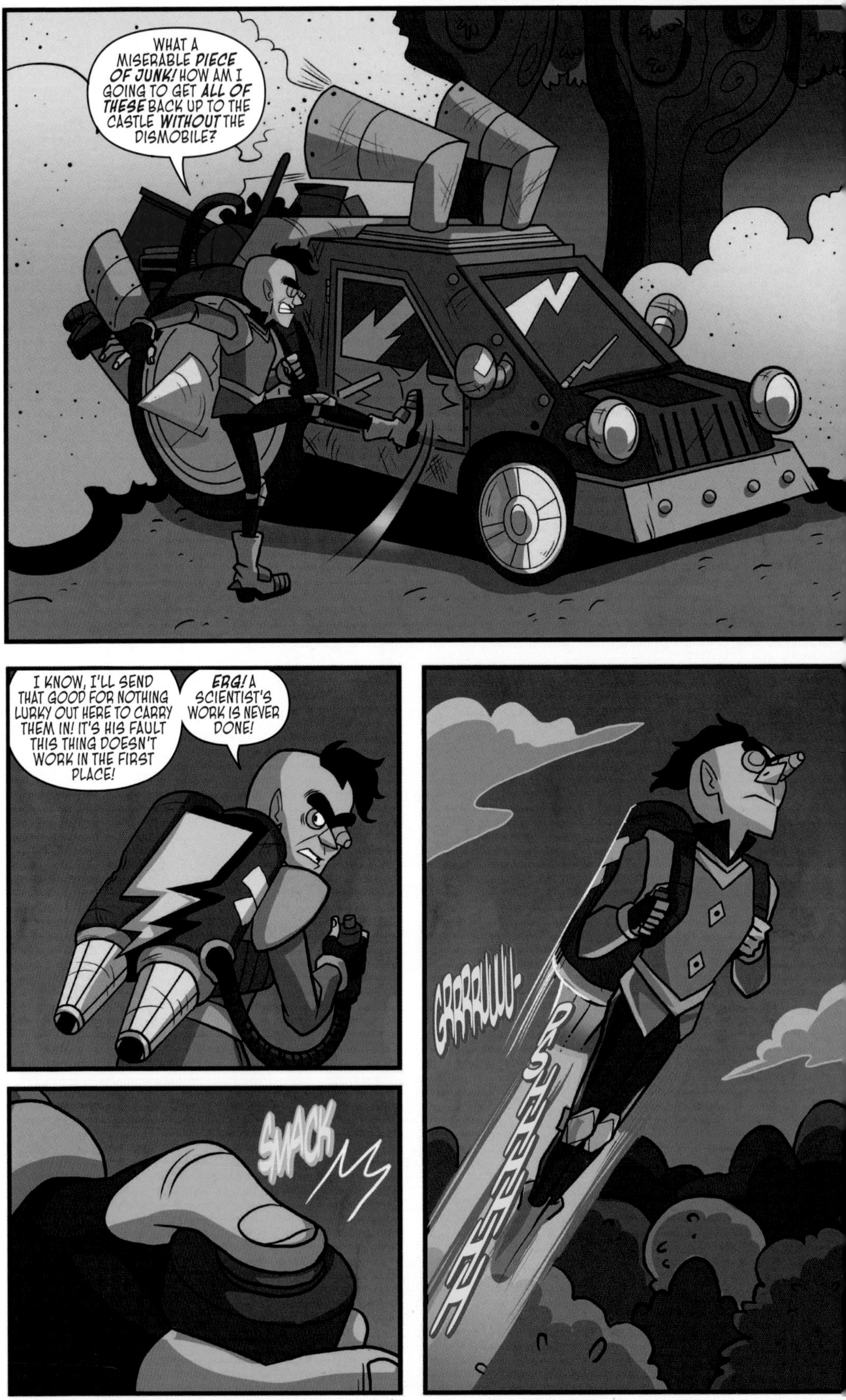
WHAT A MISERABLE PIECE OF JUNK! HOW AM I GOING TO GET ALL OF THESE BACK UP TO THE CASTLE WITHOUT THE DISMOBILE?
I KNOW, I'LL SEND THAT GOOD FOR NOTHING LURKY OUT HERE TO CARRY THEM IN! IT'S HIS FAULT THIS THING DOESN'T WORK IN THE FIRST PLACE!
ERG! A SCIENTIST'S WORK IS NEVER DONE!
SMACK
GRRRUUU-

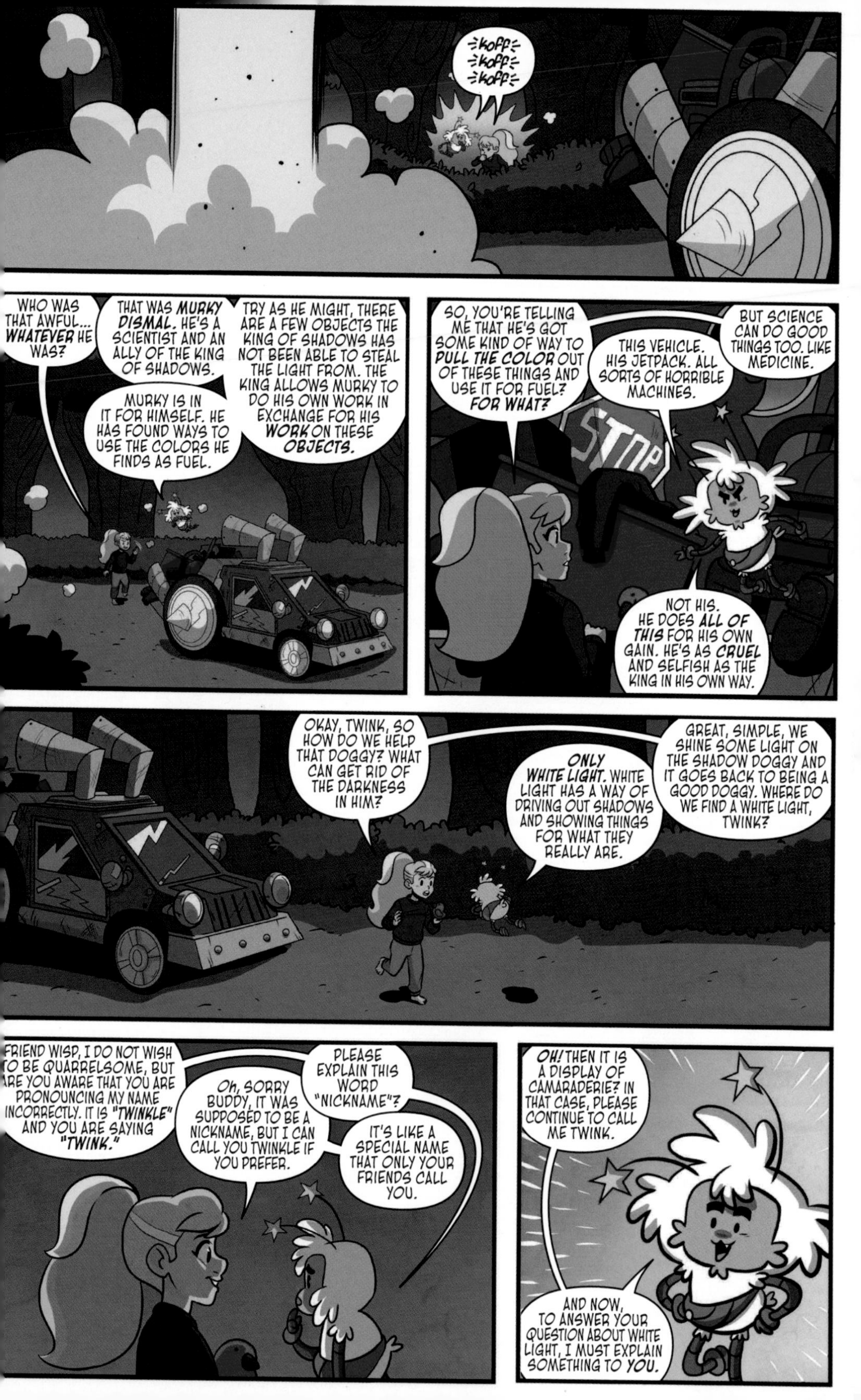

KOFF KOFF KOFF
WHO WAS THAT AWFUL... WHATEVER HE WAS?
THAT WAS MURKY DISMAL. HE'S A SCIENTIST AND AN ALLY OF THE KING OF SHADOWS.
MURKY IS IN IT FOR HIMSELF. HE HAS FOUND WAYS TO USE THE COLORS HE FINDS AS FUEL.
TRY AS HE MIGHT, THERE ARE A FEW OBJECTS THE KING OF SHADOWS HAS NOT BEEN ABLE TO STEAL THE LIGHT FROM. THE KING ALLOWS MURKY TO DO HIS OWN WORK IN EXCHANGE FOR HIS WORK ON THESE OBJECTS.
SO, YOU'RE TELLING ME THAT HE'S GOT SOME KIND OF WAY TO PULL THE COLOR OUT OF THESE THINGS AND USE IT FOR FUEL? FOR WHAT?
THIS VEHICLE. HIS JETPACK. ALL SORTS OF HORRIBLE MACHINES.
BUT SCIENCE CAN DO GOOD THINGS TOO. LIKE MEDICINE.
STOP
NOT HIS. HE DOES ALL OF THIS FOR HIS OWN GAIN. HE'S AS CRUEL AND SELFISH AS THE KING IN HIS OWN WAY.
OKAY, TWINK, SO HOW DO WE HELP THAT DOGGY? WHAT CAN GET RID OF THE DARKNESS IN HIM?
ONLY WHITE LIGHT. WHITE LIGHT HAS A WAY OF DRIVING OUT SHADOWS AND SHOWING THINGS FOR WHAT THEY REALLY ARE.
GREAT, SIMPLE, WE SHINE SOME LIGHT ON THE SHADOW DOGGY AND IT GOES BACK TO BEING A GOOD DOGGY. WHERE DO WE FIND A WHITE LIGHT, TWINK?
FRIEND WISP, I DO NOT WISH TO BE QUARRELSOME, BUT ARE YOU AWARE THAT YOU ARE PRONOUNCING MY NAME INCORRECTLY. IT IS "TWINKLE" AND YOU ARE SAYING "TWINK."
OH, SORRY BUDDY, IT WAS SUPPOSED TO BE A NICKNAME, BUT I CAN CALL YOU TWINKLE IF YOU PREFER.
PLEASE EXPLAIN THIS WORD "NICKNAME"?
IT'S LIKE A SPECIAL NAME THAT ONLY YOUR FRIENDS CALL YOU.
OH! THEN IT IS A DISPLAY OF CAMARADERIE? IN THAT CASE, PLEASE CONTINUE TO CALL ME TWINK.
AND NOW, TO ANSWER YOUR QUESTION ABOUT WHITE LIGHT, I MUST EXPLAIN SOMETHING TO YOU.

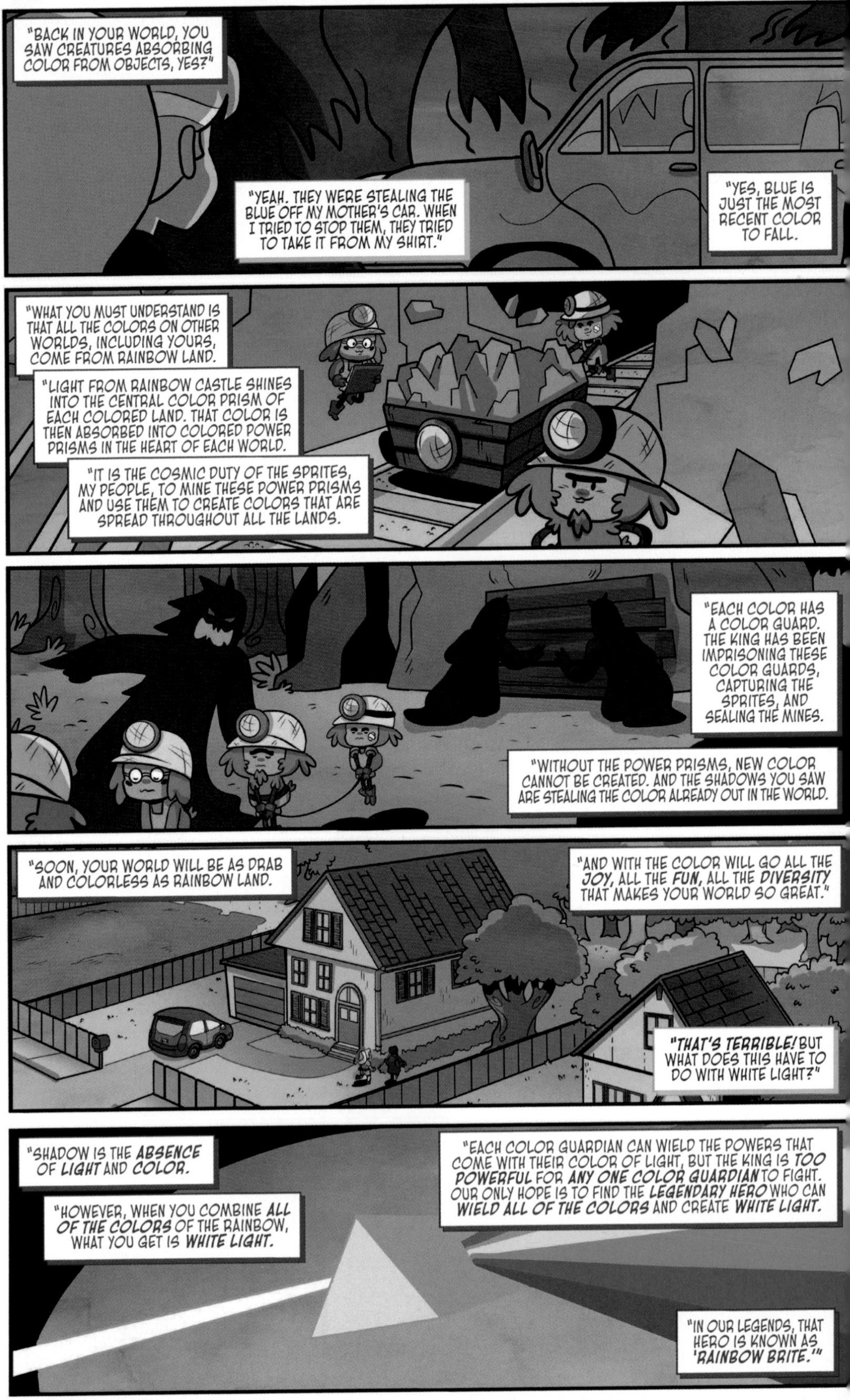
"BACK IN YOUR WORLD, YOU SAW CREATURES ABSORBING COLOR FROM OBJECTS, YES?"
"YEAH. THEY WERE STEALING THE BLUE OFF MY MOTHER'S CAR. WHEN I TRIED TO STOP THEM, THEY TRIED TO TAKE IT FROM MY SHIRT."
"YES, BLUE IS JUST THE MOST RECENT COLOR TO FALL.
"WHAT YOU MUST UNDERSTAND IS THAT ALL THE COLORS ON OTHER WORLDS, INCLUDING YOURS, COME FROM RAINBOW LAND.
"LIGHT FROM RAINBOW CASTLE SHINES INTO THE CENTRAL COLOR PRISM OF EACH COLORED LAND. THAT COLOR IS THEN ABSORBED INTO COLORED POWER PRISMS IN THE HEART OF EACH WORLD.
"IT IS THE COSMIC DUTY OF THE SPRITES, MY PEOPLE, TO MINE THESE POWER PRISMS AND USE THEM TO CREATE COLORS THAT ARE SPREAD THROUGHOUT ALL THE LANDS.
"EACH COLOR HAS A COLOR GUARD. THE KING HAS BEEN IMPRISONING THESE COLOR GUARDS, CAPTURING THE SPRITES, AND SEALING THE MINES.
"WITHOUT THE POWER PRISMS, NEW COLOR CANNOT BE CREATED. AND THE SHADOWS YOU SAW ARE STEALING THE COLOR ALREADY OUT IN THE WORLD.
"SOON, YOUR WORLD WILL BE AS DRAB AND COLORLESS AS RAINBOW LAND.
"AND WITH THE COLOR WILL GO ALL THE *JOY*, ALL THE *FUN*, ALL THE *DIVERSITY* THAT MAKES YOUR WORLD SO GREAT."
"***THAT'S TERRIBLE!*** BUT WHAT DOES THIS HAVE TO DO WITH WHITE LIGHT?"
"SHADOW IS THE ***ABSENCE*** OF ***LIGHT*** AND ***COLOR.***
"HOWEVER, WHEN YOU COMBINE ***ALL OF THE COLORS*** OF THE RAINBOW, WHAT YOU GET IS ***WHITE LIGHT.***
"EACH COLOR GUARDIAN CAN WIELD THE POWERS THAT COME WITH THEIR COLOR OF LIGHT, BUT THE KING IS ***TOO POWERFUL*** FOR ***ANY ONE COLOR GUARDIAN*** TO FIGHT. OUR ONLY HOPE IS TO FIND THE ***LEGENDARY HERO*** WHO CAN ***WIELD ALL OF THE COLORS*** AND CREATE ***WHITE LIGHT.***
"IN OUR LEGENDS, THAT HERO IS KNOWN AS ***'RAINBOW BRITE.'"***

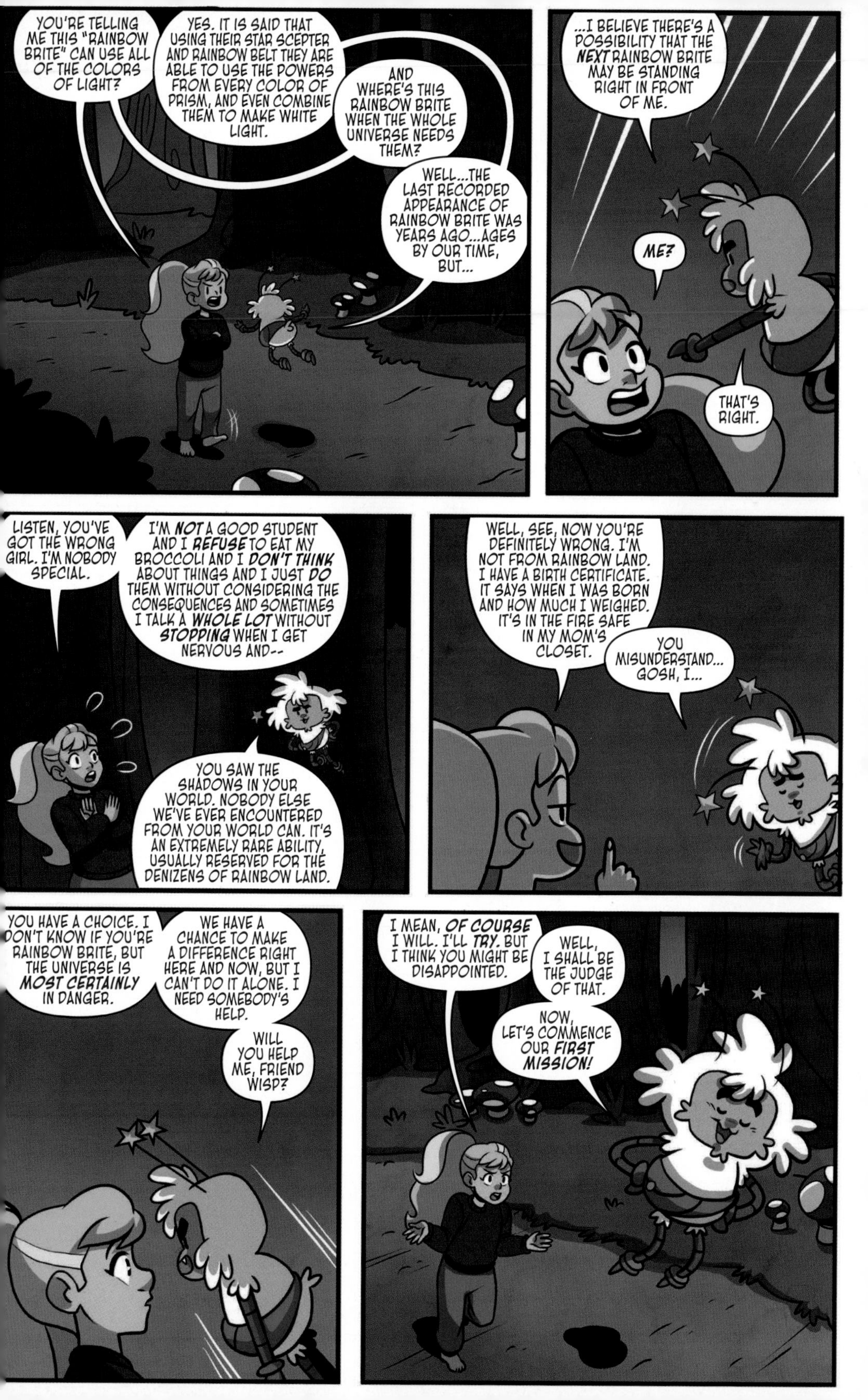
YOU'RE TELLING ME THIS "RAINBOW BRITE" CAN USE ALL OF THE COLORS OF LIGHT?
YES. IT IS SAID THAT USING THEIR STAR SCEPTER AND RAINBOW BELT THEY ARE ABLE TO USE THE POWERS FROM EVERY COLOR OF PRISM, AND EVEN COMBINE THEM TO MAKE WHITE LIGHT.
AND WHERE'S THIS RAINBOW BRITE WHEN THE WHOLE UNIVERSE NEEDS THEM?
WELL...THE LAST RECORDED APPEARANCE OF RAINBOW BRITE WAS YEARS AGO...AGES BY OUR TIME, BUT...
...I BELIEVE THERE'S A POSSIBILITY THAT THE NEXT RAINBOW BRITE MAY BE STANDING RIGHT IN FRONT OF ME.
ME?
THAT'S RIGHT.
LISTEN, YOU'VE GOT THE WRONG GIRL. I'M NOBODY SPECIAL.
I'M NOT A GOOD STUDENT AND I REFUSE TO EAT MY BROCCOLI AND I DON'T THINK ABOUT THINGS AND I JUST DO THEM WITHOUT CONSIDERING THE CONSEQUENCES AND SOMETIMES I TALK A WHOLE LOT WITHOUT STOPPING WHEN I GET NERVOUS AND--
YOU SAW THE SHADOWS IN YOUR WORLD. NOBODY ELSE WE'VE EVER ENCOUNTERED FROM YOUR WORLD CAN. IT'S AN EXTREMELY RARE ABILITY, USUALLY RESERVED FOR THE DENIZENS OF RAINBOW LAND.
WELL, SEE, NOW YOU'RE DEFINITELY WRONG. I'M NOT FROM RAINBOW LAND. I HAVE A BIRTH CERTIFICATE. IT SAYS WHEN I WAS BORN AND HOW MUCH I WEIGHED. IT'S IN THE FIRE SAFE IN MY MOM'S CLOSET.
YOU MISUNDERSTAND... GOSH, I...
YOU HAVE A CHOICE. I DON'T KNOW IF YOU'RE RAINBOW BRITE, BUT THE UNIVERSE IS MOST CERTAINLY IN DANGER.
WE HAVE A CHANCE TO MAKE A DIFFERENCE RIGHT HERE AND NOW, BUT I CAN'T DO IT ALONE. I NEED SOMEBODY'S HELP.
WILL YOU HELP ME, FRIEND WISP?
I MEAN, OF COURSE I WILL. I'LL TRY. BUT I THINK YOU MIGHT BE DISAPPOINTED.
WELL, I SHALL BE THE JUDGE OF THAT.
NOW, LET'S COMMENCE OUR FIRST MISSION!

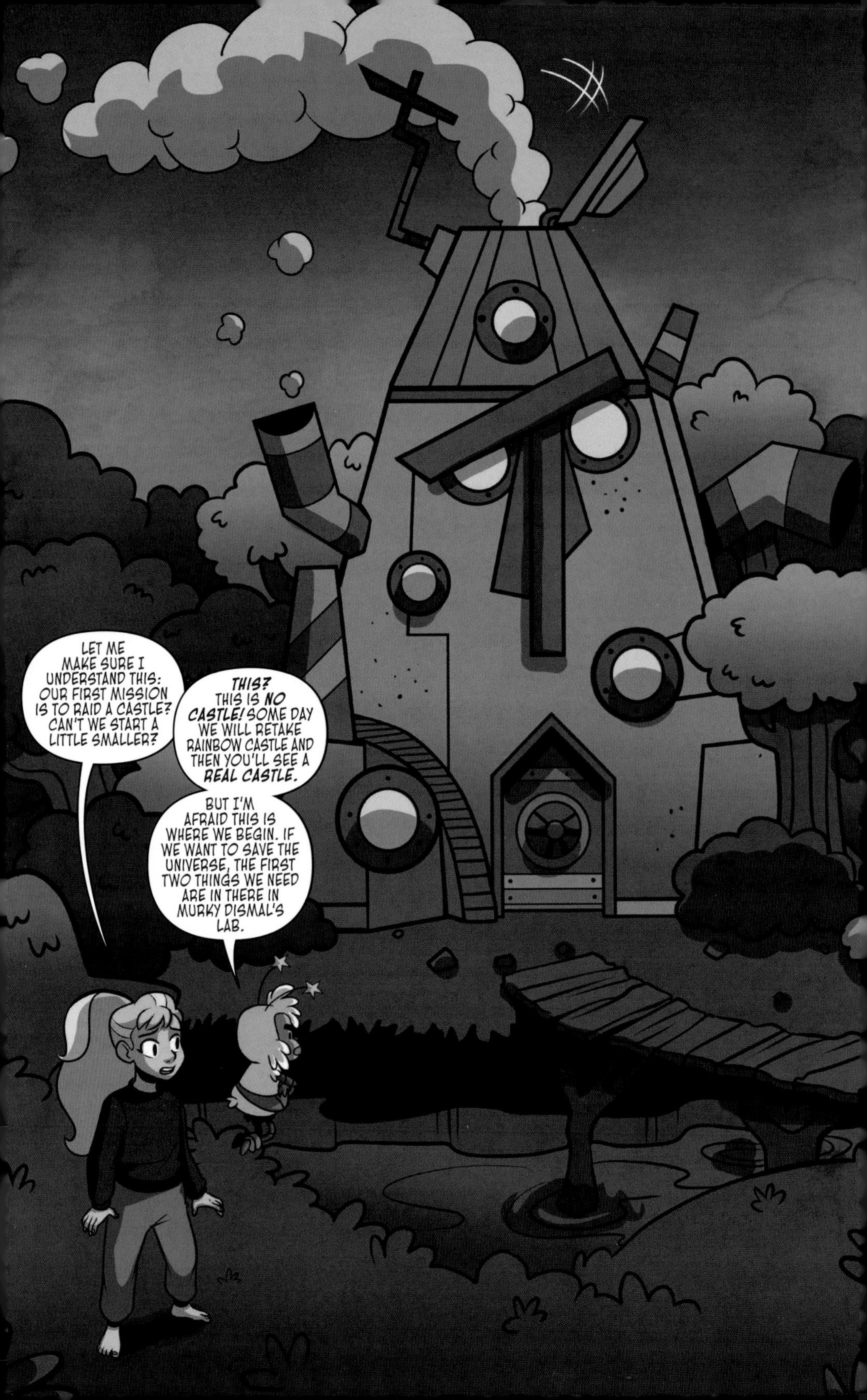
LET ME MAKE SURE I UNDERSTAND THIS: OUR FIRST MISSION IS TO RAID A CASTLE? CAN'T WE START A LITTLE SMALLER?
THIS? THIS IS NO CASTLE! SOME DAY WE WILL RETAKE RAINBOW CASTLE AND THEN YOU'LL SEE A REAL CASTLE.
BUT I'M AFRAID THIS IS WHERE WE BEGIN. IF WE WANT TO SAVE THE UNIVERSE, THE FIRST TWO THINGS WE NEED ARE IN THERE IN MURKY DISMAL'S LAB.

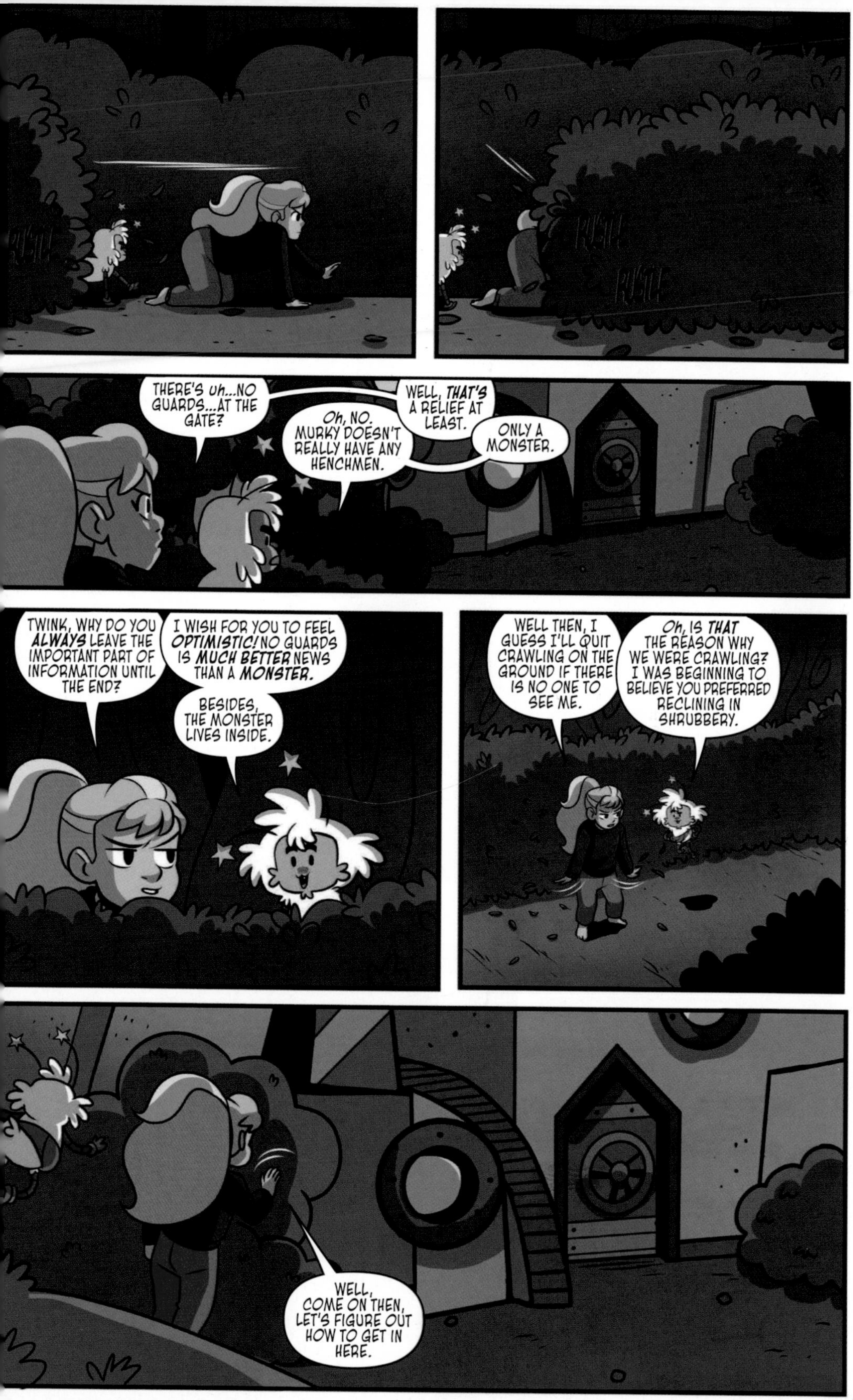
RUSTLE
RUSTLE
THERE'S *Uh*...NO GUARDS...AT THE GATE?
Oh, NO. MURKY DOESN'T REALLY HAVE ANY HENCHMEN.
WELL, ***THAT'S*** A RELIEF AT LEAST.
ONLY A MONSTER.
TWINK, WHY DO YOU ***ALWAYS*** LEAVE THE IMPORTANT PART OF INFORMATION UNTIL THE END?
I WISH FOR YOU TO FEEL ***OPTIMISTIC!*** NO GUARDS IS ***MUCH BETTER*** NEWS THAN A ***MONSTER.***
BESIDES, THE MONSTER LIVES INSIDE.
WELL THEN, I GUESS I'LL QUIT CRAWLING ON THE GROUND IF THERE IS NO ONE TO SEE ME.
Oh, IS ***THAT*** THE REASON WHY WE WERE CRAWLING? I WAS BEGINNING TO BELIEVE YOU PREFERRED RECLINING IN SHRUBBERY.
WELL, COME ON THEN, LET'S FIGURE OUT HOW TO GET IN HERE.

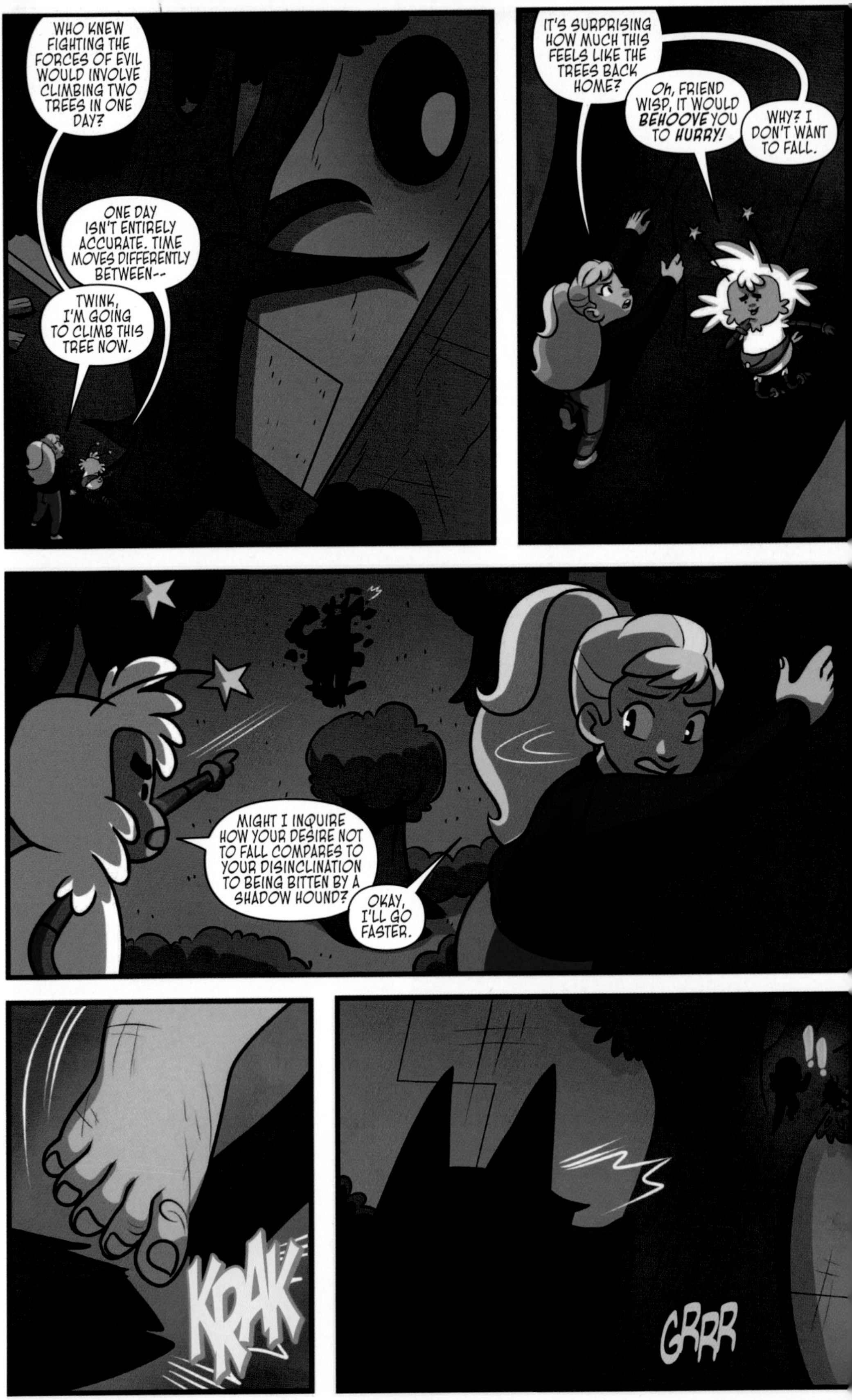
WHO KNEW FIGHTING THE FORCES OF EVIL WOULD INVOLVE CLIMBING TWO TREES IN ONE DAY?
ONE DAY ISN'T ENTIRELY ACCURATE. TIME MOVES DIFFERENTLY BETWEEN--
TWINK, I'M GOING TO CLIMB THIS TREE NOW.
IT'S SURPRISING HOW MUCH THIS FEELS LIKE THE TREES BACK HOME?
Oh, FRIEND WISP, IT WOULD BEHOOVE YOU TO HURRY!
WHY? I DON'T WANT TO FALL.
MIGHT I INQUIRE HOW YOUR DESIRE NOT TO FALL COMPARES TO YOUR DISINCLINATION TO BEING BITTEN BY A SHADOW HOUND?
OKAY, I'LL GO FASTER.
KRAK
!!
GRRR

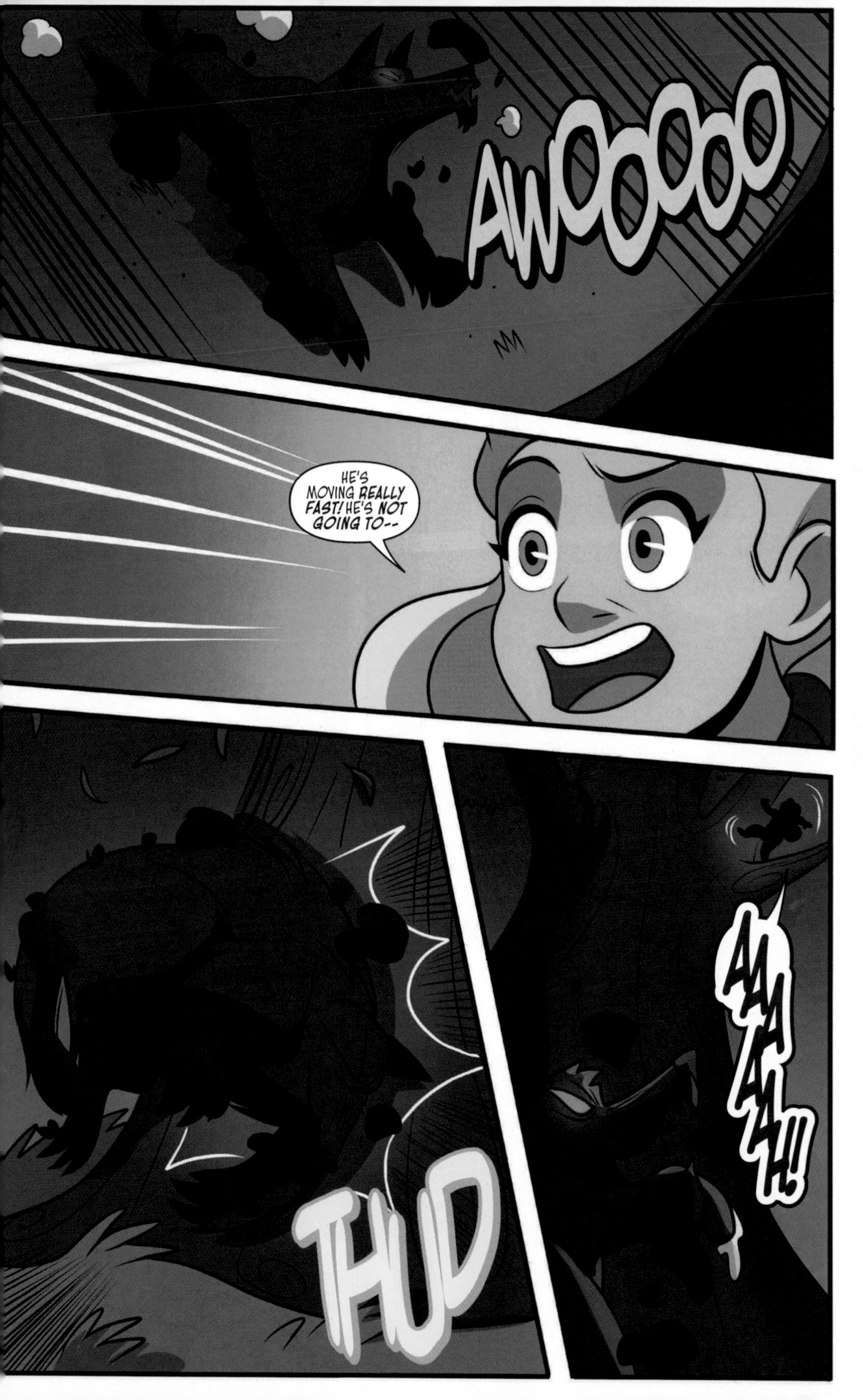
AWOOOOO
HE'S MOVING REALLY FAST! HE'S NOT GOING TO--
THUD
AAAAAAH!!

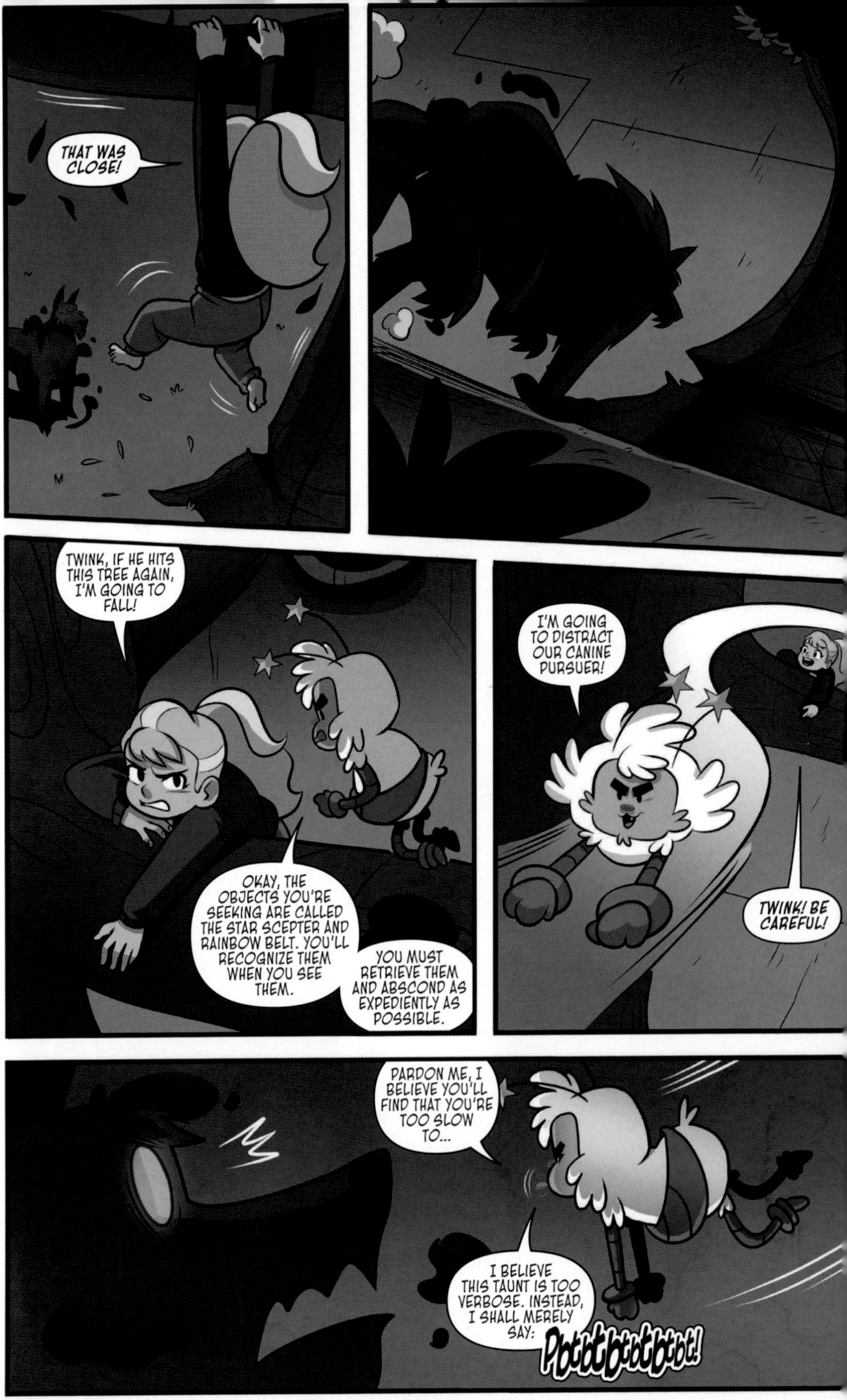
THAT WAS CLOSE!
TWINK, IF HE HITS THIS TREE AGAIN, I'M GOING TO FALL!
OKAY, THE OBJECTS YOU'RE SEEKING ARE CALLED THE STAR SCEPTER AND RAINBOW BELT. YOU'LL RECOGNIZE THEM WHEN YOU SEE THEM.
YOU MUST RETRIEVE THEM AND ABSCOND AS EXPEDIENTLY AS POSSIBLE.
I'M GOING TO DISTRACT OUR CANINE PURSUER!
TWINK! BE CAREFUL!
PARDON ME, I BELIEVE YOU'LL FIND THAT YOU'RE TOO SLOW TO...
I BELIEVE THIS TAUNT IS TOO VERBOSE. INSTEAD, I SHALL MERELY SAY:
Pbtbtbtbtbtbt!

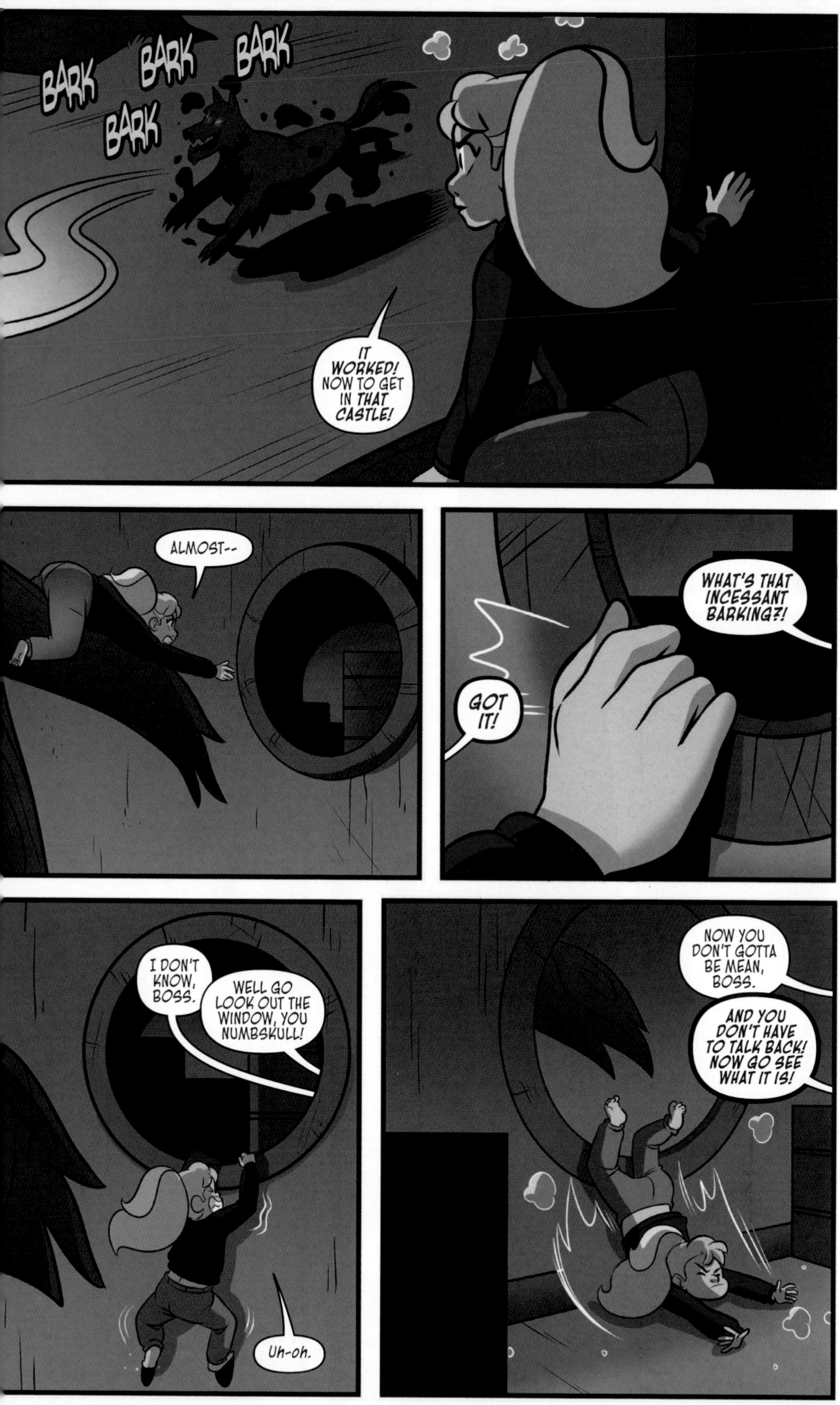
BARK
BARK
BARK
BARK
IT WORKED! NOW TO GET IN THAT CASTLE!
ALMOST--
WHAT'S THAT INCESSANT BARKING?!
GOT IT!
I DON'T KNOW, BOSS.
WELL GO LOOK OUT THE WINDOW, YOU NUMBSKULL!
Uh-oh.
NOW YOU DON'T GOTTA BE MEAN, BOSS.
AND YOU DON'T HAVE TO TALK BACK! NOW GO SEE WHAT IT IS!

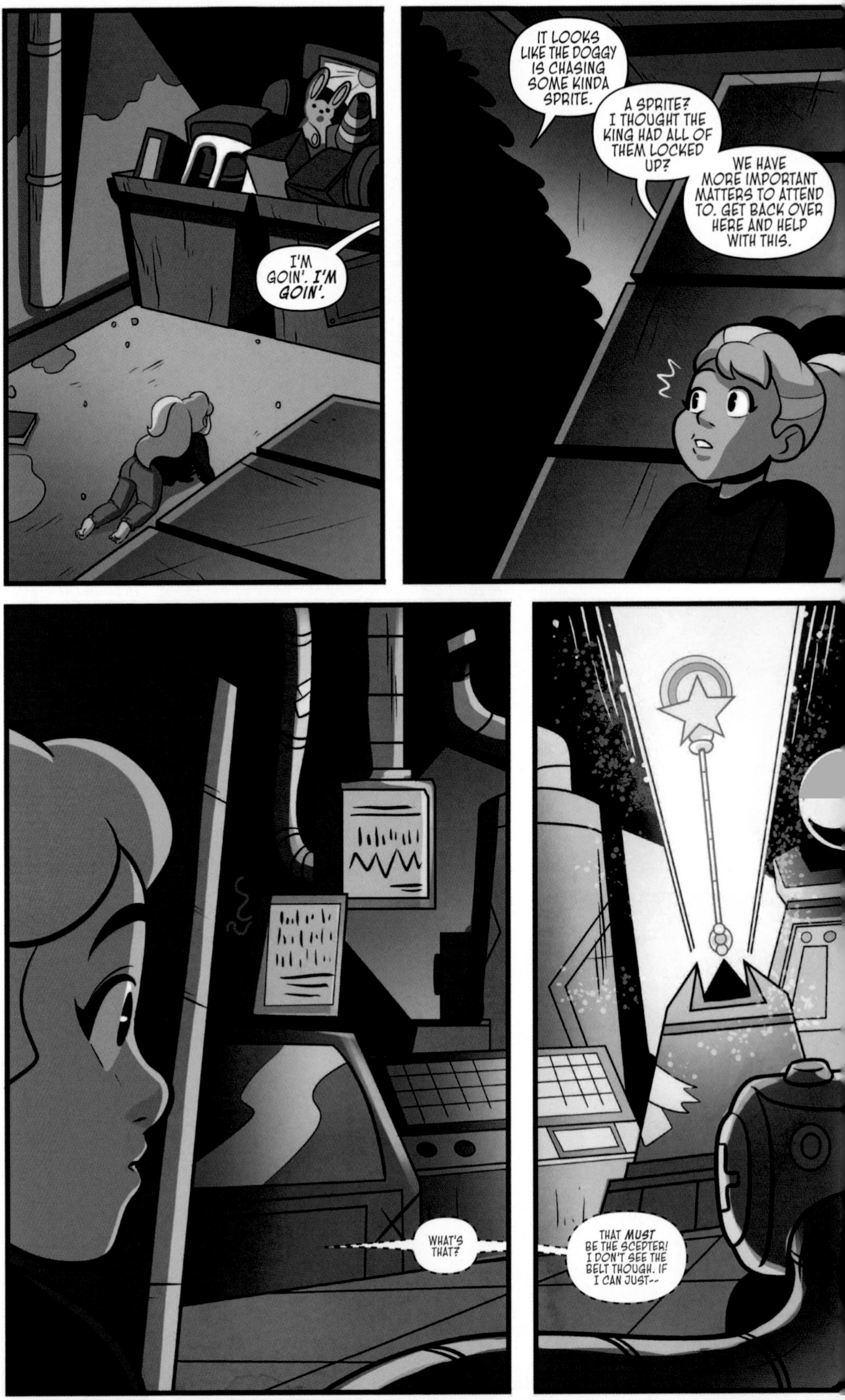
I'M GOIN'. I'M GOIN'.
IT LOOKS LIKE THE DOGGY IS CHASING SOME KINDA SPRITE.
A SPRITE? I THOUGHT THE KING HAD ALL OF THEM LOCKED UP?
WE HAVE MORE IMPORTANT MATTERS TO ATTEND TO. GET BACK OVER HERE AND HELP WITH THIS.
WHAT'S THAT?
THAT MUST BE THE SCEPTER! I DON'T SEE THE BELT THOUGH. IF I CAN JUST--

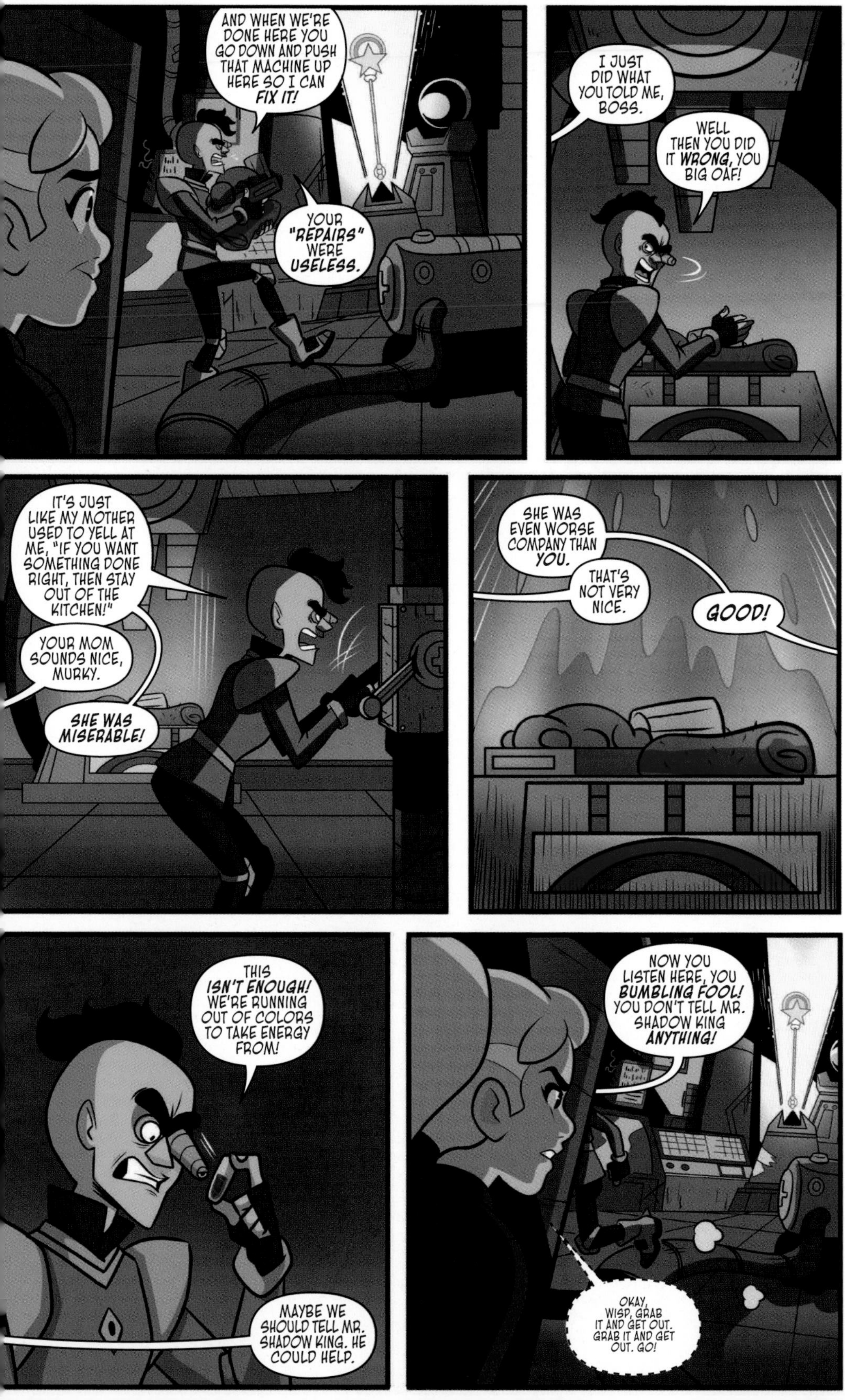
AND WHEN WE'RE DONE HERE YOU GO DOWN AND PUSH THAT MACHINE UP HERE SO I CAN FIX IT!
YOUR "REPAIRS" WERE USELESS.
I JUST DID WHAT YOU TOLD ME, BOSS.
WELL THEN YOU DID IT WRONG, YOU BIG OAF!
IT'S JUST LIKE MY MOTHER USED TO YELL AT ME, "IF YOU WANT SOMETHING DONE RIGHT, THEN STAY OUT OF THE KITCHEN!"
YOUR MOM SOUNDS NICE, MURKY.
SHE WAS MISERABLE!
SHE WAS EVEN WORSE COMPANY THAN YOU.
THAT'S NOT VERY NICE.
GOOD!
THIS ISN'T ENOUGH! WE'RE RUNNING OUT OF COLORS TO TAKE ENERGY FROM!
MAYBE WE SHOULD TELL MR. SHADOW KING. HE COULD HELP.
NOW YOU LISTEN HERE, YOU BUMBLING FOOL! YOU DON'T TELL MR. SHADOW KING ANYTHING!
OKAY, WISP, GRAB IT AND GET OUT. GRAB IT AND GET OUT. GO!

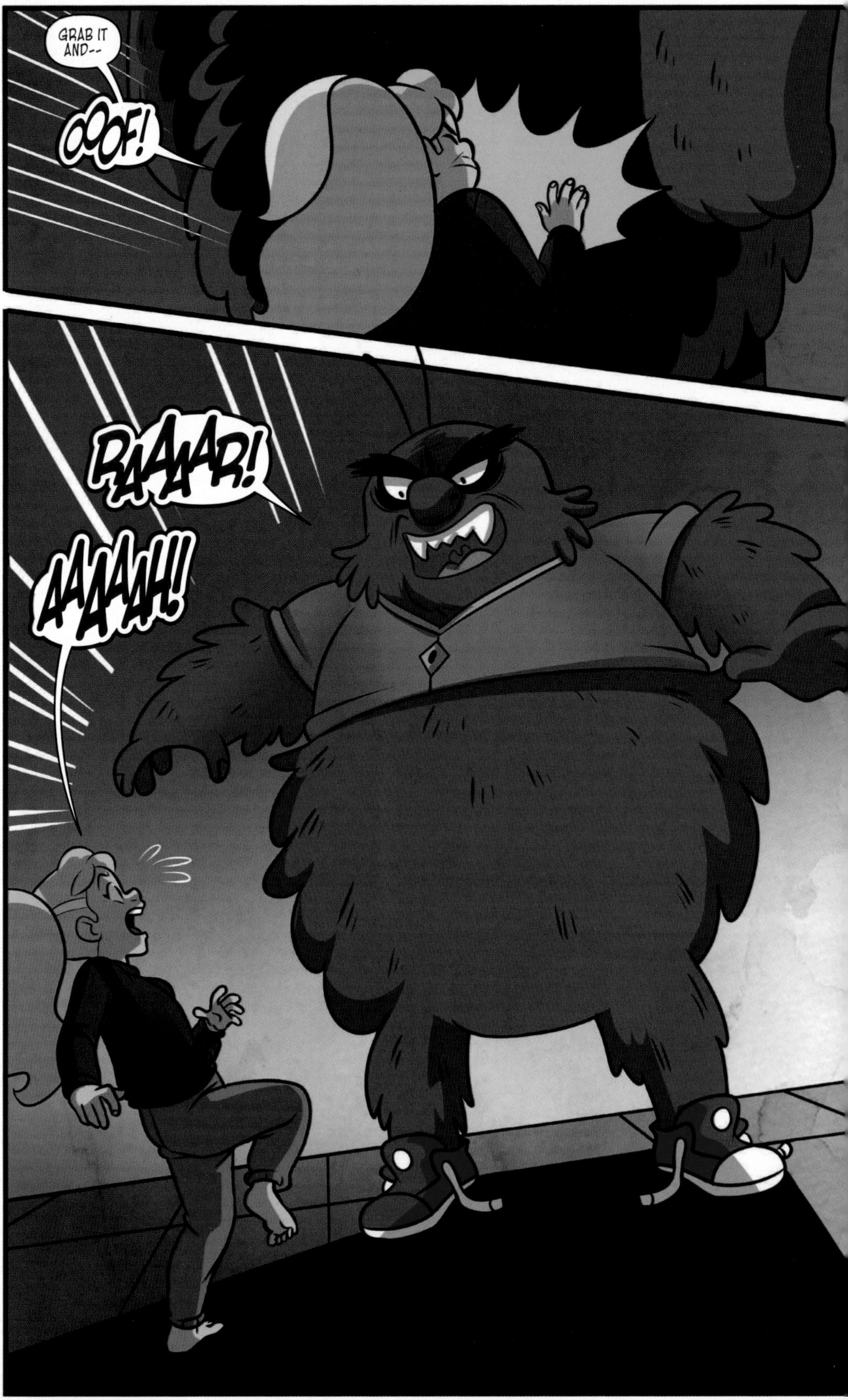
GRAB IT AND--
OOOF!
RAAAAR!
AAAAAH!

AAAAH!!
IT ATTACKED ME!
WHAT IS IT?!
SOME KIND OF MONSTER!
LOOK AT ALL THOSE COLORS!
GRAB HER!

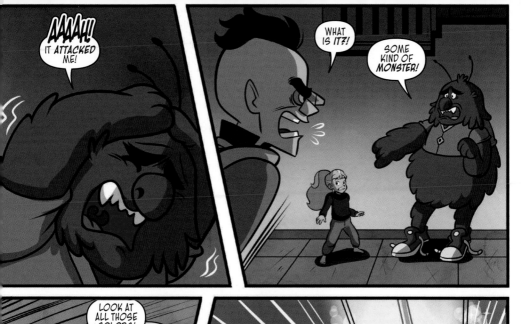

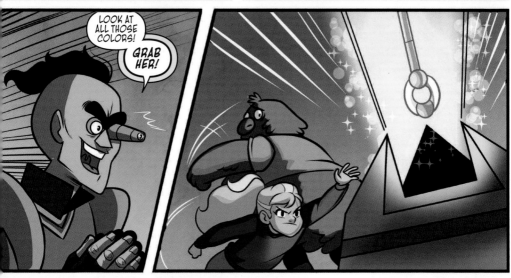

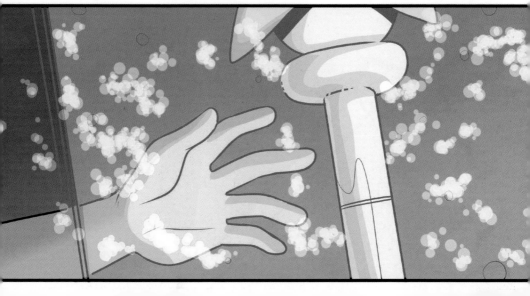

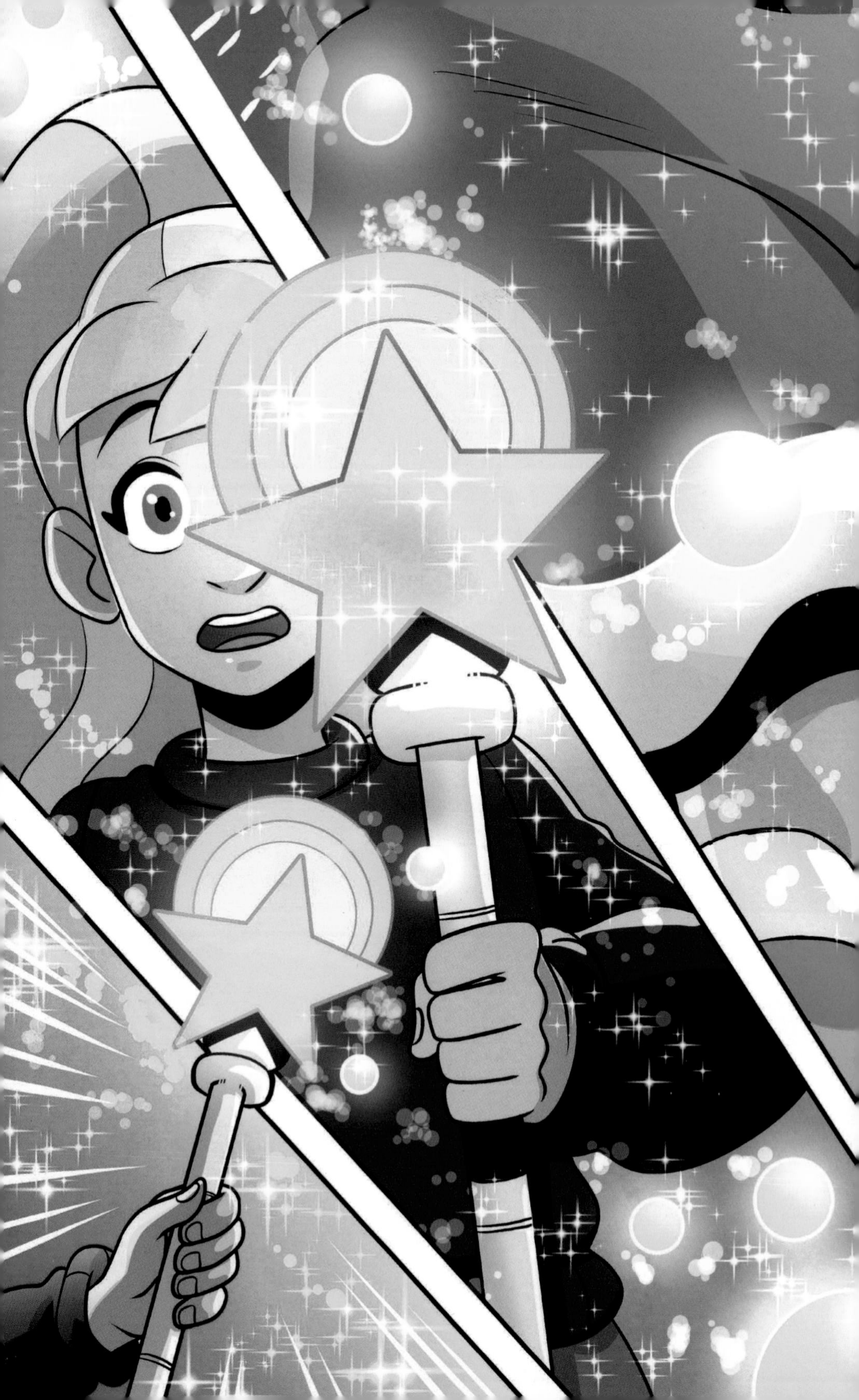

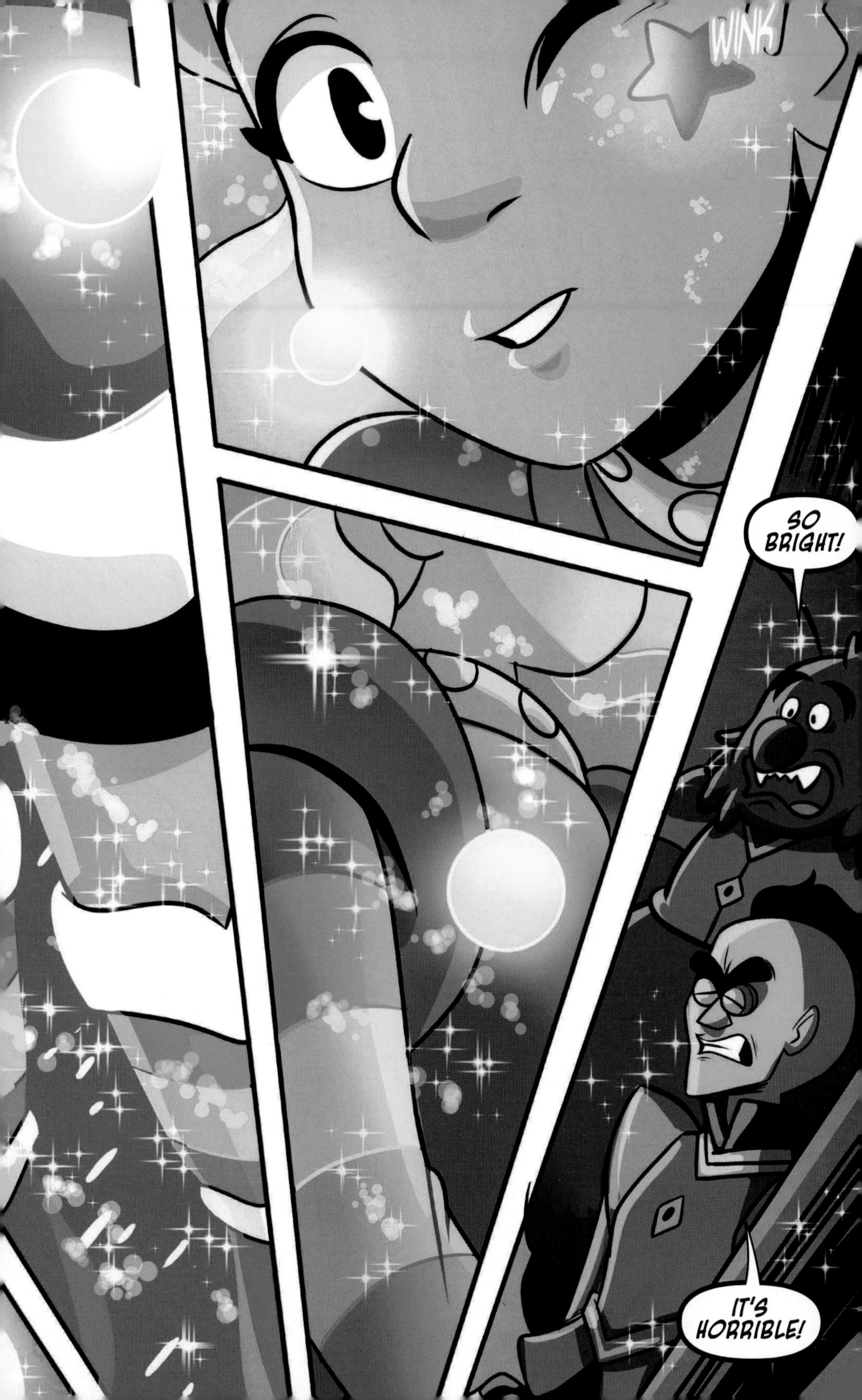
WINK
SO BRIGHT!
IT'S HORRIBLE!

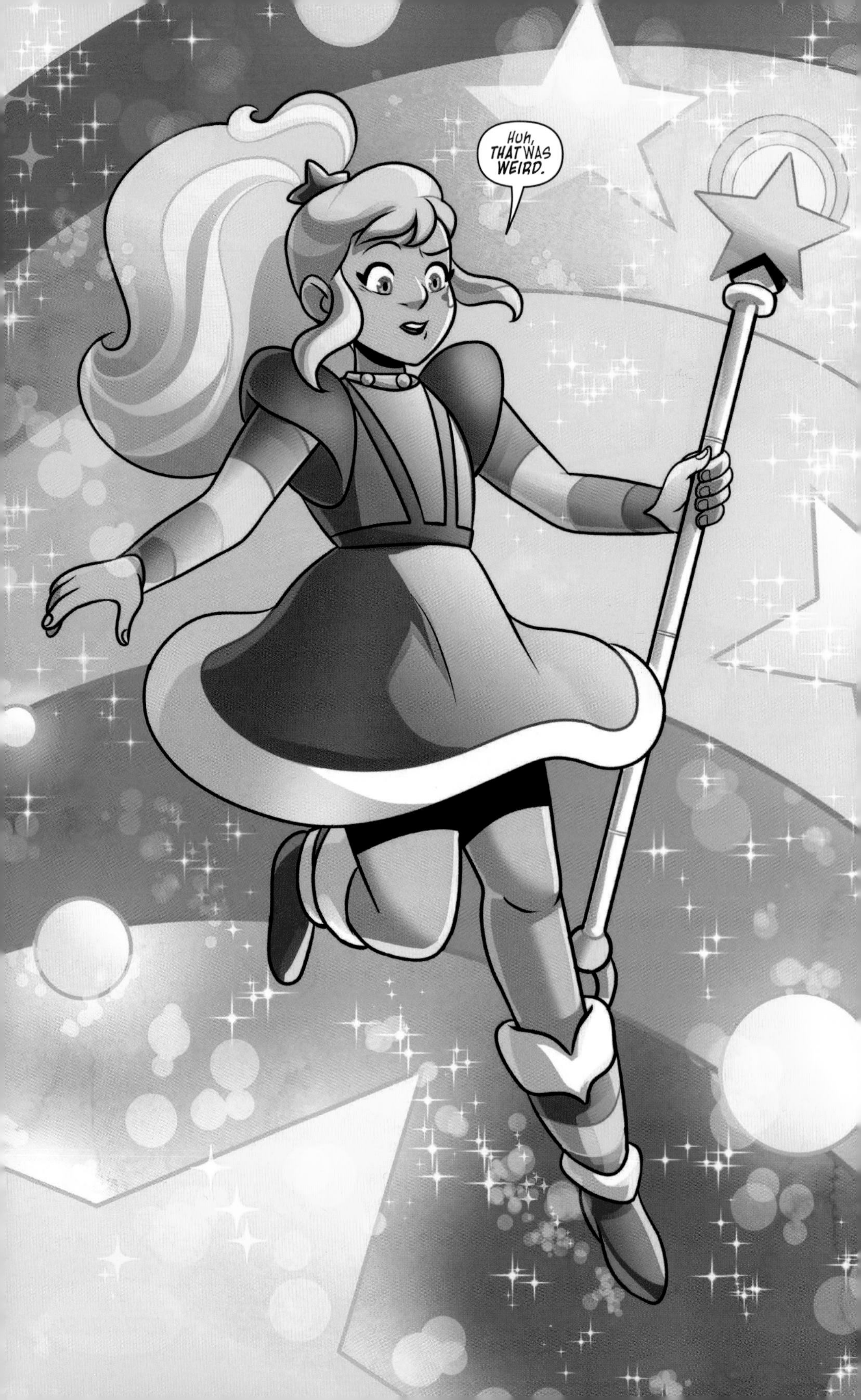
HUH, THAT WAS WEIRD.

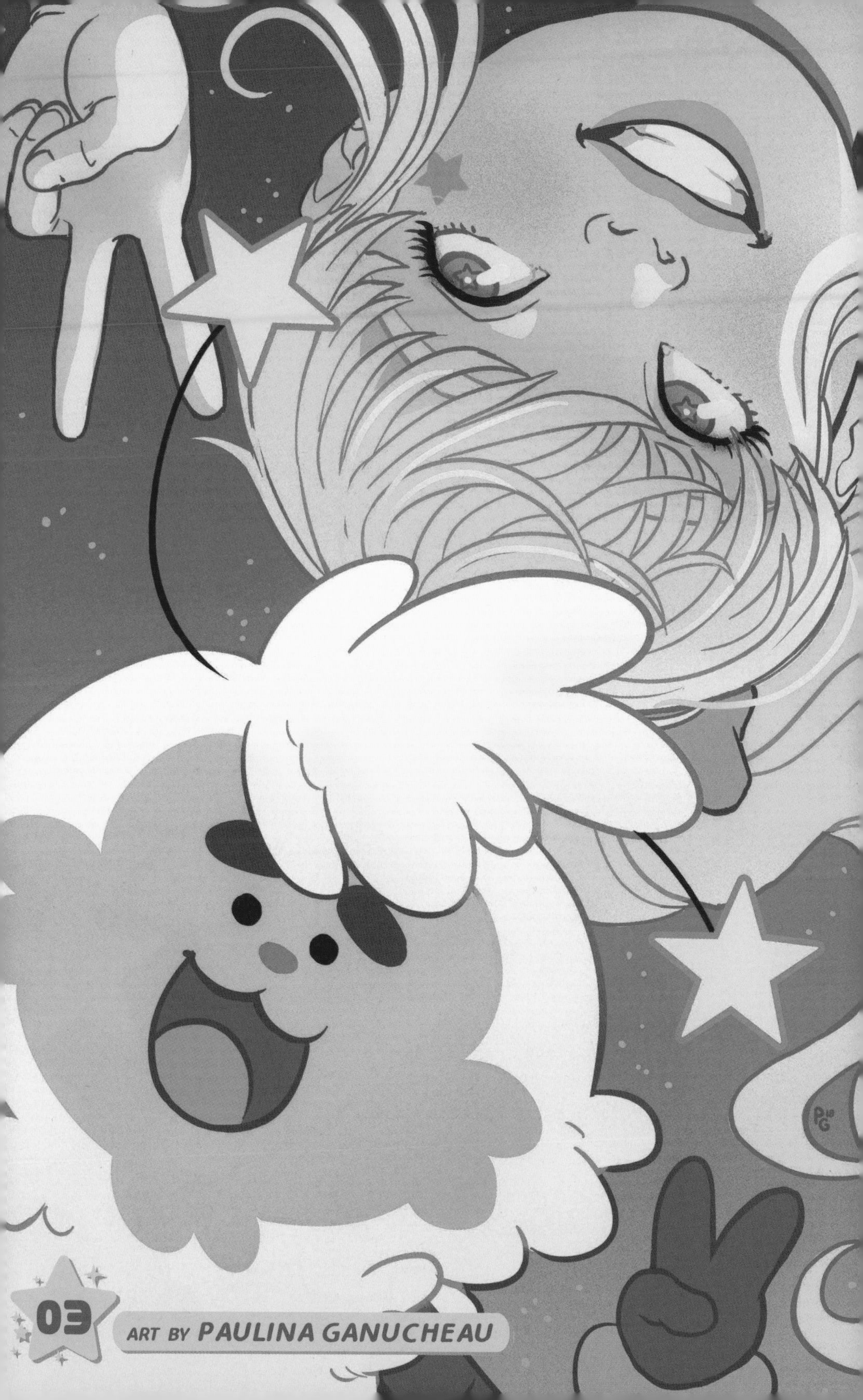

03

ART BY PAULINA GANUCHEAU

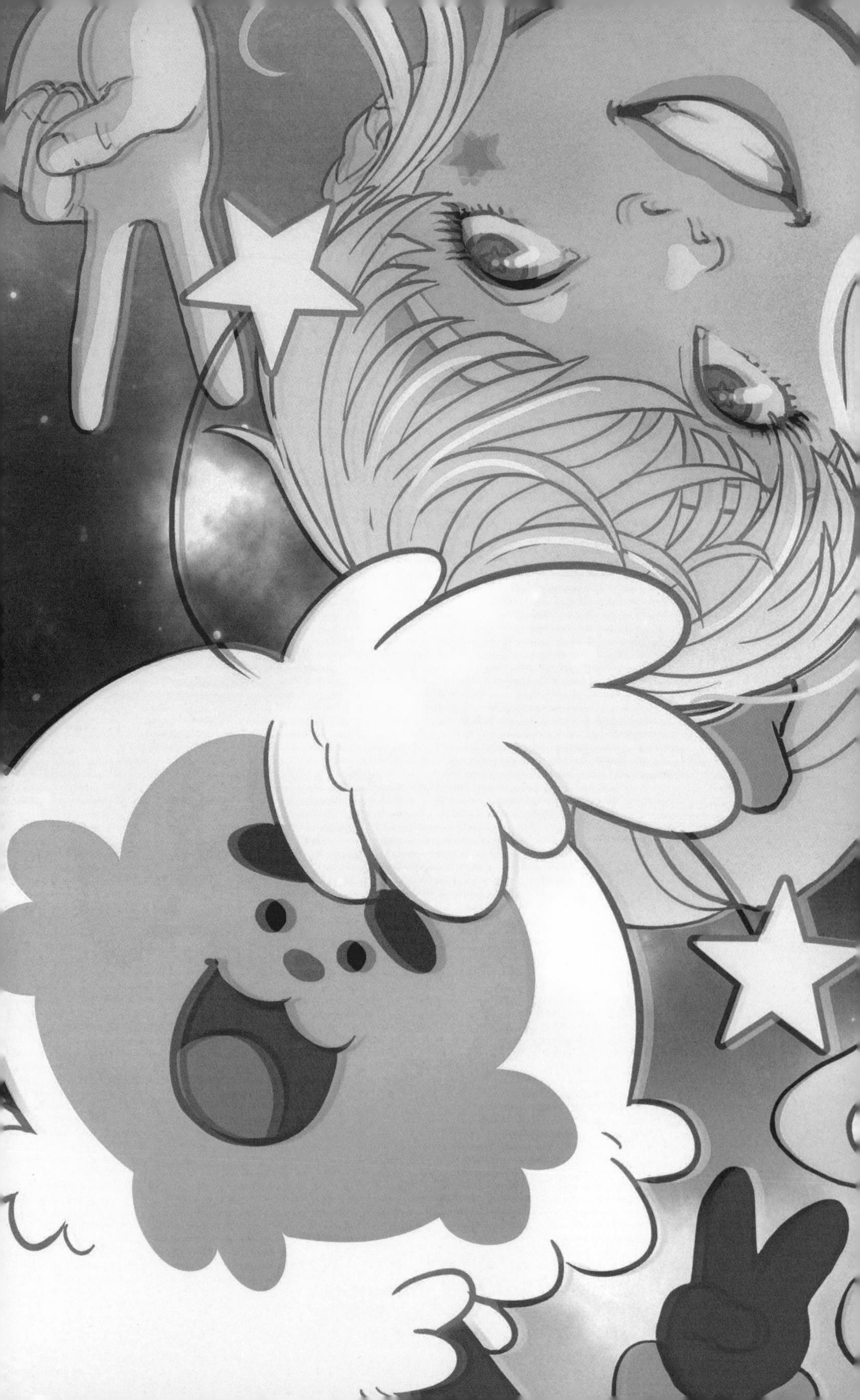

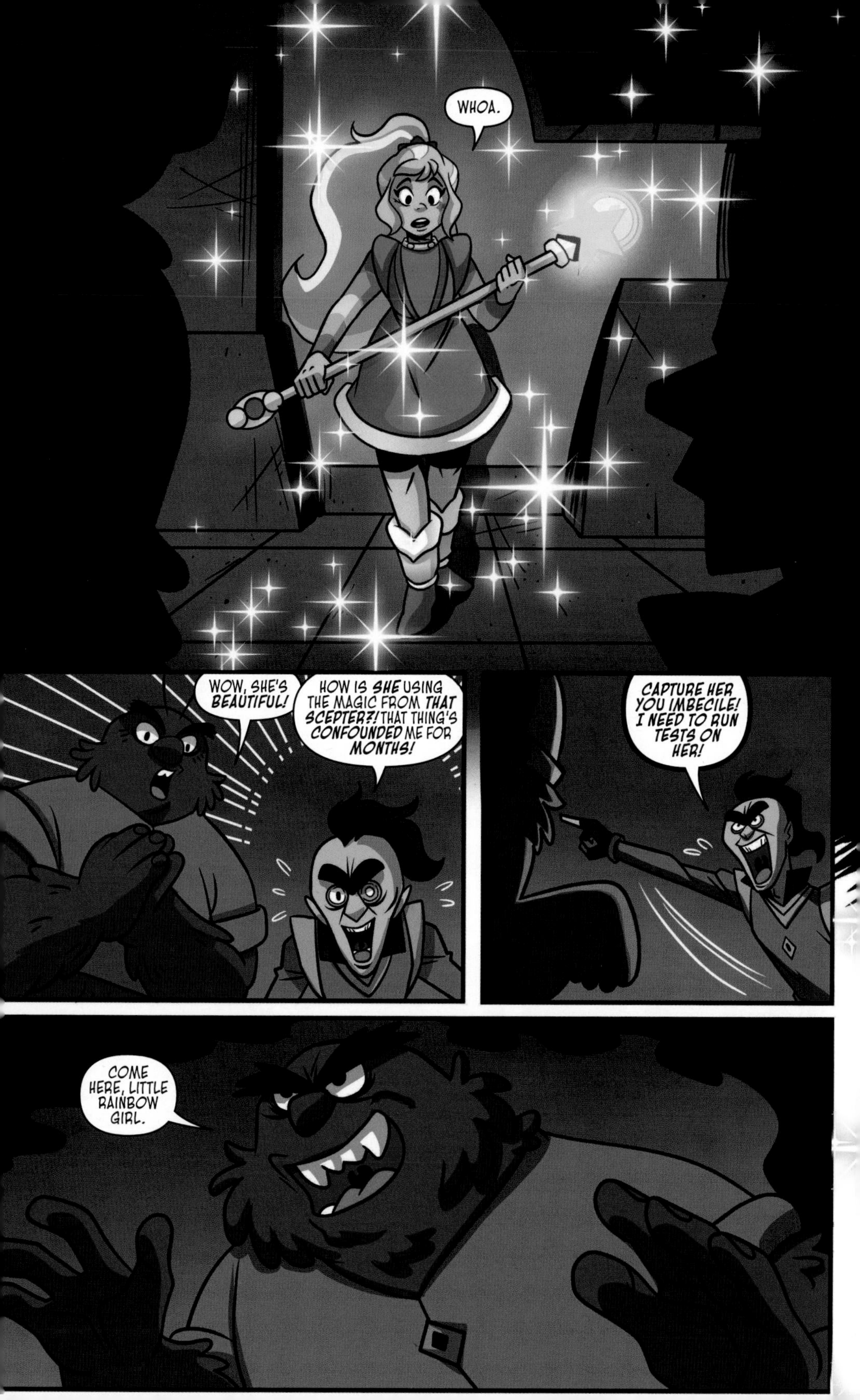
WHOA.
WOW, SHE'S BEAUTIFUL!
HOW IS SHE USING THE MAGIC FROM THAT SCEPTER?! THAT THING'S CONFOUNDED ME FOR MONTHS!
CAPTURE HER YOU IMBECILE! I NEED TO RUN TESTS ON HER!
COME HERE, LITTLE RAINBOW GIRL.

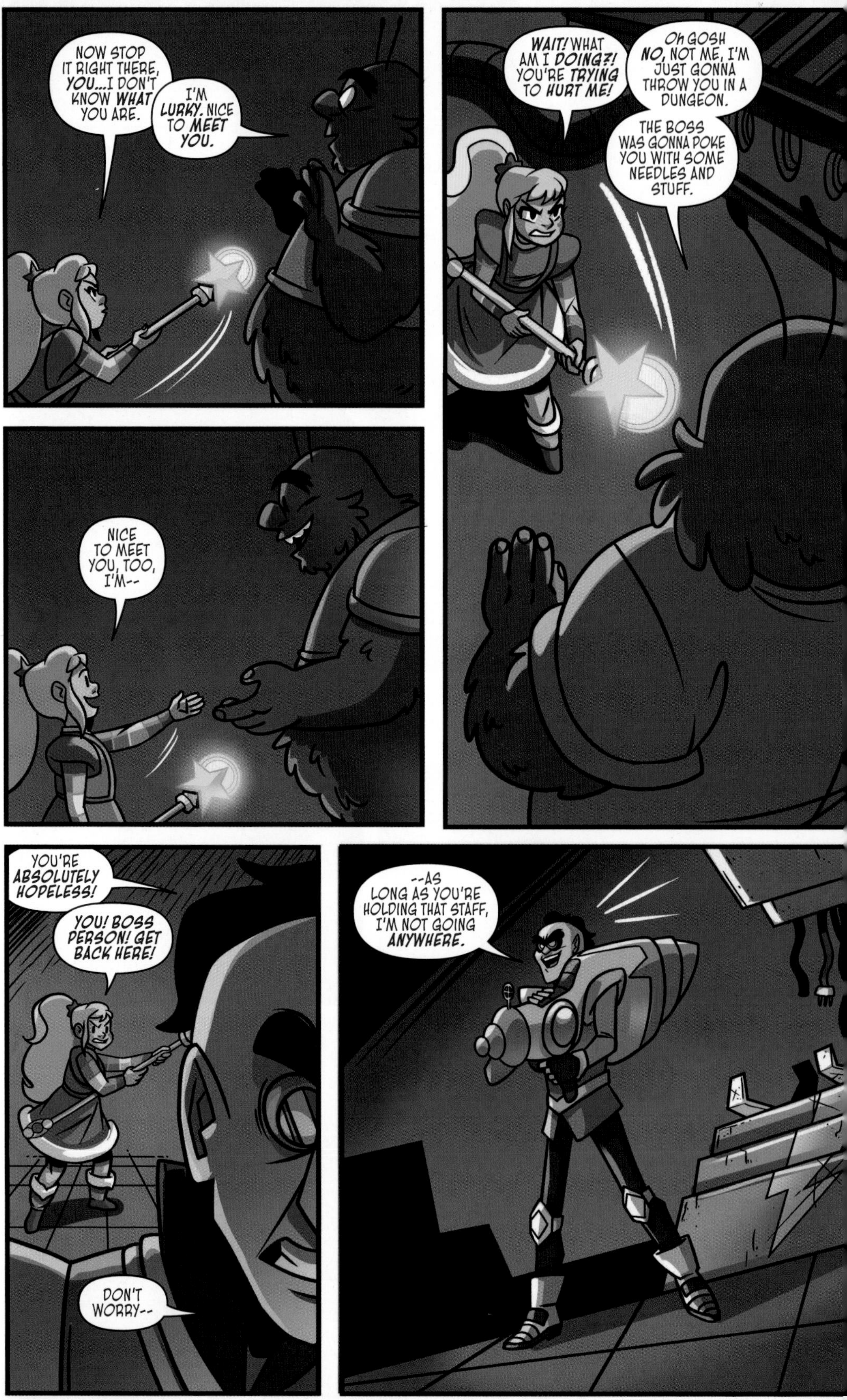
NOW STOP IT RIGHT THERE, YOU...I DON'T KNOW WHAT YOU ARE.
I'M LURKY. NICE TO MEET YOU.
NICE TO MEET YOU, TOO, I'M--
WAIT! WHAT AM I DOING?! YOU'RE TRYING TO HURT ME!
Oh GOSH NO, NOT ME, I'M JUST GONNA THROW YOU IN A DUNGEON.
THE BOSS WAS GONNA POKE YOU WITH SOME NEEDLES AND STUFF.
YOU'RE ABSOLUTELY HOPELESS!
YOU! BOSS PERSON! GET BACK HERE!
DON'T WORRY--
--AS LONG AS YOU'RE HOLDING THAT STAFF, I'M NOT GOING ANYWHERE.

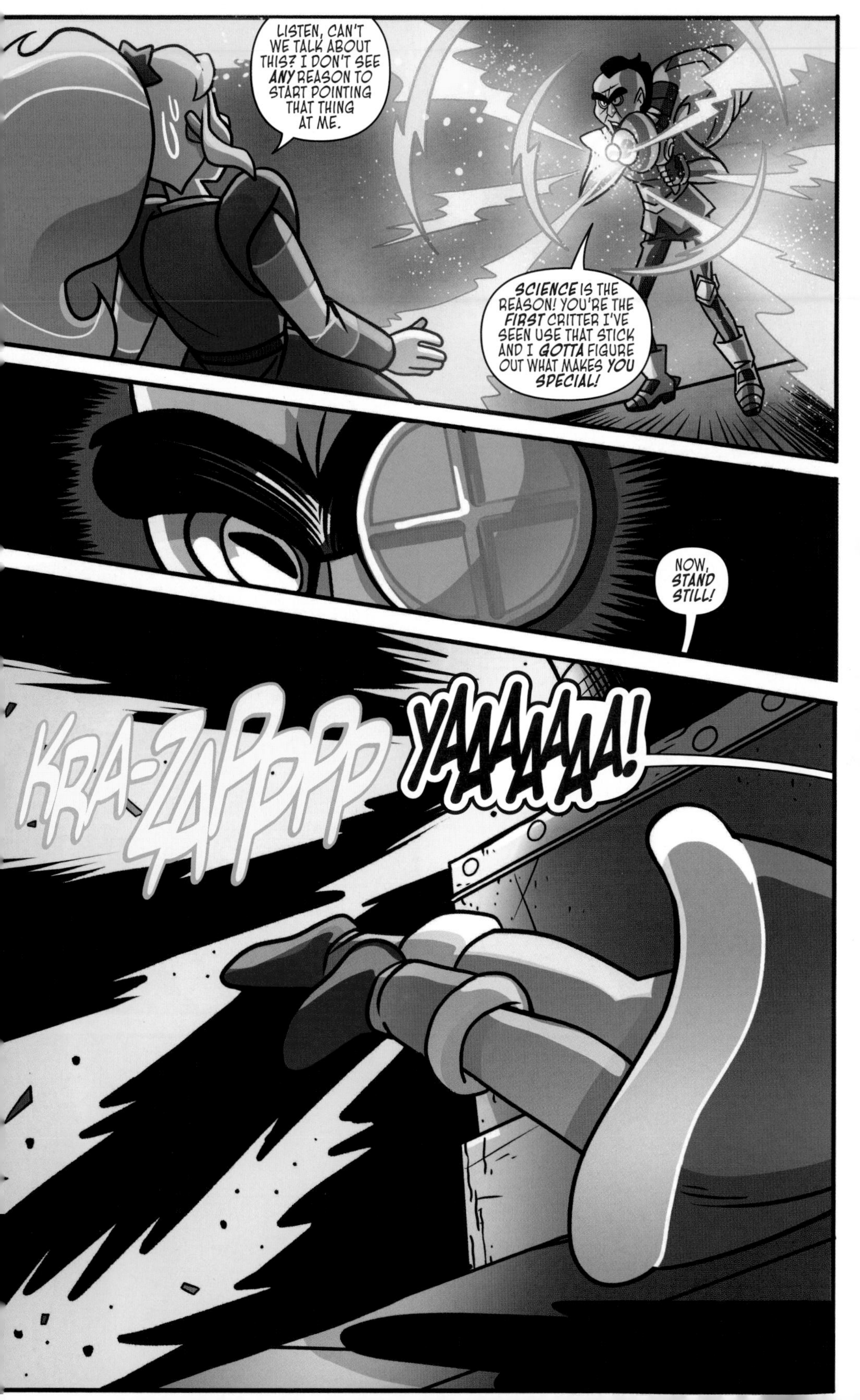
LISTEN, CAN'T WE TALK ABOUT THIS? I DON'T SEE ANY REASON TO START POINTING THAT THING AT ME.
SCIENCE IS THE REASON! YOU'RE THE FIRST CRITTER I'VE SEEN USE THAT STICK AND I GOTTA FIGURE OUT WHAT MAKES YOU SPECIAL!
NOW, STAND STILL!
KRA-ZAPPPP
YAAAAAAA!

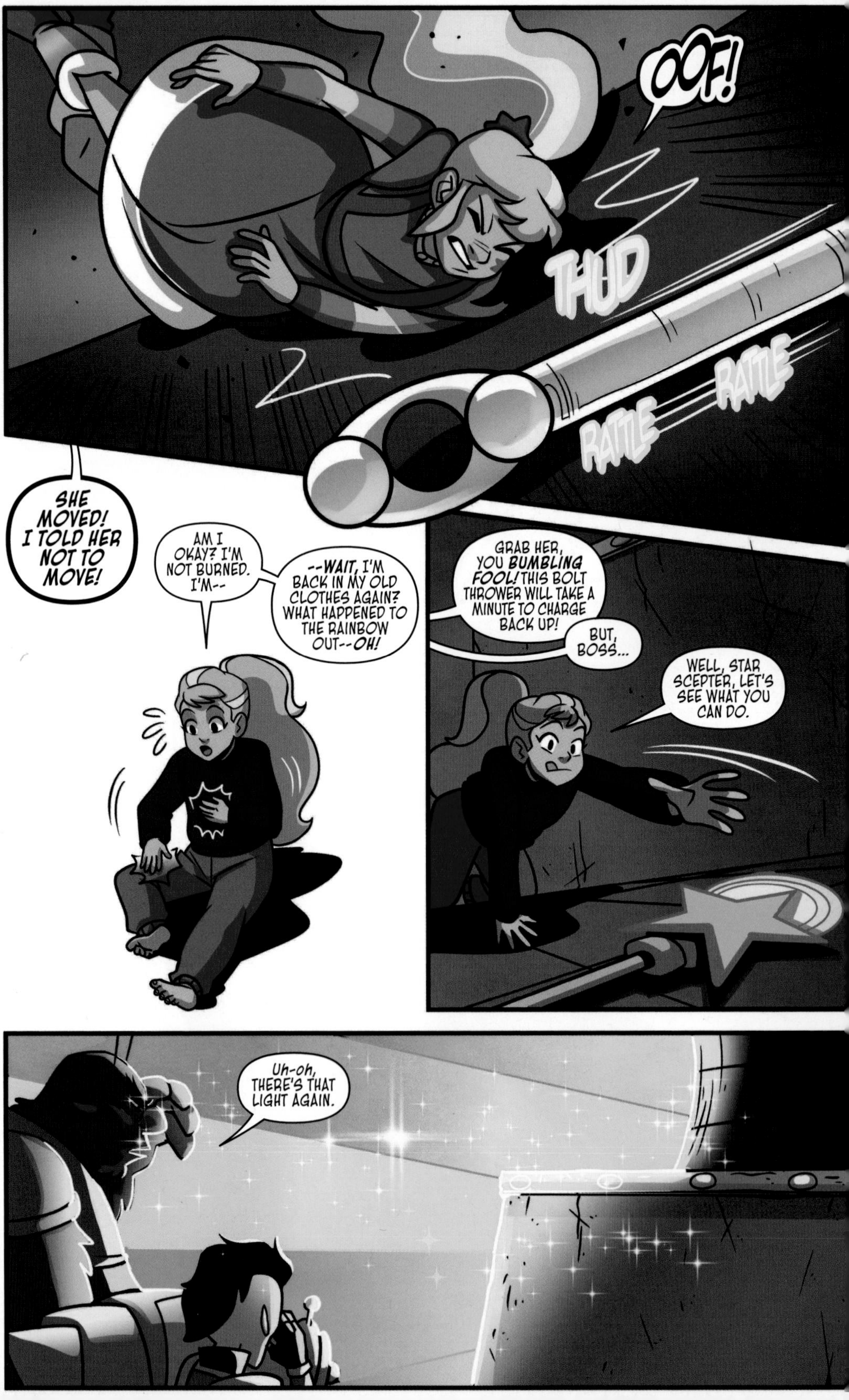
OOF!
THUD
RATTLE RATTLE
SHE MOVED! I TOLD HER NOT TO MOVE!
AM I OKAY? I'M NOT BURNED. I'M--
--WAIT, I'M BACK IN MY OLD CLOTHES AGAIN? WHAT HAPPENED TO THE RAINBOW OUT--OH!
GRAB HER, YOU BUMBLING FOOL! THIS BOLT THROWER WILL TAKE A MINUTE TO CHARGE BACK UP!
BUT, BOSS...
WELL, STAR SCEPTER, LET'S SEE WHAT YOU CAN DO.
Uh-oh, THERE'S THAT LIGHT AGAIN.

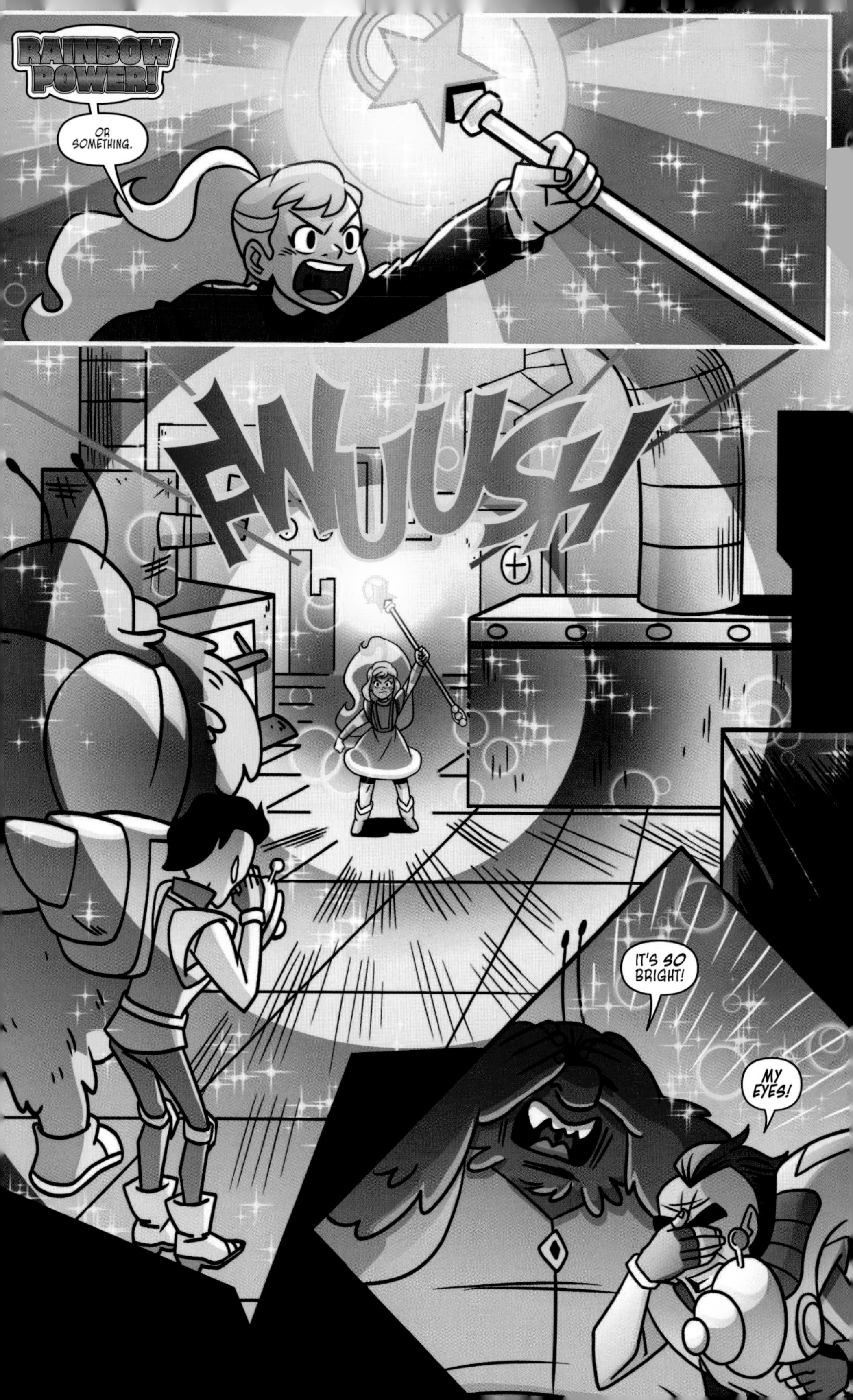
RAINBOW POWER!
OR SOMETHING.
FWUUSH
IT'S SO BRIGHT!
MY EYES!

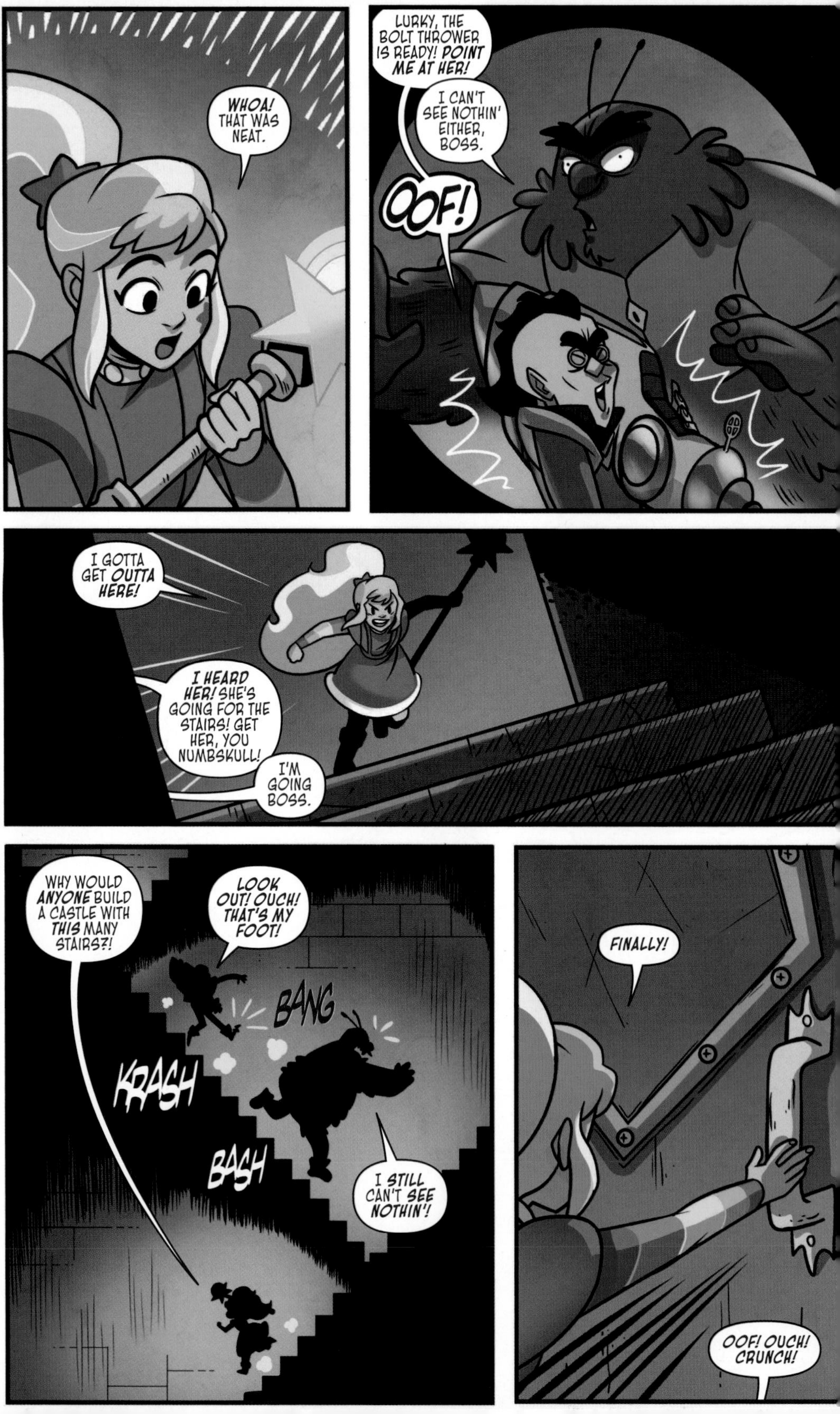
WHOA! THAT WAS NEAT.
LURKY, THE BOLT THROWER IS READY! POINT ME AT HER!
I CAN'T SEE NOTHIN' EITHER, BOSS.
OOF!
I GOTTA GET OUTTA HERE!
I HEARD HER! SHE'S GOING FOR THE STAIRS! GET HER, YOU NUMBSKULL!
I'M GOING BOSS.
WHY WOULD ANYONE BUILD A CASTLE WITH THIS MANY STAIRS?!
LOOK OUT! OUCH! THAT'S MY FOOT!
BANG
KRASH
BASH
I STILL CAN'T SEE NOTHIN'!
FINALLY!
OOF! OUCH! CRUNCH!

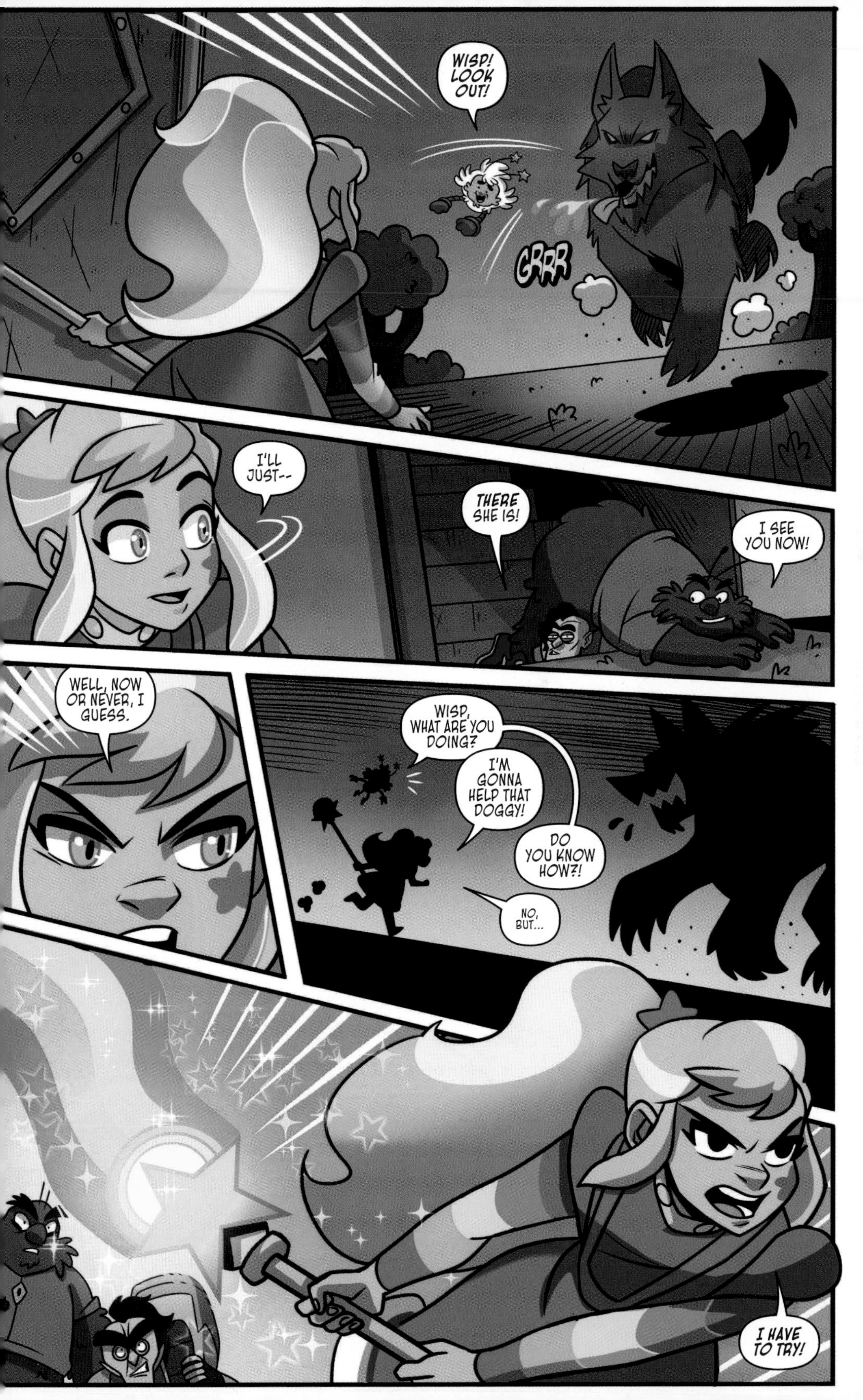
WISP! LOOK OUT!
GRRR
I'LL JUST--
THERE SHE IS!
I SEE YOU NOW!
WELL, NOW OR NEVER, I GUESS.
WISP, WHAT ARE YOU DOING?
I'M GONNA HELP THAT DOGGY!
DO YOU KNOW HOW?!
NO, BUT...
I HAVE TO TRY!

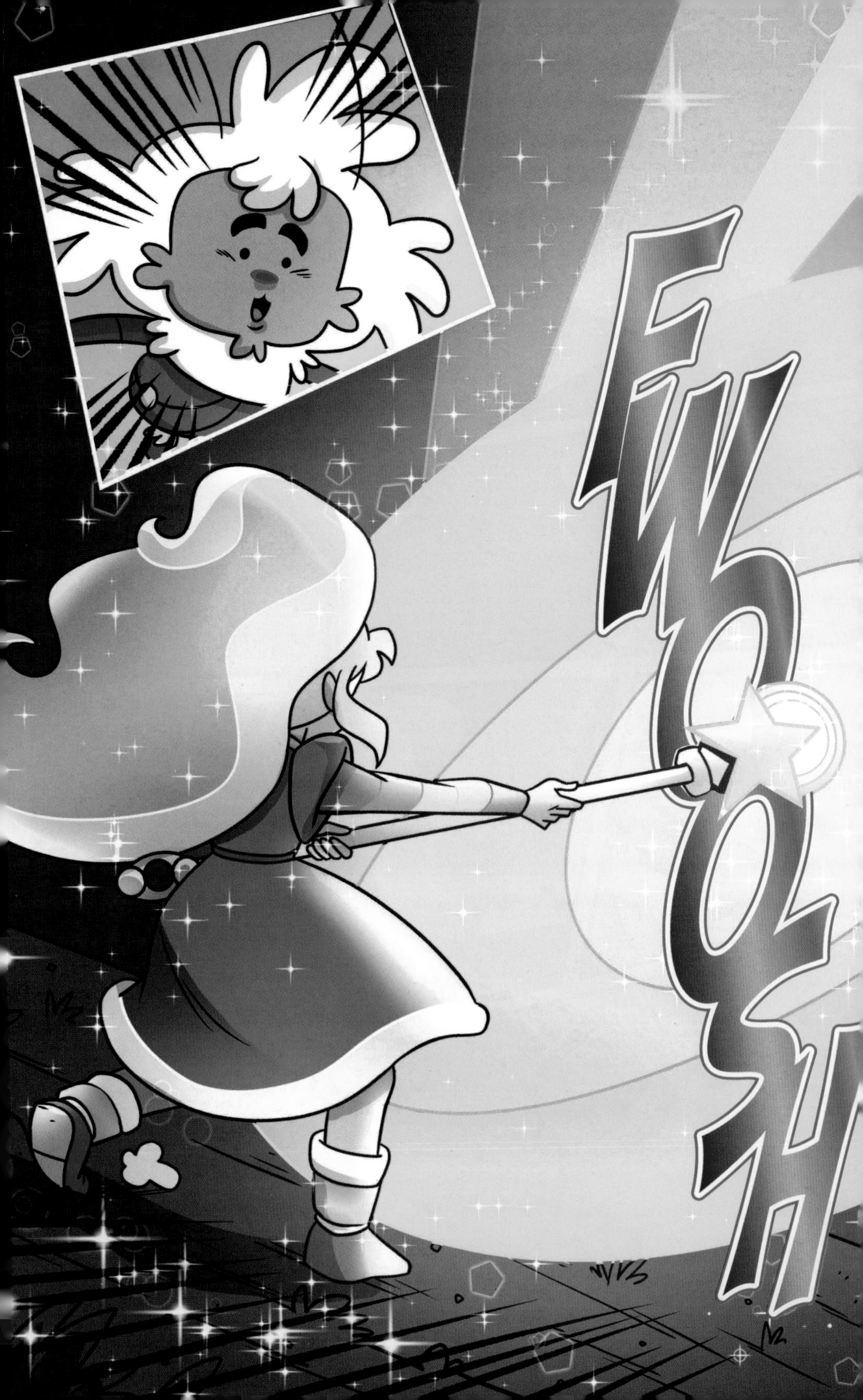
FWOOSH

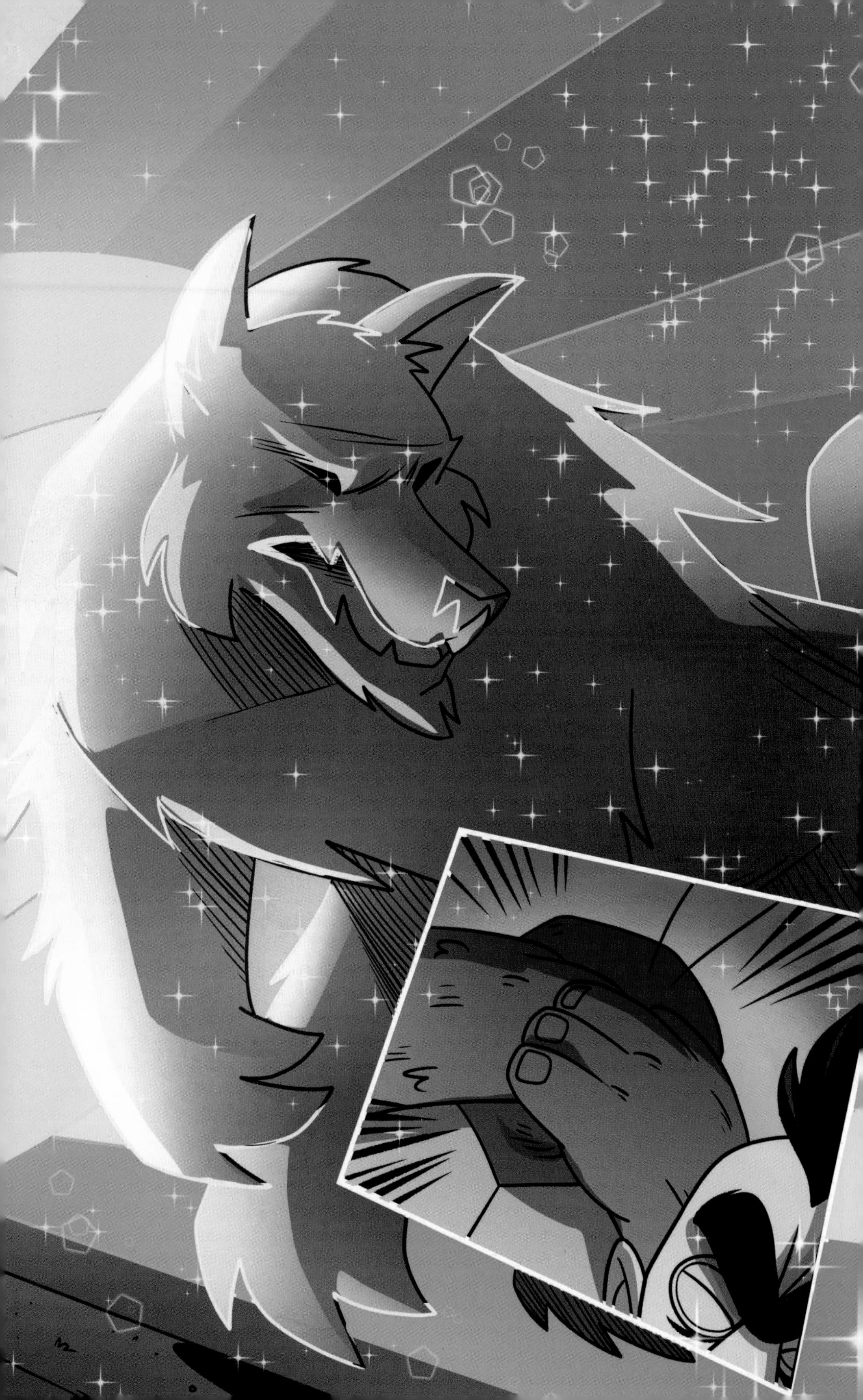

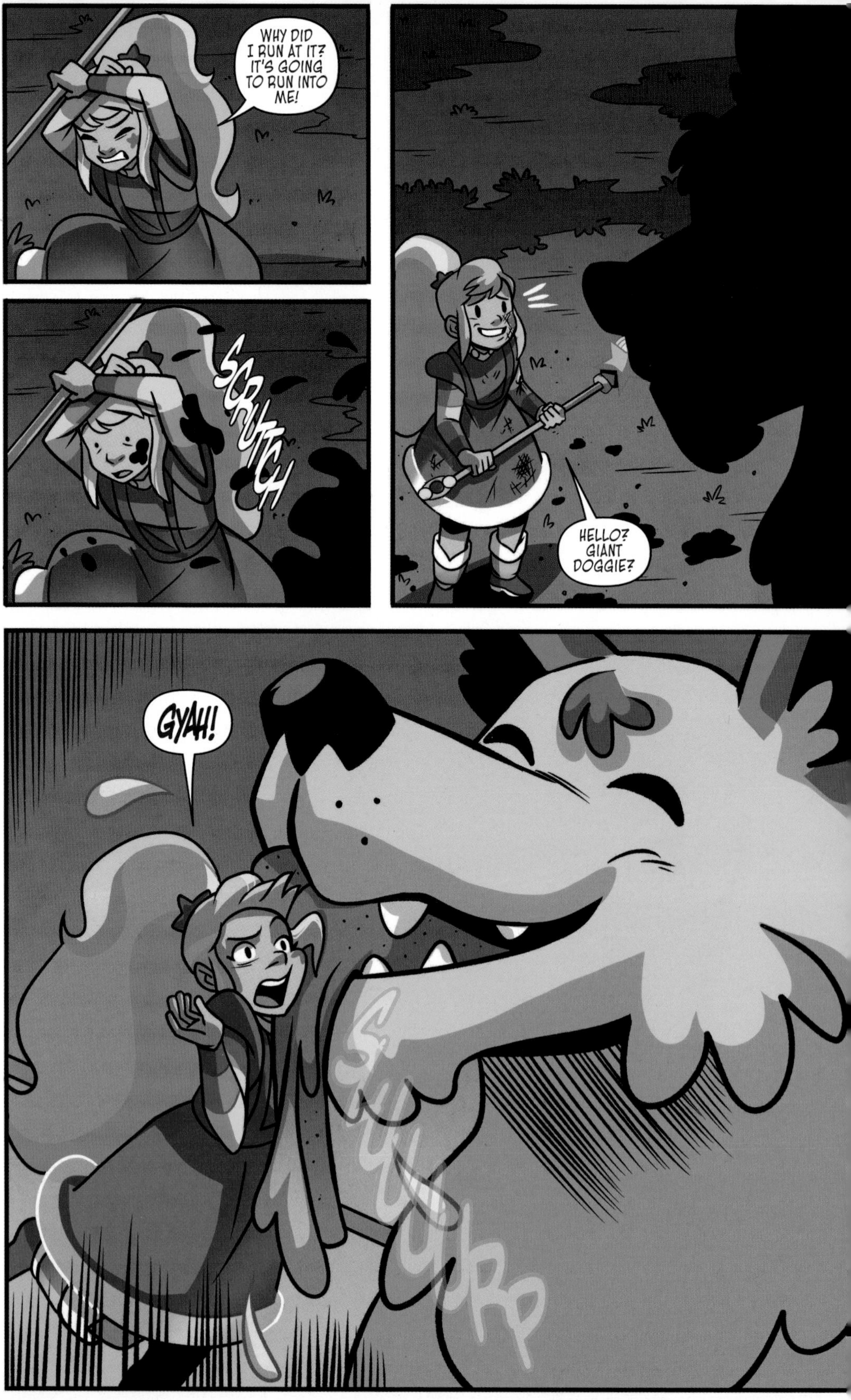
WHY DID I RUN AT IT? IT'S GOING TO RUN INTO ME!
SCRUTCH
HELLO? GIANT DOGGIE?
GYAH!
SHLLLURP

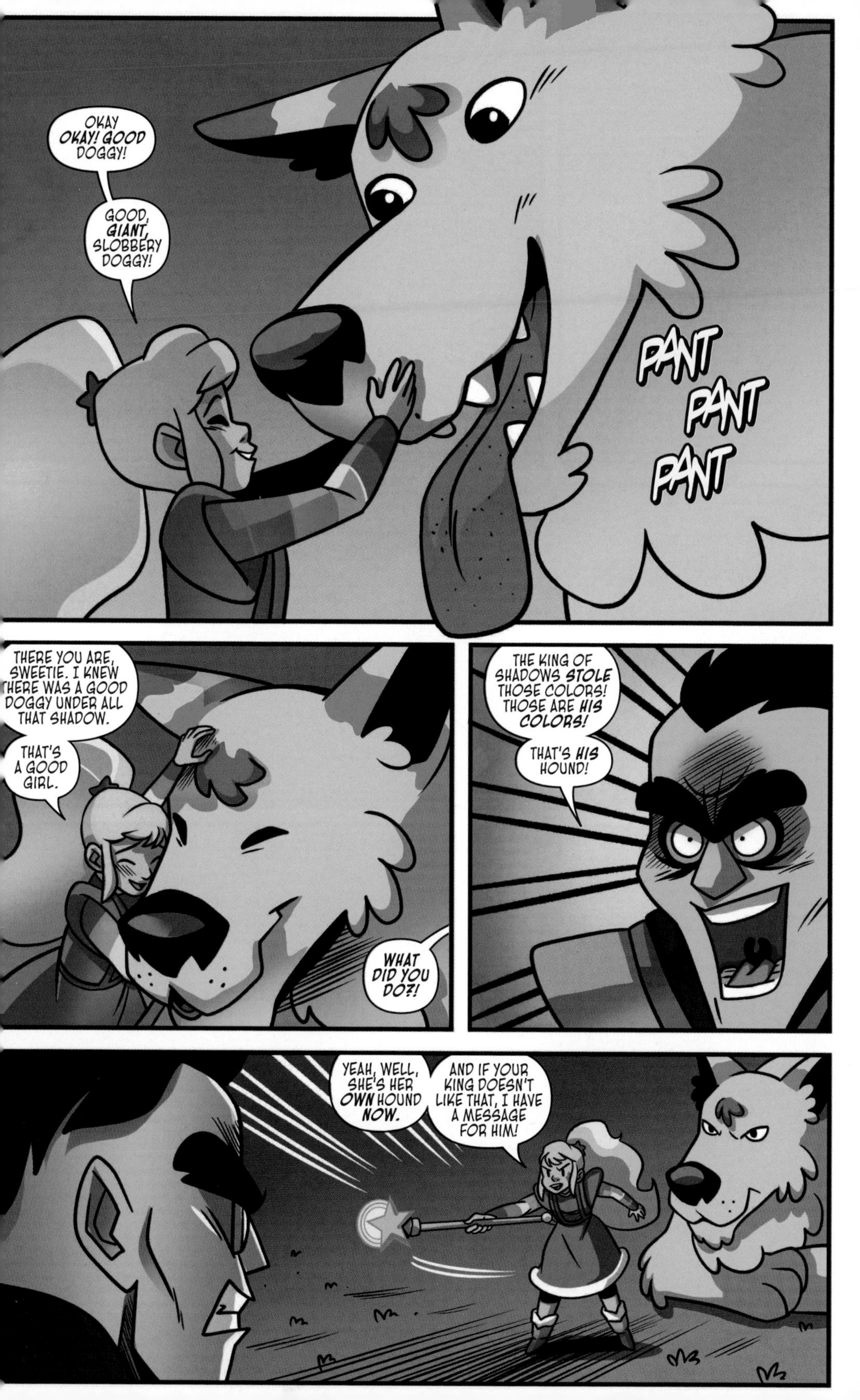
OKAY OKAY! GOOD DOGGY!
GOOD, GIANT, SLOBBERY DOGGY!
PANT PANT PANT
THERE YOU ARE, SWEETIE. I KNEW THERE WAS A GOOD DOGGY UNDER ALL THAT SHADOW.
THAT'S A GOOD GIRL.
WHAT DID YOU DO?!
THE KING OF SHADOWS STOLE THOSE COLORS! THOSE ARE HIS COLORS!
THAT'S HIS HOUND!
YEAH, WELL, SHE'S HER OWN HOUND NOW.
AND IF YOUR KING DOESN'T LIKE THAT, I HAVE A MESSAGE FOR HIM!

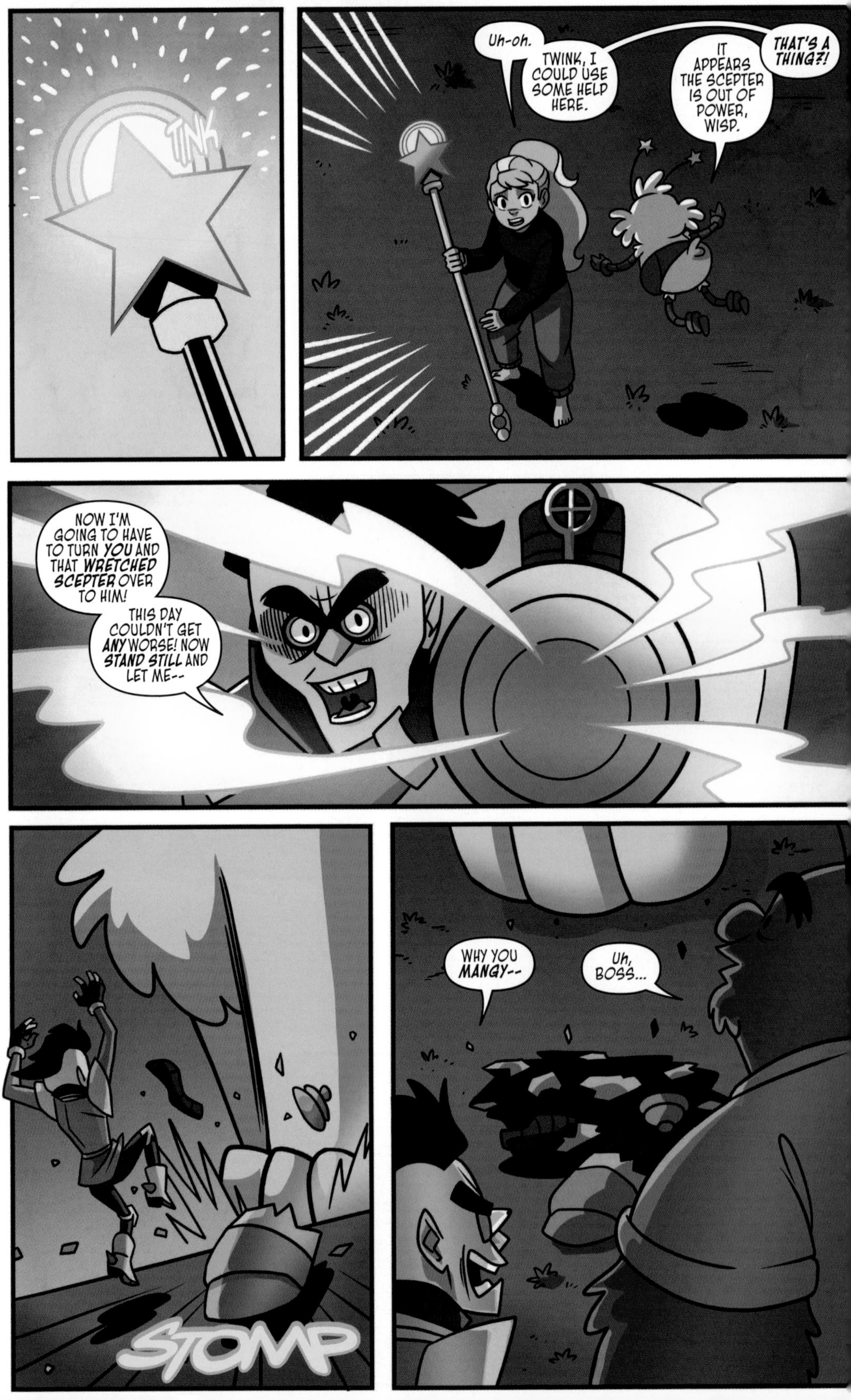
TINK
Uh-oh.
TWINK, I COULD USE SOME HELP HERE.
IT APPEARS THE SCEPTER IS OUT OF POWER, WISP.
THAT'S A THING?!
NOW I'M GOING TO HAVE TO TURN YOU AND THAT WRETCHED SCEPTER OVER TO HIM!
THIS DAY COULDN'T GET ANY WORSE! NOW STAND STILL AND LET ME--
STOMP
WHY YOU MANGY--
Uh, BOSS...

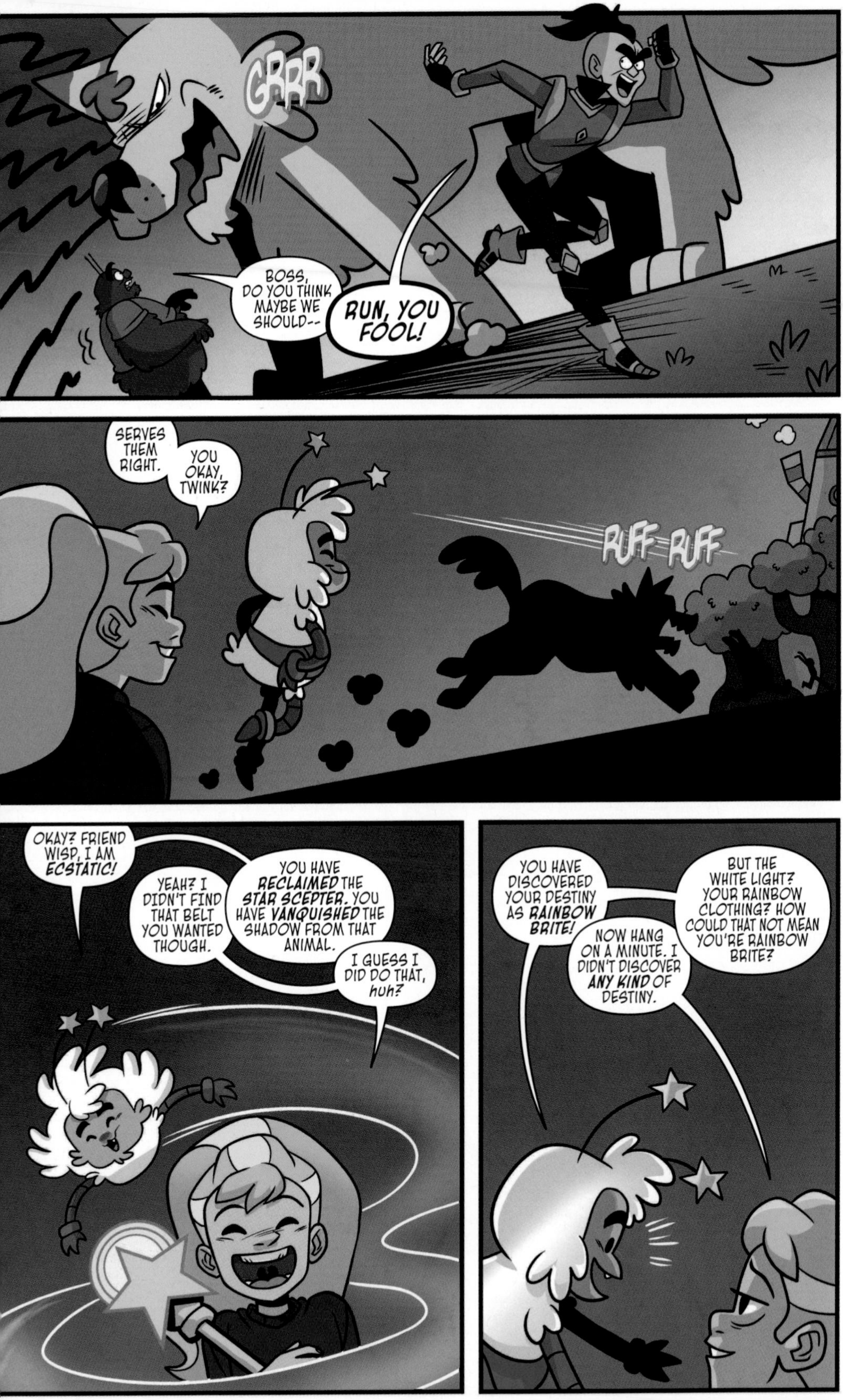
GRRR
BOSS, DO YOU THINK MAYBE WE SHOULD--
RUN, YOU FOOL!
SERVES THEM RIGHT.
YOU OKAY, TWINK?
RUFF RUFF
OKAY? FRIEND WISP, I AM ECSTATIC!
YEAH? I DIDN'T FIND THAT BELT YOU WANTED THOUGH.
YOU HAVE RECLAIMED THE STAR SCEPTER. YOU HAVE VANQUISHED THE SHADOW FROM THAT ANIMAL.
I GUESS I DID DO THAT, huh?
YOU HAVE DISCOVERED YOUR DESTINY AS RAINBOW BRITE!
NOW HANG ON A MINUTE. I DIDN'T DISCOVER ANY KIND OF DESTINY.
BUT THE WHITE LIGHT? YOUR RAINBOW CLOTHING? HOW COULD THAT NOT MEAN YOU'RE RAINBOW BRITE?

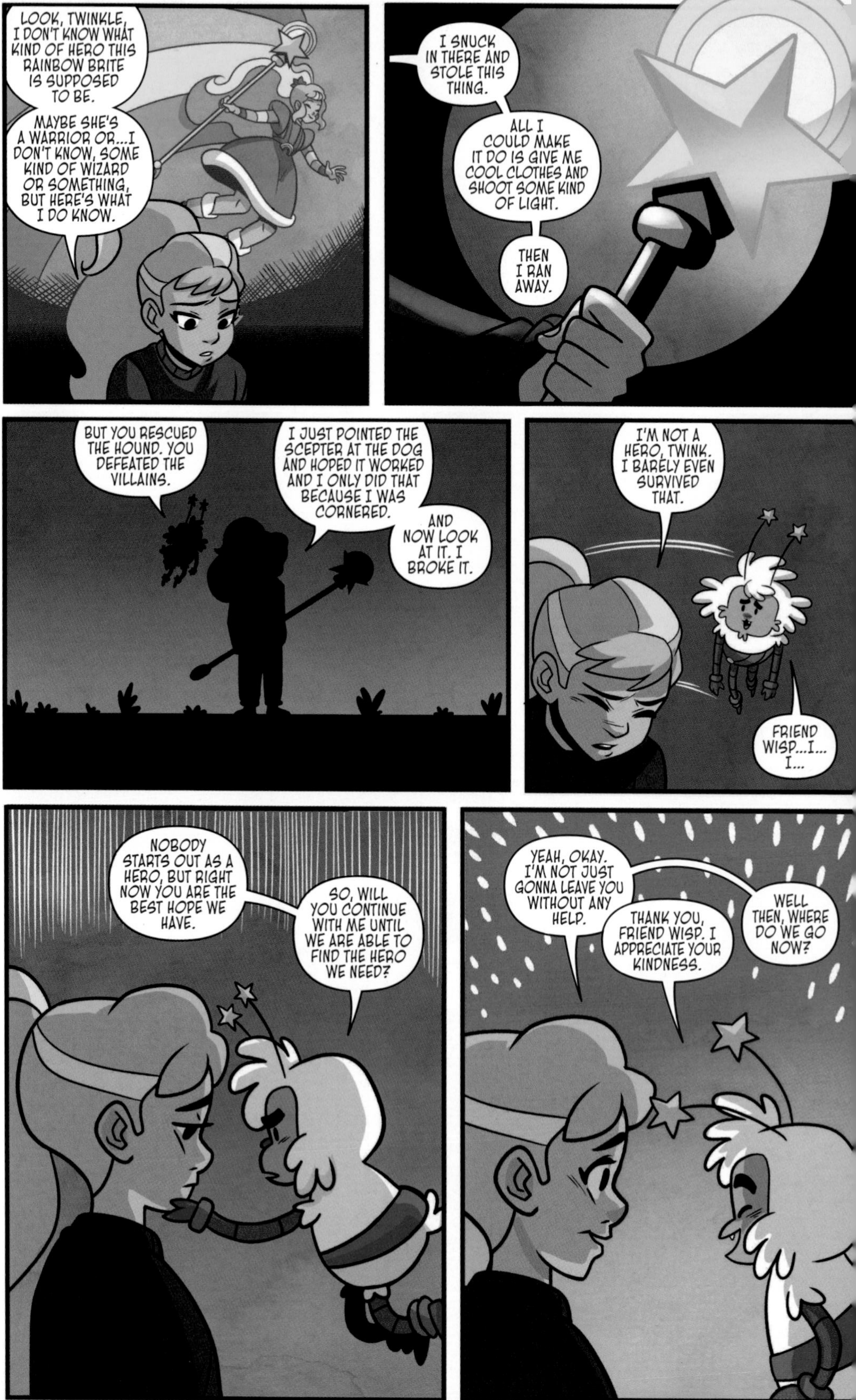
LOOK, TWINKLE, I DON'T KNOW WHAT KIND OF HERO THIS RAINBOW BRITE IS SUPPOSED TO BE.
MAYBE SHE'S A WARRIOR OR...I DON'T KNOW, SOME KIND OF WIZARD OR SOMETHING, BUT HERE'S WHAT I DO KNOW.
I SNUCK IN THERE AND STOLE THIS THING.
ALL I COULD MAKE IT DO IS GIVE ME COOL CLOTHES AND SHOOT SOME KIND OF LIGHT.
THEN I RAN AWAY.
BUT YOU RESCUED THE HOUND. YOU DEFEATED THE VILLAINS.
I JUST POINTED THE SCEPTER AT THE DOG AND HOPED IT WORKED AND I ONLY DID THAT BECAUSE I WAS CORNERED.
AND NOW LOOK AT IT. I BROKE IT.
I'M NOT A HERO, TWINK. I BARELY EVEN SURVIVED THAT.
FRIEND WISP...I... I...
NOBODY STARTS OUT AS A HERO, BUT RIGHT NOW YOU ARE THE BEST HOPE WE HAVE.
SO, WILL YOU CONTINUE WITH ME UNTIL WE ARE ABLE TO FIND THE HERO WE NEED?
YEAH, OKAY. I'M NOT JUST GONNA LEAVE YOU WITHOUT ANY HELP.
THANK YOU, FRIEND WISP. I APPRECIATE YOUR KINDNESS.
WELL THEN, WHERE DO WE GO NOW?

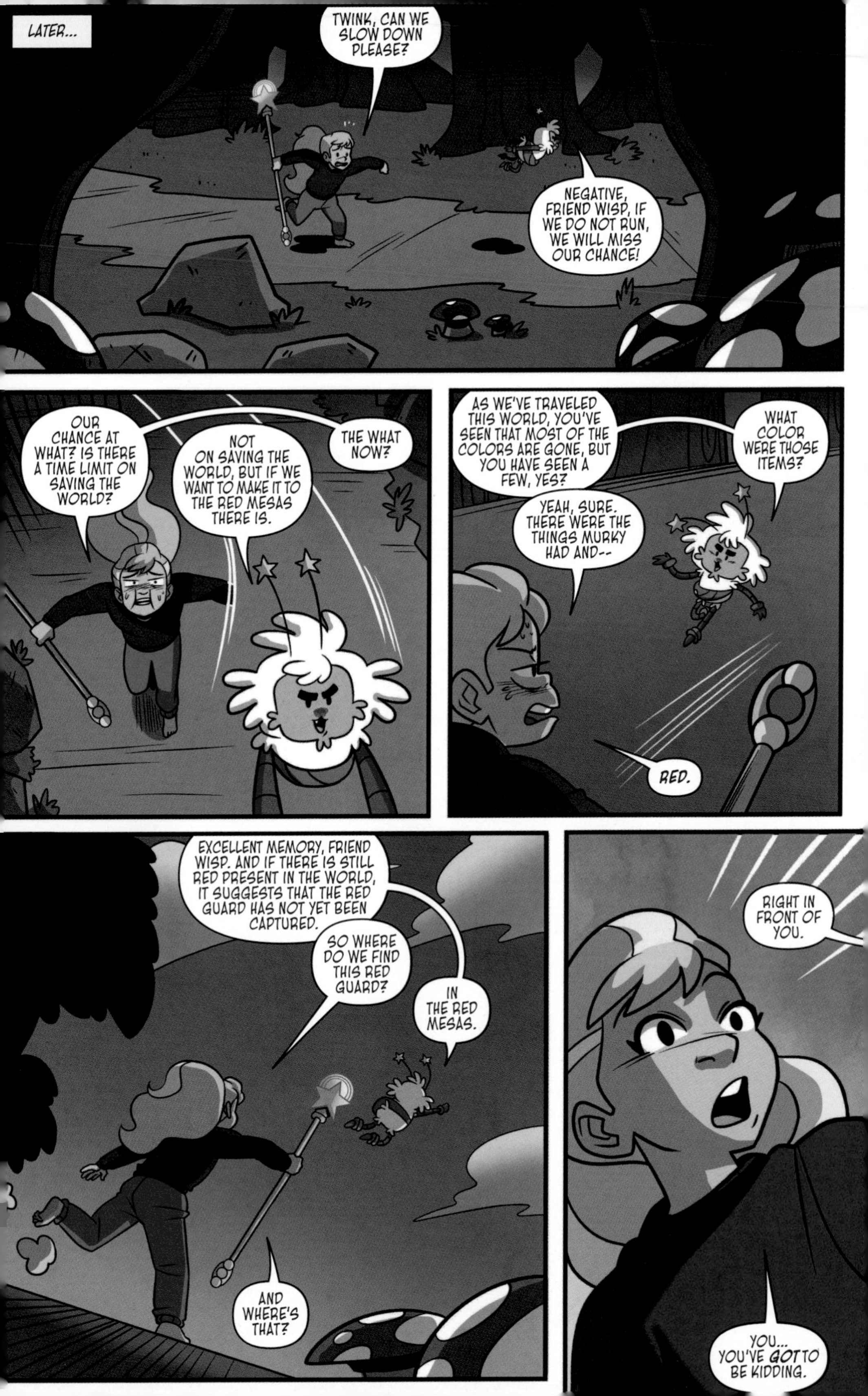
LATER...
TWINK, CAN WE SLOW DOWN PLEASE?
NEGATIVE, FRIEND WISP, IF WE DO NOT RUN, WE WILL MISS OUR CHANCE!
OUR CHANCE AT WHAT? IS THERE A TIME LIMIT ON SAVING THE WORLD?
NOT ON SAVING THE WORLD, BUT IF WE WANT TO MAKE IT TO THE RED MESAS THERE IS.
THE WHAT NOW?
AS WE'VE TRAVELED THIS WORLD, YOU'VE SEEN THAT MOST OF THE COLORS ARE GONE, BUT YOU HAVE SEEN A FEW, YES?
YEAH, SURE. THERE WERE THE THINGS MURKY HAD AND--
WHAT COLOR WERE THOSE ITEMS?
RED.
EXCELLENT MEMORY, FRIEND WISP. AND IF THERE IS STILL RED PRESENT IN THE WORLD, IT SUGGESTS THAT THE RED GUARD HAS NOT YET BEEN CAPTURED.
SO WHERE DO WE FIND THIS RED GUARD?
IN THE RED MESAS.
AND WHERE'S THAT?
RIGHT IN FRONT OF YOU.
YOU... YOU'VE GOT TO BE KIDDING.

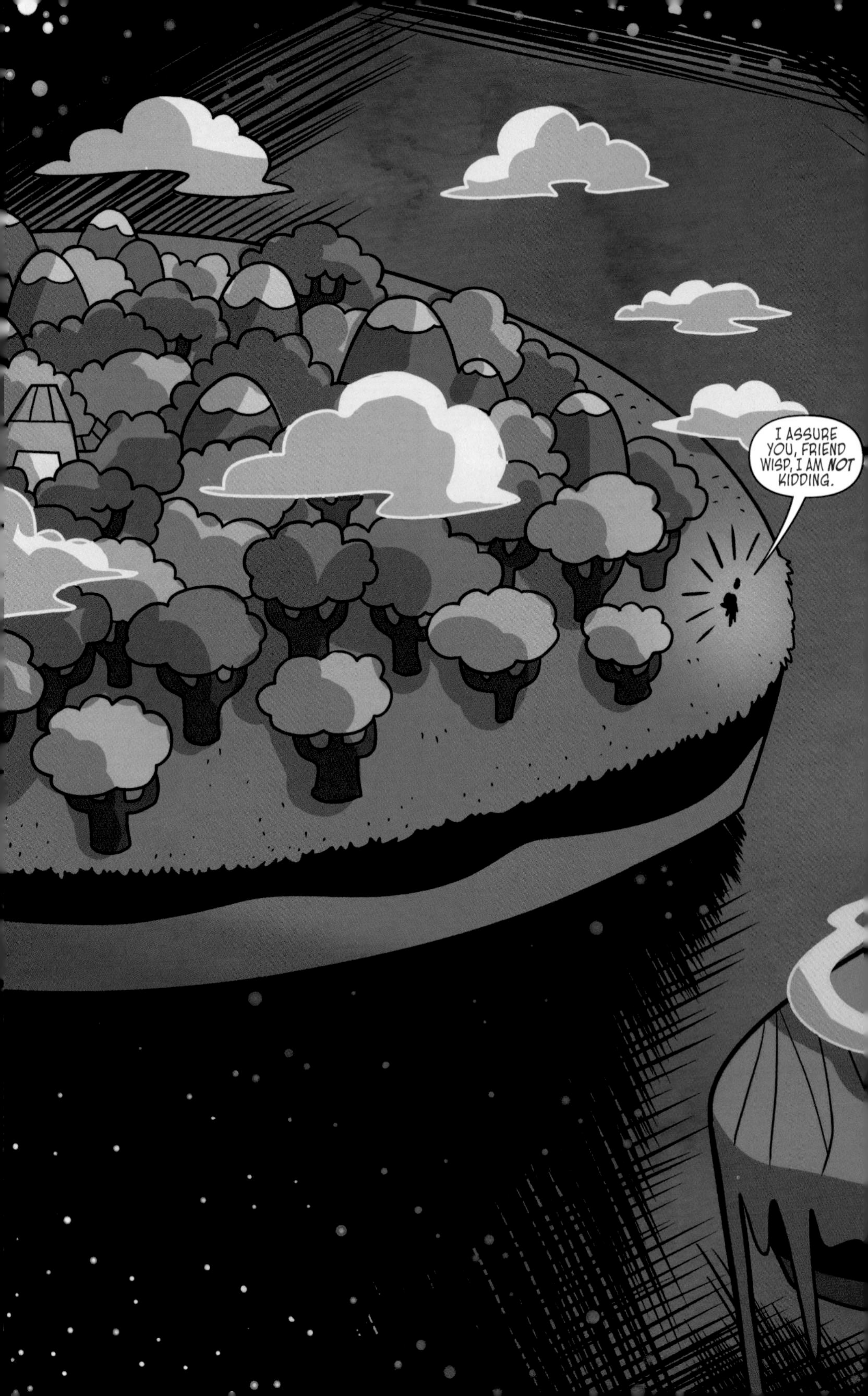
I ASSURE YOU, FRIEND WISP, I AM *NOT* KIDDING.

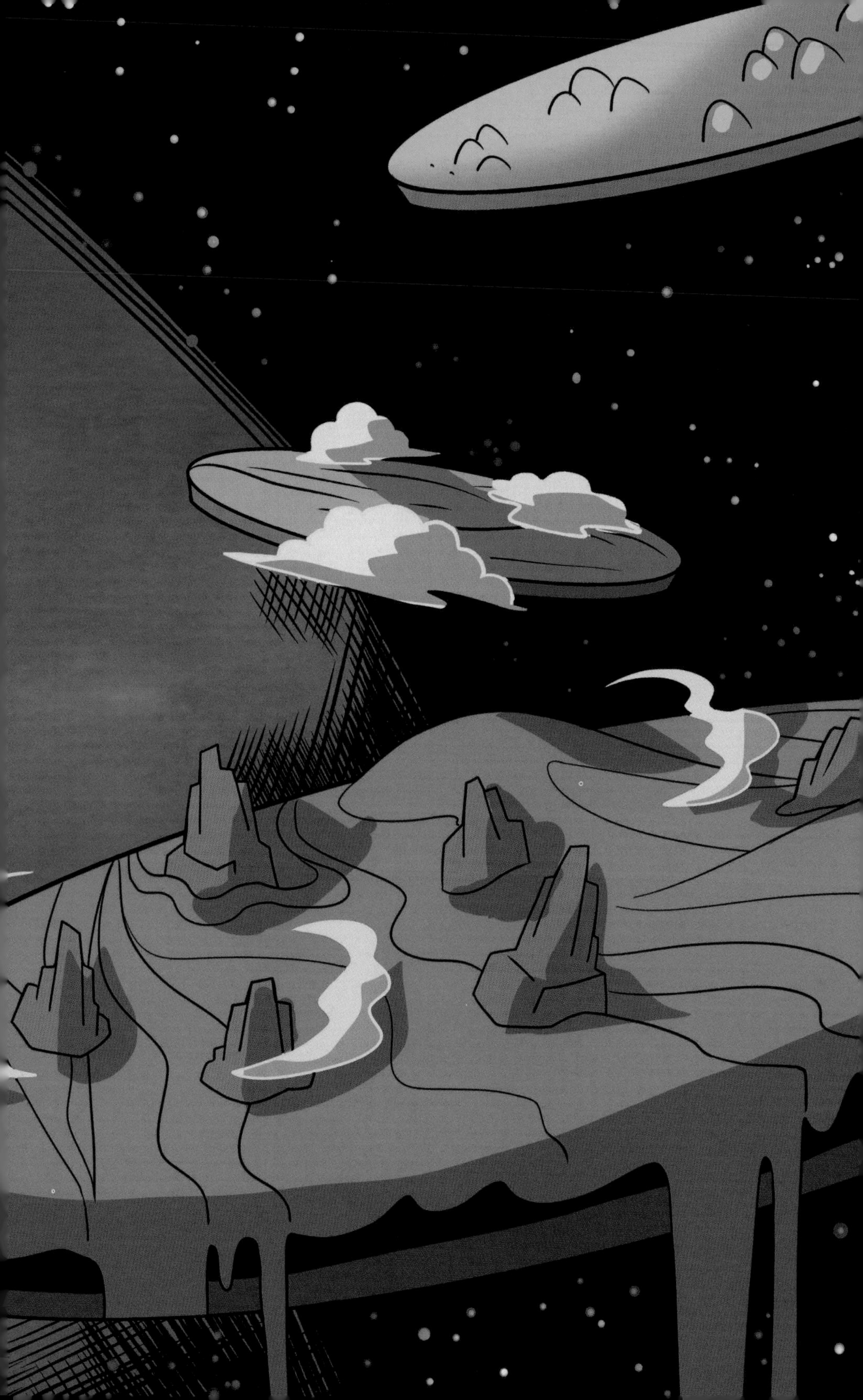

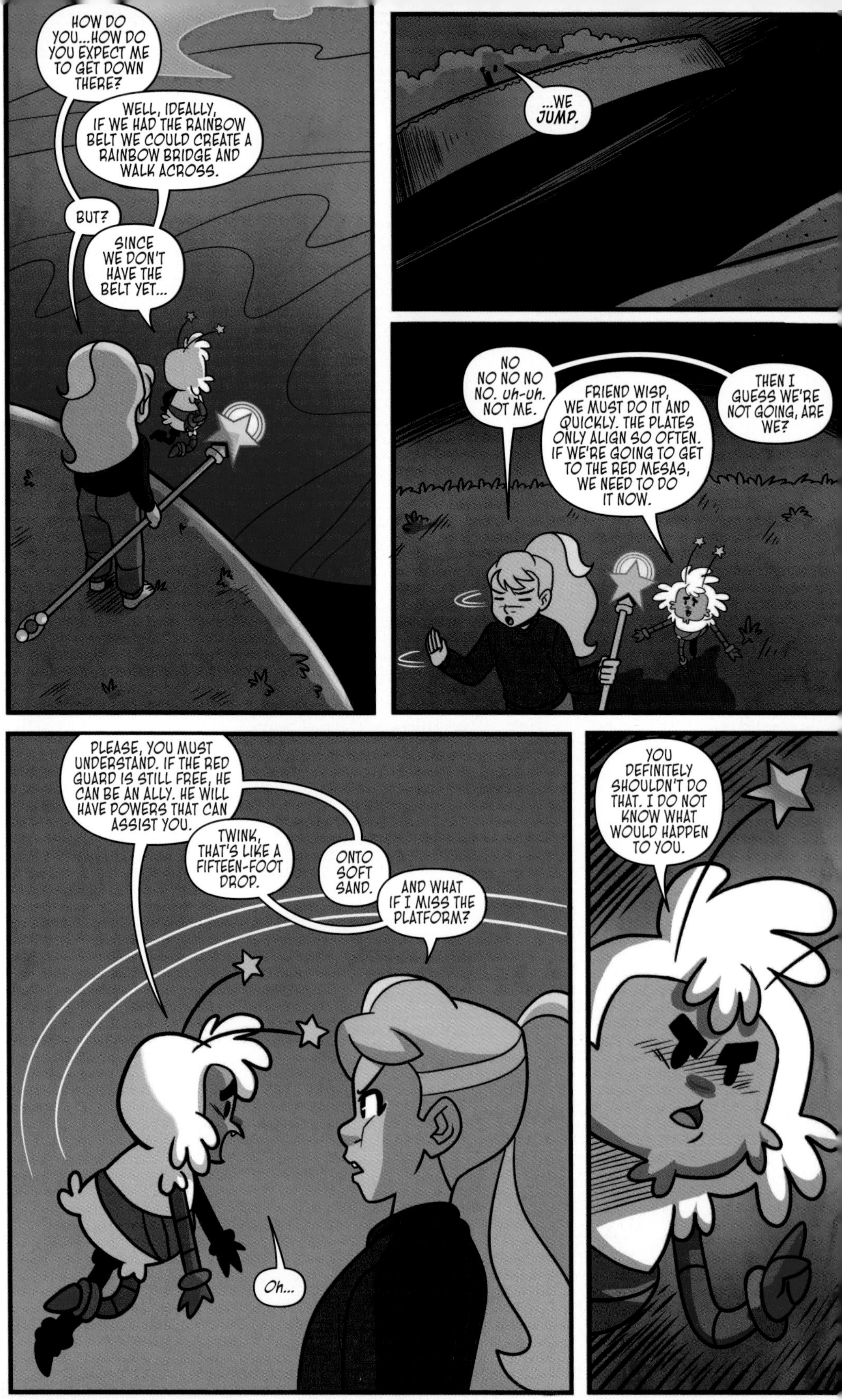
HOW DO YOU...HOW DO YOU EXPECT ME TO GET DOWN THERE?
WELL, IDEALLY, IF WE HAD THE RAINBOW BELT WE COULD CREATE A RAINBOW BRIDGE AND WALK ACROSS.
BUT?
SINCE WE DON'T HAVE THE BELT YET...
...WE JUMP.
NO NO NO NO NO. Uh-uh. NOT ME.
FRIEND WISP, WE MUST DO IT AND QUICKLY. THE PLATES ONLY ALIGN SO OFTEN. IF WE'RE GOING TO GET TO THE RED MESAS, WE NEED TO DO IT NOW.
THEN I GUESS WE'RE NOT GOING, ARE WE?
PLEASE, YOU MUST UNDERSTAND. IF THE RED GUARD IS STILL FREE, HE CAN BE AN ALLY. HE WILL HAVE POWERS THAT CAN ASSIST YOU.
TWINK, THAT'S LIKE A FIFTEEN-FOOT DROP.
ONTO SOFT SAND.
AND WHAT IF I MISS THE PLATFORM?
Oh...
YOU DEFINITELY SHOULDN'T DO THAT. I DO NOT KNOW WHAT WOULD HAPPEN TO YOU.

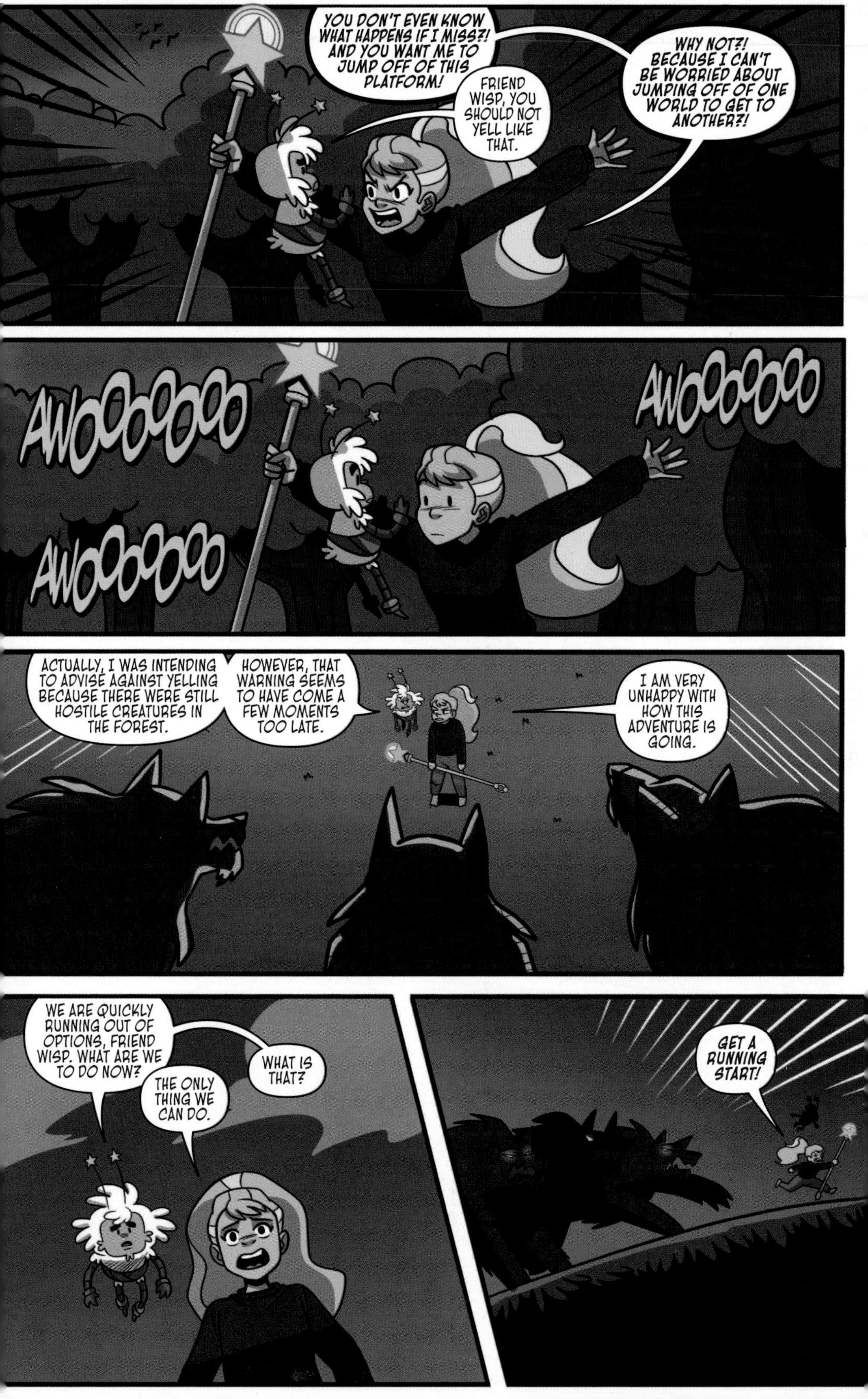
YOU DON'T EVEN KNOW WHAT HAPPENS IF I MISS?! AND YOU WANT ME TO JUMP OFF OF THIS PLATFORM!
WHY NOT?! BECAUSE I CAN'T BE WORRIED ABOUT JUMPING OFF OF ONE WORLD TO GET TO ANOTHER?!
FRIEND WISP, YOU SHOULD NOT YELL LIKE THAT.
AWOOOOOOO
AWOOOOOOO
AWOOOOOOO
ACTUALLY, I WAS INTENDING TO ADVISE AGAINST YELLING BECAUSE THERE WERE STILL HOSTILE CREATURES IN THE FOREST.
HOWEVER, THAT WARNING SEEMS TO HAVE COME A FEW MOMENTS TOO LATE.
I AM VERY UNHAPPY WITH HOW THIS ADVENTURE IS GOING.
WE ARE QUICKLY RUNNING OUT OF OPTIONS, FRIEND WISP. WHAT ARE WE TO DO NOW?
THE ONLY THING WE CAN DO.
WHAT IS THAT?
GET A RUNNING START!

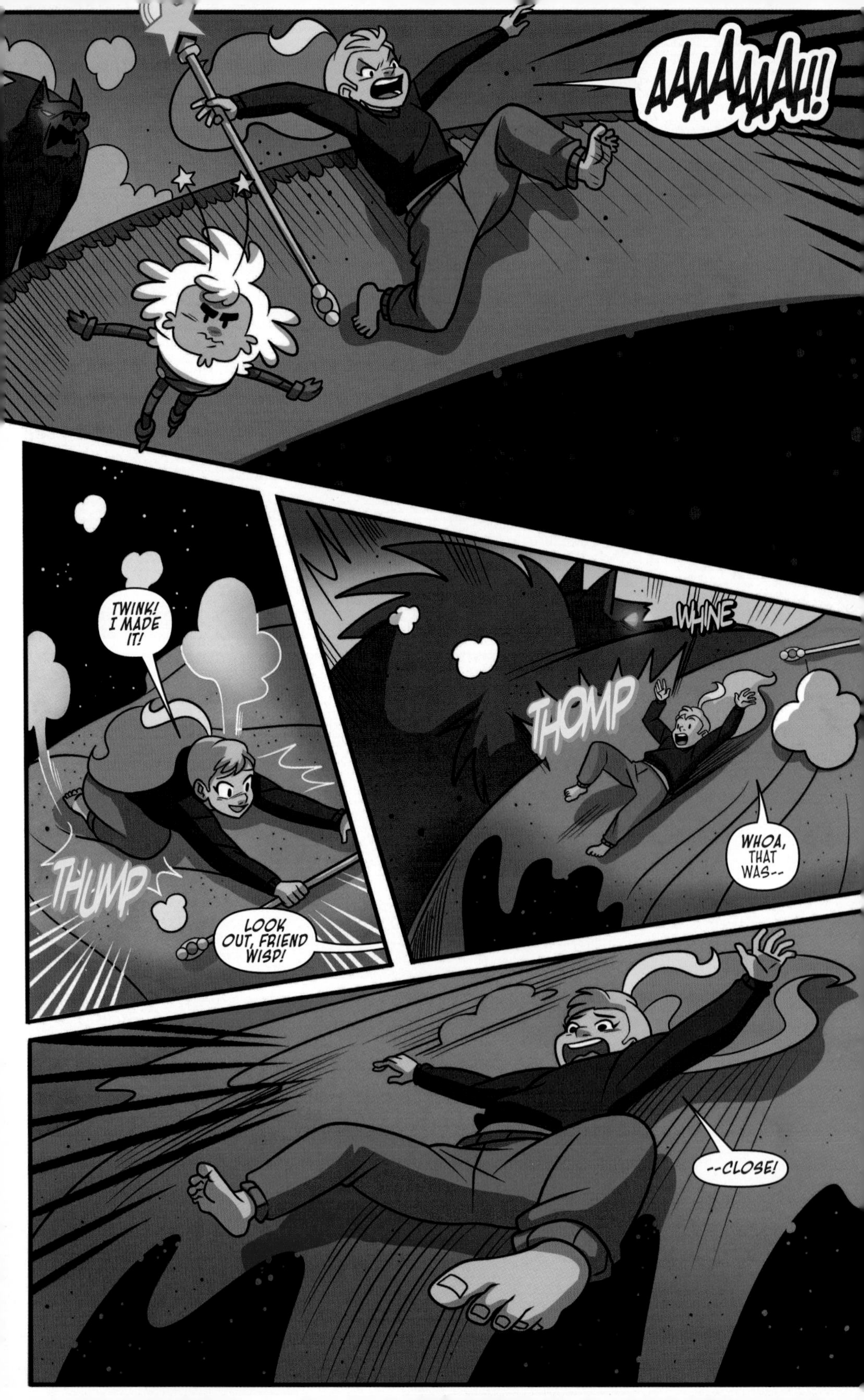
AAAAAAAH!!
TWINK! I MADE IT!
THUMP
LOOK OUT, FRIEND WISP!
WHINE
THOMP
WHOA, THAT WAS--
--CLOSE!

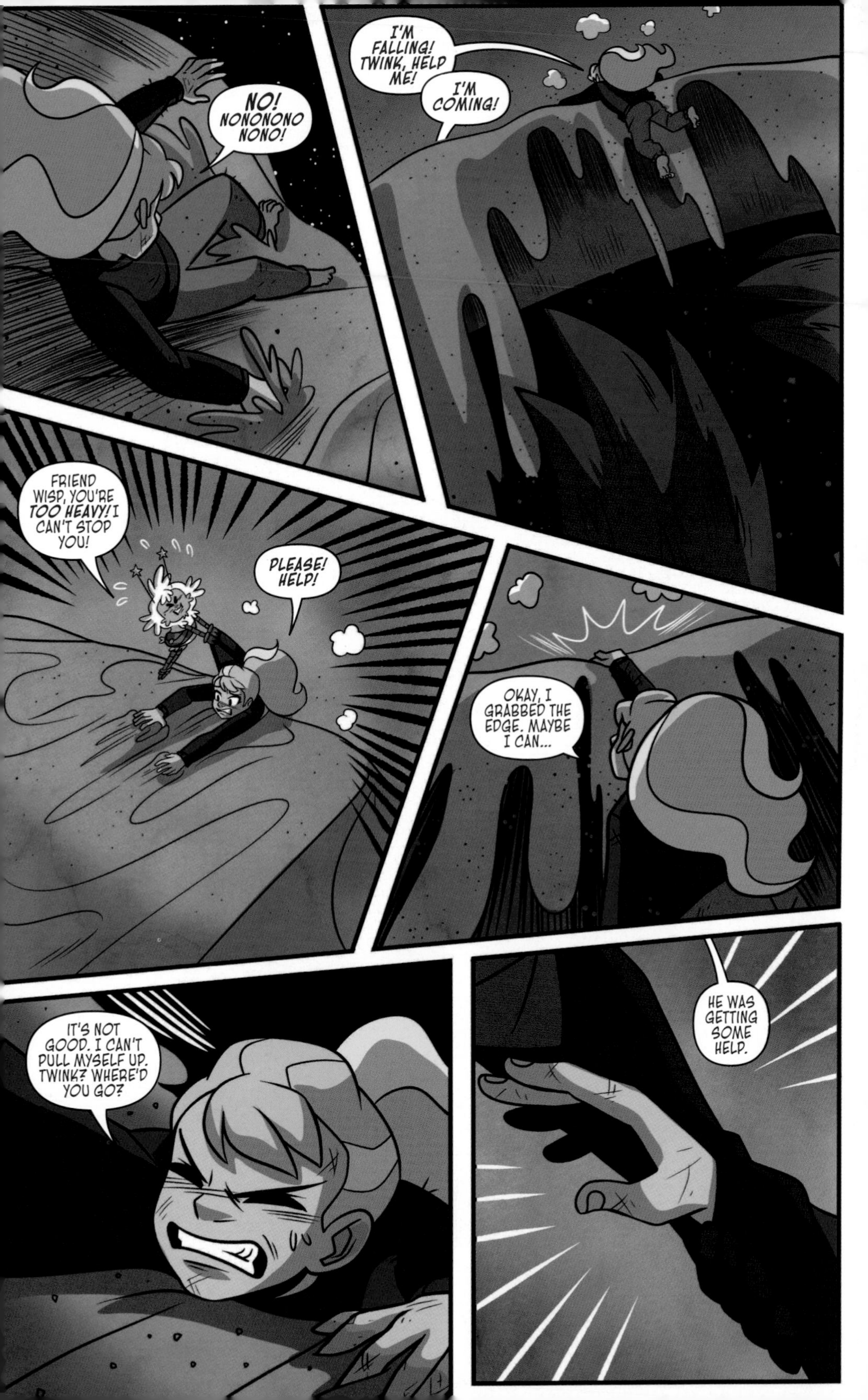
NO! NONONONO NONO!
I'M FALLING! TWINK, HELP ME!
I'M COMING!
FRIEND WISP, YOU'RE TOO HEAVY! I CAN'T STOP YOU!
PLEASE! HELP!
OKAY, I GRABBED THE EDGE. MAYBE I CAN...
IT'S NOT GOOD. I CAN'T PULL MYSELF UP. TWINK? WHERE'D YOU GO?
HE WAS GETTING SOME HELP.

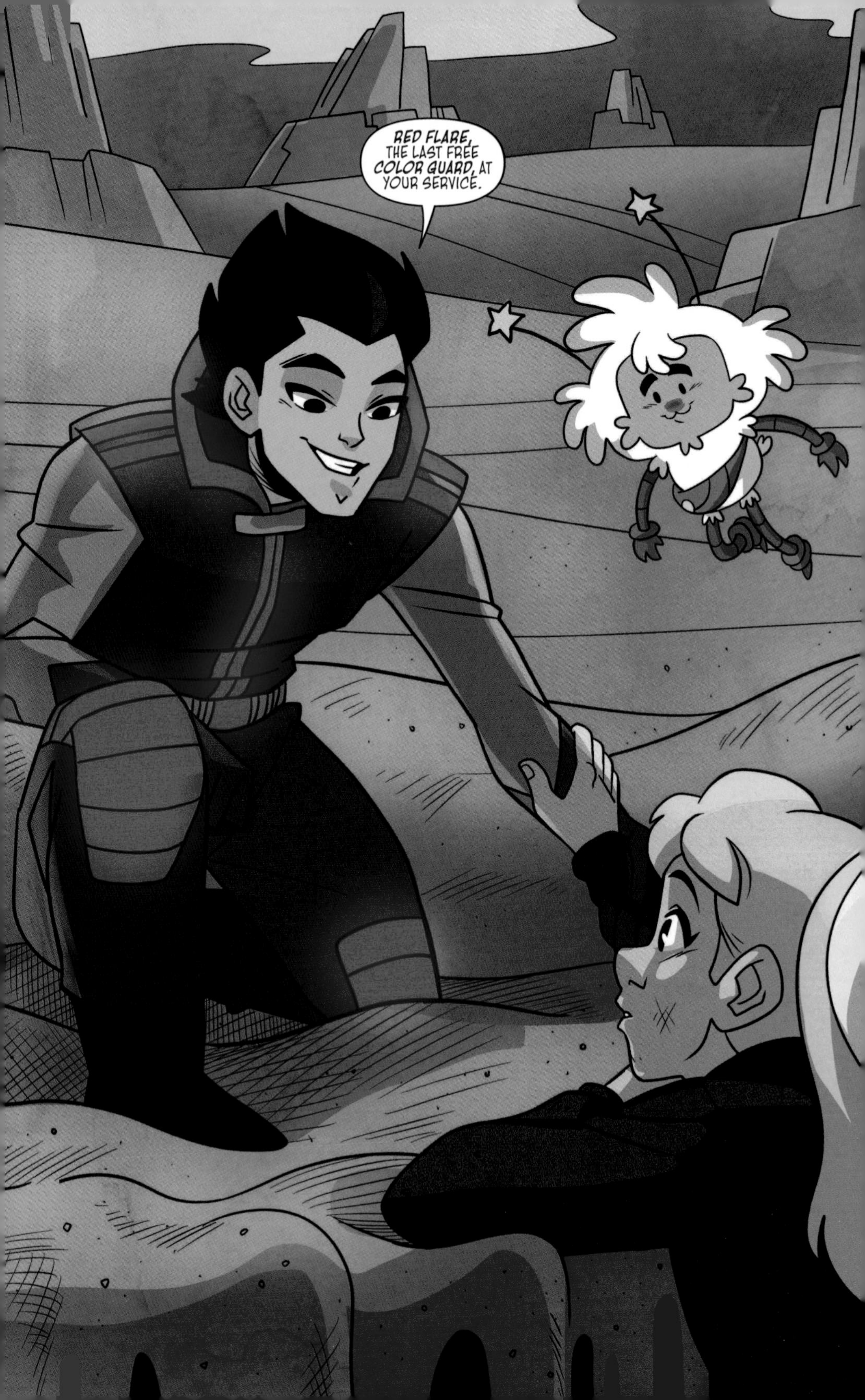
RED FLARE, THE LAST FREE COLOR GUARD, AT YOUR SERVICE.

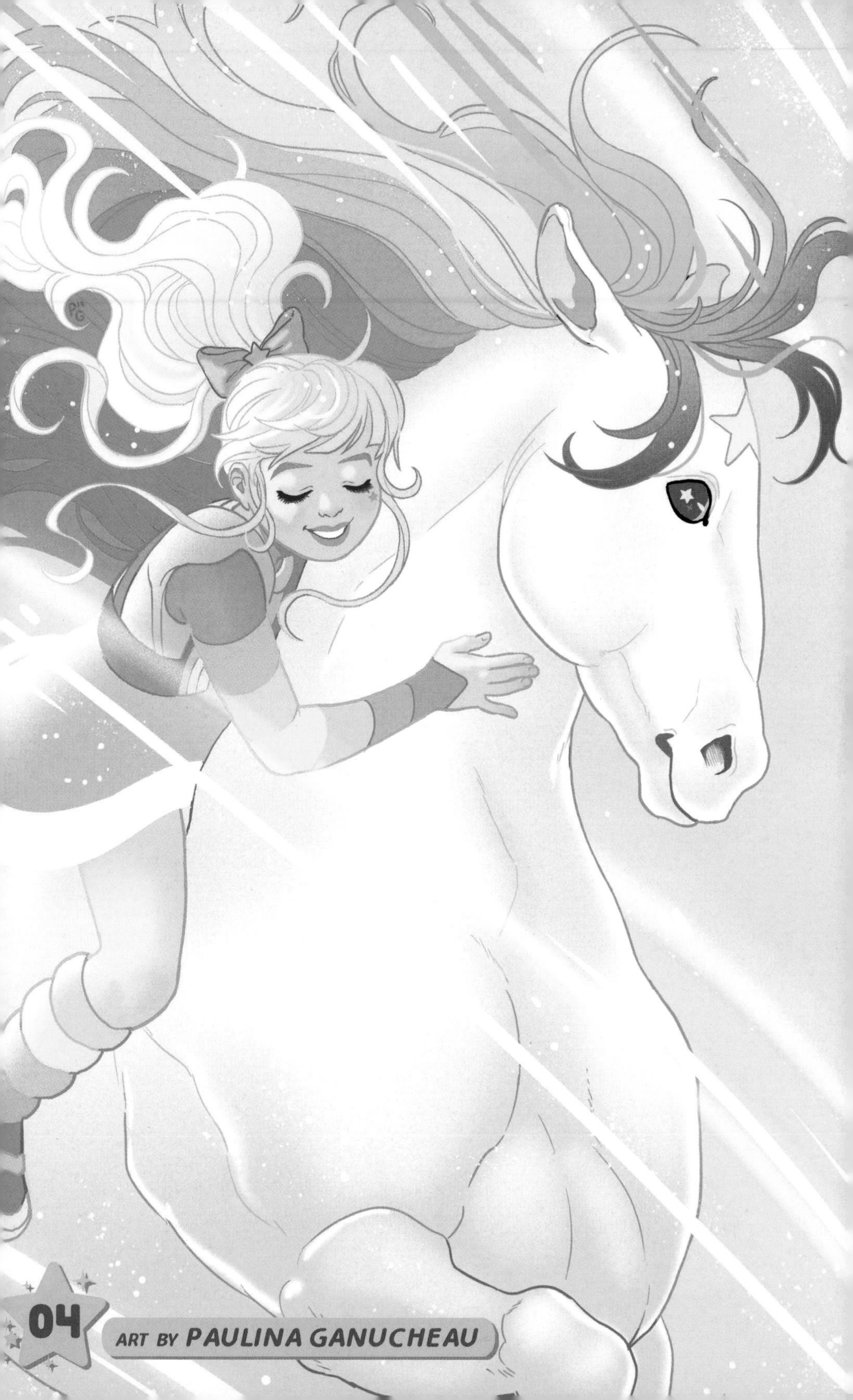
P G

04 ART BY PAULINA GANUCHEAU

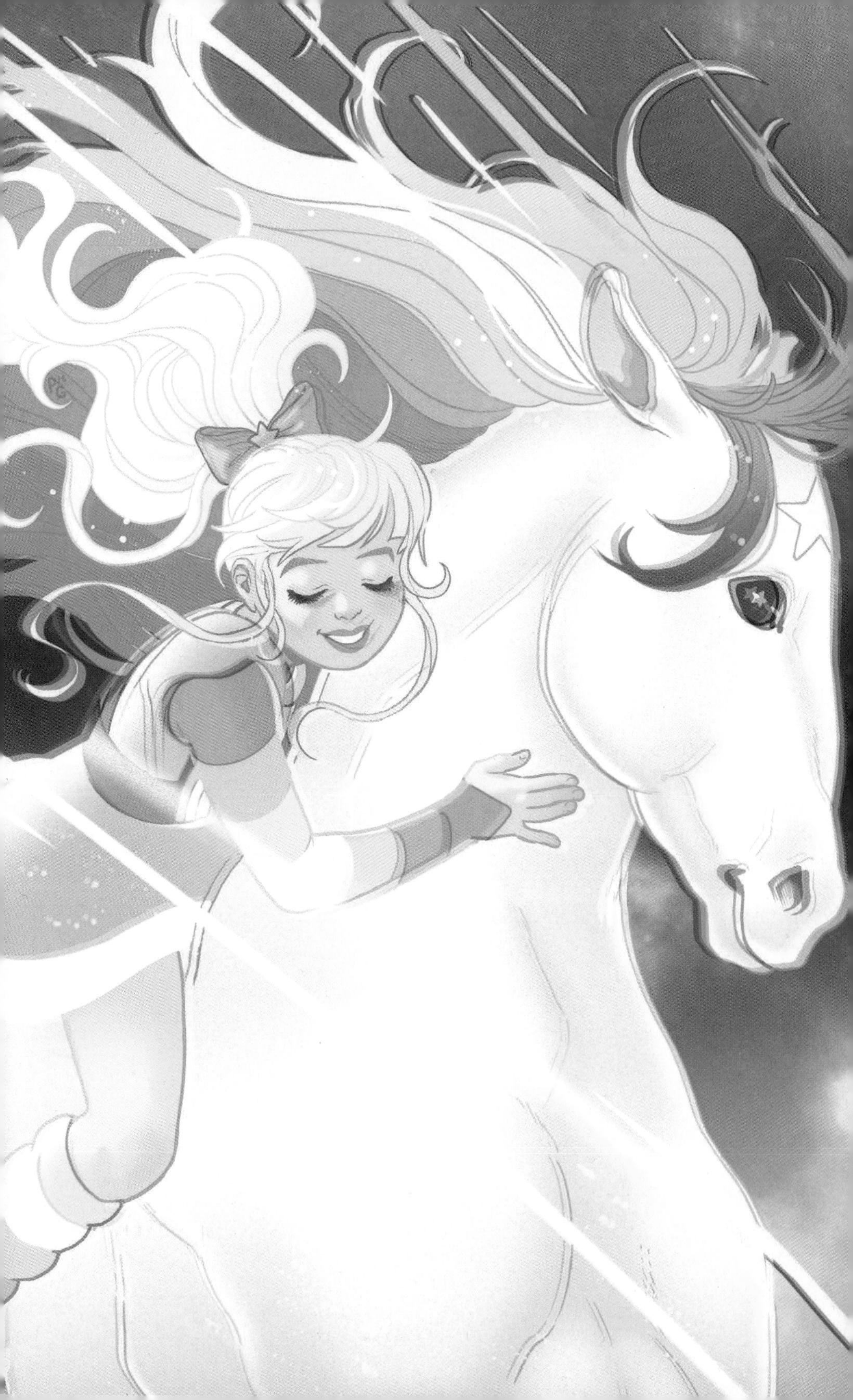

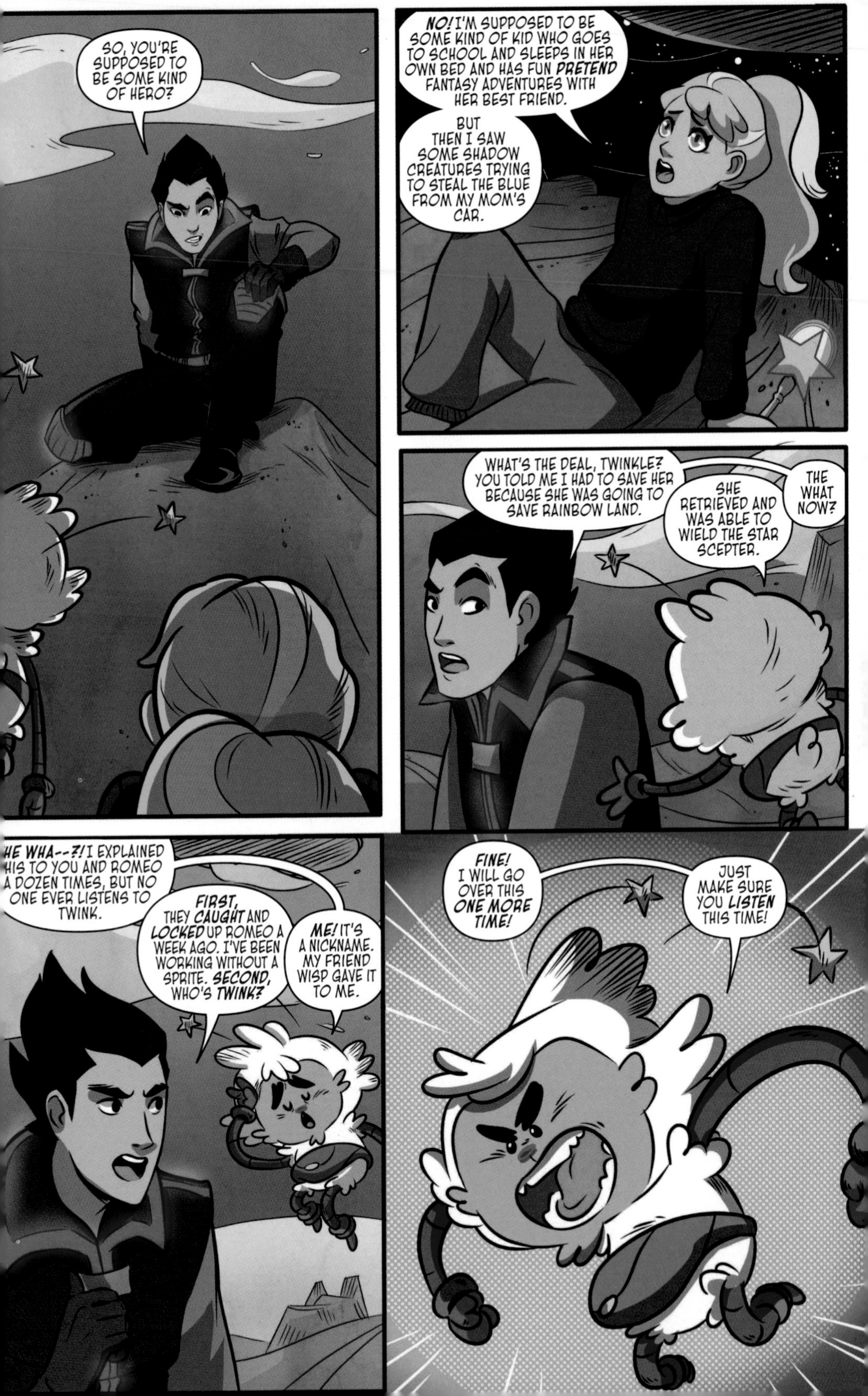
SO, YOU'RE SUPPOSED TO BE SOME KIND OF HERO?
NO! I'M SUPPOSED TO BE SOME KIND OF KID WHO GOES TO SCHOOL AND SLEEPS IN HER OWN BED AND HAS FUN PRETEND FANTASY ADVENTURES WITH HER BEST FRIEND.
BUT THEN I SAW SOME SHADOW CREATURES TRYING TO STEAL THE BLUE FROM MY MOM'S CAR.
WHAT'S THE DEAL, TWINKLE? YOU TOLD ME I HAD TO SAVE HER BECAUSE SHE WAS GOING TO SAVE RAINBOW LAND.
SHE RETRIEVED AND WAS ABLE TO WIELD THE STAR SCEPTER.
THE WHAT NOW?
HE WHA--?! I EXPLAINED HIS TO YOU AND ROMEO A DOZEN TIMES, BUT NO ONE EVER LISTENS TO TWINK.
FIRST, THEY CAUGHT AND LOCKED UP ROMEO A WEEK AGO. I'VE BEEN WORKING WITHOUT A SPRITE. SECOND, WHO'S TWINK?
ME! IT'S A NICKNAME. MY FRIEND WISP GAVE IT TO ME.
FINE! I WILL GO OVER THIS ONE MORE TIME!
JUST MAKE SURE YOU LISTEN THIS TIME!

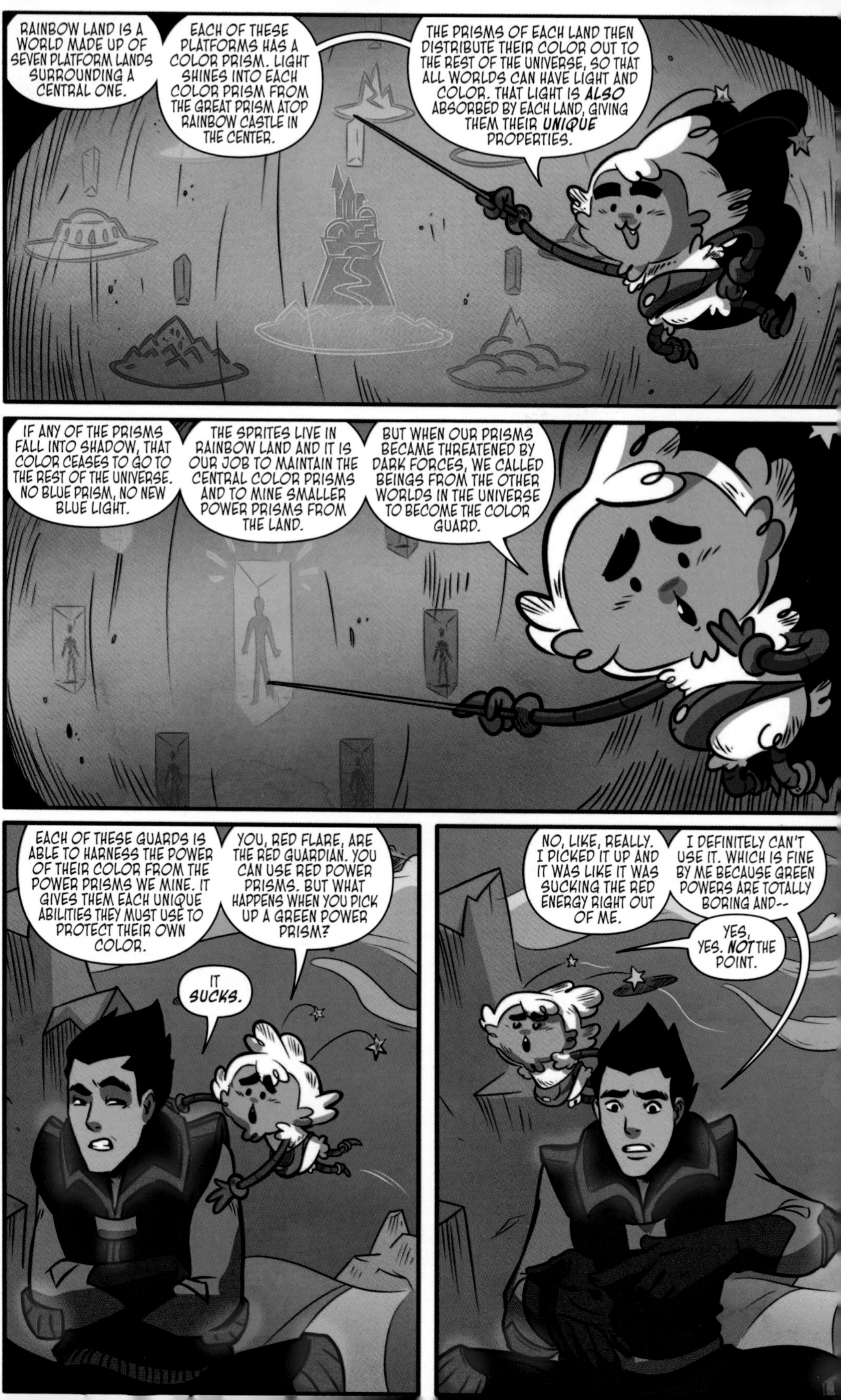
RAINBOW LAND IS A WORLD MADE UP OF SEVEN PLATFORM LANDS SURROUNDING A CENTRAL ONE.
EACH OF THESE PLATFORMS HAS A COLOR PRISM. LIGHT SHINES INTO EACH COLOR PRISM FROM THE GREAT PRISM ATOP RAINBOW CASTLE IN THE CENTER.
THE PRISMS OF EACH LAND THEN DISTRIBUTE THEIR COLOR OUT TO THE REST OF THE UNIVERSE, SO THAT ALL WORLDS CAN HAVE LIGHT AND COLOR. THAT LIGHT IS ALSO ABSORBED BY EACH LAND, GIVING THEM THEIR UNIQUE PROPERTIES.
IF ANY OF THE PRISMS FALL INTO SHADOW, THAT COLOR CEASES TO GO TO THE REST OF THE UNIVERSE. NO BLUE PRISM, NO NEW BLUE LIGHT.
THE SPRITES LIVE IN RAINBOW LAND AND IT IS OUR JOB TO MAINTAIN THE CENTRAL COLOR PRISMS AND TO MINE SMALLER POWER PRISMS FROM THE LAND.
BUT WHEN OUR PRISMS BECAME THREATENED BY DARK FORCES, WE CALLED BEINGS FROM THE OTHER WORLDS IN THE UNIVERSE TO BECOME THE COLOR GUARD.
EACH OF THESE GUARDS IS ABLE TO HARNESS THE POWER OF THEIR COLOR FROM THE POWER PRISMS WE MINE. IT GIVES THEM EACH UNIQUE ABILITIES THEY MUST USE TO PROTECT THEIR OWN COLOR.
YOU, RED FLARE, ARE THE RED GUARDIAN. YOU CAN USE RED POWER PRISMS. BUT WHAT HAPPENS WHEN YOU PICK UP A GREEN POWER PRISM?
IT SUCKS.
NO, LIKE, REALLY. I PICKED IT UP AND IT WAS LIKE IT WAS SUCKING THE RED ENERGY RIGHT OUT OF ME.
I DEFINITELY CAN'T USE IT. WHICH IS FINE BY ME BECAUSE GREEN POWERS ARE TOTALLY BORING AND--
YES, YES. NOT THE POINT.

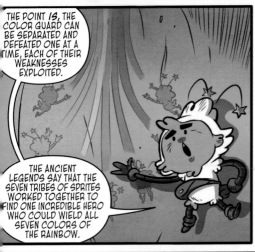

THE POINT *IS*, THE COLOR GUARD CAN BE SEPARATED AND DEFEATED ONE AT A TIME, EACH OF THEIR WEAKNESSES EXPLOITED.

THE ANCIENT LEGENDS SAY THAT THE SEVEN TRIBES OF SPRITES WORKED TOGETHER TO FIND ONE INCREDIBLE HERO WHO COULD WIELD ALL SEVEN COLORS OF THE RAINBOW.

THE LEGEND SAYS THAT NOT ONLY WAS THE HERO THEY FOUND ABLE TO WIELD ALL SEVEN PRISMS AND THEIR POWERS--

--BUT THEY WERE ABLE TO WIELD WHITE STARLIGHT, WHICH COULD FIGHT BACK SHADOW AND UNCOVER TRUTH.

THE HERO DID THIS USING THE STAR SCEPTER AND THE RAINBOW BELT. THEY WERE KNOWN AS RAINBOW BRITE AND THEY SAVED ALL COLOR IN THE UNIVERSE.

SO, YOU THINK THIS KID WHO'S BEEN HYPERVENTILATING HERE SINCE I KEPT HER FROM FALLING IN THE PITS IS, WHAT, SOME ANCIENT RAINBOW HERO?

SHE LOOKS PRETTY YOUNG FOR AN "ANCIENT HERO" TO ME.

I DON'T THINK SHE'S THE *SAME PERSON!* JUST LIKE I DON'T THINK YOU'RE THE *FIRST* RED COLOR GUARD.

STOP *PULLING* ME. I NEED TO LAY HERE SOME MORE.

BUT JUST LIKE MY COUSIN *ROMEO* FOUND YOU AND DETERMINED YOU HAD THE POWER TO USE THE RED PRISM, I THINK *WISP* HAS THE POTENTIAL TO BE *RAINBOW BRITE.*

YEAH, WELL, I DON'T KNOW, TWINKLE.

DON'T KNOW WHAT?

I HEAR YOU SAYING SHE'S THIS AND THAT, BUT WHAT DOES SHE SAY? IF I'M GONNA PUT MYSELF ON THE LINE FOR SOME KID WITH A MAGIC STICK, THAT KID BETTER BE PRETTY SPECIAL.

WHAT DO YOU SAY, WISP? WHY SHOULD I FOLLOW YOU?

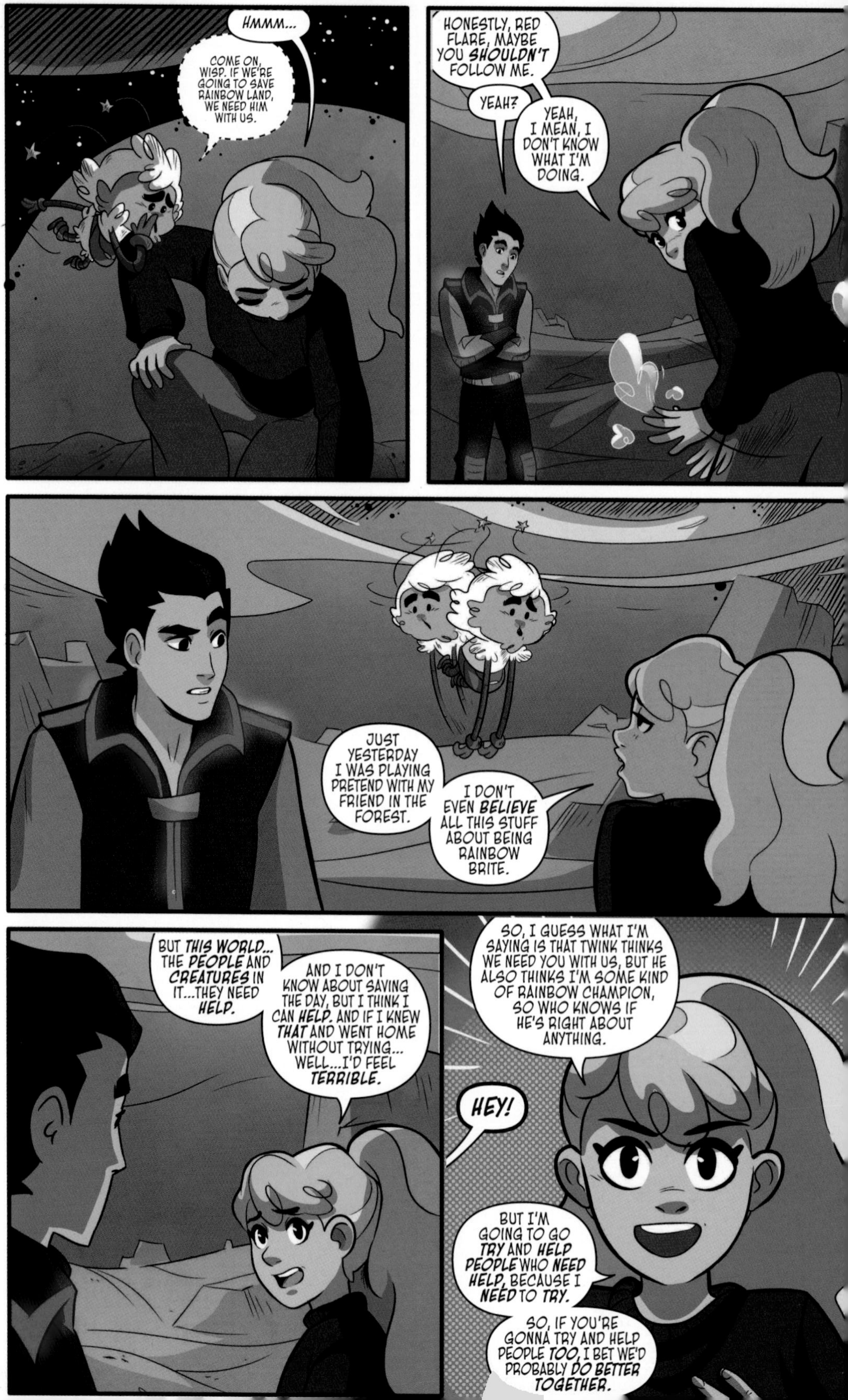
HMMM...
COME ON, WISP. IF WE'RE GOING TO SAVE RAINBOW LAND, WE NEED HIM WITH US.
HONESTLY, RED FLARE, MAYBE YOU SHOULDN'T FOLLOW ME.
YEAH?
YEAH, I MEAN, I DON'T KNOW WHAT I'M DOING.
JUST YESTERDAY I WAS PLAYING PRETEND WITH MY FRIEND IN THE FOREST.
I DON'T EVEN BELIEVE ALL THIS STUFF ABOUT BEING RAINBOW BRITE.
BUT THIS WORLD... THE PEOPLE AND CREATURES IN IT...THEY NEED HELP.
AND I DON'T KNOW ABOUT SAVING THE DAY, BUT I THINK I CAN HELP. AND IF I KNEW THAT AND WENT HOME WITHOUT TRYING... WELL...I'D FEEL TERRIBLE.
SO, I GUESS WHAT I'M SAYING IS THAT TWINK THINKS WE NEED YOU WITH US, BUT HE ALSO THINKS I'M SOME KIND OF RAINBOW CHAMPION, SO WHO KNOWS IF HE'S RIGHT ABOUT ANYTHING.
HEY!
BUT I'M GOING TO GO TRY AND HELP PEOPLE WHO NEED HELP, BECAUSE I NEED TO TRY.
SO, IF YOU'RE GONNA TRY AND HELP PEOPLE TOO, I BET WE'D PROBABLY DO BETTER TOGETHER.

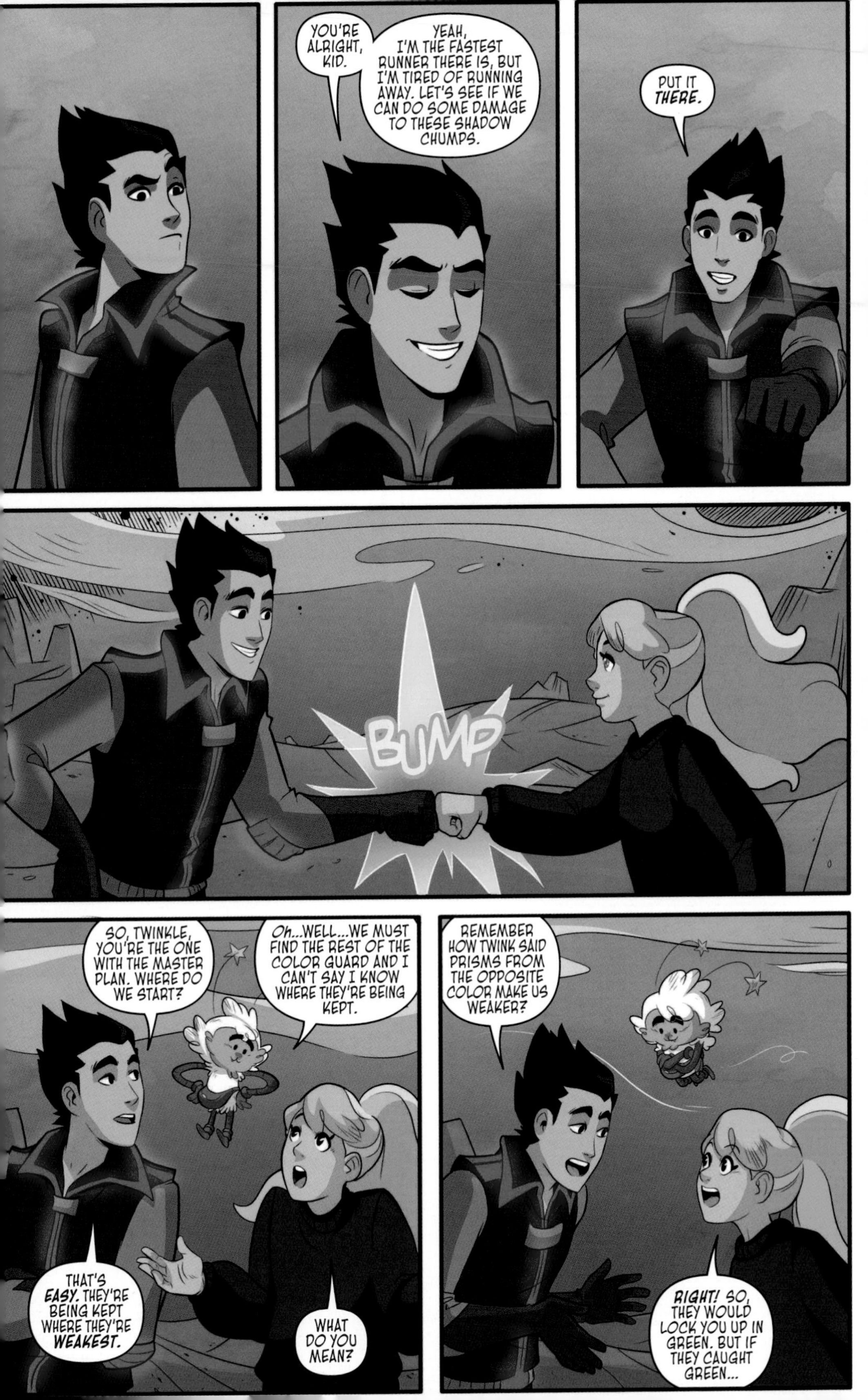
YOU'RE ALRIGHT, KID.
YEAH, I'M THE FASTEST RUNNER THERE IS, BUT I'M TIRED OF RUNNING AWAY. LET'S SEE IF WE CAN DO SOME DAMAGE TO THESE SHADOW CHUMPS.
PUT IT THERE.
BUMP
SO, TWINKLE, YOU'RE THE ONE WITH THE MASTER PLAN. WHERE DO WE START?
Oh...WELL...WE MUST FIND THE REST OF THE COLOR GUARD AND I CAN'T SAY I KNOW WHERE THEY'RE BEING KEPT.
THAT'S EASY. THEY'RE BEING KEPT WHERE THEY'RE WEAKEST.
WHAT DO YOU MEAN?
REMEMBER HOW TWINK SAID PRISMS FROM THE OPPOSITE COLOR MAKE US WEAKER?
RIGHT! SO, THEY WOULD LOCK YOU UP IN GREEN. BUT IF THEY CAUGHT GREEN...

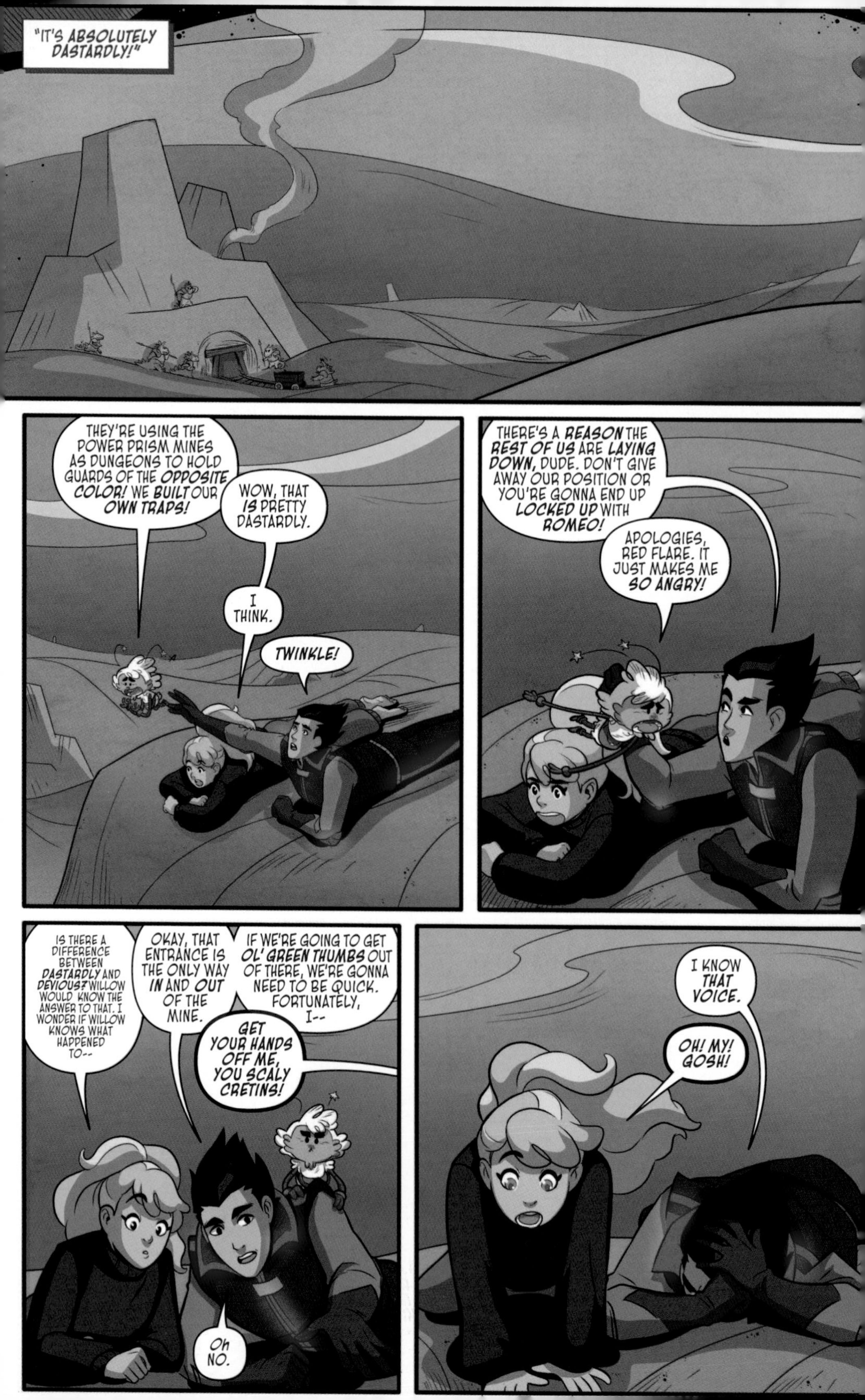
"IT'S ABSOLUTELY DASTARDLY!"
THEY'RE USING THE POWER PRISM MINES AS DUNGEONS TO HOLD GUARDS OF THE OPPOSITE COLOR! WE BUILT OUR OWN TRAPS!
WOW, THAT IS PRETTY DASTARDLY.
I THINK.
TWINKLE!
THERE'S A REASON THE REST OF US ARE LAYING DOWN, DUDE. DON'T GIVE AWAY OUR POSITION OR YOU'RE GONNA END UP LOCKED UP WITH ROMEO!
APOLOGIES, RED FLARE. IT JUST MAKES ME SO ANGRY!
IS THERE A DIFFERENCE BETWEEN DASTARDLY AND DEVIOUS? WILLOW WOULD KNOW THE ANSWER TO THAT. I WONDER IF WILLOW KNOWS WHAT HAPPENED TO--
OKAY, THAT ENTRANCE IS THE ONLY WAY IN AND OUT OF THE MINE.
IF WE'RE GOING TO GET OL' GREEN THUMBS OUT OF THERE, WE'RE GONNA NEED TO BE QUICK. FORTUNATELY, I--
GET YOUR HANDS OFF ME, YOU SCALY CRETINS!
Oh NO.
I KNOW THAT VOICE.
OH! MY! GOSH!

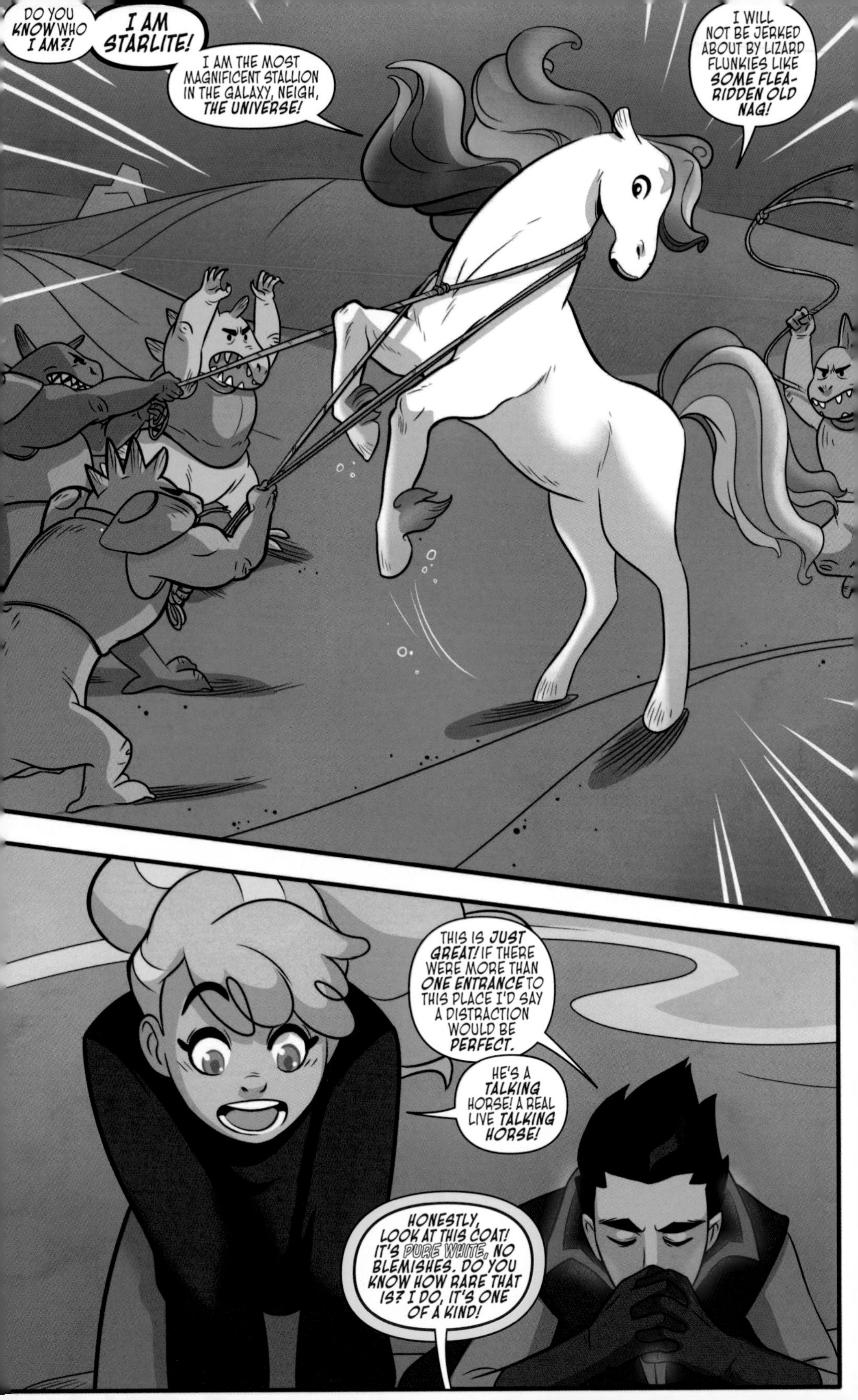
DO YOU KNOW WHO I AM?!
I AM STARLITE!
I AM THE MOST MAGNIFICENT STALLION IN THE GALAXY, NEIGH, THE UNIVERSE!
I WILL NOT BE JERKED ABOUT BY LIZARD FLUNKIES LIKE SOME FLEA-RIDDEN OLD NAG!
THIS IS JUST GREAT! IF THERE WERE MORE THAN ONE ENTRANCE TO THIS PLACE I'D SAY A DISTRACTION WOULD BE PERFECT.
HE'S A TALKING HORSE! A REAL LIVE TALKING HORSE!
HONESTLY, LOOK AT THIS COAT! IT'S PURE WHITE, NO BLEMISHES. DO YOU KNOW HOW RARE THAT IS? I DO, IT'S ONE OF A KIND!

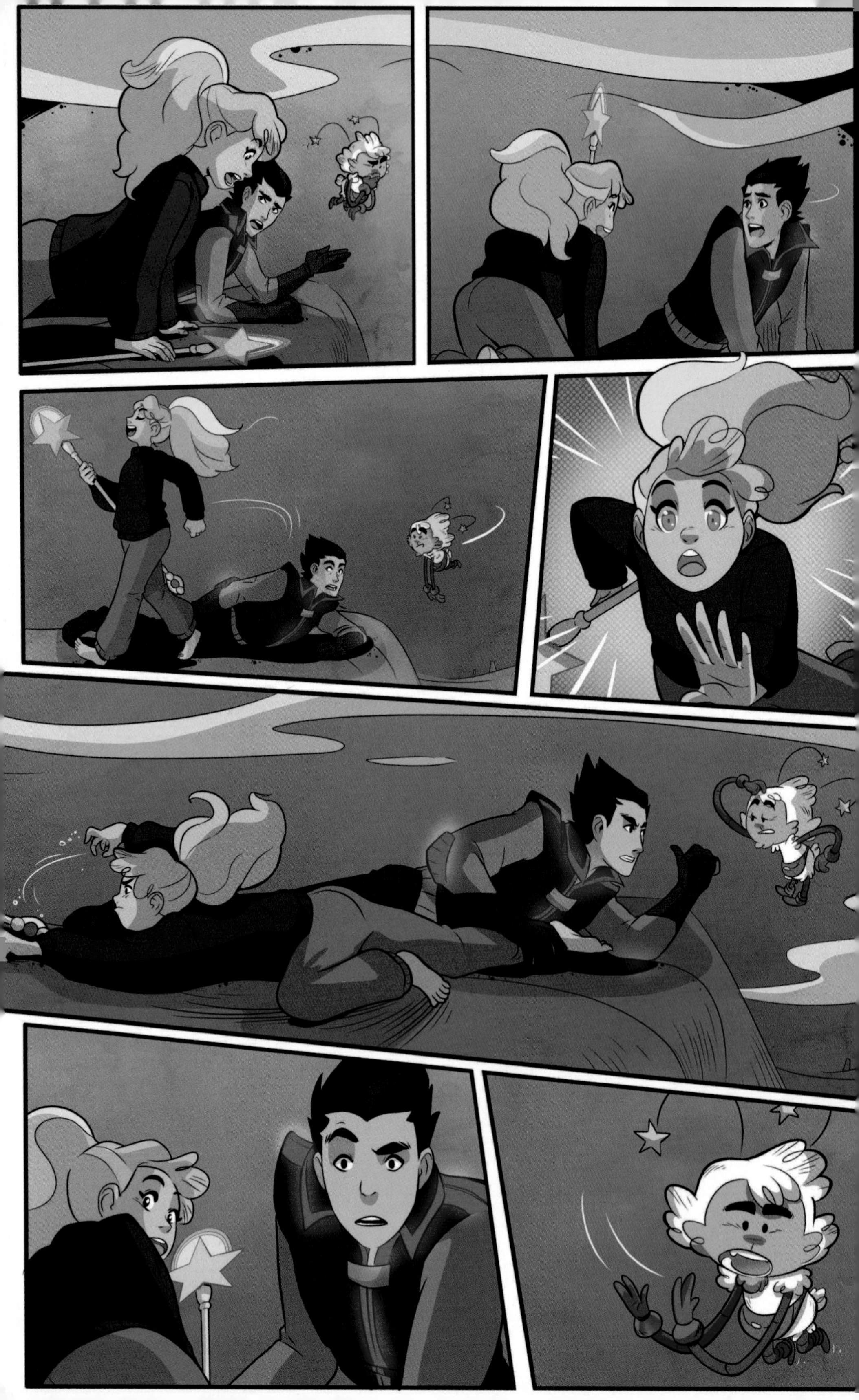

THAT MIGHT *ACTUALLY* WORK.

OKAY, FIRST, *YAY.* MY IDEA WAS *GOOD.* BUT NOW THAT I'M THINKING ABOUT IT, THERE'S *NO MAGIC LEFT* IN THE *SCEPTER.* HOW AM I SUPPOSED TO *TAKE ON* THOSE LIZARD MEN?

Oh, YES. THEY'RE STRONGER THAN MOST HUMANS. YOU WOULD NEED SOME KIND OF ADVANTAGE.

WELL, TWINKLE, YOU SAID SHE CAN USE *ANY COLOR* POWER PRISM, RIGHT?

IN THEORY, IF SHE *IS* THE LEGENDARY HERO, THEN--

WELL, DUDES, LET'S PUT THE THEORY TO THE TEST.

OH! WISP, HOLD UP THE *STAR SCEPTER!*

IT'S LIKE THE SCEPTER IS PULLING ME TO IT. TWINK, I'M *NOT SURE--*

FWIP

DOES SHE *ALWAYS* DO THAT?

I DON'T KNOW. I'VE NEVER SEEN IT BEFORE.

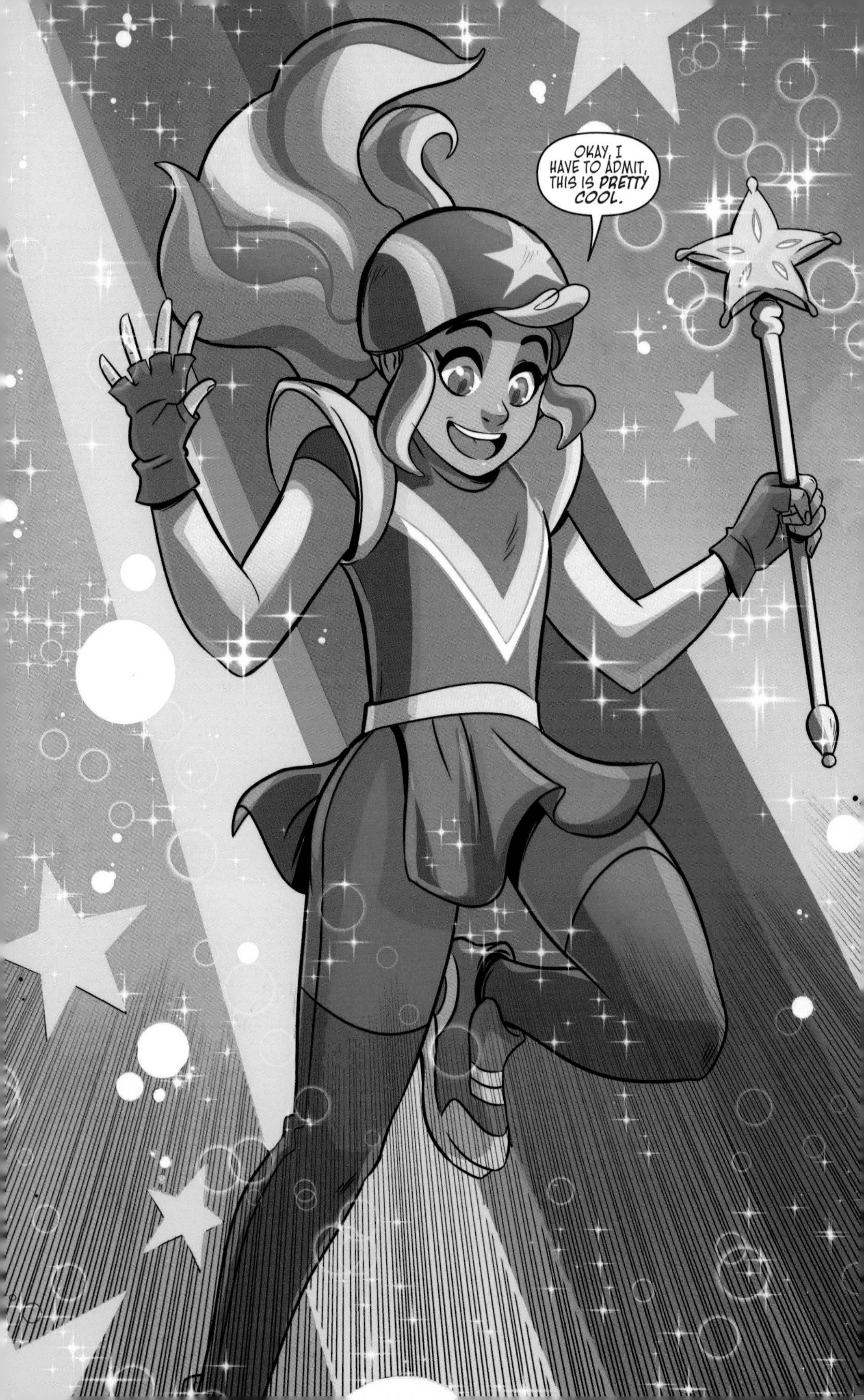
OKAY, I HAVE TO ADMIT, THIS IS PRETTY COOL.

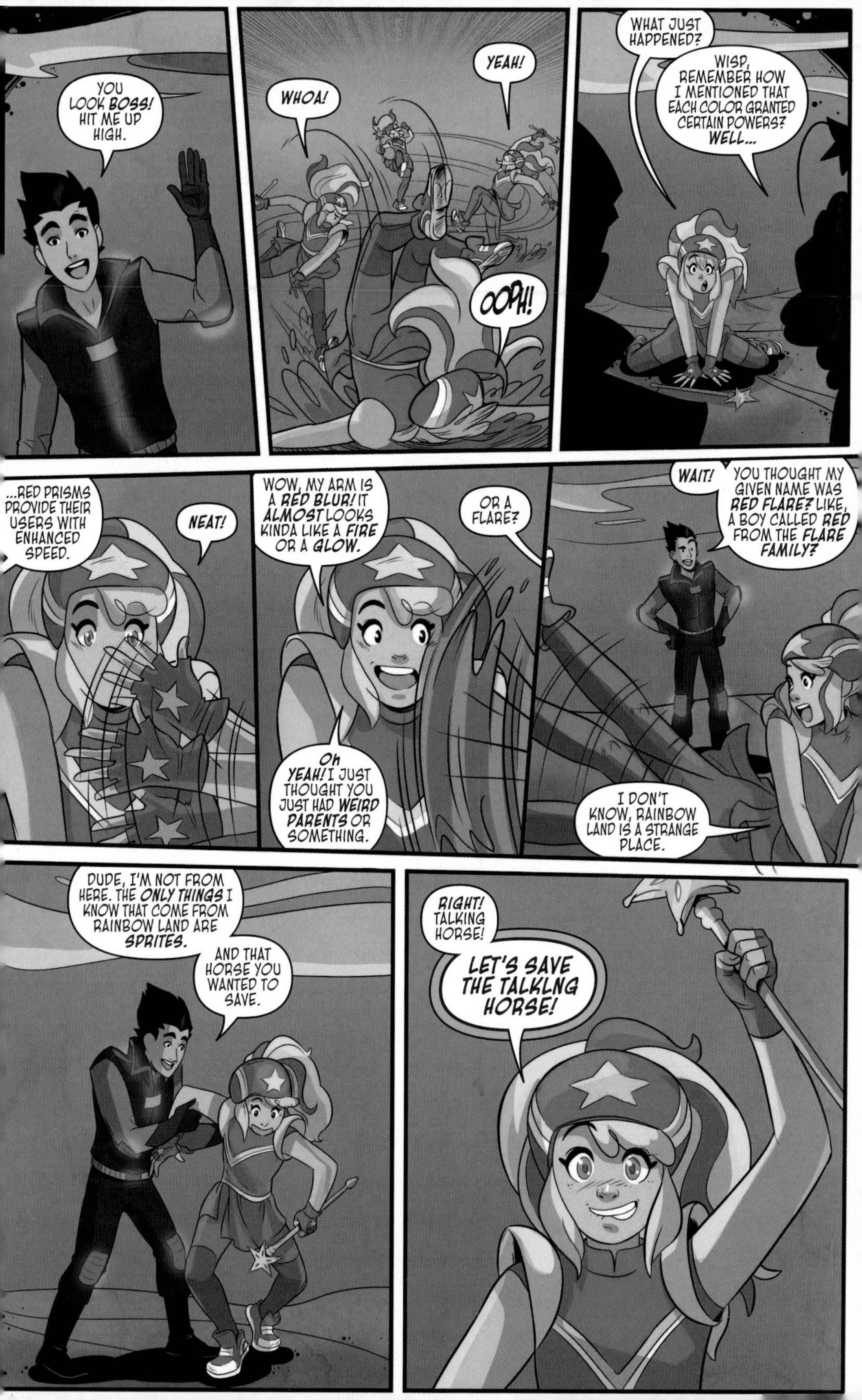
YOU LOOK BOSS! HIT ME UP HIGH.
WHOA!
YEAH!
OOPH!
WHAT JUST HAPPENED?
WISP, REMEMBER HOW I MENTIONED THAT EACH COLOR GRANTED CERTAIN POWERS? WELL...
...RED PRISMS PROVIDE THEIR USERS WITH ENHANCED SPEED.
NEAT!
WOW, MY ARM IS A RED BLUR! IT ALMOST LOOKS KINDA LIKE A FIRE OR A GLOW.
OR A FLARE?
Oh YEAH! I JUST THOUGHT YOU JUST HAD WEIRD PARENTS OR SOMETHING.
WAIT!
YOU THOUGHT MY GIVEN NAME WAS RED FLARE? LIKE, A BOY CALLED RED FROM THE FLARE FAMILY?
I DON'T KNOW, RAINBOW LAND IS A STRANGE PLACE.
DUDE, I'M NOT FROM HERE. THE ONLY THINGS I KNOW THAT COME FROM RAINBOW LAND ARE SPRITES.
AND THAT HORSE YOU WANTED TO SAVE.
RIGHT! TALKING HORSE!
LET'S SAVE THE TALKLNG HORSE!

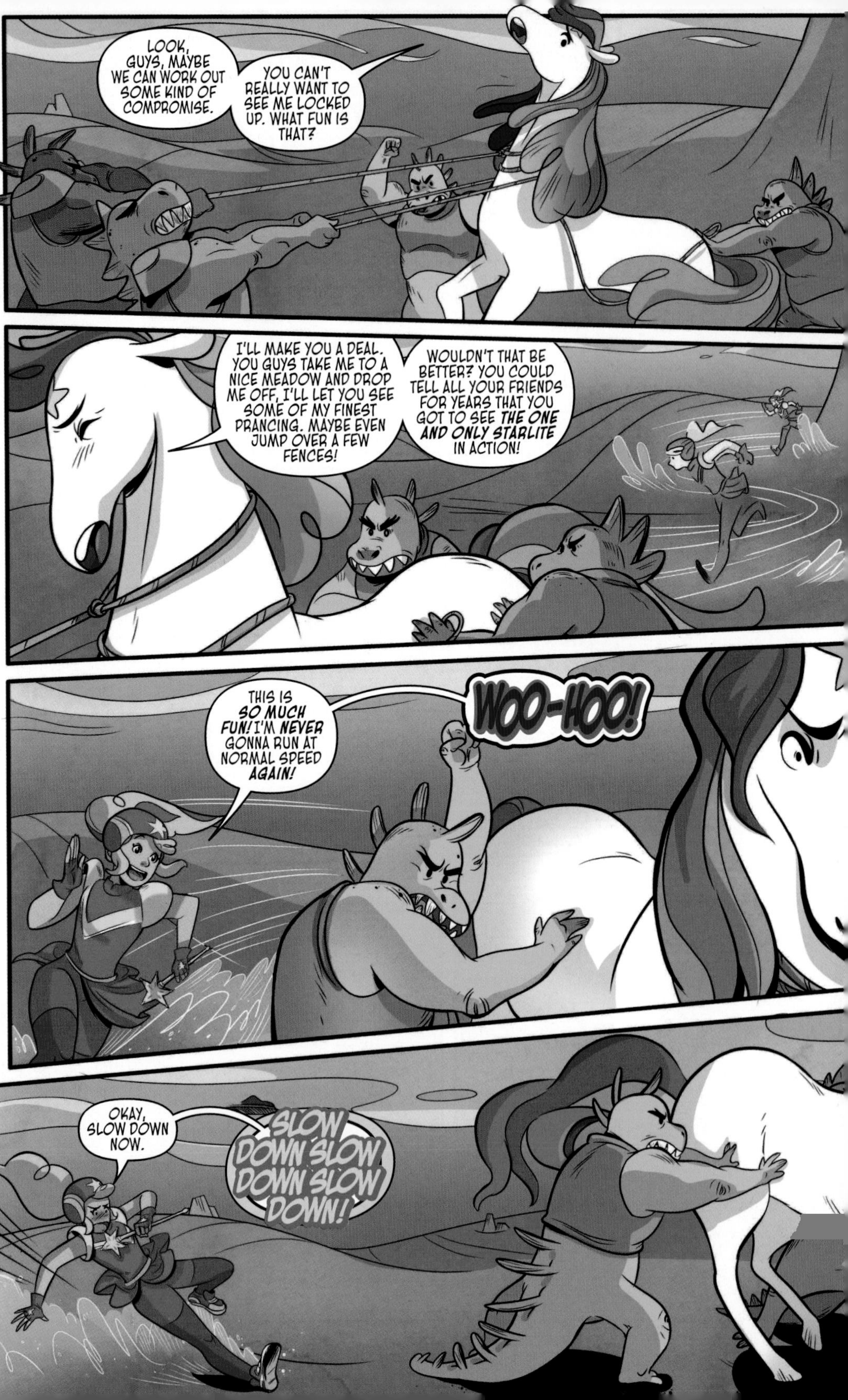
LOOK, GUYS, MAYBE WE CAN WORK OUT SOME KIND OF COMPROMISE.
YOU CAN'T REALLY WANT TO SEE ME LOCKED UP. WHAT FUN IS THAT?
I'LL MAKE YOU A DEAL. YOU GUYS TAKE ME TO A NICE MEADOW AND DROP ME OFF, I'LL LET YOU SEE SOME OF MY FINEST PRANCING. MAYBE EVEN JUMP OVER A FEW FENCES!
WOULDN'T THAT BE BETTER? YOU COULD TELL ALL YOUR FRIENDS FOR YEARS THAT YOU GOT TO SEE THE ONE AND ONLY STARLITE IN ACTION!
THIS IS SO MUCH FUN! I'M NEVER GONNA RUN AT NORMAL SPEED AGAIN!
WOO-HOO!
OKAY, SLOW DOWN NOW.
SLOW DOWN SLOW DOWN SLOW DOWN!

HSSS!

AAAHHHH!

HSSS!

HSSS!

WHOA! WHERE DID EVERYBODY GO?

WHAT IN RAINBOW LAND ARE YOU SUPPOSED TO BE?

HI, STARLITE. I'M WISP.

DO WE HAVE A NEW RED GUARD? NOBODY TELLS ME ANYTHING. I MEAN, GOOD BECAUSE THAT BRO WE HAD BEFORE--

OH NO, I'M NOT THE RED GUARD, BUT I DID COME TO RESCUE YOU.

WELL, YOU PROBABLY BETTER DO SOMETHING ABOUT THESE GUYS AND THEIR ROPES THEN.

OH!

DON'T WORRY. I CAN UNTIE THESE KNOTS AND THEN--

YOU BETTER DO IT FAST, FLIP, BECAUSE THESE LIZARD GUYS ARE PRETTY TOUGH.

IT'S WISP, NOT FLIP, BUT THAT'S OKAY.

I THINK I'M GETTING THE HANG OF THIS.

GREAT. LET'S CHAT ABOUT IT AFTER WE'RE AWAY FROM HERE, 'KAY?

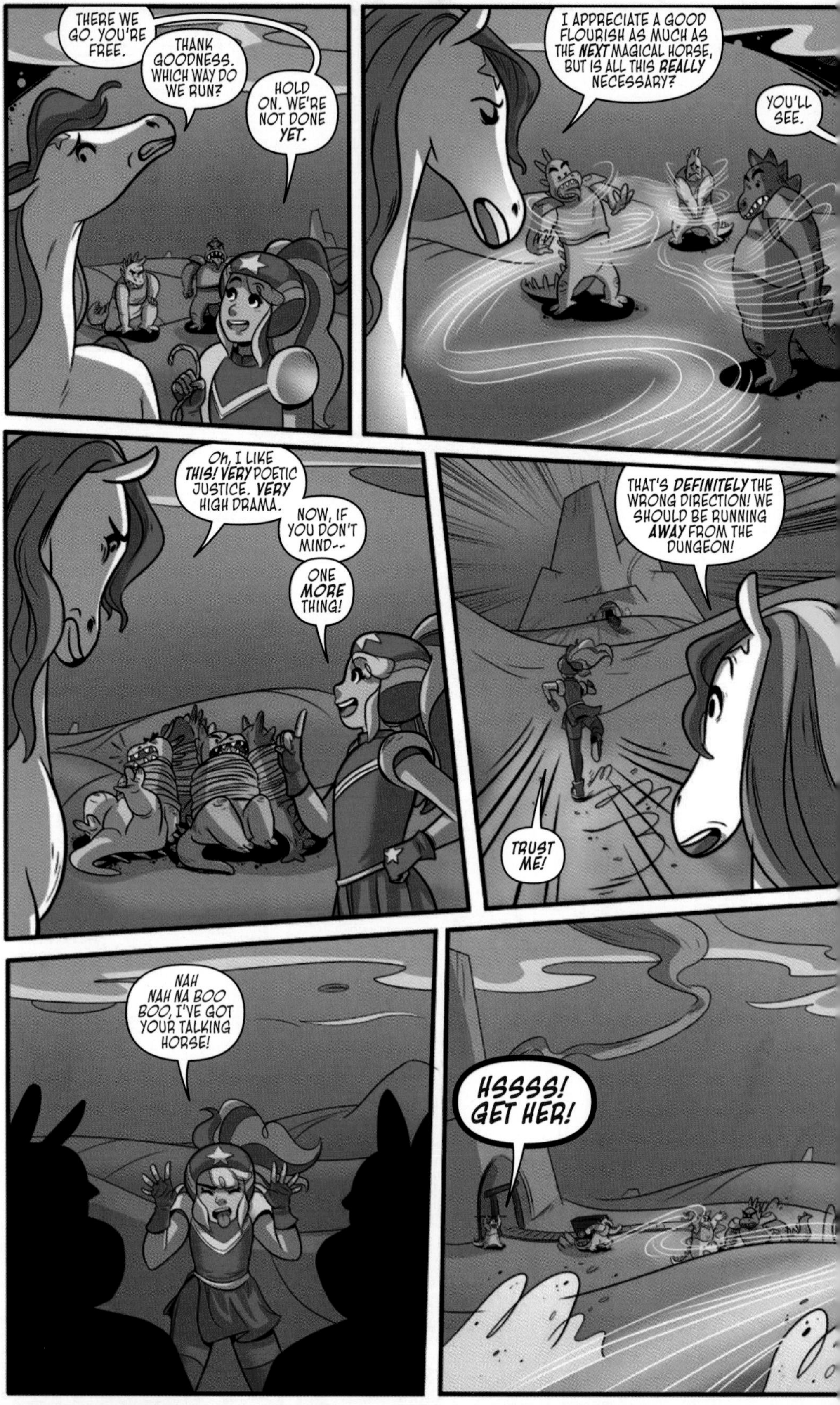
THERE WE GO. YOU'RE FREE.
THANK GOODNESS. WHICH WAY DO WE RUN?
HOLD ON. WE'RE NOT DONE YET.
I APPRECIATE A GOOD FLOURISH AS MUCH AS THE NEXT MAGICAL HORSE, BUT IS ALL THIS REALLY NECESSARY?
YOU'LL SEE.
Oh, I LIKE THIS! VERY POETIC JUSTICE. VERY HIGH DRAMA.
NOW, IF YOU DON'T MIND--
ONE MORE THING!
THAT'S DEFINITELY THE WRONG DIRECTION! WE SHOULD BE RUNNING AWAY FROM THE DUNGEON!
TRUST ME!
NAH NAH NA BOO BOO, I'VE GOT YOUR TALKING HORSE!
HSSSS! GET HER!

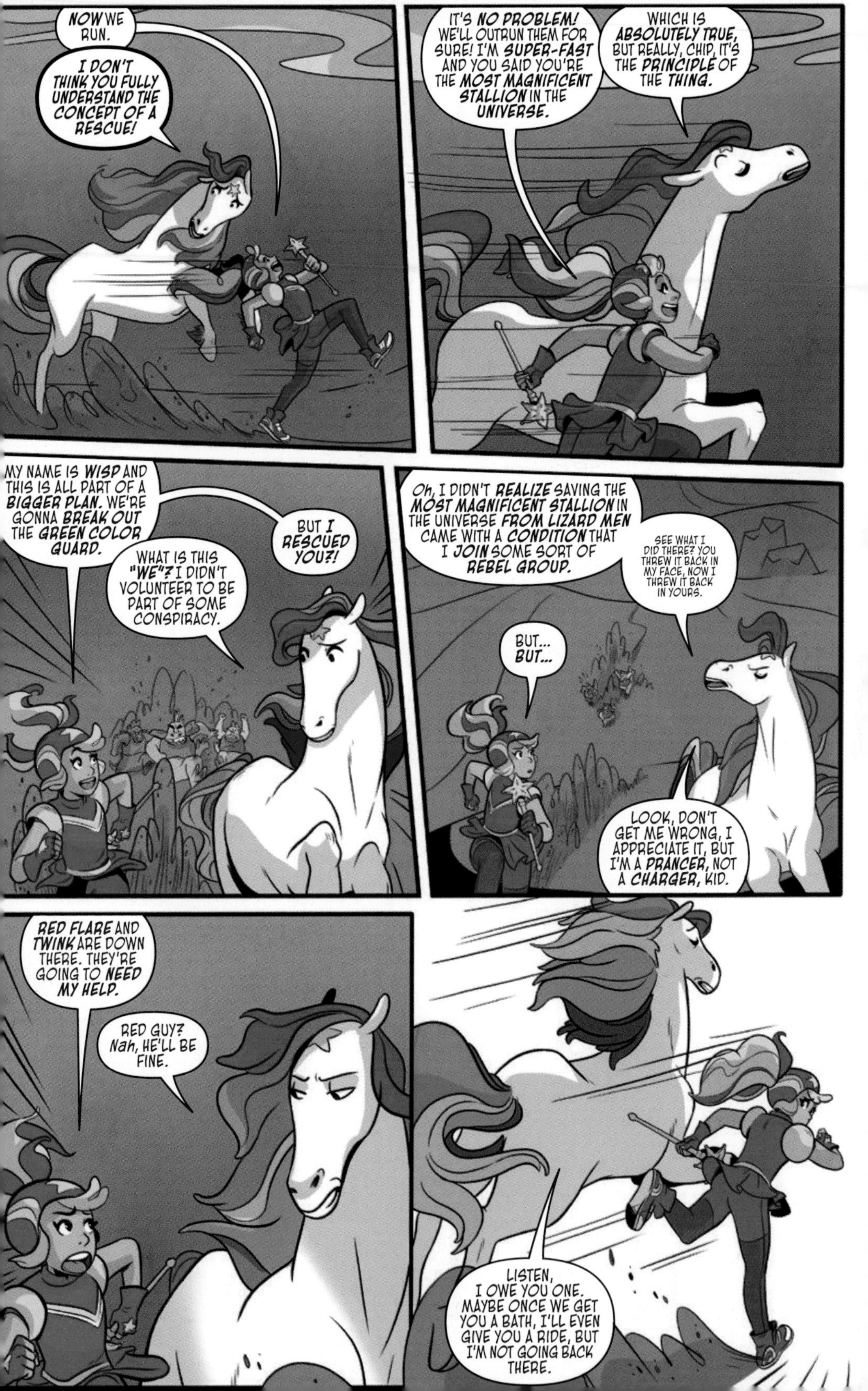
NOW WE RUN.
I DON'T THINK YOU FULLY UNDERSTAND THE CONCEPT OF A RESCUE!
IT'S NO PROBLEM! WE'LL OUTRUN THEM FOR SURE! I'M SUPER-FAST AND YOU SAID YOU'RE THE MOST MAGNIFICENT STALLION IN THE UNIVERSE.
WHICH IS ABSOLUTELY TRUE, BUT REALLY, CHIP, IT'S THE PRINCIPLE OF THE THING.
MY NAME IS WISP AND THIS IS ALL PART OF A BIGGER PLAN. WE'RE GONNA BREAK OUT THE GREEN COLOR GUARD.
WHAT IS THIS "WE"? I DIDN'T VOLUNTEER TO BE PART OF SOME CONSPIRACY.
BUT I RESCUED YOU?!
Oh, I DIDN'T REALIZE SAVING THE MOST MAGNIFICENT STALLION IN THE UNIVERSE FROM LIZARD MEN CAME WITH A CONDITION THAT I JOIN SOME SORT OF REBEL GROUP.
SEE WHAT I DID THERE? YOU THREW IT BACK IN MY FACE, NOW I THREW IT BACK IN YOURS.
BUT... BUT...
LOOK, DON'T GET ME WRONG, I APPRECIATE IT, BUT I'M A PRANCER, NOT A CHARGER, KID.
RED FLARE AND TWINK ARE DOWN THERE. THEY'RE GOING TO NEED MY HELP.
RED GUY? Nah, HE'LL BE FINE.
LISTEN, I OWE YOU ONE. MAYBE ONCE WE GET YOU A BATH, I'LL EVEN GIVE YOU A RIDE, BUT I'M NOT GOING BACK THERE.

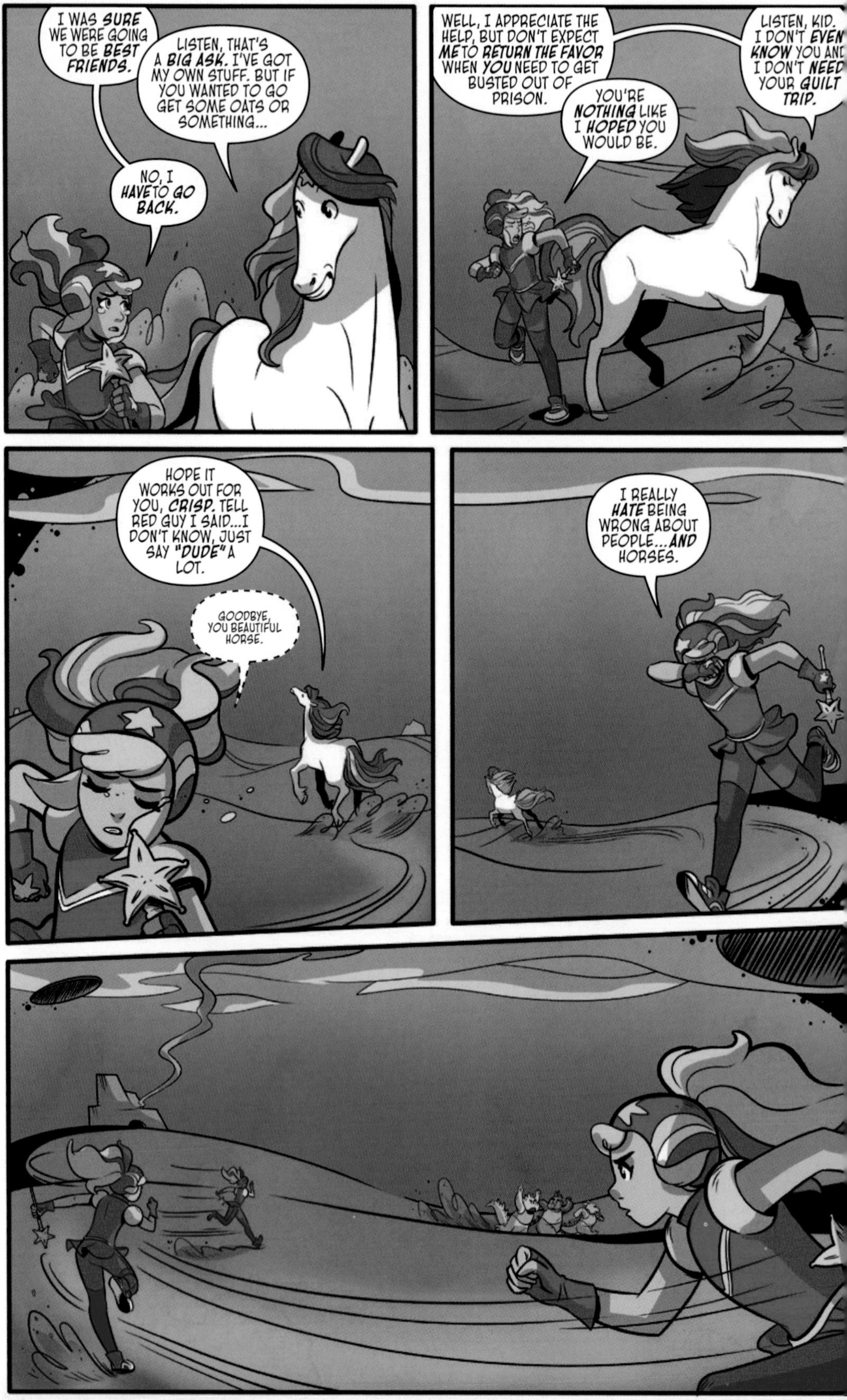
I WAS SURE WE WERE GOING TO BE BEST FRIENDS.
LISTEN, THAT'S A BIG ASK. I'VE GOT MY OWN STUFF. BUT IF YOU WANTED TO GO GET SOME OATS OR SOMETHING...
NO, I HAVE TO GO BACK.
WELL, I APPRECIATE THE HELP, BUT DON'T EXPECT ME TO RETURN THE FAVOR WHEN YOU NEED TO GET BUSTED OUT OF PRISON.
YOU'RE NOTHING LIKE I HOPED YOU WOULD BE.
LISTEN, KID. I DON'T EVEN KNOW YOU AND I DON'T NEED YOUR GUILT TRIP.
HOPE IT WORKS OUT FOR YOU, CRISP. TELL RED GUY I SAID...I DON'T KNOW, JUST SAY "DUDE" A LOT.
GOODBYE, YOU BEAUTIFUL HORSE.
I REALLY HATE BEING WRONG ABOUT PEOPLE...AND HORSES.

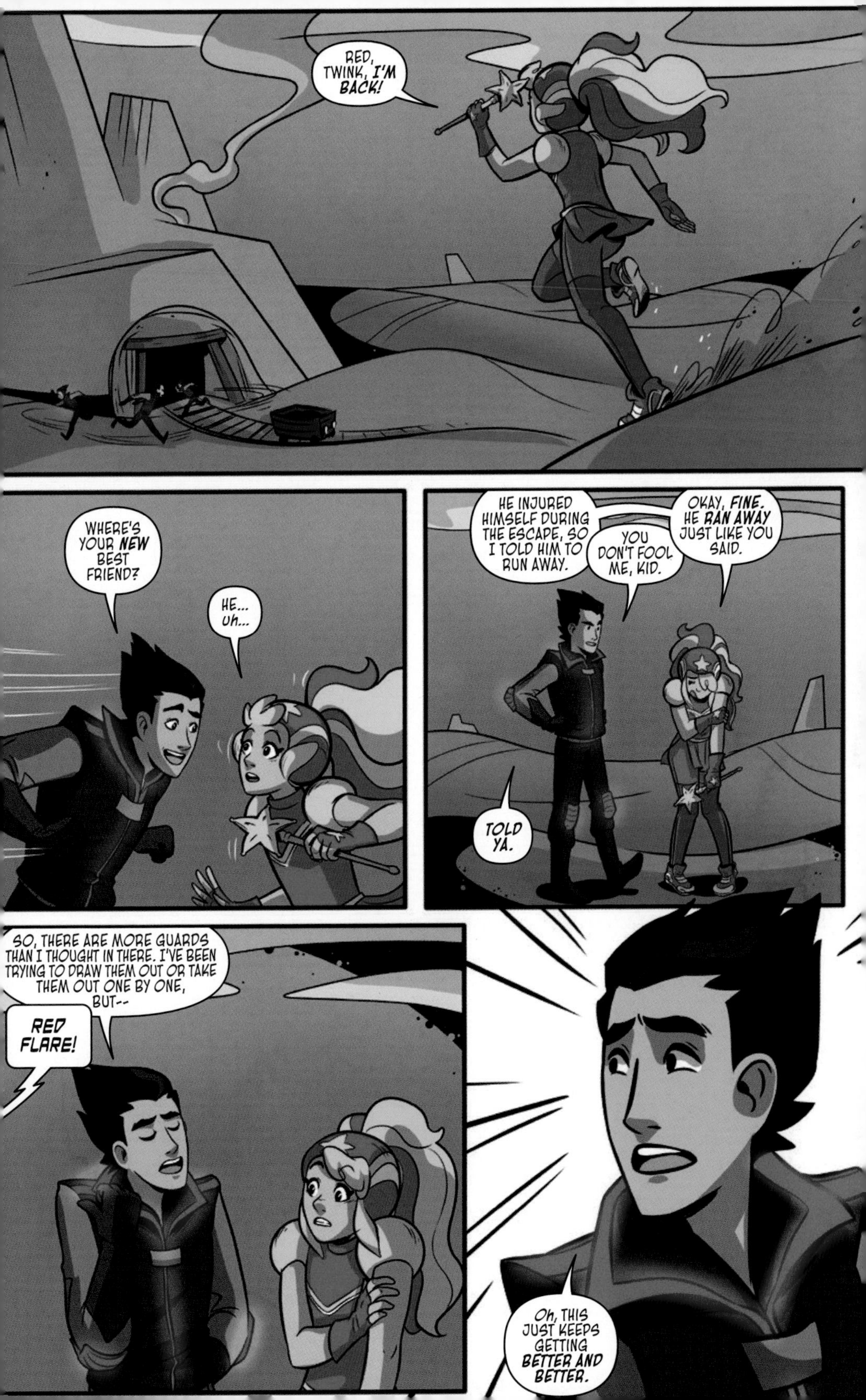
RED, TWINK, I'M BACK!
WHERE'S YOUR NEW BEST FRIEND?
HE... Uh...
HE INJURED HIMSELF DURING THE ESCAPE, SO I TOLD HIM TO RUN AWAY.
YOU DON'T FOOL ME, KID.
OKAY, FINE. HE RAN AWAY JUST LIKE YOU SAID.
TOLD YA.
SO, THERE ARE MORE GUARDS THAN I THOUGHT IN THERE. I'VE BEEN TRYING TO DRAW THEM OUT OR TAKE THEM OUT ONE BY ONE, BUT--
RED FLARE!
Oh, THIS JUST KEEPS GETTING BETTER AND BETTER.

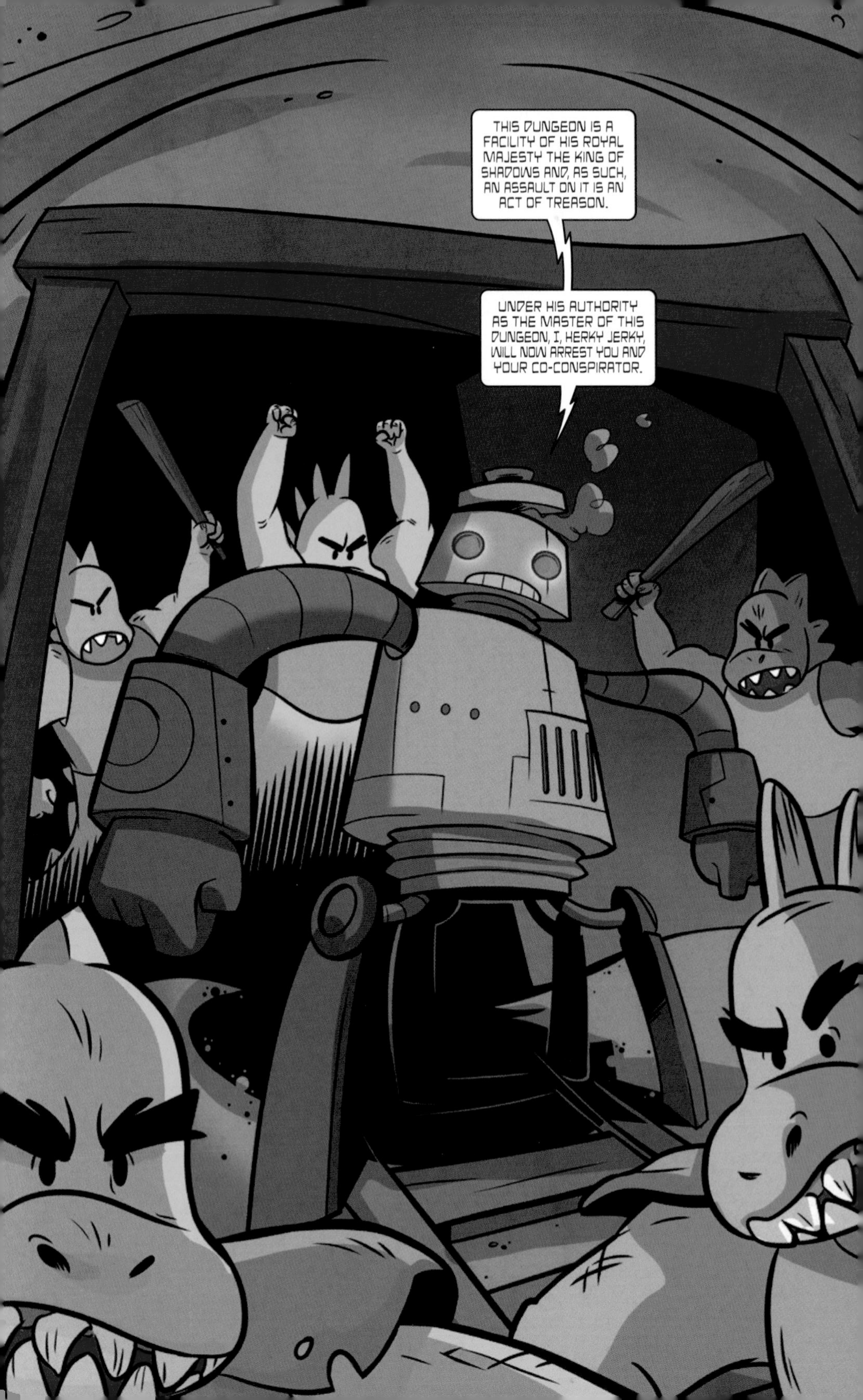
THIS DUNGEON IS A FACILITY OF HIS ROYAL MAJESTY THE KING OF SHADOWS AND, AS SUCH, AN ASSAULT ON IT IS AN ACT OF TREASON.
UNDER HIS AUTHORITY AS THE MASTER OF THIS DUNGEON, I, HERKY JERKY, WILL NOW ARREST YOU AND YOUR CO-CONSPIRATOR.

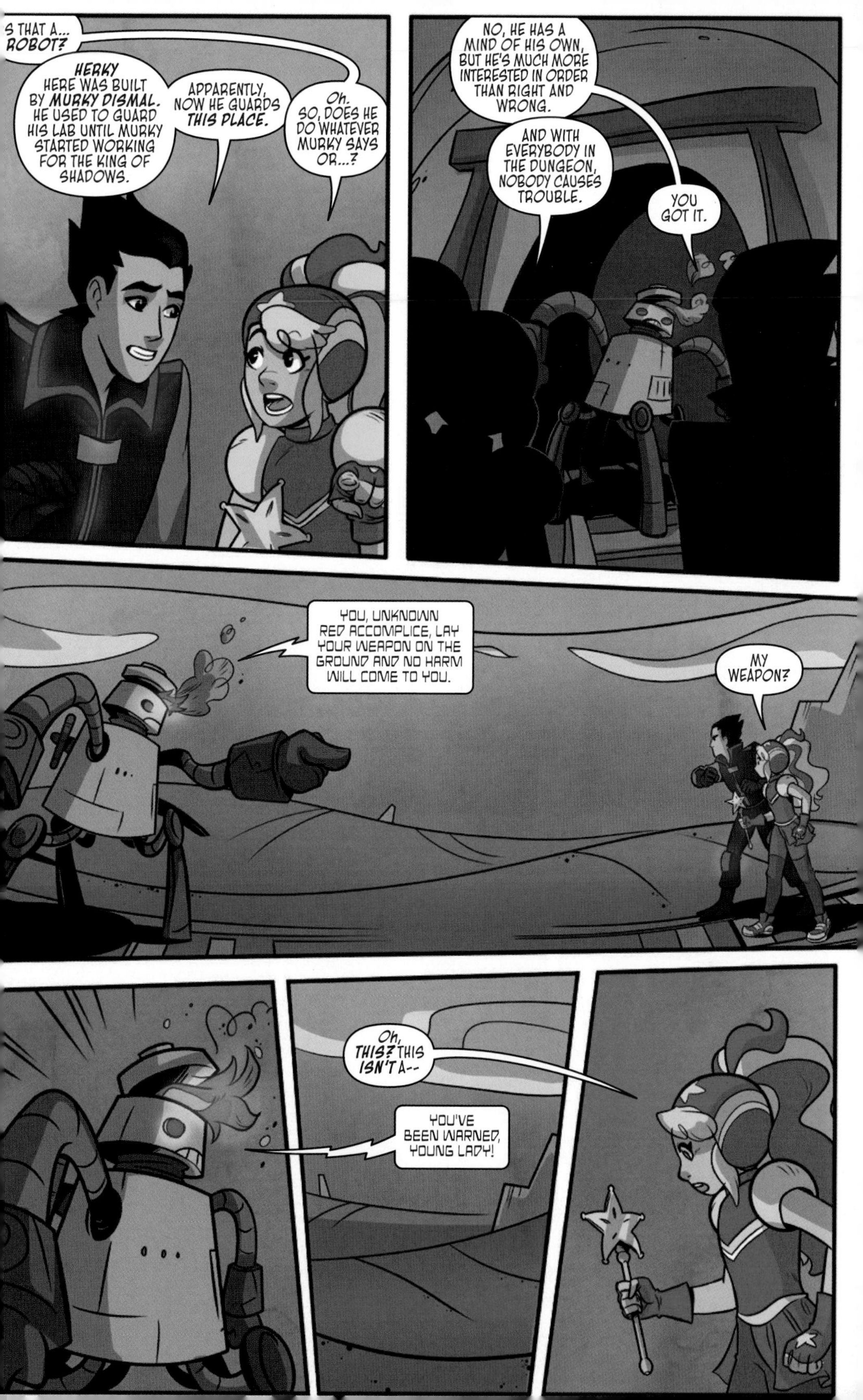
S THAT A... ROBOT?
HERKY HERE WAS BUILT BY MURKY DISMAL. HE USED TO GUARD HIS LAB UNTIL MURKY STARTED WORKING FOR THE KING OF SHADOWS.
APPARENTLY, NOW HE GUARDS THIS PLACE.
Oh. SO, DOES HE DO WHATEVER MURKY SAYS OR...?
NO, HE HAS A MIND OF HIS OWN, BUT HE'S MUCH MORE INTERESTED IN ORDER THAN RIGHT AND WRONG.
AND WITH EVERYBODY IN THE DUNGEON, NOBODY CAUSES TROUBLE.
YOU GOT IT.
YOU, UNKNOWN RED ACCOMPLICE, LAY YOUR WEAPON ON THE GROUND AND NO HARM WILL COME TO YOU.
MY WEAPON?
Oh, THIS? THIS ISN'T A--
YOU'VE BEEN WARNED, YOUNG LADY!

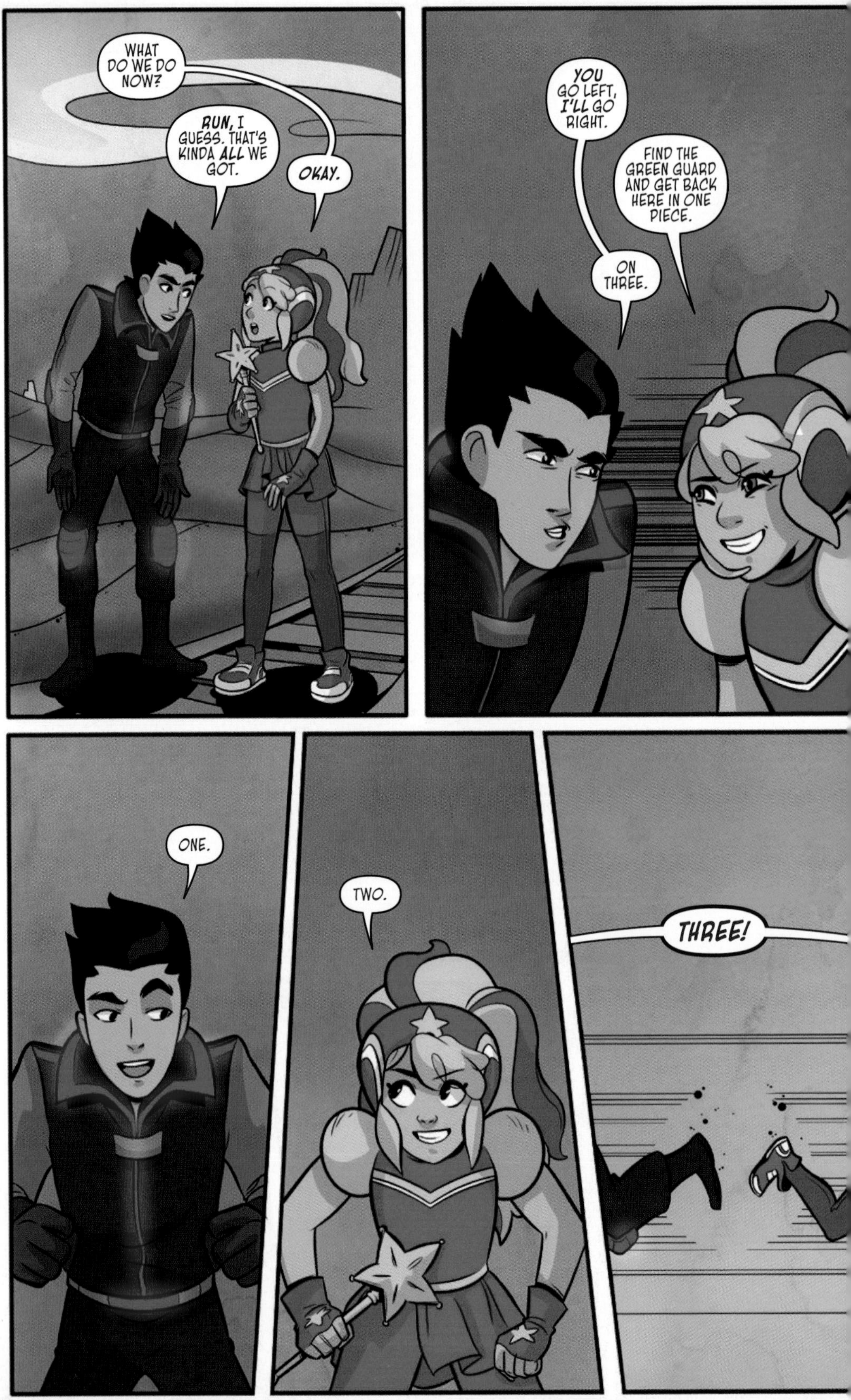
WHAT DO WE DO NOW?
RUN, I GUESS. THAT'S KINDA ALL WE GOT.
OKAY.
YOU GO LEFT, I'LL GO RIGHT.
FIND THE GREEN GUARD AND GET BACK HERE IN ONE PIECE.
ON THREE.
ONE.
TWO.
THREE!

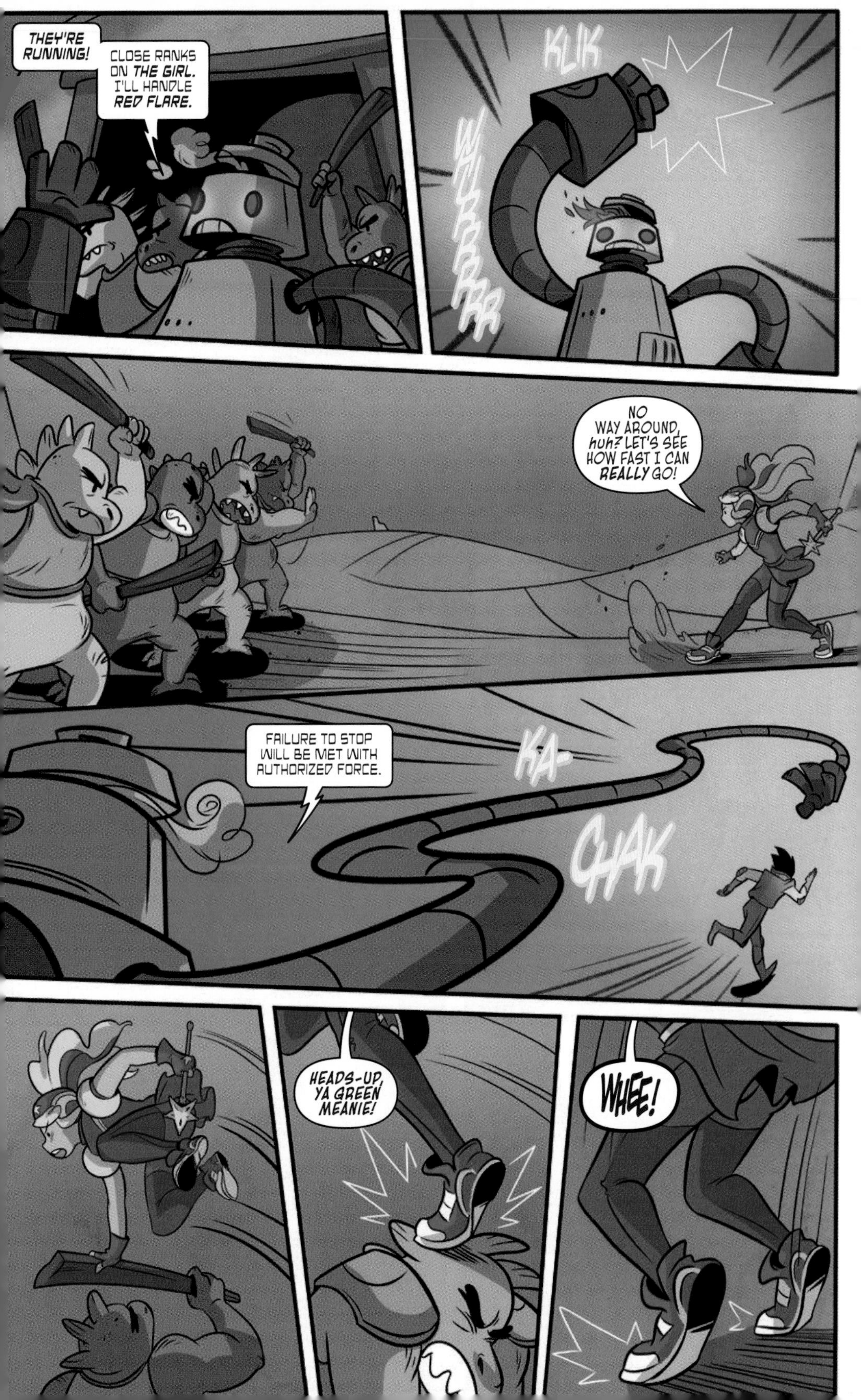
THEY'RE RUNNING!
CLOSE RANKS ON THE GIRL. I'LL HANDLE RED FLARE.
KLIK
WHURRRRRR
NO WAY AROUND, huh? LET'S SEE HOW FAST I CAN REALLY GO!
FAILURE TO STOP WILL BE MET WITH AUTHORIZED FORCE.
KA-CHAK
HEADS-UP, YA GREEN MEANIE!
WHEE!

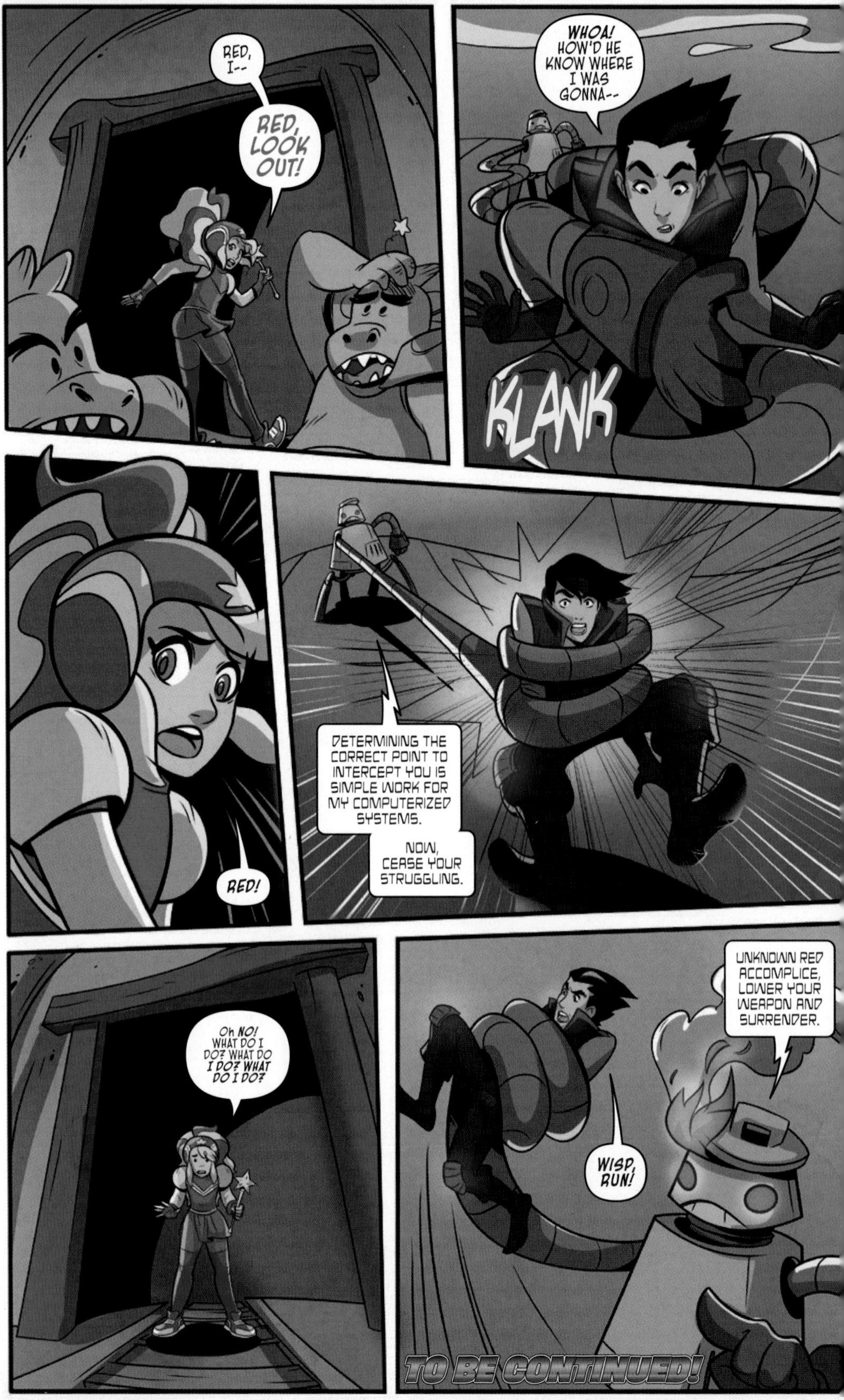
RED, I--
RED, LOOK OUT!
WHOA! HOW'D HE KNOW WHERE I WAS GONNA--
KLANK
RED!
DETERMINING THE CORRECT POINT TO INTERCEPT YOU IS SIMPLE WORK FOR MY COMPUTERIZED SYSTEMS.
NOW, CEASE YOUR STRUGGLING.
Oh NO! WHAT DO I DO? WHAT DO I DO? WHAT DO I DO?
UNKNOWN RED ACCOMPLICE, LOWER YOUR WEAPON AND SURRENDER.
WISP, RUN!
TO BE CONTINUED!

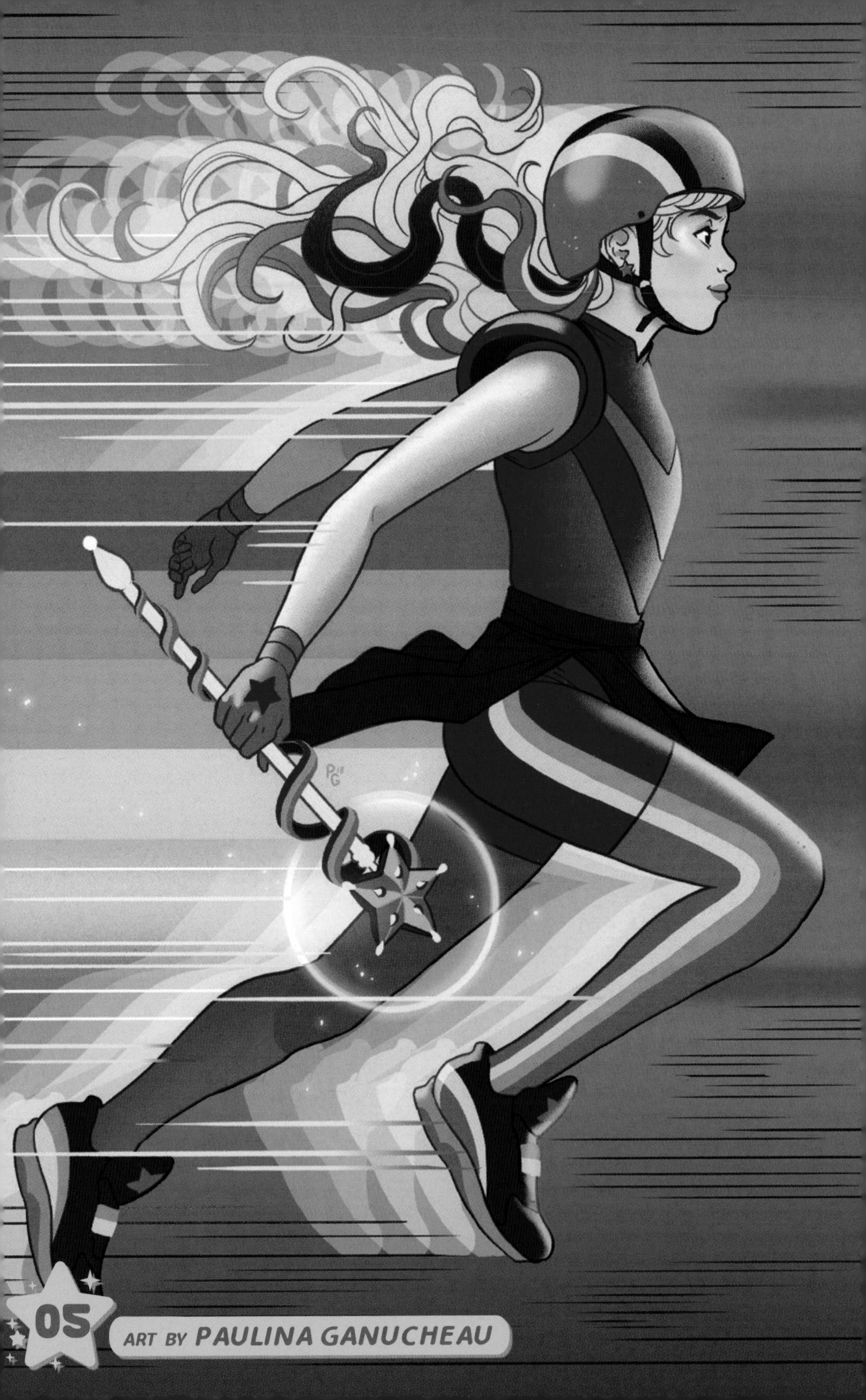

05

ART BY PAULINA GANUCHEAU

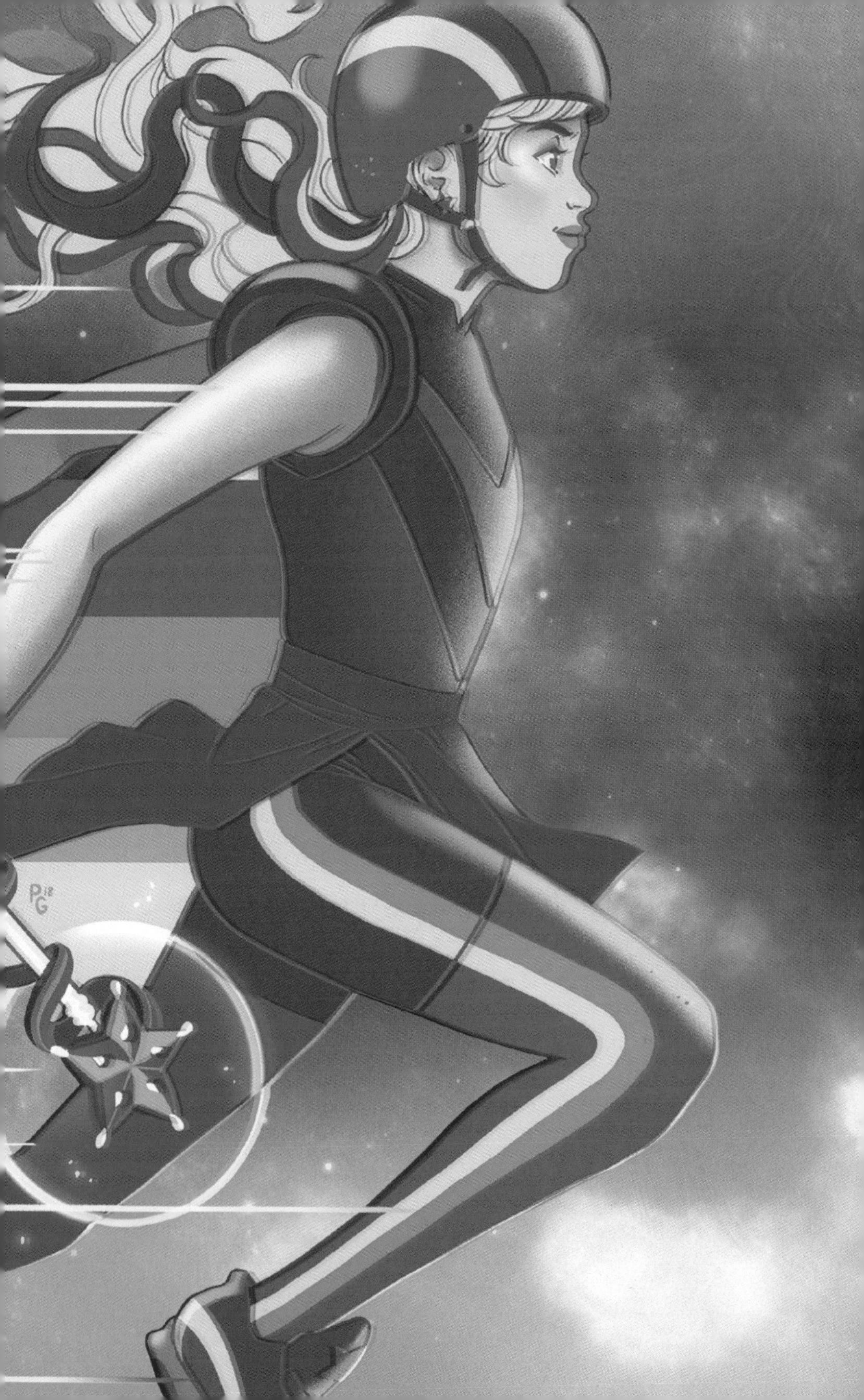

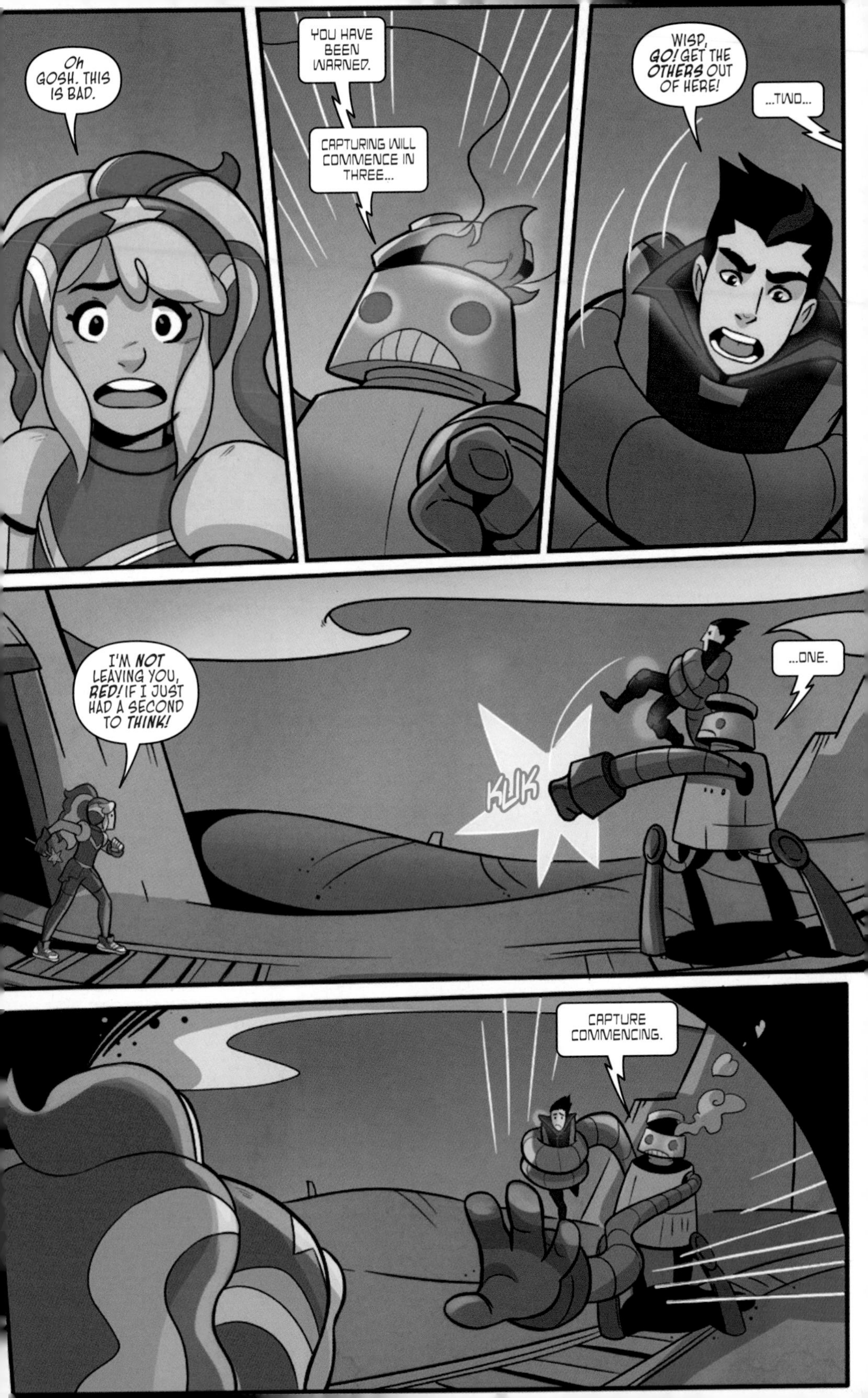
Oh GOSH. THIS IS BAD.
YOU HAVE BEEN WARNED.
CAPTURING WILL COMMENCE IN THREE...
WISP, GO! GET THE OTHERS OUT OF HERE!
...TWO...
I'M NOT LEAVING YOU, RED! IF I JUST HAD A SECOND TO THINK!
...ONE.
KLIK
CAPTURE COMMENCING.

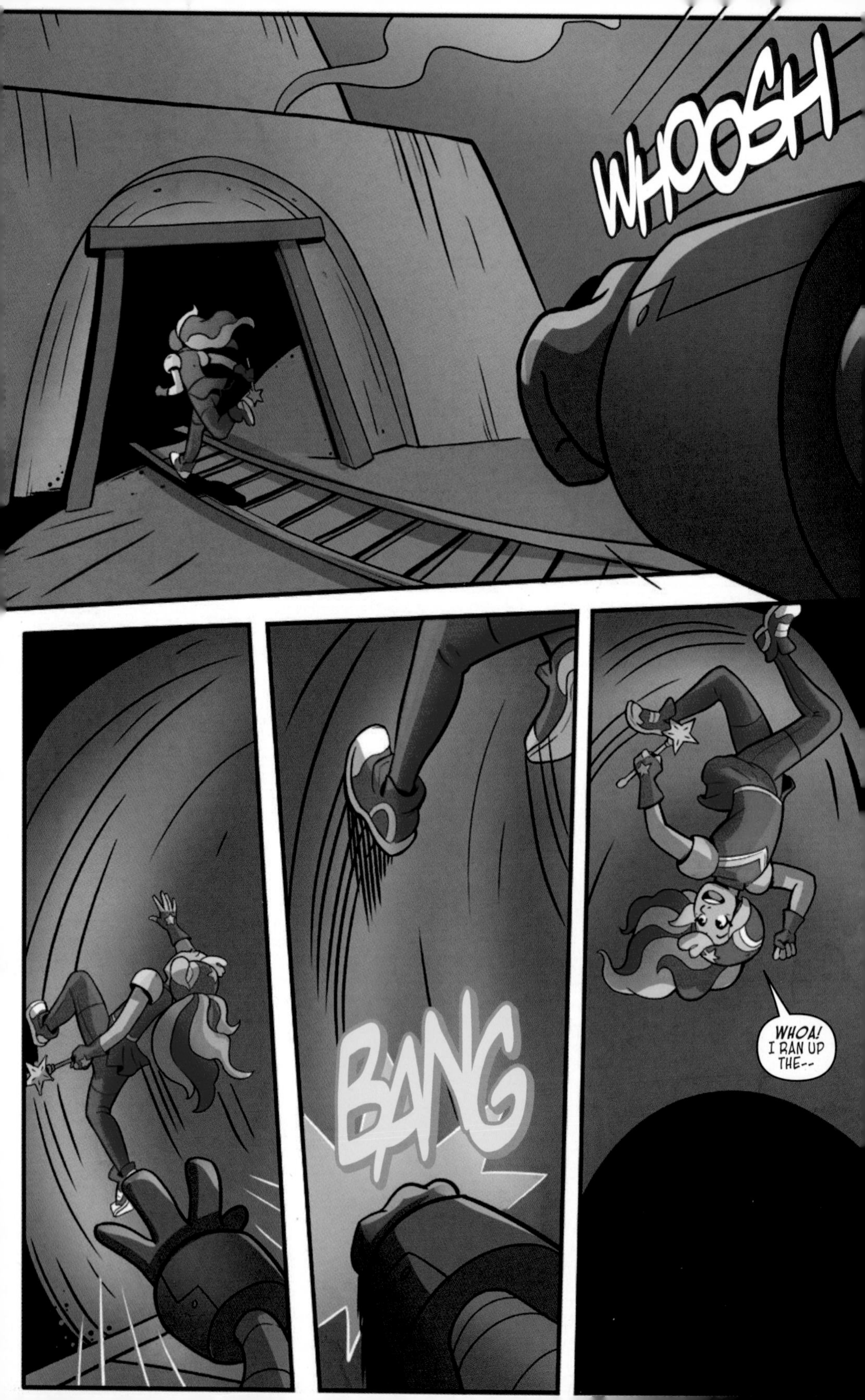
WHOOSH
BANG
WHOA!
I RAN UP
THE--

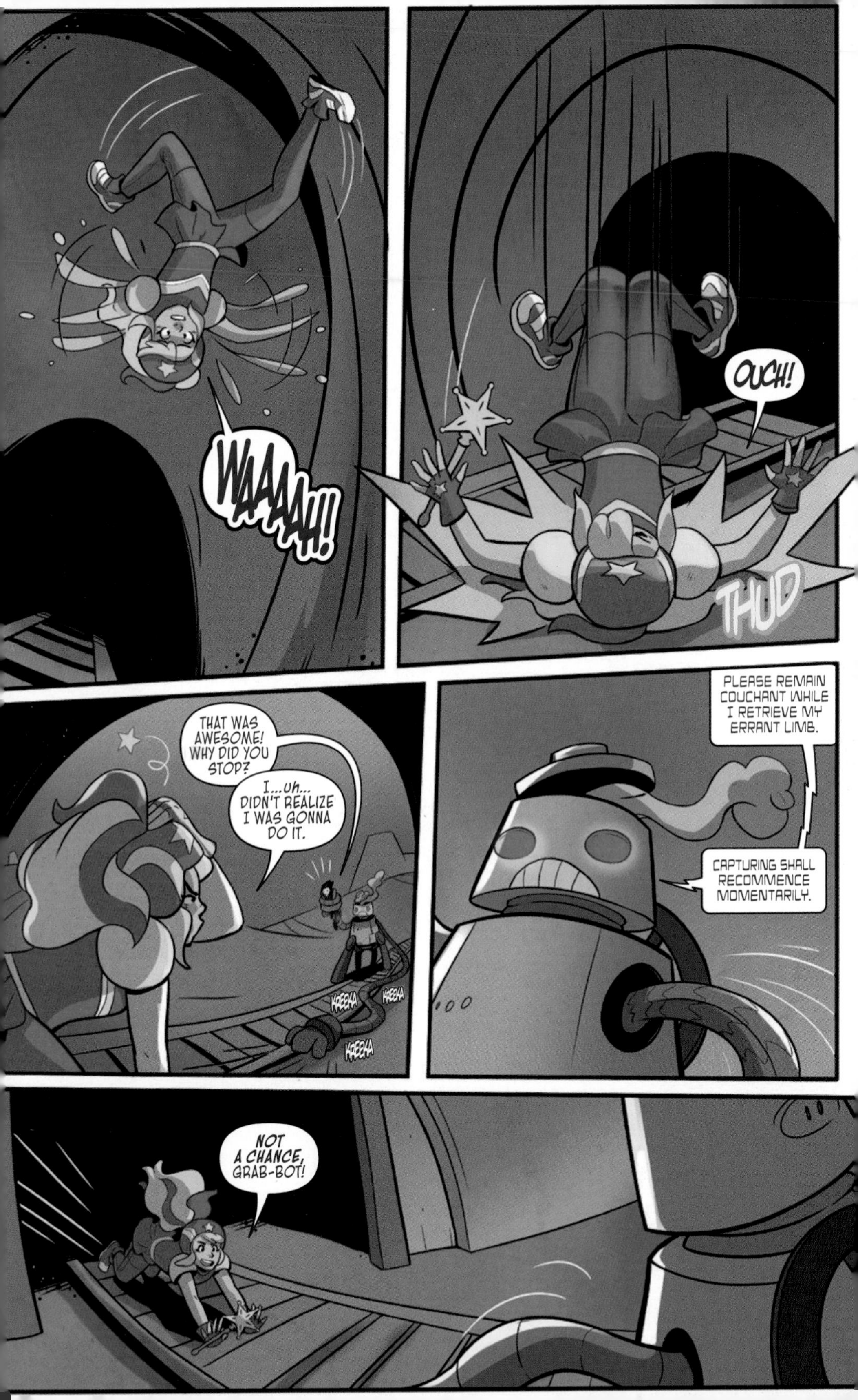
WAAAAH!!
OUCH!
THUD
THAT WAS AWESOME! WHY DID YOU STOP?
I...uh... DIDN'T REALIZE I WAS GONNA DO IT.
KREEKA
KREEKA
KREEKA
PLEASE REMAIN COUCHANT WHILE I RETRIEVE MY ERRANT LIMB.
CAPTURING SHALL RECOMMENCE MOMENTARILY.
NOT A CHANCE, GRAB-BOT!

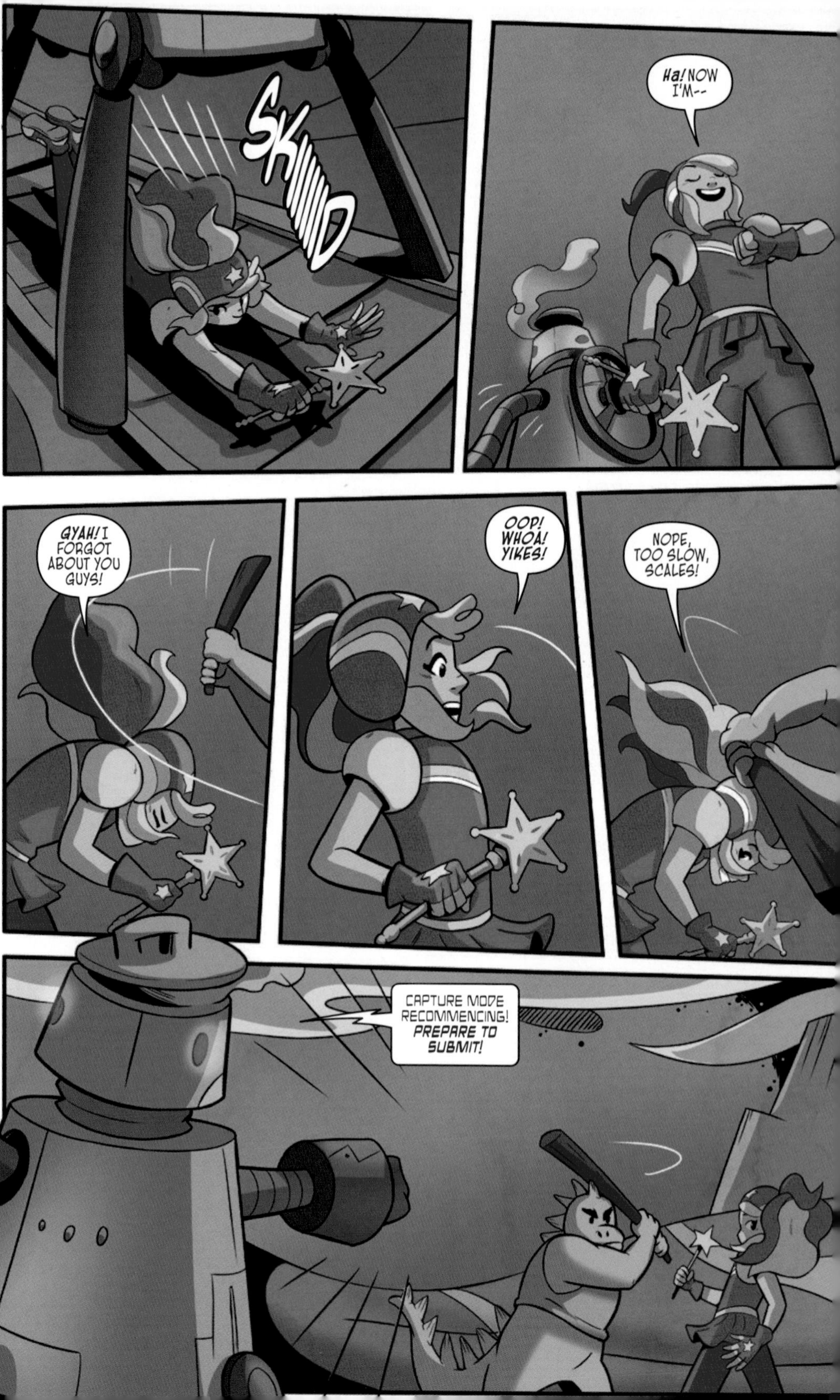
SKIIIID
Ha! NOW I'M--
GYAH! I FORGOT ABOUT YOU GUYS!
OOP! WHOA! YIKES!
NOPE, TOO SLOW, SCALES!
CAPTURE MODE RECOMMENCING! PREPARE TO SUBMIT!

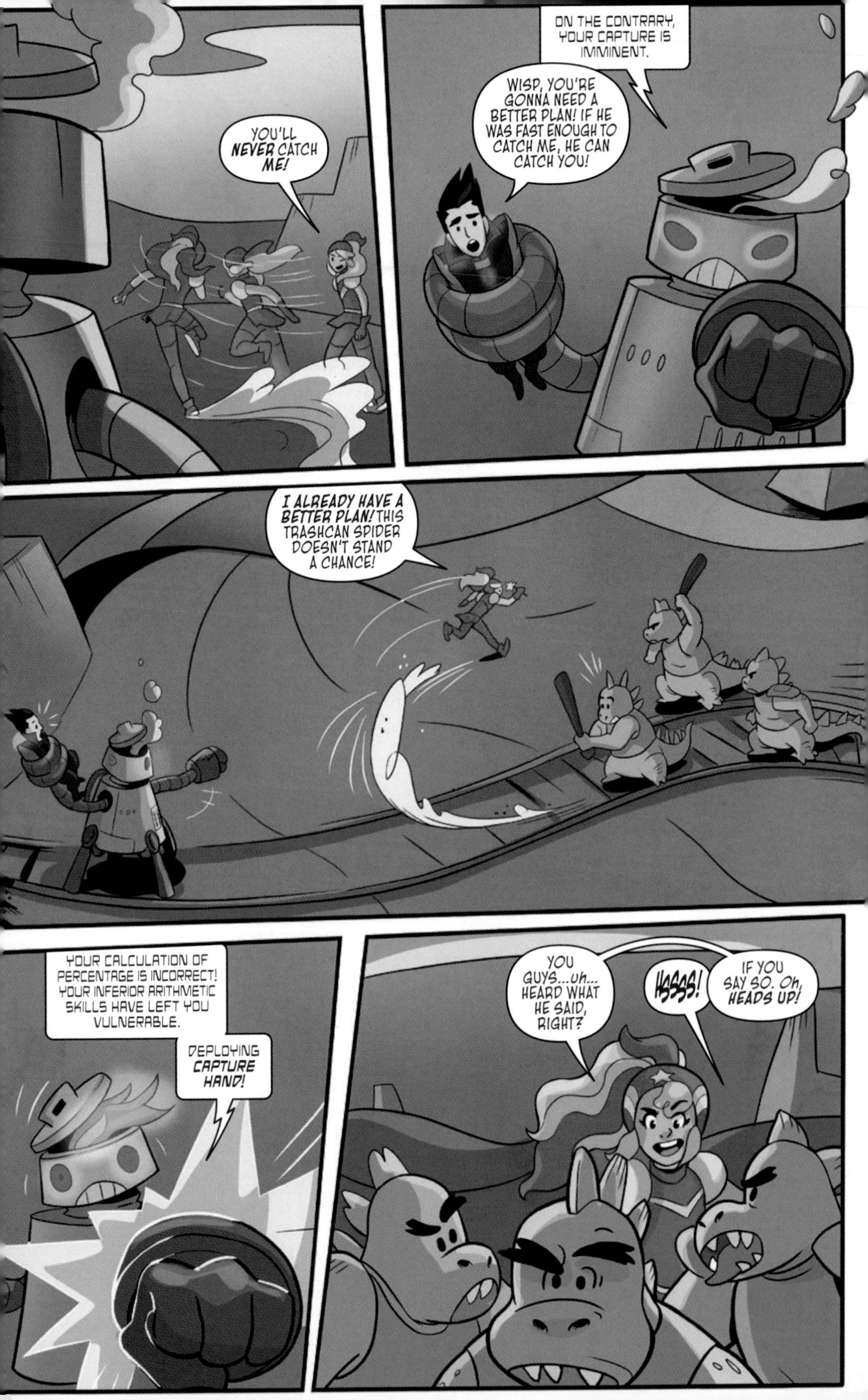
YOU'LL NEVER CATCH ME!
ON THE CONTRARY, YOUR CAPTURE IS IMMINENT.
WISP, YOU'RE GONNA NEED A BETTER PLAN! IF HE WAS FAST ENOUGH TO CATCH ME, HE CAN CATCH YOU!
I ALREADY HAVE A BETTER PLAN! THIS TRASHCAN SPIDER DOESN'T STAND A CHANCE!
YOUR CALCULATION OF PERCENTAGE IS INCORRECT! YOUR INFERIOR ARITHMETIC SKILLS HAVE LEFT YOU VULNERABLE.
DEPLOYING CAPTURE HAND!
YOU GUYS...uh... HEARD WHAT HE SAID, RIGHT?
HSSSS!
IF YOU SAY SO. Oh, HEADS UP!

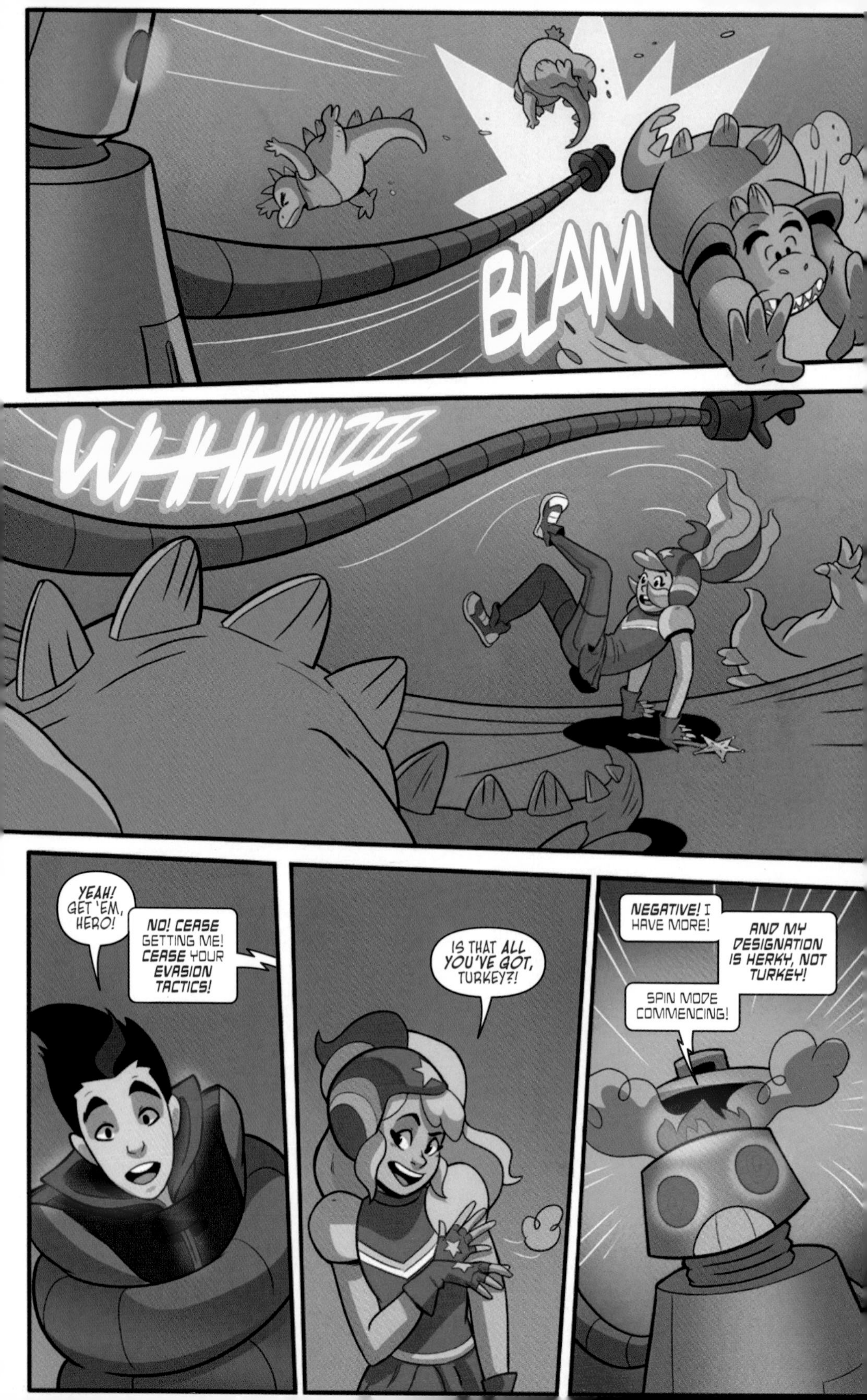
BLAM
WHHIIIIZZZ
YEAH! GET 'EM, HERO!
NO! CEASE GETTING ME! CEASE YOUR EVASION TACTICS!
IS THAT ALL YOU'VE GOT, TURKEY?!
NEGATIVE! I HAVE MORE!
AND MY DESIGNATION IS HERKY, NOT TURKEY!
SPIN MODE COMMENCING!

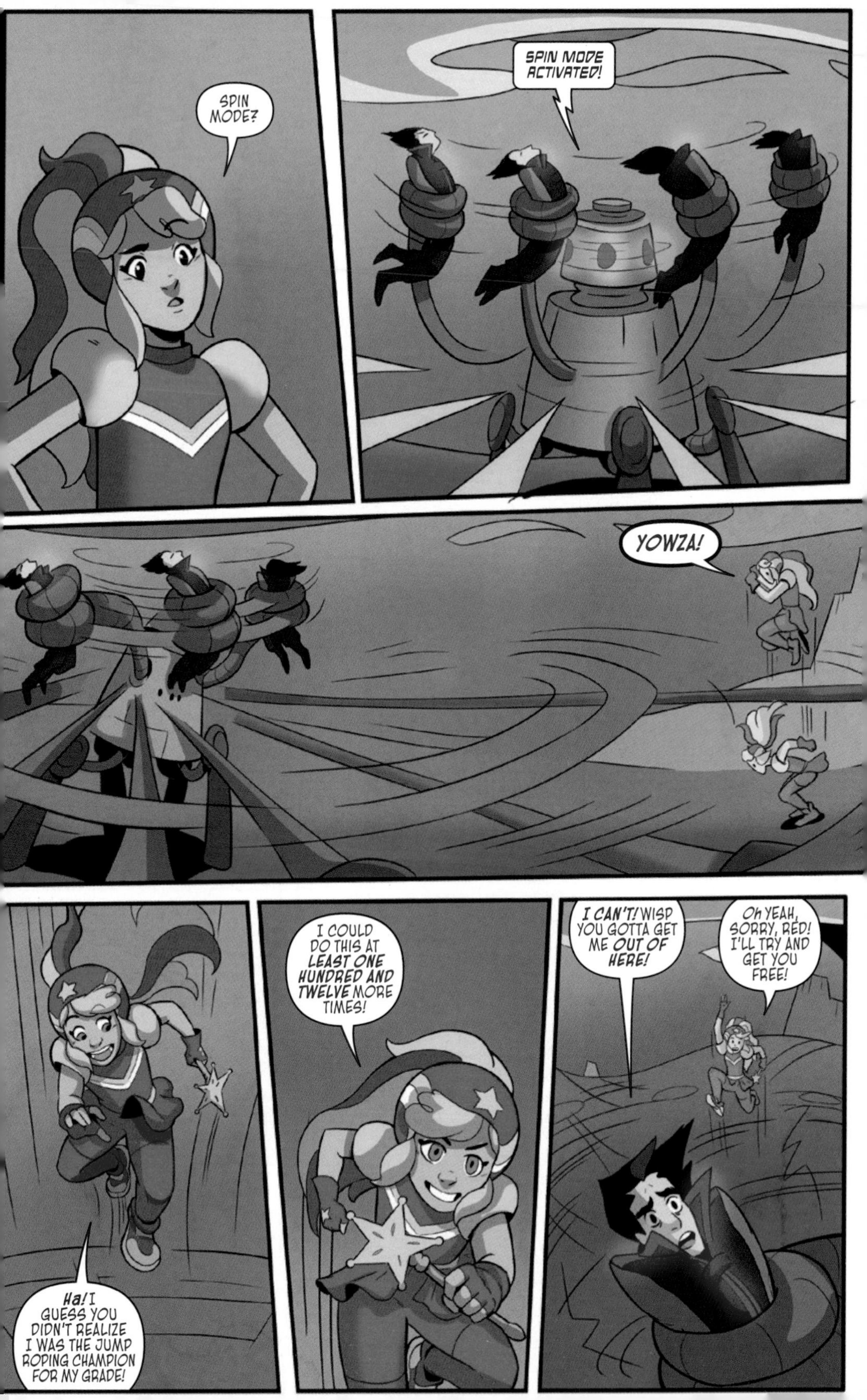
SPIN MODE?
SPIN MODE ACTIVATED!
YOWZA!
Ha! I GUESS YOU DIDN'T REALIZE I WAS THE JUMP ROPING CHAMPION FOR MY GRADE!
I COULD DO THIS AT LEAST ONE HUNDRED AND TWELVE MORE TIMES!
I CAN'T! WISP YOU GOTTA GET ME OUT OF HERE!
Oh YEAH, SORRY, RED! I'LL TRY AND GET YOU FREE!

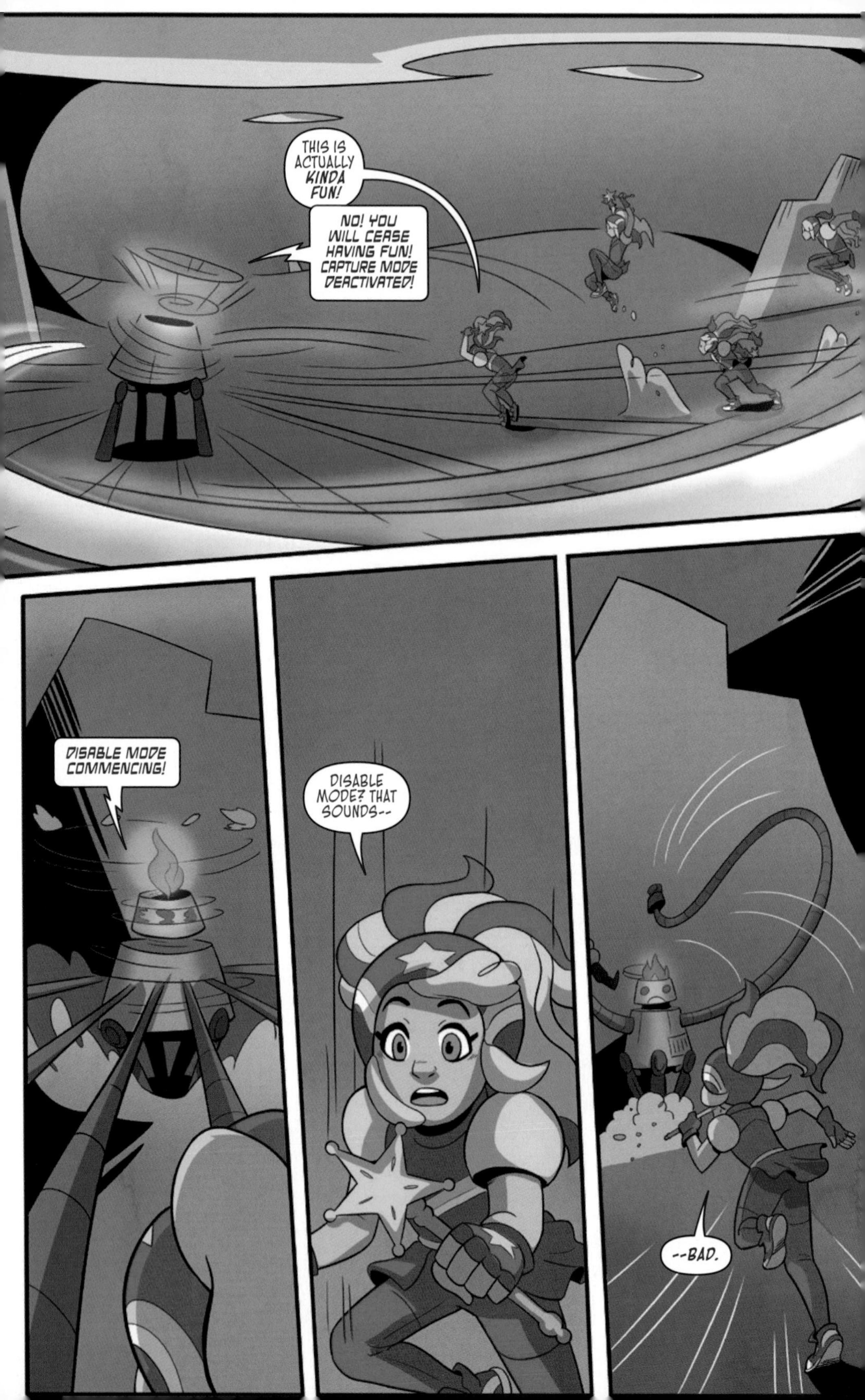
THIS IS ACTUALLY KINDA FUN!
NO! YOU WILL CEASE HAVING FUN! CAPTURE MODE DEACTIVATED!
DISABLE MODE COMMENCING!
DISABLE MODE? THAT SOUNDS--
--BAD.

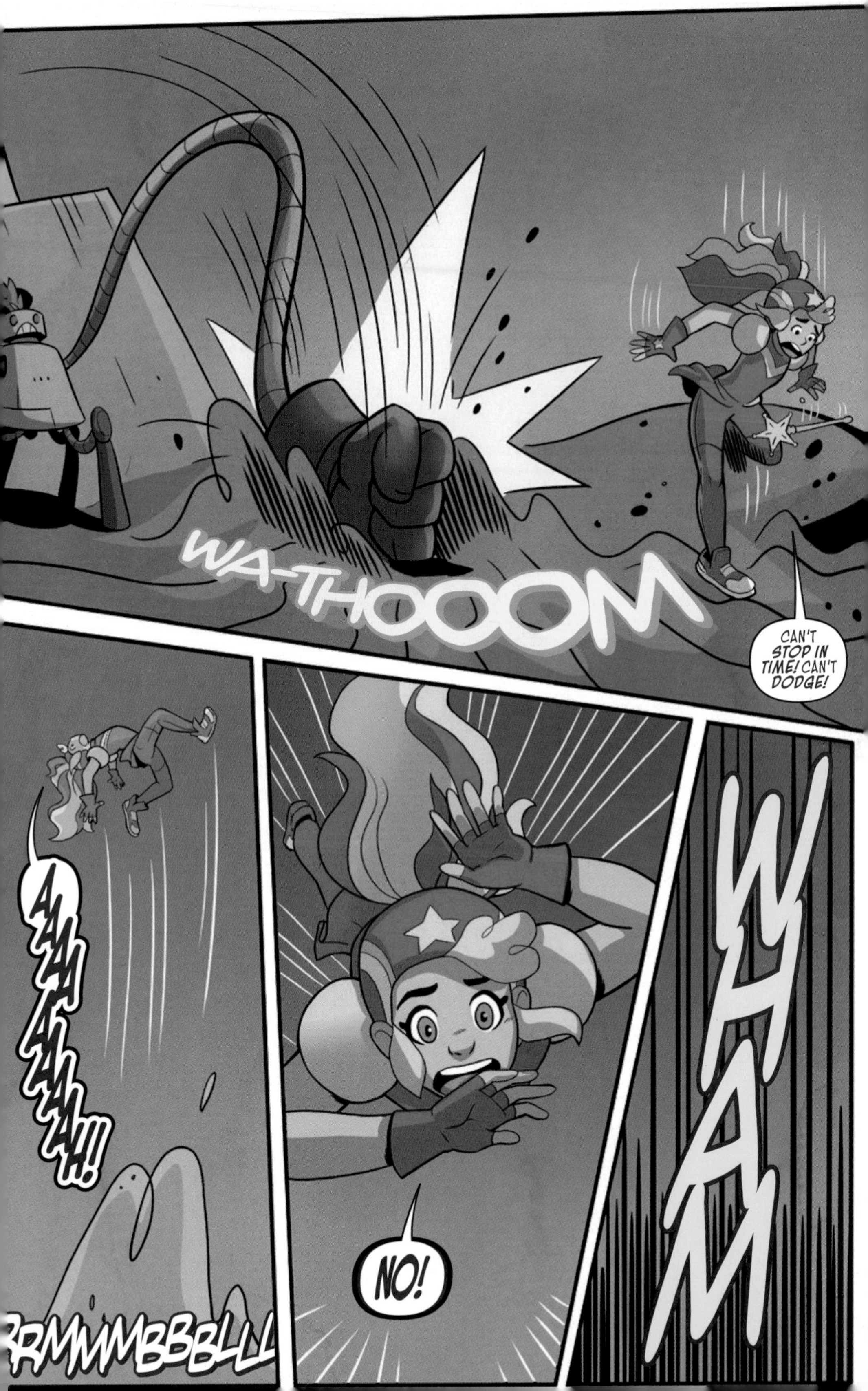
WA-THOOOM
CAN'T STOP IN TIME! CAN'T DODGE!
AAAAAAAAAAAAH!!
RRMMMBBBLLL
NO!
WHAM

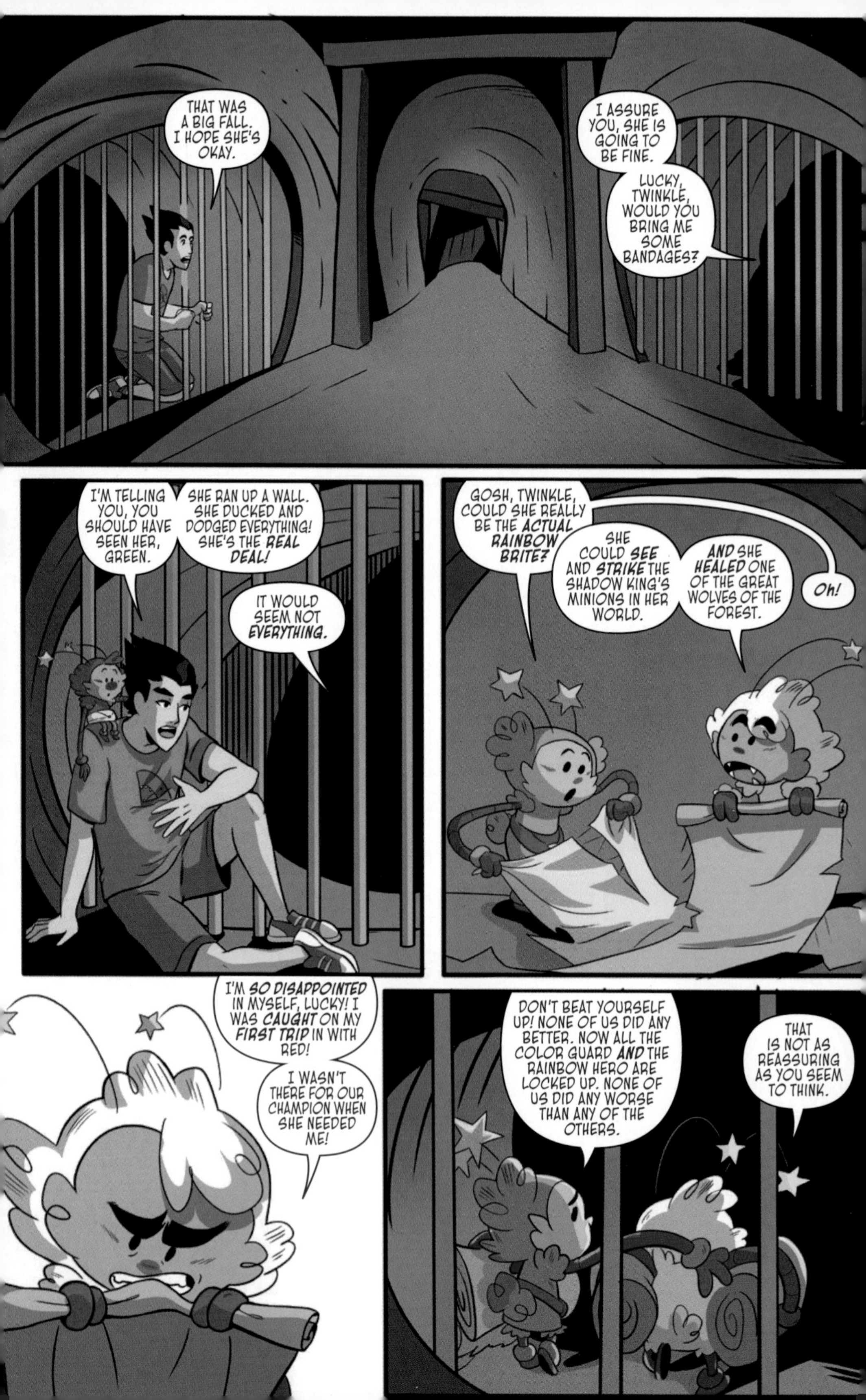
THAT WAS A BIG FALL. I HOPE SHE'S OKAY.
I ASSURE YOU, SHE IS GOING TO BE FINE.
LUCKY, TWINKLE, WOULD YOU BRING ME SOME BANDAGES?
I'M TELLING YOU, YOU SHOULD HAVE SEEN HER, GREEN.
SHE RAN UP A WALL. SHE DUCKED AND DODGED EVERYTHING! SHE'S THE REAL DEAL!
IT WOULD SEEM NOT EVERYTHING.
GOSH, TWINKLE, COULD SHE REALLY BE THE ACTUAL RAINBOW BRITE?
SHE COULD SEE AND STRIKE THE SHADOW KING'S MINIONS IN HER WORLD.
AND SHE HEALED ONE OF THE GREAT WOLVES OF THE FOREST.
Oh!
I'M SO DISAPPOINTED IN MYSELF, LUCKY! I WAS CAUGHT ON MY FIRST TRIP IN WITH RED!
I WASN'T THERE FOR OUR CHAMPION WHEN SHE NEEDED ME!
DON'T BEAT YOURSELF UP! NONE OF US DID ANY BETTER. NOW ALL THE COLOR GUARD AND THE RAINBOW HERO ARE LOCKED UP. NONE OF US DID ANY WORSE THAN ANY OF THE OTHERS.
THAT IS NOT AS REASSURING AS YOU SEEM TO THINK.

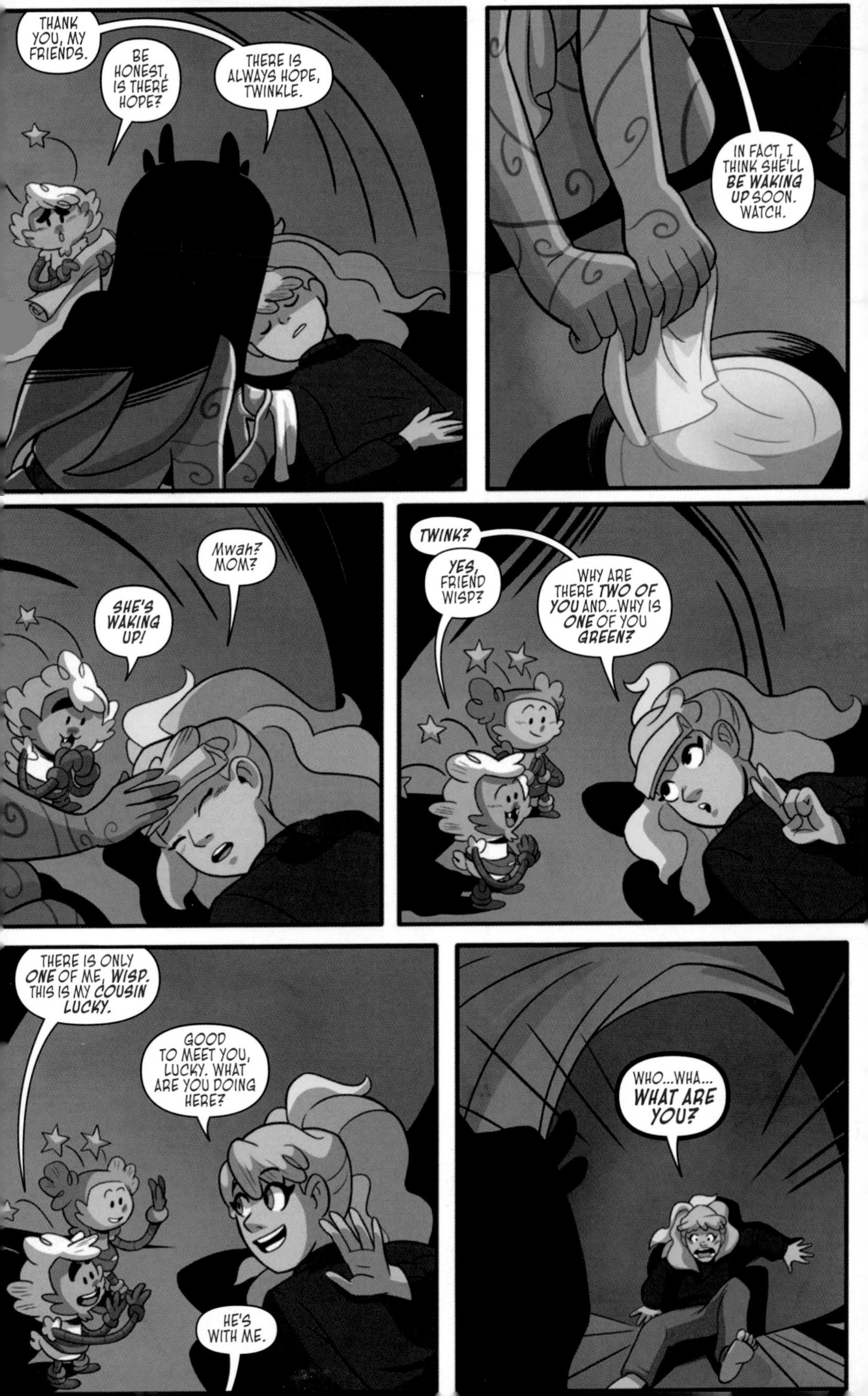
THANK YOU, MY FRIENDS.
BE HONEST, IS THERE HOPE?
THERE IS ALWAYS HOPE, TWINKLE.
IN FACT, I THINK SHE'LL BE WAKING UP SOON. WATCH.
Mwah? MOM?
SHE'S WAKING UP!
TWINK?
YES, FRIEND WISP?
WHY ARE THERE TWO OF YOU AND...WHY IS ONE OF YOU GREEN?
THERE IS ONLY ONE OF ME, WISP. THIS IS MY COUSIN LUCKY.
GOOD TO MEET YOU, LUCKY. WHAT ARE YOU DOING HERE?
HE'S WITH ME.
WHO...WHA... WHAT ARE YOU?

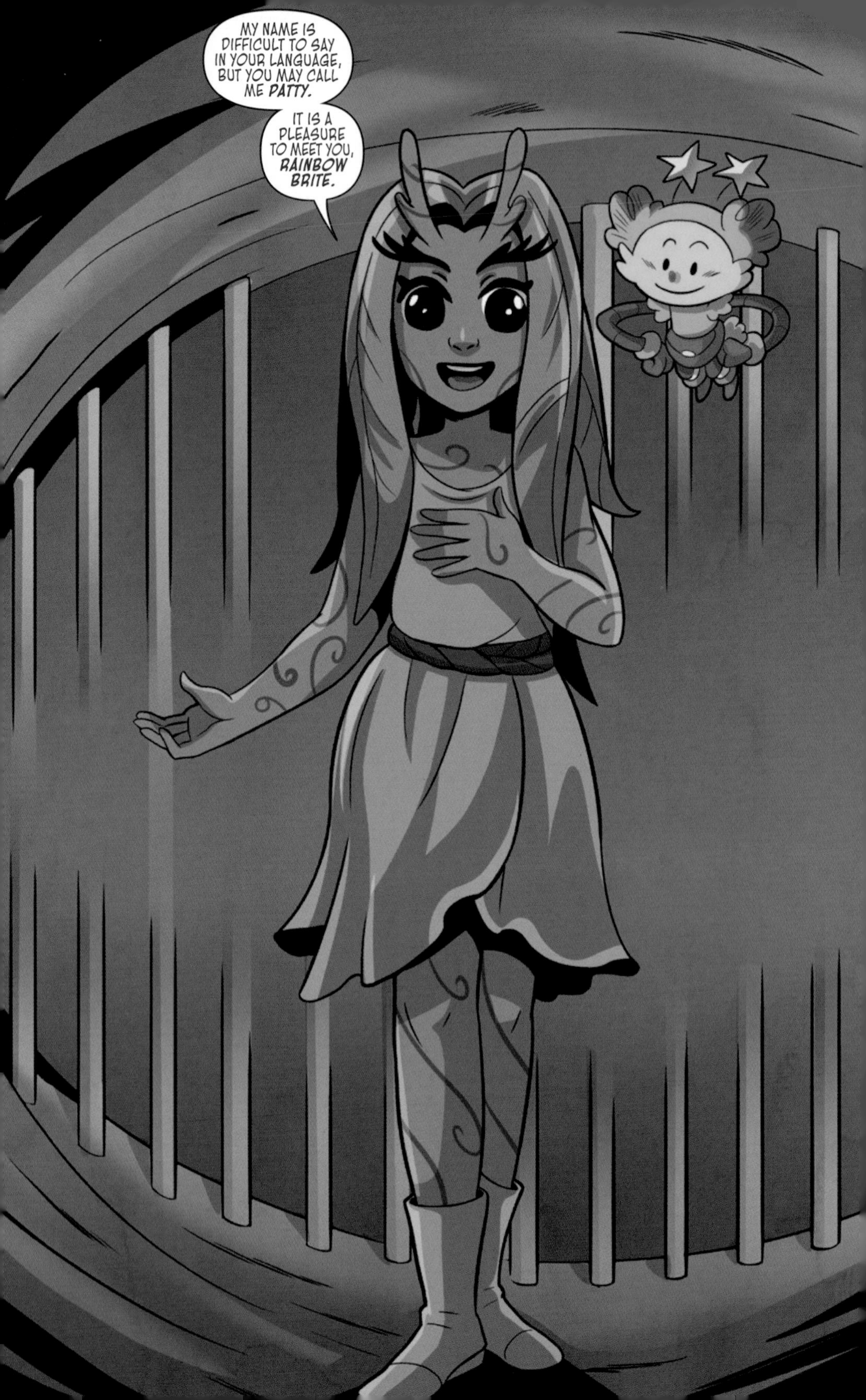
MY NAME IS DIFFICULT TO SAY IN YOUR LANGUAGE, BUT YOU MAY CALL ME **PATTY.**
IT IS A PLEASURE TO MEET YOU, **RAINBOW BRITE.**

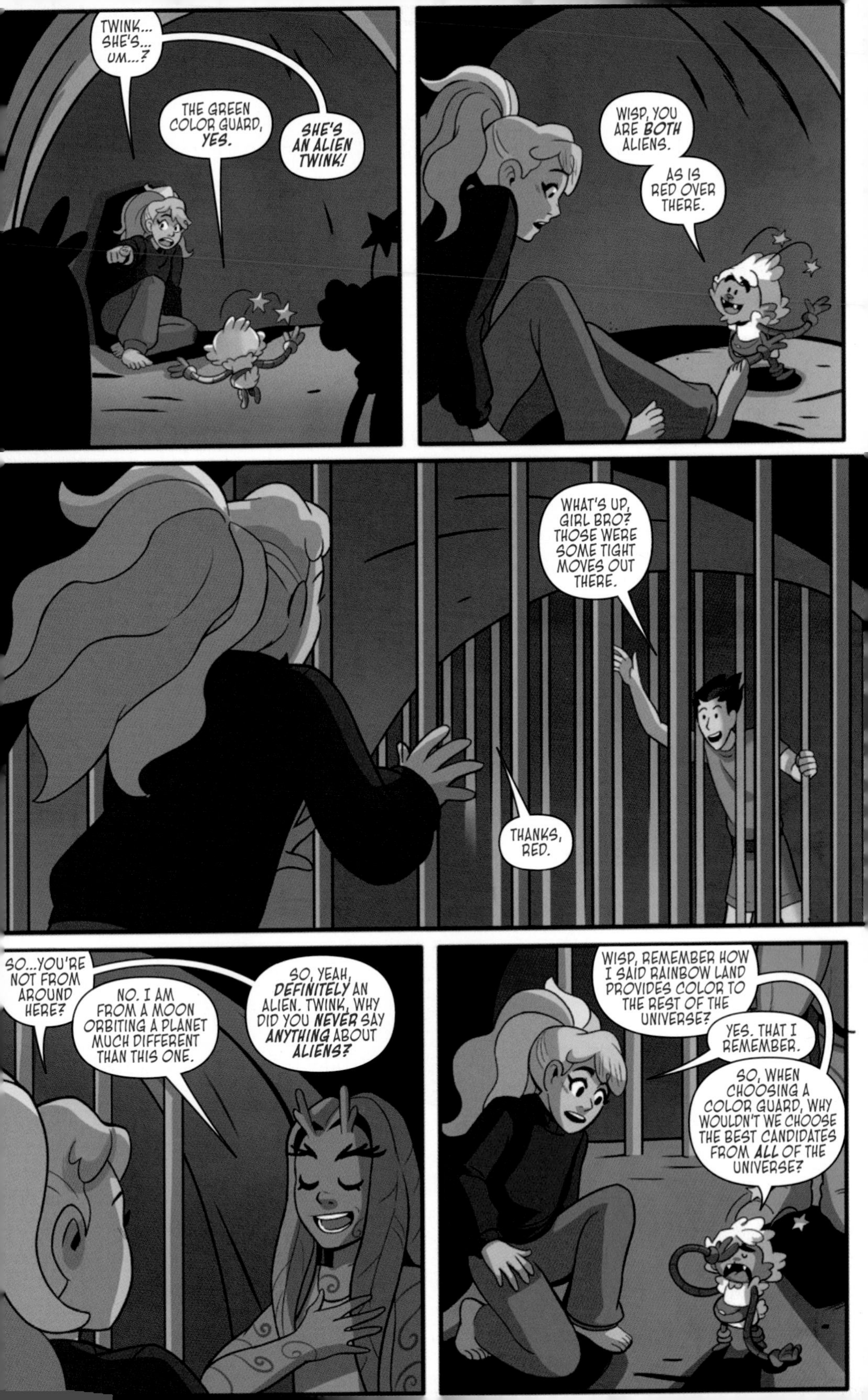
TWINK... SHE'S... UM...?
THE GREEN COLOR GUARD, YES.
SHE'S AN ALIEN TWINK!
WISP, YOU ARE BOTH ALIENS.
AS IS RED OVER THERE.
WHAT'S UP, GIRL BRO? THOSE WERE SOME TIGHT MOVES OUT THERE.
THANKS, RED.
SO...YOU'RE NOT FROM AROUND HERE?
NO. I AM FROM A MOON ORBITING A PLANET MUCH DIFFERENT THAN THIS ONE.
SO, YEAH, DEFINITELY AN ALIEN. TWINK, WHY DID YOU NEVER SAY ANYTHING ABOUT ALIENS?
WISP, REMEMBER HOW I SAID RAINBOW LAND PROVIDES COLOR TO THE REST OF THE UNIVERSE?
YES. THAT I REMEMBER.
SO, WHEN CHOOSING A COLOR GUARD, WHY WOULDN'T WE CHOOSE THE BEST CANDIDATES FROM ALL OF THE UNIVERSE?

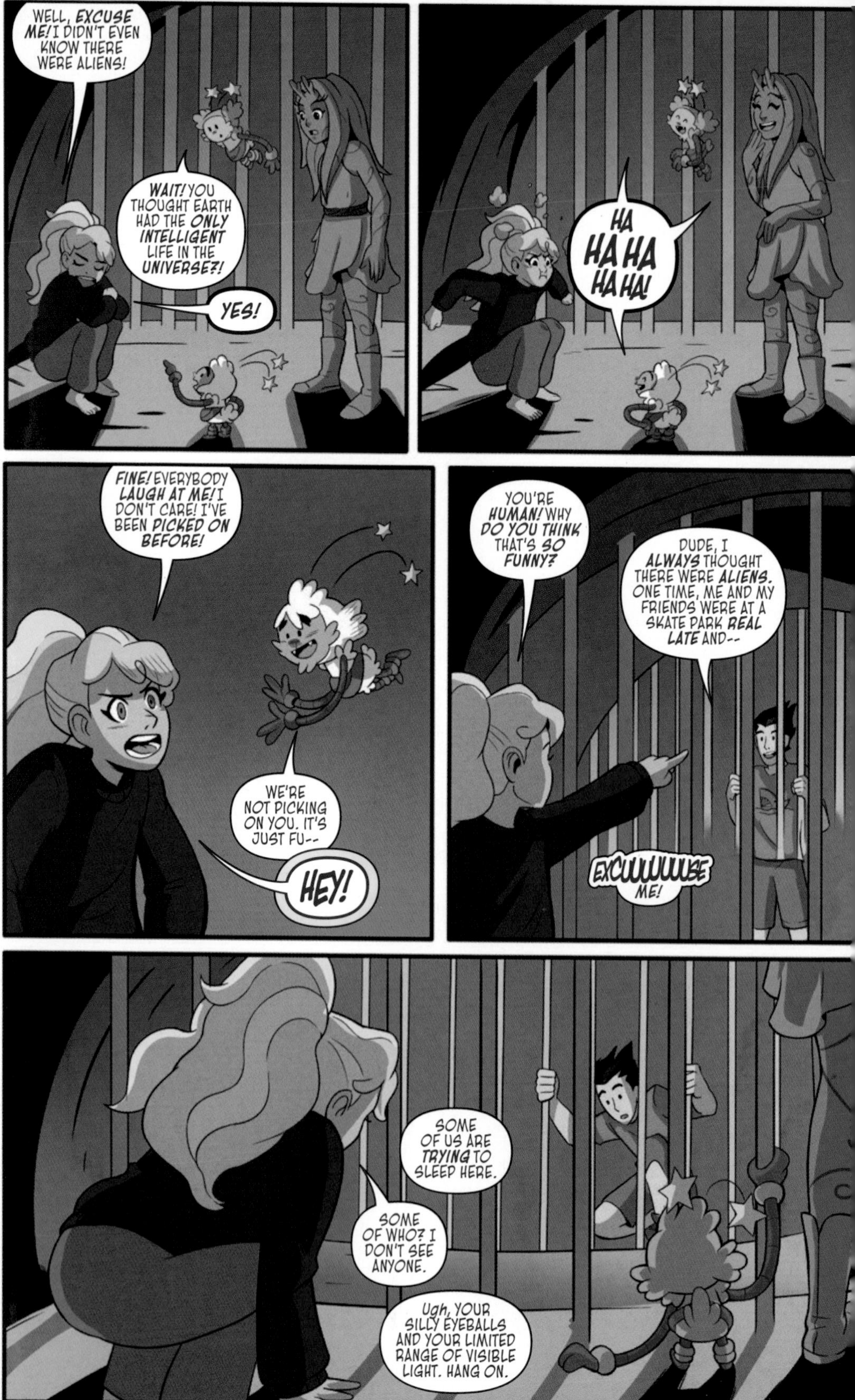
WELL, EXCUSE ME! I DIDN'T EVEN KNOW THERE WERE ALIENS!
WAIT! YOU THOUGHT EARTH HAD THE ONLY INTELLIGENT LIFE IN THE UNIVERSE?!
YES!
HA HA HA HA HA!
FINE! EVERYBODY LAUGH AT ME! I DON'T CARE! I'VE BEEN PICKED ON BEFORE!
WE'RE NOT PICKING ON YOU. IT'S JUST FU--
HEY!
YOU'RE HUMAN! WHY DO YOU THINK THAT'S SO FUNNY?
DUDE, I ALWAYS THOUGHT THERE WERE ALIENS. ONE TIME, ME AND MY FRIENDS WERE AT A SKATE PARK REAL LATE AND--
EXCUUUUUUSE ME!
SOME OF US ARE TRYING TO SLEEP HERE.
SOME OF WHO? I DON'T SEE ANYONE.
Ugh, YOUR SILLY EYEBALLS AND YOUR LIMITED RANGE OF VISIBLE LIGHT. HANG ON.

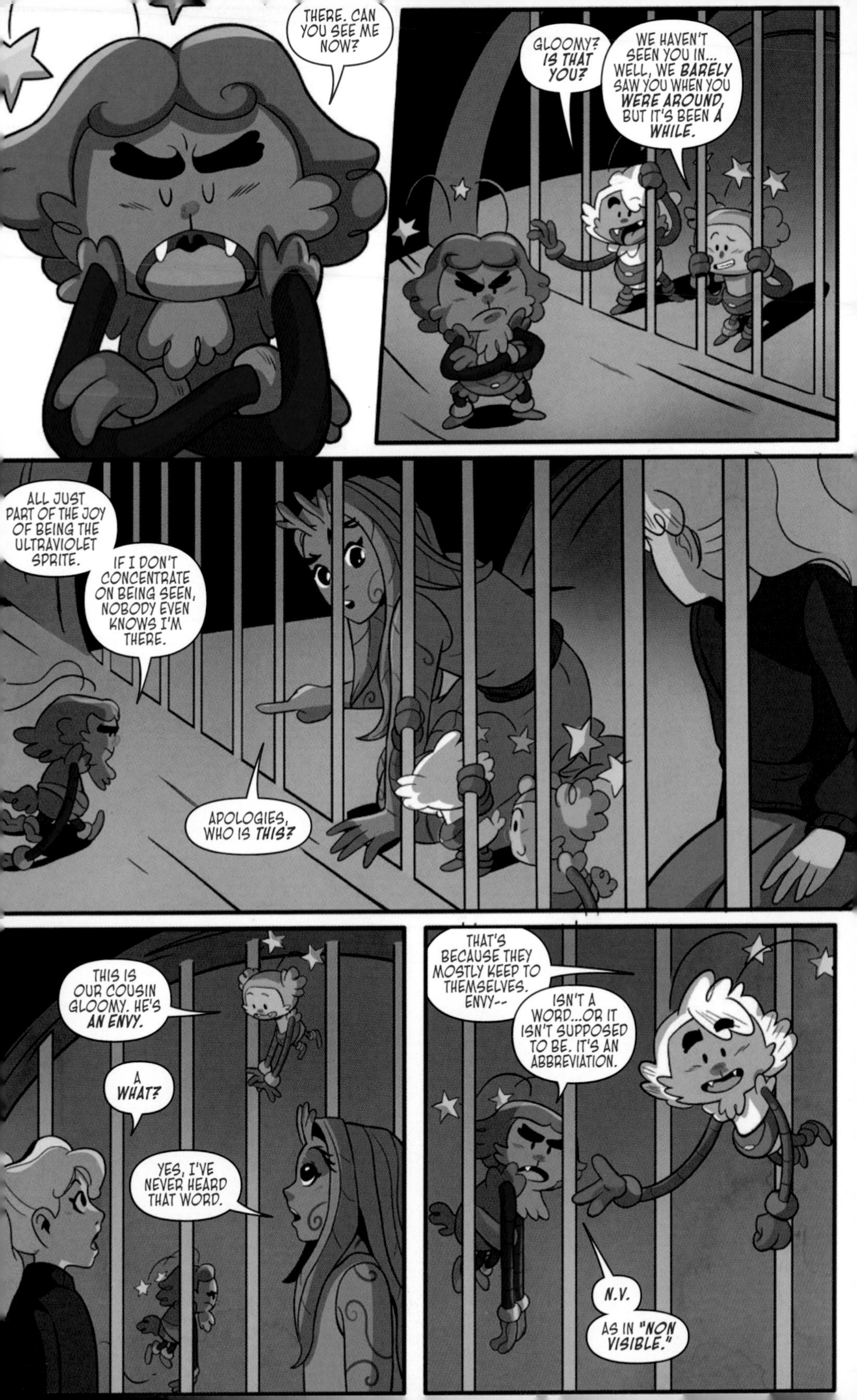
THERE. CAN YOU SEE ME NOW?
GLOOMY? IS THAT YOU?
WE HAVEN'T SEEN YOU IN... WELL, WE BARELY SAW YOU WHEN YOU WERE AROUND, BUT IT'S BEEN A WHILE.
ALL JUST PART OF THE JOY OF BEING THE ULTRAVIOLET SPRITE.
IF I DON'T CONCENTRATE ON BEING SEEN, NOBODY EVEN KNOWS I'M THERE.
APOLOGIES, WHO IS THIS?
THIS IS OUR COUSIN GLOOMY. HE'S AN ENVY.
A WHAT?
YES, I'VE NEVER HEARD THAT WORD.
THAT'S BECAUSE THEY MOSTLY KEEP TO THEMSELVES. ENVY--
ISN'T A WORD...OR IT ISN'T SUPPOSED TO BE. IT'S AN ABBREVIATION.
N.V.
AS IN "NON VISIBLE."

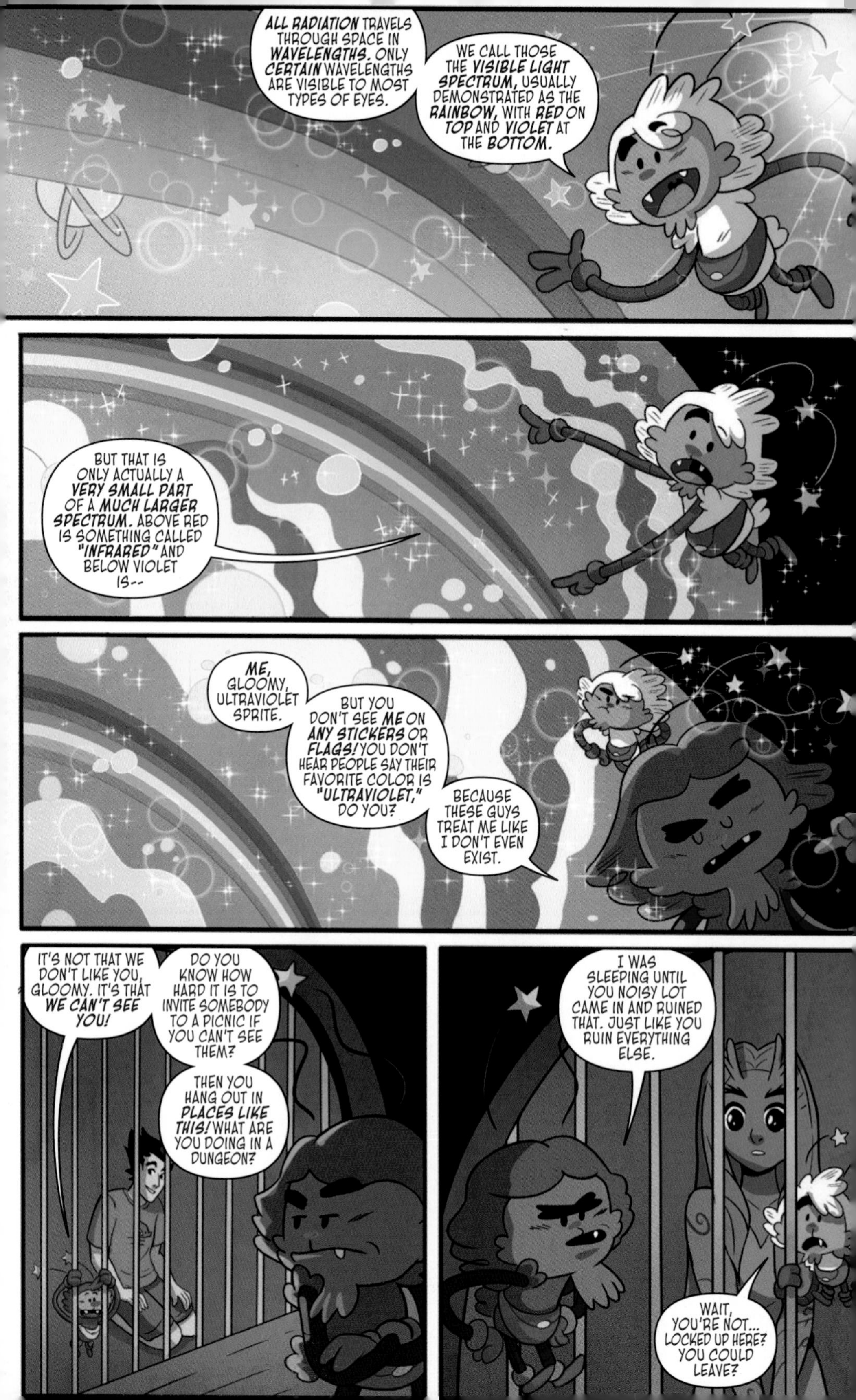
ALL RADIATION TRAVELS THROUGH SPACE IN WAVELENGTHS. ONLY CERTAIN WAVELENGTHS ARE VISIBLE TO MOST TYPES OF EYES.
WE CALL THOSE THE VISIBLE LIGHT SPECTRUM, USUALLY DEMONSTRATED AS THE RAINBOW, WITH RED ON TOP AND VIOLET AT THE BOTTOM.
BUT THAT IS ONLY ACTUALLY A VERY SMALL PART OF A MUCH LARGER SPECTRUM. ABOVE RED IS SOMETHING CALLED "INFRARED" AND BELOW VIOLET IS--
ME, GLOOMY, ULTRAVIOLET SPRITE.
BUT YOU DON'T SEE ME ON ANY STICKERS OR FLAGS! YOU DON'T HEAR PEOPLE SAY THEIR FAVORITE COLOR IS "ULTRAVIOLET," DO YOU?
BECAUSE THESE GUYS TREAT ME LIKE I DON'T EVEN EXIST.
IT'S NOT THAT WE DON'T LIKE YOU, GLOOMY. IT'S THAT WE CAN'T SEE YOU!
DO YOU KNOW HOW HARD IT IS TO INVITE SOMEBODY TO A PICNIC IF YOU CAN'T SEE THEM?
THEN YOU HANG OUT IN PLACES LIKE THIS! WHAT ARE YOU DOING IN A DUNGEON?
I WAS SLEEPING UNTIL YOU NOISY LOT CAME IN AND RUINED THAT. JUST LIKE YOU RUIN EVERYTHING ELSE.
WAIT, YOU'RE NOT... LOCKED UP HERE? YOU COULD LEAVE?

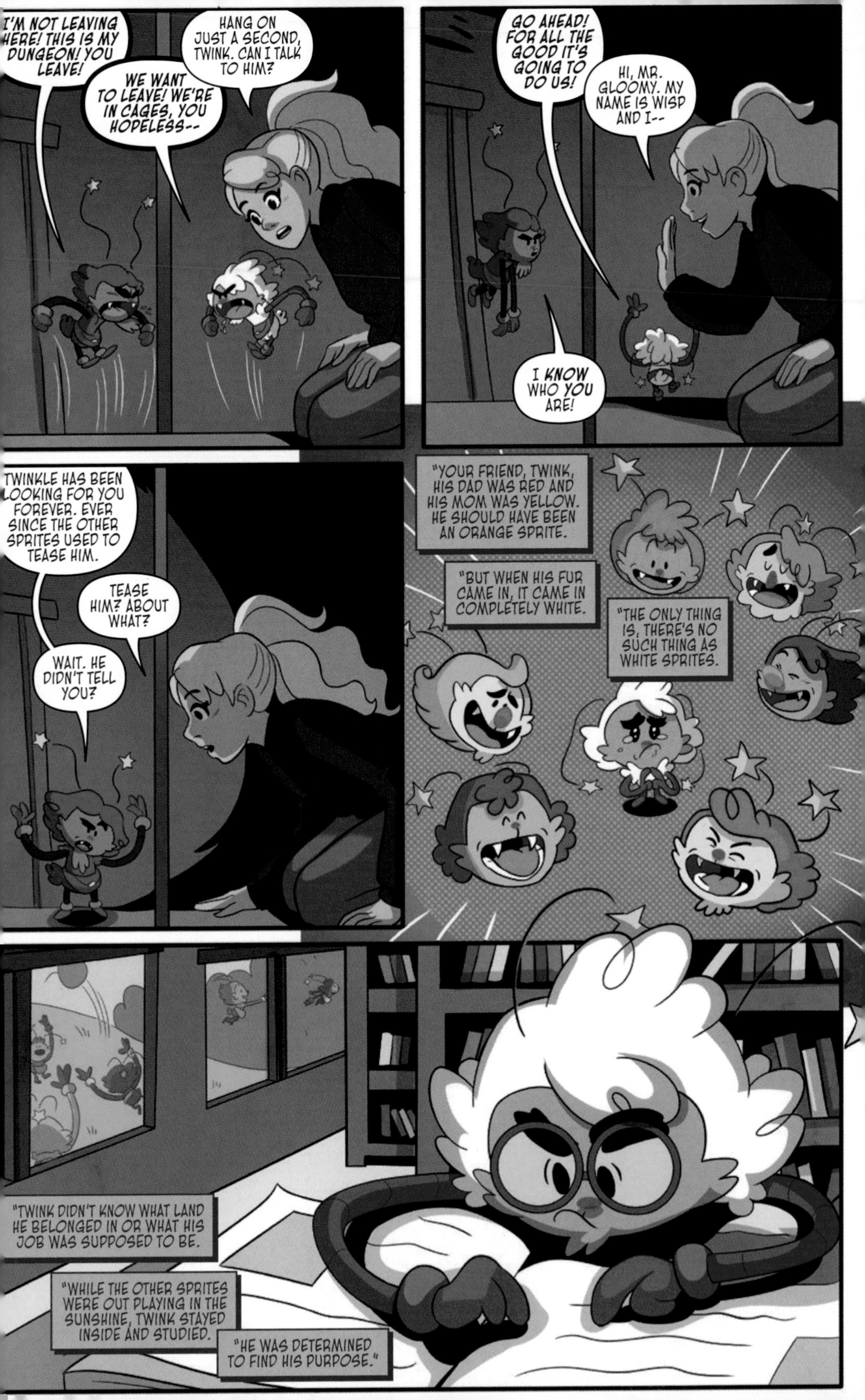
I'M NOT LEAVING HERE! THIS IS MY DUNGEON! YOU LEAVE!
WE WANT TO LEAVE! WE'RE IN CAGES, YOU HOPELESS--
HANG ON JUST A SECOND, TWINK. CAN I TALK TO HIM?
GO AHEAD! FOR ALL THE GOOD IT'S GOING TO DO US!
HI, MR. GLOOMY. MY NAME IS WISP AND I--
I KNOW WHO YOU ARE!
TWINKLE HAS BEEN LOOKING FOR YOU FOREVER. EVER SINCE THE OTHER SPRITES USED TO TEASE HIM.
TEASE HIM? ABOUT WHAT?
WAIT. HE DIDN'T TELL YOU?
"YOUR FRIEND, TWINK, HIS DAD WAS RED AND HIS MOM WAS YELLOW. HE SHOULD HAVE BEEN AN ORANGE SPRITE.
"BUT WHEN HIS FUR CAME IN, IT CAME IN COMPLETELY WHITE.
"THE ONLY THING IS, THERE'S NO SUCH THING AS WHITE SPRITES.
"TWINK DIDN'T KNOW WHAT LAND HE BELONGED IN OR WHAT HIS JOB WAS SUPPOSED TO BE.
"WHILE THE OTHER SPRITES WERE OUT PLAYING IN THE SUNSHINE, TWINK STAYED INSIDE AND STUDIED.
"HE WAS DETERMINED TO FIND HIS PURPOSE."

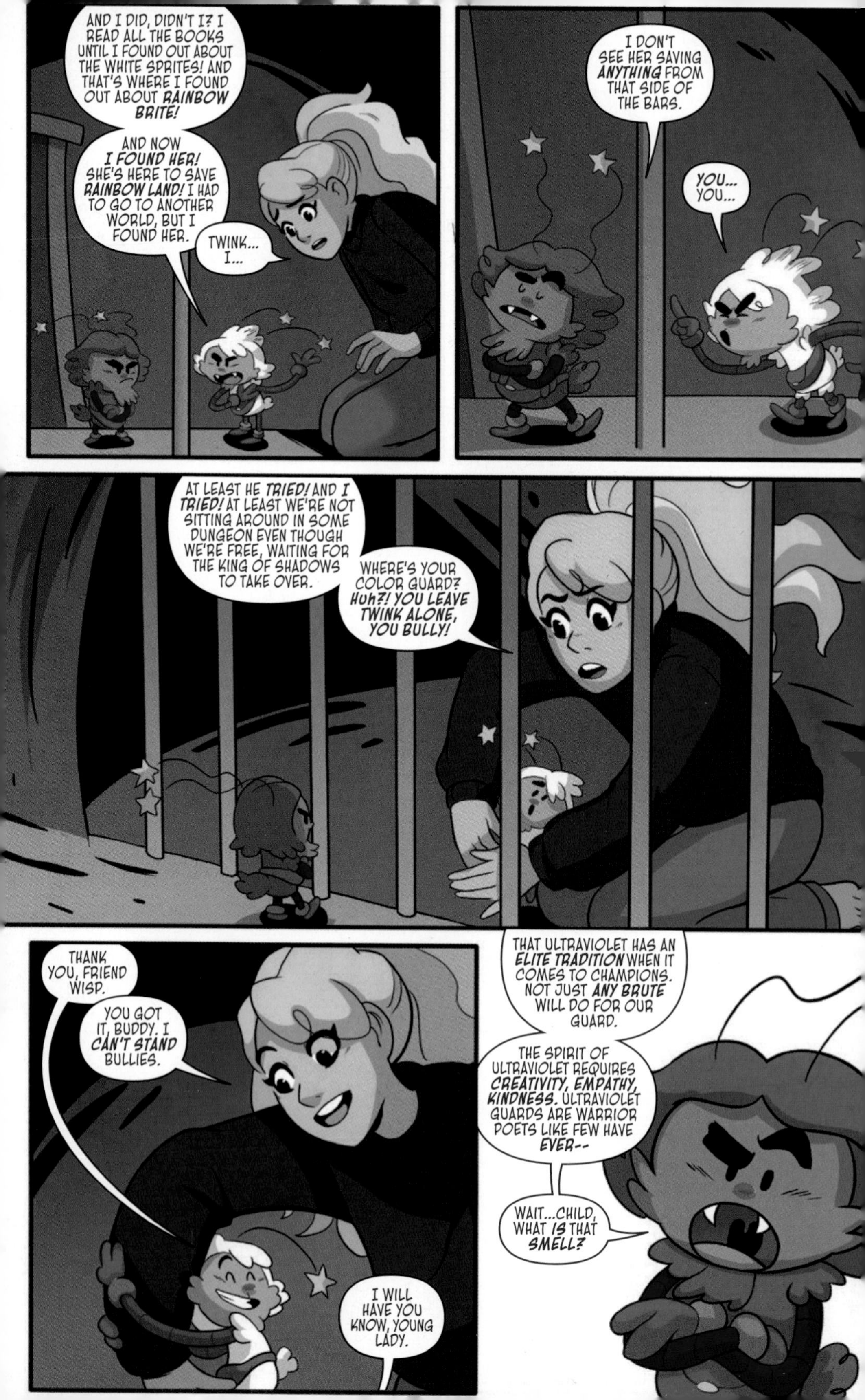
AND I DID, DIDN'T I? I READ ALL THE BOOKS UNTIL I FOUND OUT ABOUT THE WHITE SPRITES! AND THAT'S WHERE I FOUND OUT ABOUT RAINBOW BRITE!
AND NOW I FOUND HER! SHE'S HERE TO SAVE RAINBOW LAND! I HAD TO GO TO ANOTHER WORLD, BUT I FOUND HER.
TWINK... I...
I DON'T SEE HER SAVING ANYTHING FROM THAT SIDE OF THE BARS.
YOU... YOU...
AT LEAST HE TRIED! AND I TRIED! AT LEAST WE'RE NOT SITTING AROUND IN SOME DUNGEON EVEN THOUGH WE'RE FREE, WAITING FOR THE KING OF SHADOWS TO TAKE OVER.
WHERE'S YOUR COLOR GUARD? Huh?! YOU LEAVE TWINK ALONE, YOU BULLY!
THANK YOU, FRIEND WISP.
YOU GOT IT, BUDDY. I CAN'T STAND BULLIES.
I WILL HAVE YOU KNOW, YOUNG LADY.
THAT ULTRAVIOLET HAS AN ELITE TRADITION WHEN IT COMES TO CHAMPIONS. NOT JUST ANY BRUTE WILL DO FOR OUR GUARD.
THE SPIRIT OF ULTRAVIOLET REQUIRES CREATIVITY, EMPATHY, KINDNESS. ULTRAVIOLET GUARDS ARE WARRIOR POETS LIKE FEW HAVE EVER--
WAIT...CHILD, WHAT IS THAT SMELL?

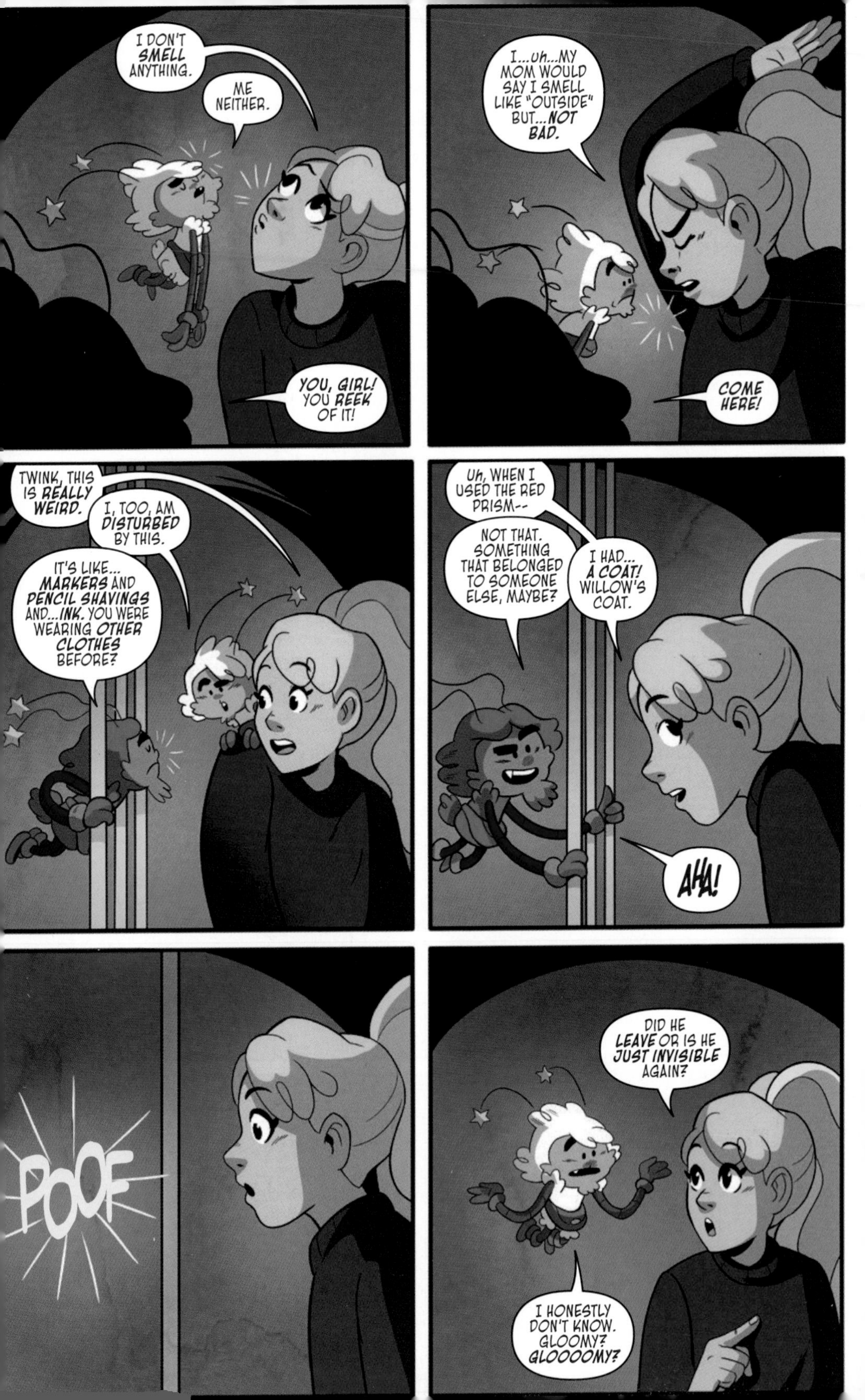
I DON'T SMELL ANYTHING.
ME NEITHER.
YOU, GIRL! YOU REEK OF IT!
I...uh...MY MOM WOULD SAY I SMELL LIKE "OUTSIDE" BUT...NOT BAD.
COME HERE!
TWINK, THIS IS REALLY WEIRD.
I, TOO, AM DISTURBED BY THIS.
IT'S LIKE... MARKERS AND PENCIL SHAVINGS AND...INK. YOU WERE WEARING OTHER CLOTHES BEFORE?
Uh, WHEN I USED THE RED PRISM--
NOT THAT. SOMETHING THAT BELONGED TO SOMEONE ELSE, MAYBE?
I HAD... A COAT! WILLOW'S COAT.
AHA!
POOF
DID HE LEAVE OR IS HE JUST INVISIBLE AGAIN?
I HONESTLY DON'T KNOW. GLOOMY? GLOOOOMY?

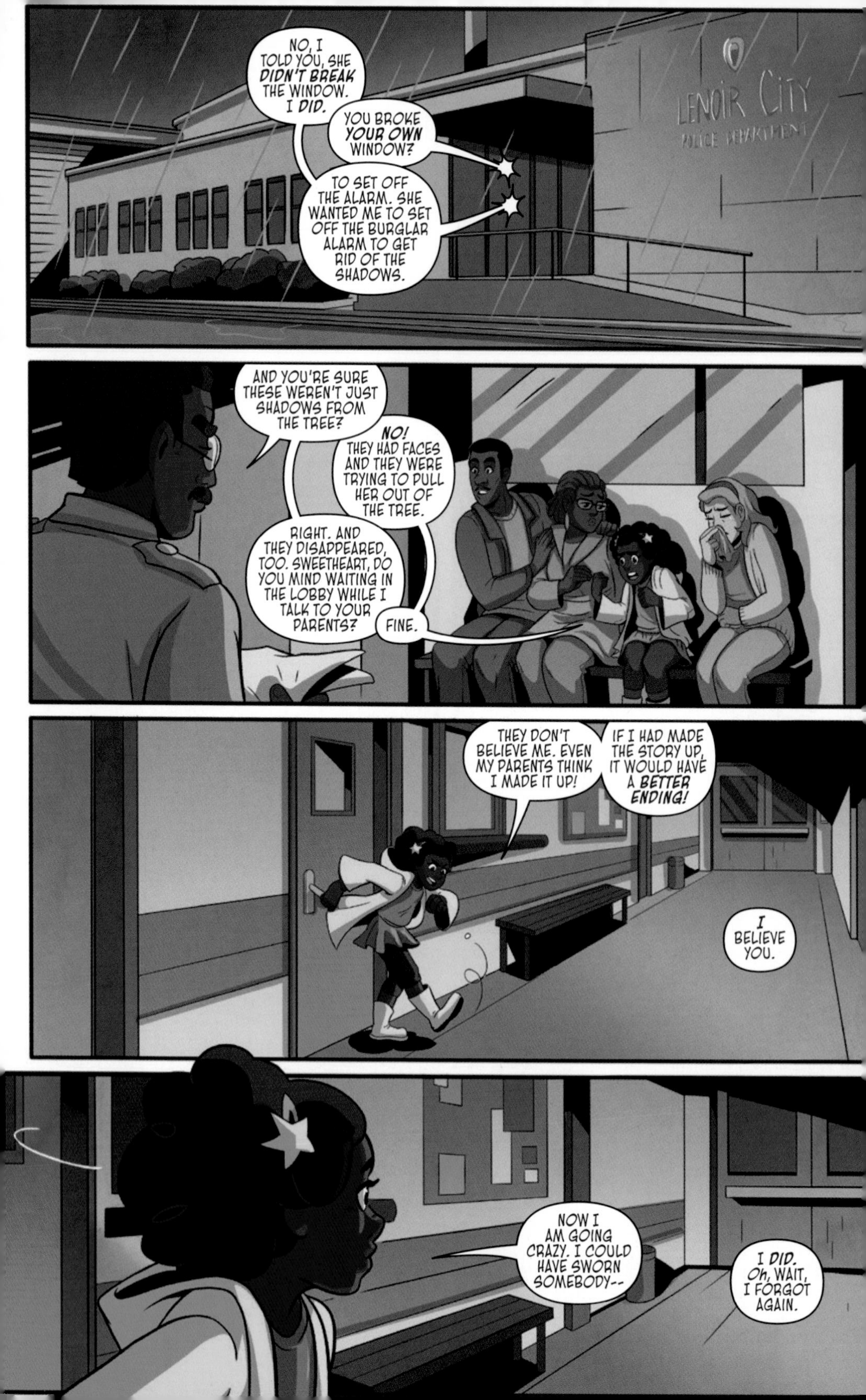
LENOIR CITY
POLICE DEPARTMENT
NO, I TOLD YOU, SHE *DIDN'T BREAK* THE WINDOW. I *DID.*
YOU BROKE *YOUR OWN* WINDOW?
TO SET OFF THE ALARM. SHE WANTED ME TO SET OFF THE BURGLAR ALARM TO GET RID OF THE SHADOWS.
AND YOU'RE SURE THESE WEREN'T JUST SHADOWS FROM THE TREE?
NO! THEY HAD FACES AND THEY WERE TRYING TO PULL HER OUT OF THE TREE.
RIGHT. AND THEY DISAPPEARED, TOO. SWEETHEART, DO YOU MIND WAITING IN THE LOBBY WHILE I TALK TO YOUR PARENTS?
FINE.
THEY DON'T BELIEVE ME. EVEN MY PARENTS THINK I MADE IT UP!
IF I HAD MADE THE STORY UP, IT WOULD HAVE A *BETTER ENDING!*
I BELIEVE YOU.
NOW I AM GOING CRAZY. I COULD HAVE SWORN SOMEBODY--
I *DID.* *Oh,* WAIT, I FORGOT AGAIN.

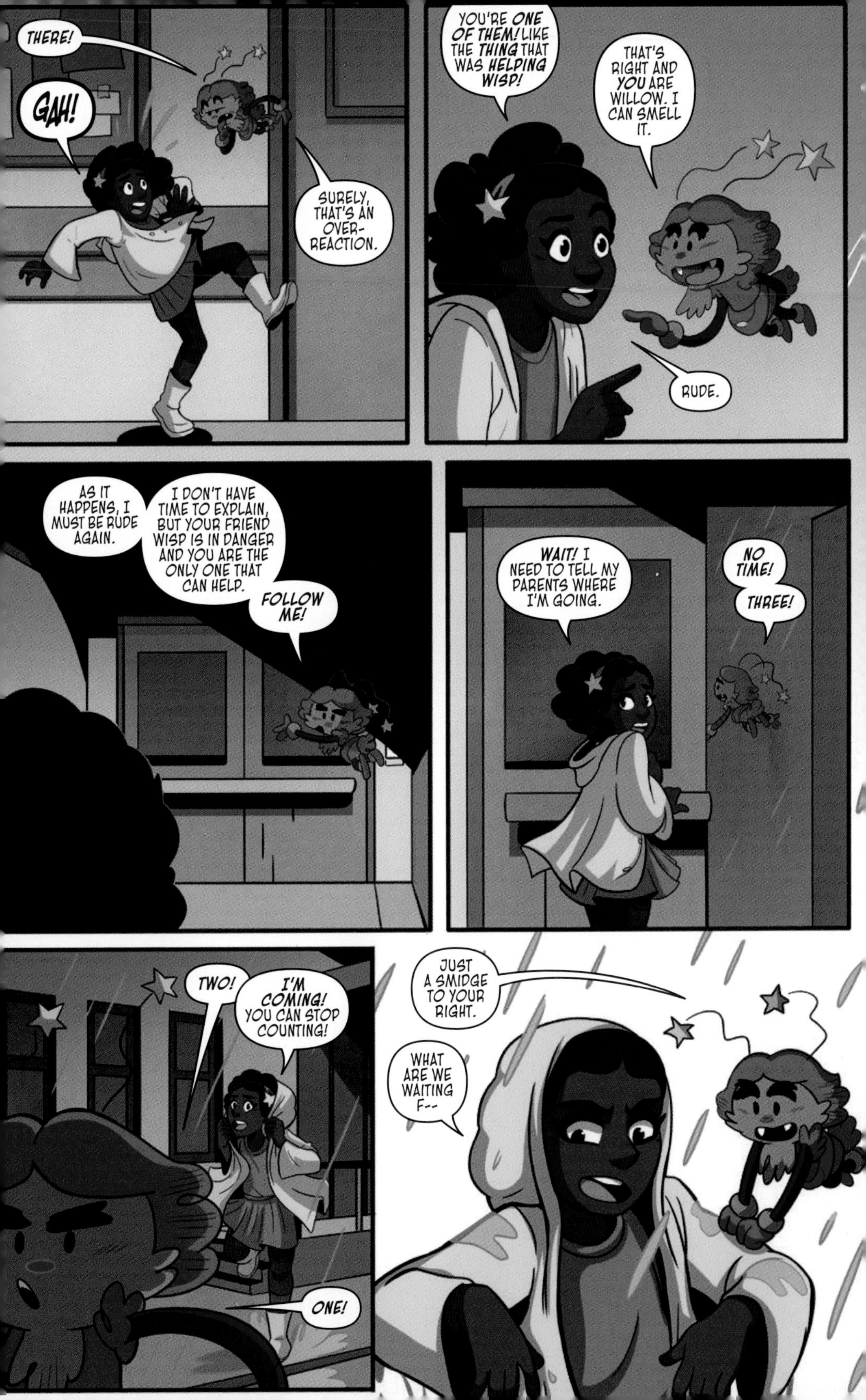
THERE!
GAH!
SURELY, THAT'S AN OVER-REACTION.
YOU'RE ONE OF THEM! LIKE THE THING THAT WAS HELPING WISP!
THAT'S RIGHT AND YOU ARE WILLOW. I CAN SMELL IT.
RUDE.
AS IT HAPPENS, I MUST BE RUDE AGAIN.
I DON'T HAVE TIME TO EXPLAIN, BUT YOUR FRIEND WISP IS IN DANGER AND YOU ARE THE ONLY ONE THAT CAN HELP.
FOLLOW ME!
WAIT! I NEED TO TELL MY PARENTS WHERE I'M GOING.
NO TIME!
THREE!
TWO!
I'M COMING! YOU CAN STOP COUNTING!
ONE!
JUST A SMIDGE TO YOUR RIGHT.
WHAT ARE WE WAITING F--

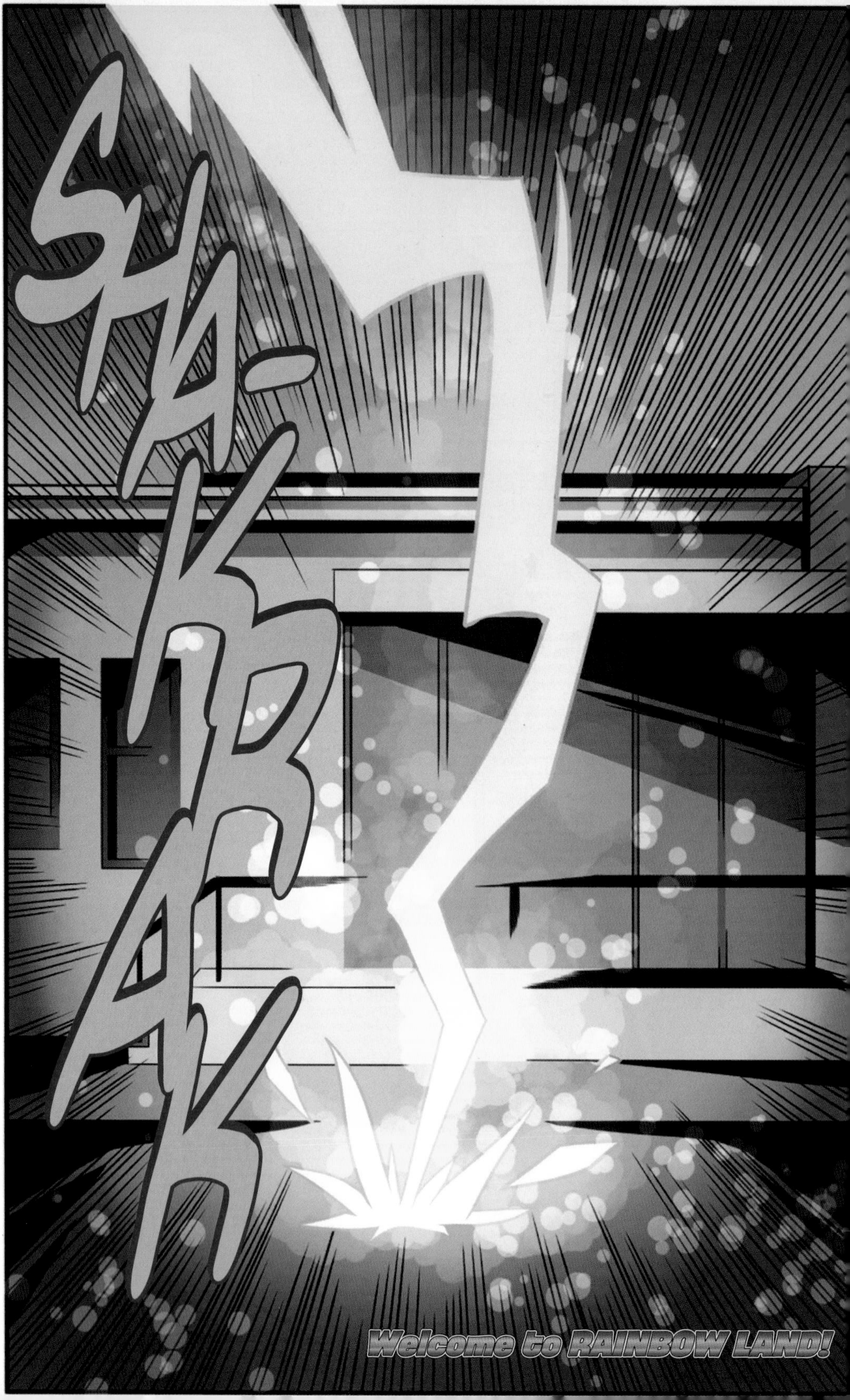
SHA-KRAAK

Cover Gallery

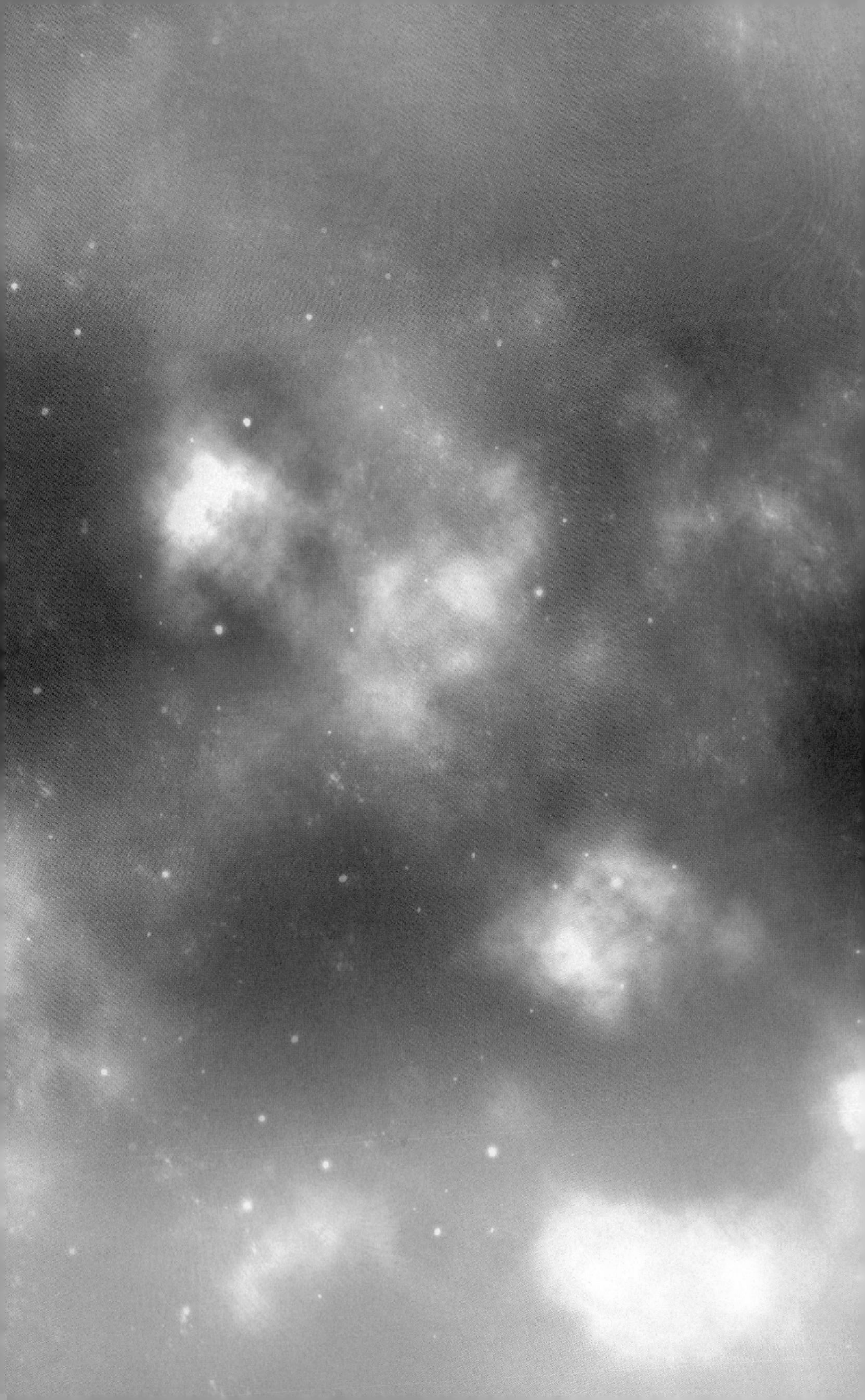

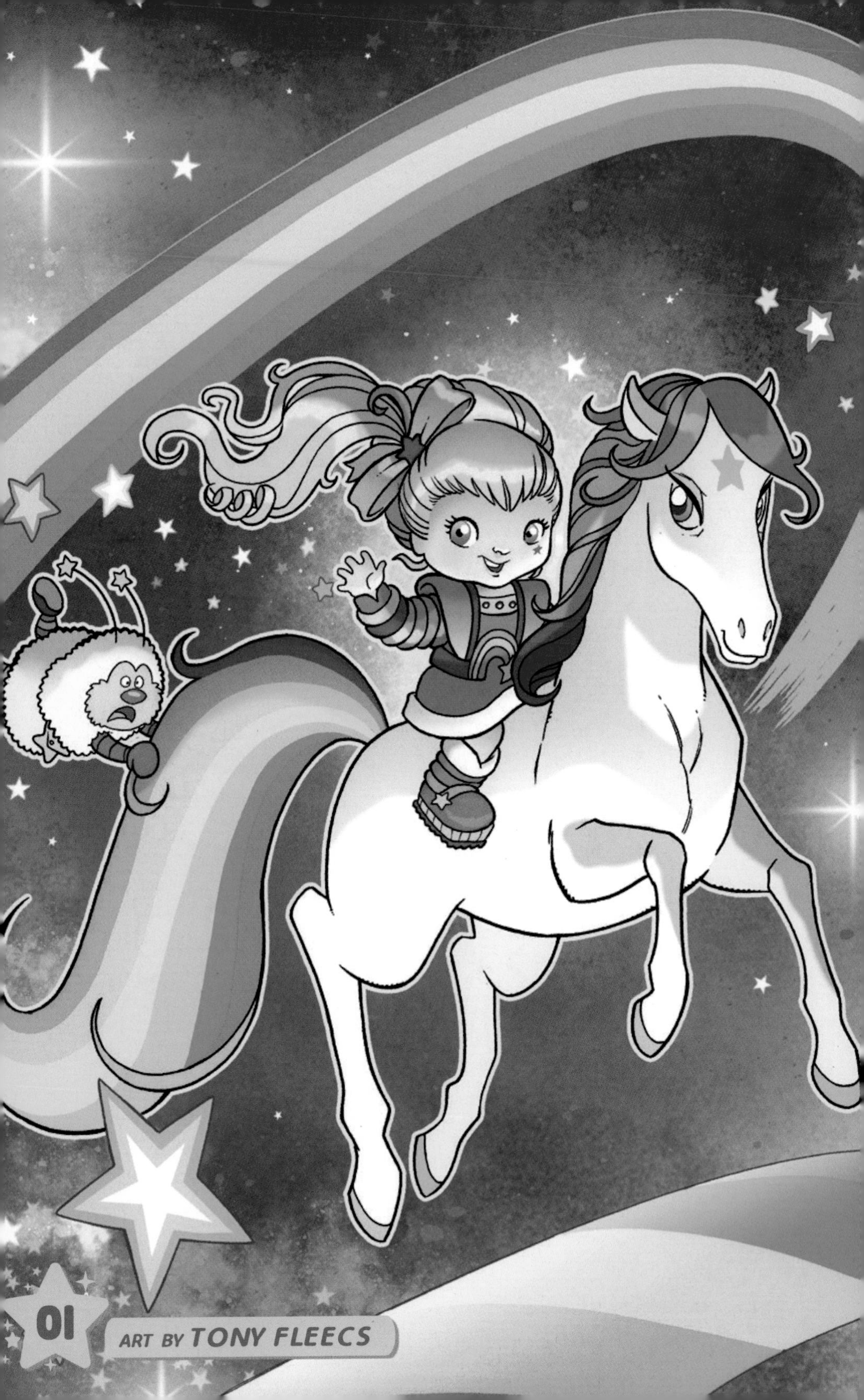
01
ART BY TONY FLEECS

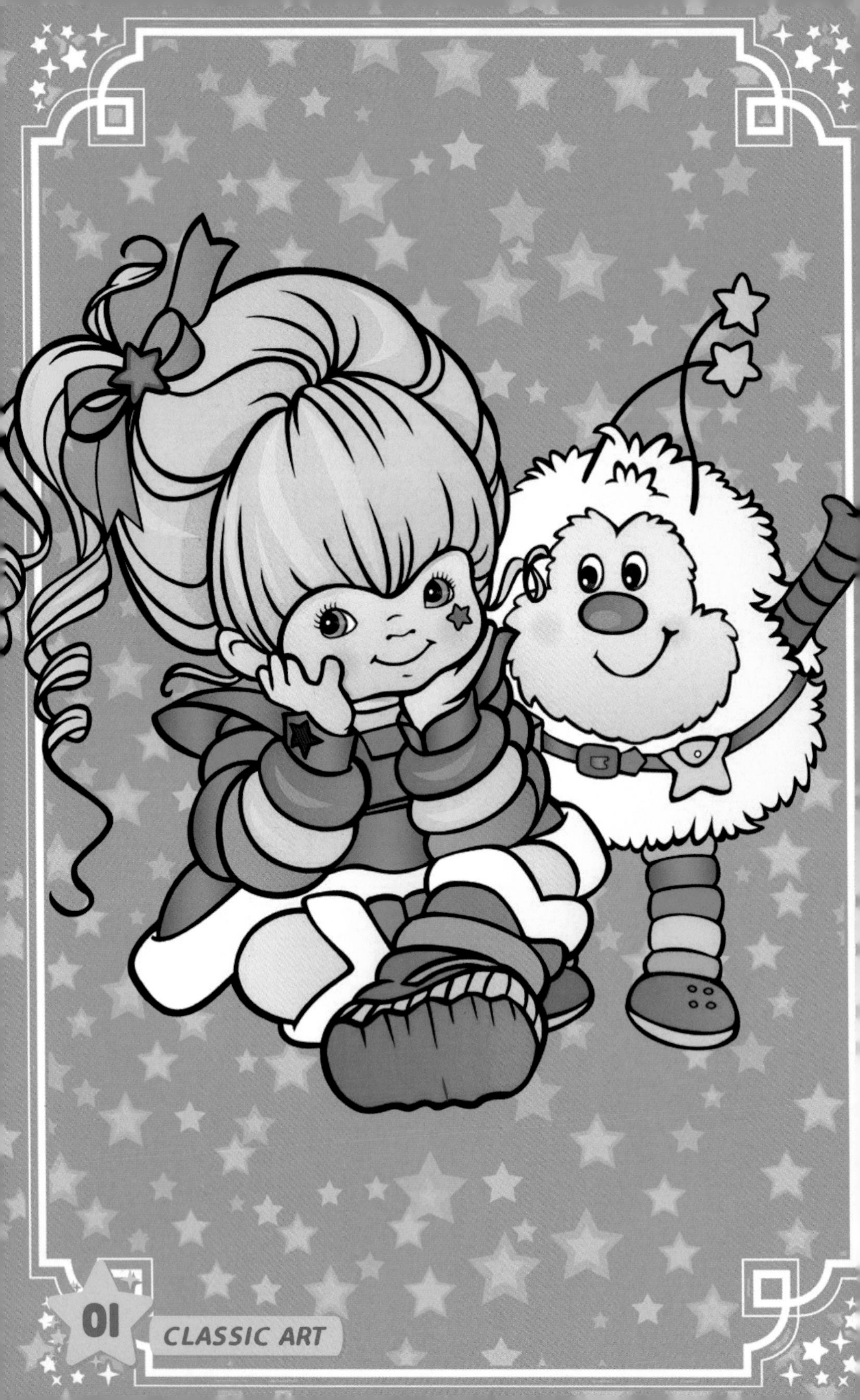
01
CLASSIC ART

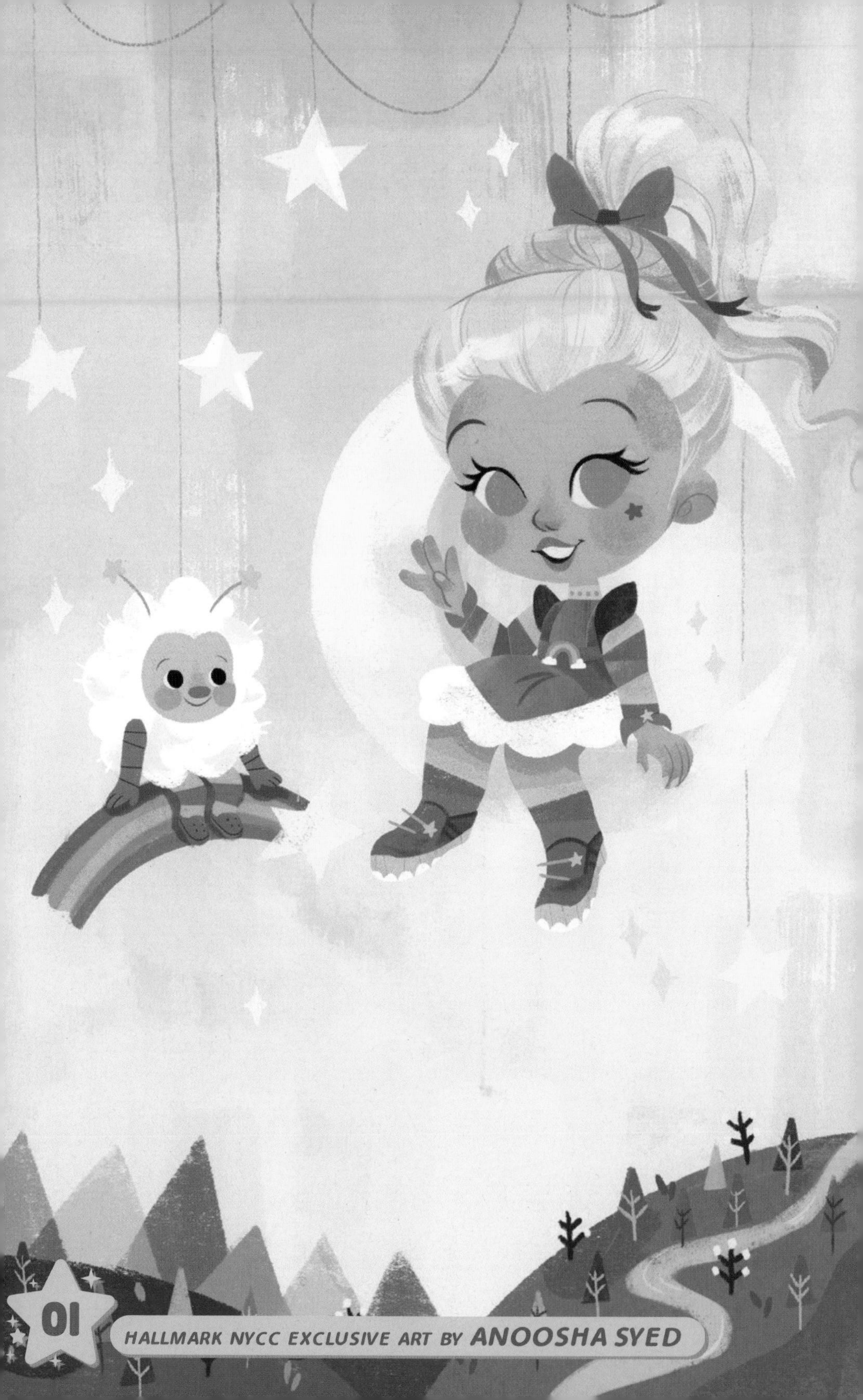
01
HALLMARK NYCC EXCLUSIVE ART BY ANOOSHA SYED

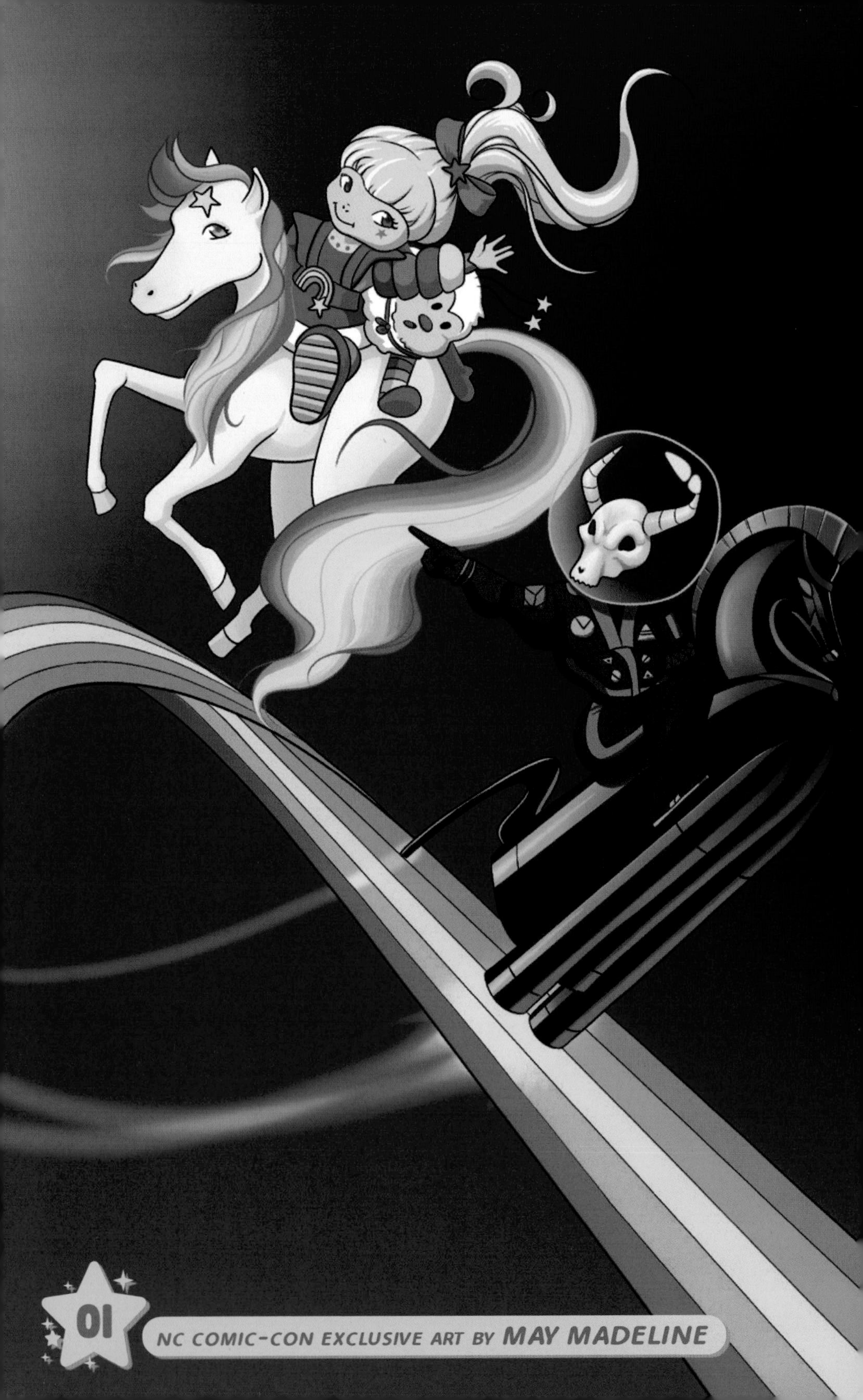

01
NC COMIC-CON EXCLUSIVE ART BY MAY MADELINE

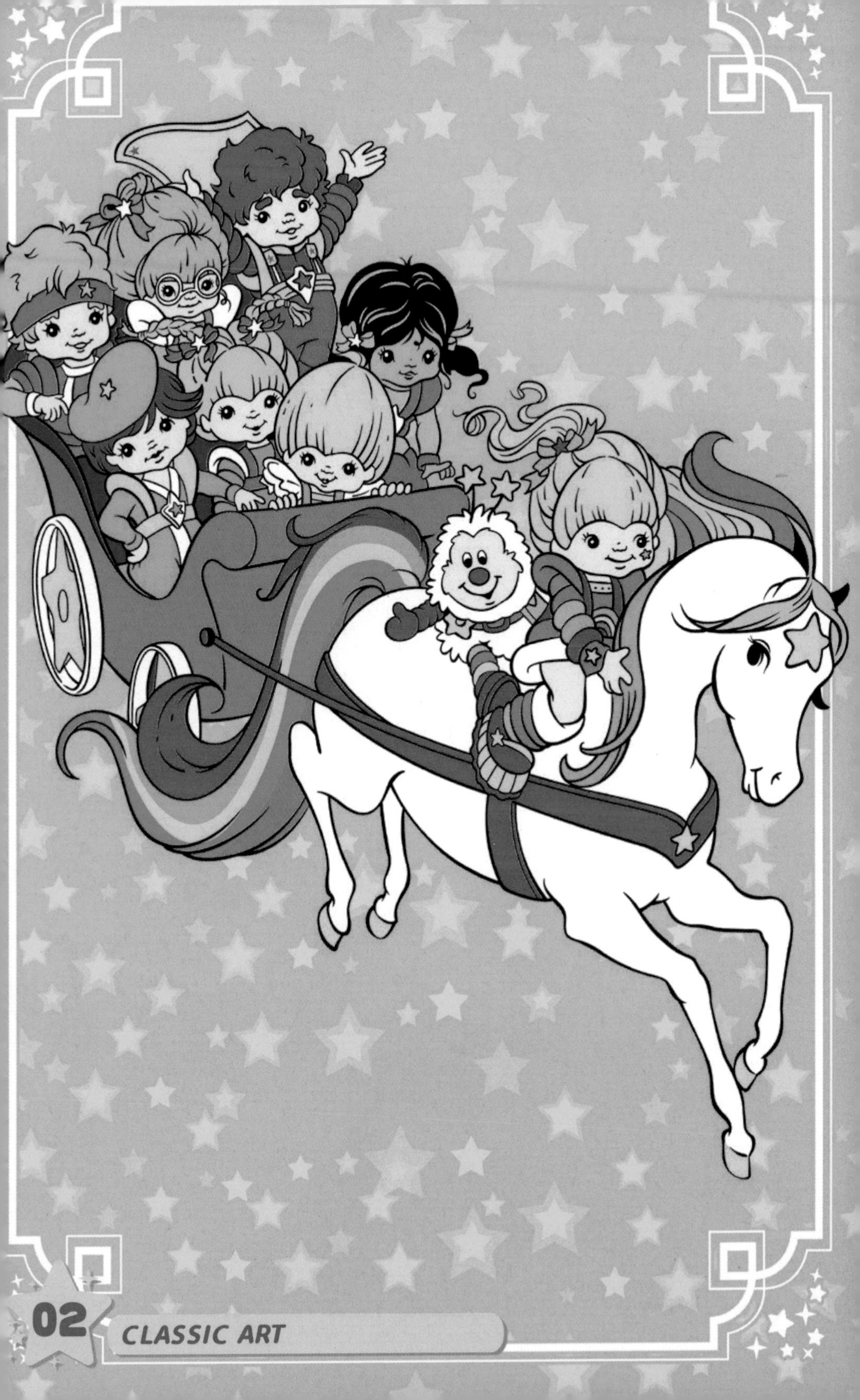

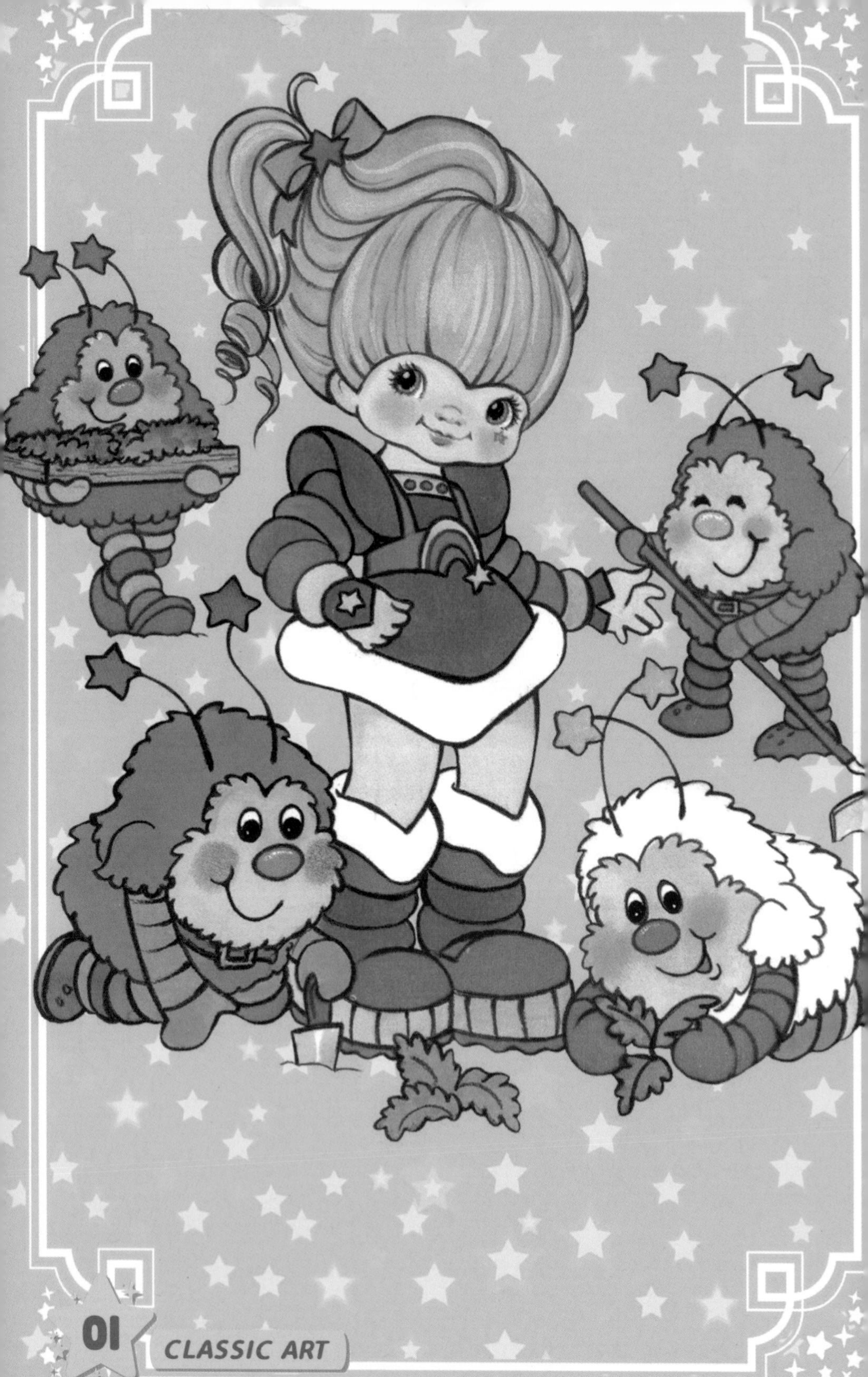

01 CLASSIC ART

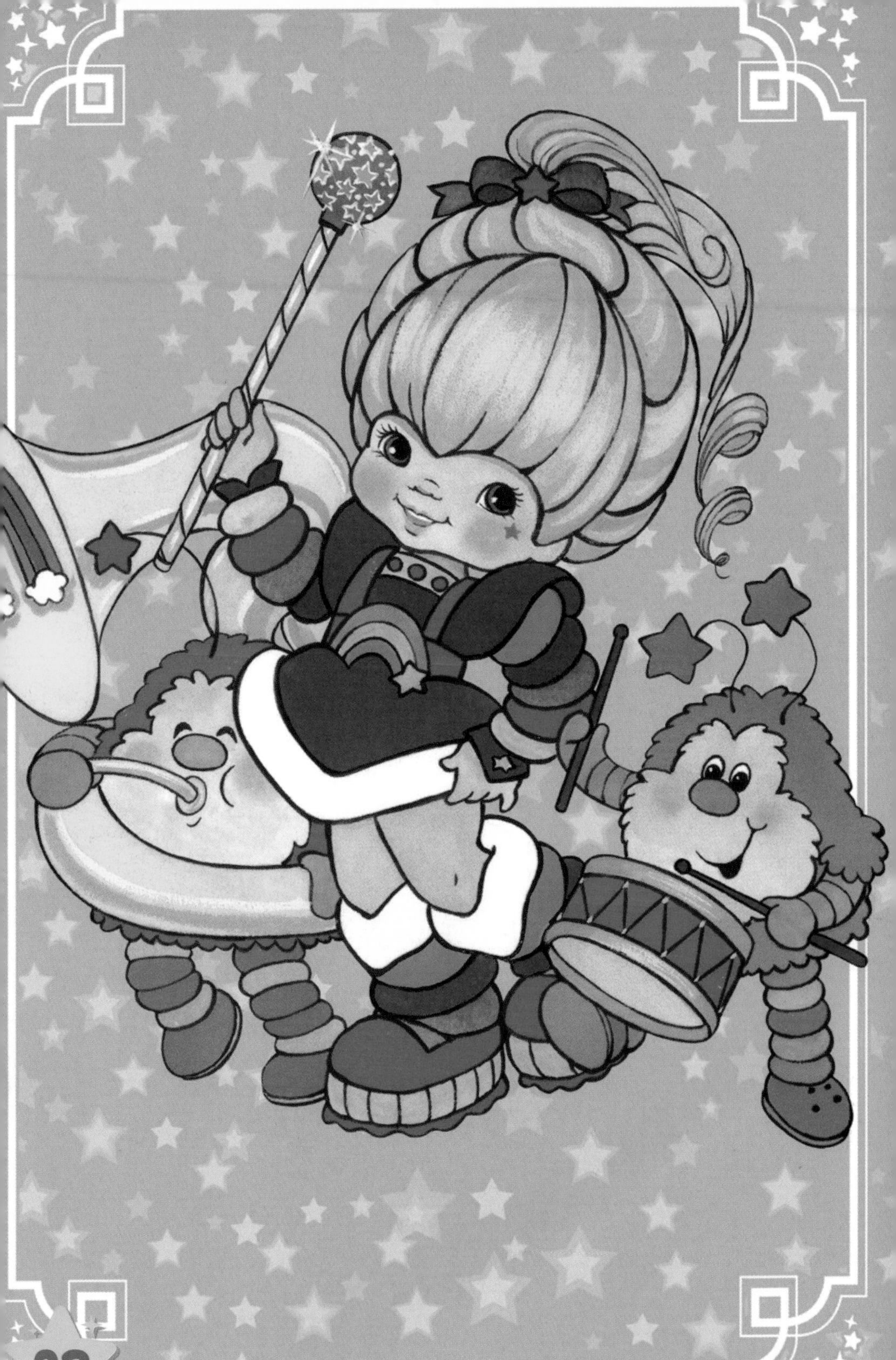

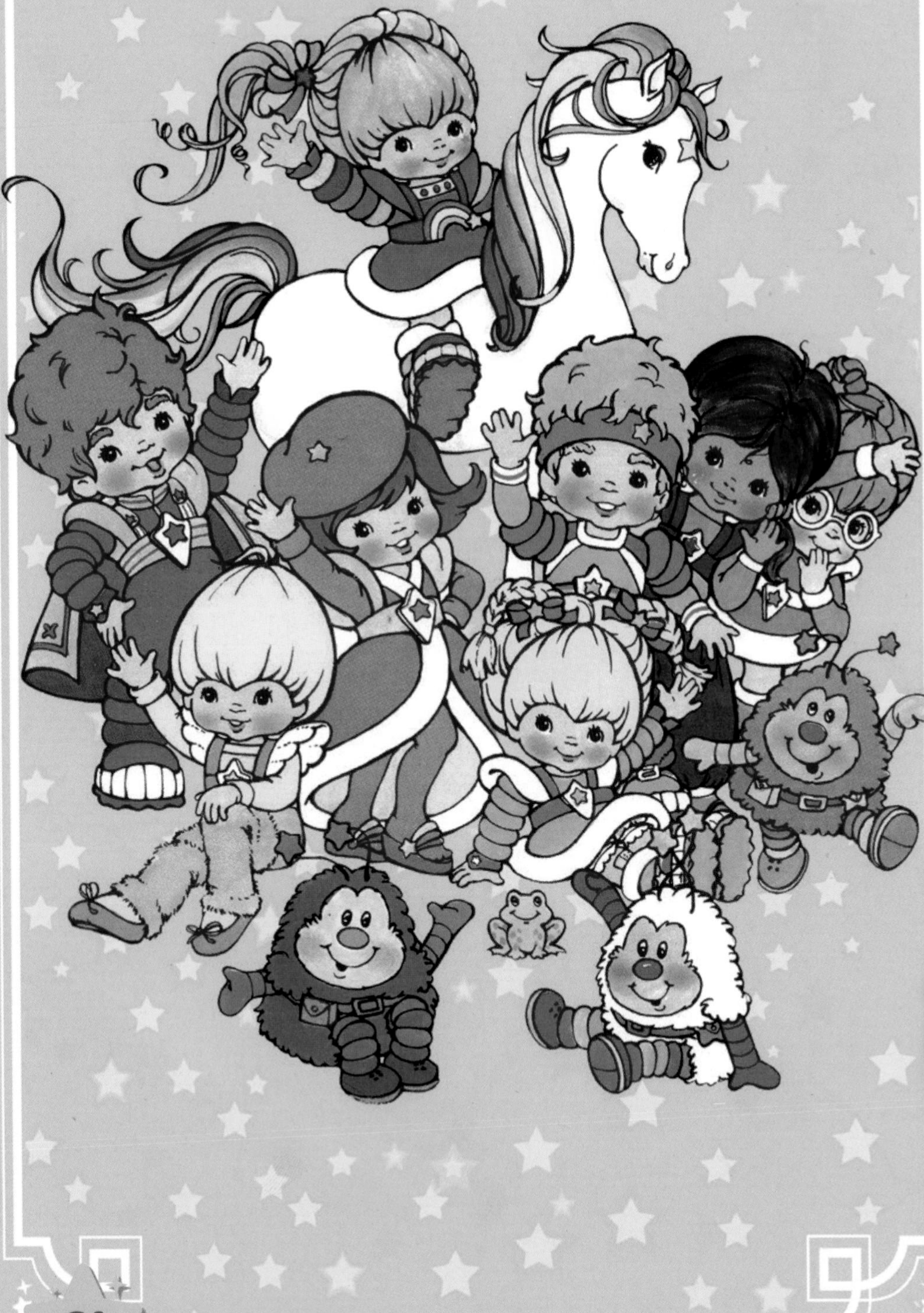

01 CLASSIC ART